...ussell,
...nately you
...oved the nukes. Now
you need to head to Kal
and work in the Super Pit :)
Stay safe.
Jim.

The Agreement

Gallows Gold Series
Book 1

Written by James Scott Thomson

Action and Adventure Novel

THE AGREEMENT
Gallows Gold Series Book 1

Published by FutureWest Publishing 2022
Perth, W.A., Australia
www.futurewest.com.au/JamesThomson

For permissions contact:
James Thomson at James@futurewest.com.au

Cover photography from Shutterstock.com

Book and cover design by Steven Schaffert

Australian map is courtesy of Bruce Jones Design and FreeUSandWorldMaps.com

ISBN: 978-0-6454800-2-3 (Paperback 2nd Ed)
ISBN: 978-0-6454800-1-6 (eBook)
Second Edition 2022

Dedicated to all those who have supported or served in the Defence Force, Fire Service, Police Force, Ambulance Service, State Emergency Service, or Health Service.

Thank you for your Support and Service!

PROLOGUE

World War One

On June 28, 1914, Archduke Franz Ferdinand of Austria was assassinated by the Bosnian Serb nationalist Gavrilo Princip. The assassination led to a war across Europe. During the conflict - Germany, Austria-Hungary, Bulgaria, and the Ottoman Empire (the Central Powers) fought against Great Britain, France, Italy, Russia, Romania, Australia, Japan, and the United States (the Allied Powers). The war ended on November 11, 1918, leaving an estimated seventeen million people dead.

World War Two

An unprecedented rise to power by Adolf Hitler led to Germany's invasion of Poland on September 1, 1939. Great Britain and France declared war on Germany. Germany, Italy, and Japan (Axis Powers) fought Great Britain, France, Australia, the United States, China, and the Soviet Union (Allies). The war ended on September the 2, 1945, leaving an estimated seventy million people dead. The bombing of Hiroshima and Nagasaki marked the first time atomic weapons were used in war.

World War Three

Tensions in the South China Sea led to conflict between China and the Philippines on August 8, 2031. South Korea engaged in the conflict by assisting the Philippine Navy. The United States declared war on China on August 17, 2031. During the conflict, the United States, South Korea, Israel, India, Japan, the United Kingdom and Australia (Allies) fought China, Russia, North Korea, Pakistan, Iran, and Vietnam (Central Allies). The war ended on October 22, 2033, leaving an estimated 2.7 billion people dead. This time, both the Allies and Central Allies resorted to the use of nuclear weapons during the conflict. Hundreds of cities worldwide were destroyed by missile strikes or deserted due to radioactive fallout.

Chapter One

Tuesday January 15, 2041 – Archie

I woke at dawn and peered through the flaps of my canvas tent. Like the surface of Mars, undulating plains of red dirt stretched as far as the eye could see. The morning heat promised a searing summer day in the desert, twenty-five kilometres east of Kalgoorlie in Western Australia. My lack of funds and wounded ego fuelled my resolve to capture a fugitive that had evaded my grasp for almost two months.

Crawling from my tent, I stood up to hear a deafening craaack! A sharp pain exploded on the right side of my head. Dazed and confused, I instinctively touched my temple. As I contemplated the fresh slippery blood dripping from my fingertips, I hurtled towards the desert floor.

When I opened my crusty eyelids, the harsh glare of the sun made me squint. I could have been unconscious for two seconds or two hours. I was being dragged on my back through the bush scrub, my shirt pulled up under my armpits, with bits of sharp gravel scoring my skin. As I lifted my head, I immediately regretted the decision when a piercing migraine overwhelmed me. It didn't help that I was looking at the back of an enormous outlaw, standing at six-foot-five and 130 kilograms. I didn't realise he had a ponytail from his mug shot. He gripped my right ankle, hauling me with ease like a ten-kilogram bag of salt, dragging me around termite mounds, large boulders and rusted mining machinery abandoned in the sand. This was not helping my state of mind.

Once again, I reflected on how I ended up in these situations. Before the War, many considered me an up-coming contract lawyer, practising out of McGlennon and Graff Legal, a respected law firm in Perth. That old saying is right on the money – 'You don't know what you have until it's gone'. I'd just won the rising star award at the firm, was newly married to the loveliest woman in the country, and moving up the ranks in the Army Reserves. And then the War started.

We may have won the War, but like many others, I lost everything - my wife, mother and father are dead, along with most of my mates. Bloody hell! How life has changed. The War resulted in over two billion deaths, the crash of the world's economy, and the destruction of almost all orbiting satellites and undersea communication cables. The Internet is now a tool of the past. My law career ended after the economic collapse. Now I'm reduced to apprehending fugitives to scrape out a living.

I returned my attention to my current dilemma. I'd finally located my bounty, but unfortunately, he found me first. To be locked up in this day in age, you have to either be a psychotic deviant or desperate enough to murder, rob or kidnap. Billy Spratt wasn't desperate. His latest escapade involved kidnapping three ten-year-old girls for the purpose of holding them for ransom. All three happened to be related to influential citizens - the mayor, a respected farmer, and a wealthy miner. The constabulary attempted to apprehend Billy at a brothel. But the arrest went awry when he fatally shot two officers and escaped out the back. In his depraved mind, they were mere obstacles that deserved to die for ruining his plans.

I considered the best course of action and reached for my revolver and then my knife. Both were missing. Billy wasn't that stupid. Ignoring the thumping migraine, I scuttled my backside towards Billy and hooked my left foot around his left ankle. Billy fell forwards. Breaking his fall with both hands, he jumped up to his feet from a push-up position with surprising speed. He moved like a world wrestling superstar of old, swiftly closing the distance as I raised myself up from my knees. His knee connected with one of my floating ribs, forcing me to fall onto all fours.

Now, I'm only a lean 80 kilograms at just over six-foot-two, but I have one slight advantage over Billy, I'm a highly skilled fighter who's often underestimated. I had an old man that saw shadows amongst shadows, a former soldier who fought in Iraq and Afghanistan. He thought it was imperative for his son to face physical and mental adversity. Dad enrolled me into mixed martial arts at a tender age, and spent his spare time manipulating my joints, kicking, punching, and choking me. He'd be considered a child abuser by most people. But if you'd asked my old man, he'd tell you that he was just doing his job as a father. There's no doubt I have mixed feelings on the matter, but I'd be a liar if I told you that the skills weren't helpful in my current career, especially in situations like this one.

Pushing the pain of my ribs to the back of my mind, I dived forwards for a double leg takedown, driving my shoulder deep into Billy's stomach, propelling the air from his lungs - Oooffff! As he doubled over in pain, I grabbed him behind both knees and completed the move by pulling his legs out from underneath him. Billy groaned as he came crashing down onto his back, destroying a termite mound as he fell. There are three essential rules to restraining an adversary on the ground. First, circumnavigate their legs without being kicked or tripped, second, attain a controlled position, and then third, choke them unconscious or knock them out.

Upon issuing the 'Alive' contract, the bondsman made it crystal clear that nothing short of a public hanging was an acceptable punishment for Billy's heinous crimes. My hammer fist strikes broke his nose and caved in his front two teeth. Payback can be sweet! When he turned away from me to avoid further punishment, I wrapped my arm around his neck, squeezing his arteries to stop the blood supply to his brain, only releasing the pressure after losing consciousness.

Billy had dragged me about 300 metres from my temporary camp, lugging me towards an old mine shaft. The landscape was riddled with similar abandoned mines, with estimates of 10,000 discarded claims in the Eastern Goldfields alone. Early prospectors would dig a square shaft straight down, thirty metres or more deep.

The perfect spot out here to get rid of a body.

To ensure Billy didn't escape, I hogtied him, securing his wrists to the back of his ankles and rolled him onto his side. There have been stories of bounty hunters leaving unconscious fugitives in a face down prone position, only to find them dead from positional asphyxia. I needed Billy alive to claim the full bounty. If I returned to the station with a corpse, I'd only receive a quarter of the reward I was entitled to. The incentive to claim an '*Alive*' bounty was substantial, especially when the authorities desire a public execution. It doesn't take a rocket scientist to recognise the political benefits of allowing citizens to witness justice being delivered.

The authorities may be politicly shrewd, but they are also pragmatic. A '*Dead or Alive*' bounty is issued when the cost of delivering the offender with a pulse outweighs the political benefits. Think of it as your classic risk versus reward scenario - if the hunter considers the risk of an '*Alive*' contract is too high, they'll simply wait for the next job. In fact, a majority of hunters will only accept '*Dead or Alive*' contracts, so they can shoot the offender from a distance, thereby reducing their risk. To top it off, the reward for a '*Dead or Alive*' contract does not alter in value whether the hunter escorts the culprit back kicking and screaming, or just delivers their head. In the grand scheme of things I prefer to bring the culprits back alive, as I don't consider myself an executioner. And it helps me sleep better at night.

Roger stamped his hoof as I hitched Billy atop of the saddle. My slightly disgruntled horse demands attention, and quite frankly, it's tiring having to constantly pander to his needs. However, it doesn't change the fact that I love the silly bugger, all 500 kilos of him. As I secured Billy, I felt Roger's wet nose shove my shoulder, "Come on mate, I've got a splitting head-ache, I'm tired and hungry." Roger made a high-pitched whinny. "Okay mate, I get the message." I grabbed him some feed before I commenced packing up my tent and belongings.

My possessions may be meagre, but they're critical to my survival. I picked up my .38 Smith and Wesson revolver and knife from the dirt and slid them into my holster and sheath respectively. Billy had stripped me of the weapons after knocking me out; items that he would have eventually sold. But first he would have displayed them like trophies, bragging to anyone that would listen – *'Do ya want to hear how I killed a hunter?'* I made a solemn oath to give them a good and thorough clean upon returning to my lodgings.

After I retrieved my silver flask from my pack, I swallowed a blue oxycodone pill with a gulp of whisky. Before we commenced our long walk back to town, I wrapped a makeshift bandage around my noggin to stem the bleeding. It was forty degrees Celsius, but it felt like it was fifty. I waved the voracious flies from my face and scanned the desert. It appeared desolate, but there were critters everywhere – lizards, spiders and snakes can give you a fright if you step or sit blindly unaware.

It didn't take long to locate Billy's tent. It was pitched just three kilometres west of my campsite. I searched through his belongings, taking items of value – three litres of potable water, a compass, spade, map book, and some playing cards. Billy didn't complain, he was still unconscious and blissfully unaware of his dramatic reversal of fortune.

We were making good time and were almost halfway into our return journey to Kalgoorlie, when Billy muttered a desperate plea, "Let me go and I'll give ya my *thash* of nuggets, I have twenty ountheth." Billy now spoke with a lisp due to his missing teeth. If it were not for his horrid treatment of the young girls he kidnapped, I would have probably considered his offer.

Twenty ounces of gold would greatly assist me in achieving my dream of settling near Darwin in the top end of the Northern Territory and opening a small brewing company. My lack of funds is a major barrier to achieving this dream. Crypto traders weren't the only ones that had heart attacks when the Internet and electronic systems were destroyed. Every person or business with a bank account lost all of their wealth in an instant. On the flip side, mortgages and personal loans also disappeared without a trace. High inflation and the inability to print cash forced the government to search for alternative currencies. Gold, silver, and bartering were now used to purchase goods and services. Coins are still minted, but their supply is carefully controlled by the State Government to avoid hyperinflation.

I shook my head and turned towards him, "Shut up Billy, you deserve to hang for what you did to those girls."

Billy's following tirade of abuse and threats would have impressed the roughest and toughest of stockmen.

We finally arrived in Kalgoorlie late in the afternoon. Before heading to the hotel to quench my thirst, I stopped off at the cop shop to deliver Billy. I tied Roger to the hitching post out front and left him to drink the clear water from the trough. The local sergeant is a horse tragic and a man after my own heart, hence the equine population is provided cleaner water than most of the local residents. Just one of the reasons why beer is so popular.

Prospectors arrived in Kalgoorlie in 1893 during the Western Australian Gold Rush. The city's name is derived from the word *Kulgooluh*, a word from the Wongatha people, meaning place of the silky pears. The silky pear, also known as the bush banana, is a native plant eaten by the Indigenous people. Due to the shortage of food, bush tucker is becoming popular with the non-indigenous population - native fruits, vegetables, nuts, grubs, insects and animals (goanna, snakes, kangaroo and emu).

Water was scarce when prospectors first hit the red dirt with their pickaxe in search for gold. Their poor knowledge of the land made survival challenging in the harsh and unforgiving conditions. The government of the day hired a talented engineer by the name of C. Y O'Connor, who envisaged a pipe pumping water 590 kilometres from Perth to Kalgoorlie. In 1902 the heralded engineer killed himself less than twelve months prior to 'liquid gold' pouring from the thirty-inch pipe. This ready access to clean water supported the thousands of people who participated in the Gold Rush, and continued to do so until 2033. Grandad used to swear that C.Y. O'Connor was a distant relation of ours. When Grandad wasn't looking, Dad would shake his head to dismiss the notion.

Nuclear missiles struck the City of Perth on the 22 of February 2033. The Kalgoorlie residents continued to drink and bathe in the water delivered by the pipeline. Thousands of residents were sick from radiation poisoning and hundreds died. Kalgoorlie is still populated by miners and associated industries because of the promise of gold. Locals are now relying on trains to transport water from the Avon River in Northam, a distance of 495 kilometres. The irony is not lost on local historians, as this was the method used prior to O'Connor's pipe, almost 140 years earlier. It's not surprising that water in Kalgoorlie is not only rationed, but also priced higher than oil.

I took my .223 Remington rifle from the scabbard and hung it over my shoulder. With Billy in tow I approached the police station's front counter. Senior Constable Atkins leaned against the counter attempting to complete a crossword puzzle. He had a look of deep concentration and mild frustration. The demise of the Internet and smart phones has resulted in a resurgence in paper-based media and entertainment. One thing I'll never miss from the old world is the annoying buzz of my work phone. That, and social media.

Atkins is an athletic looking man in his late twenties, with shaggy blonde hair and blue eyes. Give him a wetsuit and a board and he wouldn't look out of place in the big surf of the expansive west coast beaches. He's awfully popular with the ladies; until they get to know him.

I peered down at the puzzle, before flipping it around and contemplating the two missing words. "Ten across is aardvark."

Atkins glared at me. "Did I ask for your assistance Archie?"

With a fist full of Billy's ponytail, I tilted my head towards the enraged reprobate, "I'm not just helping you with your puzzles mate. As you can see, I've dragged back your favourite escapee."

Billy spat out across the counter yelping, "Get off me ya dog!" Atkins pointed to the side counter entrance and asked me to bring him out the back. I dragged Billy by the scruff of his neck to the cell door and pushed him towards the far wall. As Atkins locked the cell door he muttered, "I'll meet you at the counter and fix you up."

I took one last glance at Billy. "I don't mean to rub salt into your wounds, but I'm hoping we don't meet again, in this life or the next." Billy spat towards me, falling short, just like he did in life.

It took just three months after the War's end for the Australian States and Territories to fracture and secede from the Federal Commonwealth. The decimation of the population, the destruction of the communication systems and the crash of the global economy, caused untold stress on Government structures, including law and order. One of the consequences of the increase in violent crimes was the contracting of bounty hunters to chase down the most violent of offenders.

After returning to the front counter, Senior Constable Atkins passed me the completed handover documentation, which I required to prove to the bondsman that I had honoured the contract. It was time to get paid. But first I needed a much-deserved alcoholic beverage. I led Roger to Heidrick's Stables and handed over the reins to the stable boy. Roger's agistment cost me one twentieth of an ounce of gold per month. Because I love the silly fella, I paid extra for his rub down, walk around the yard, and better-quality feed.

It was reported that during the War, the United States, India, China, and Russia, used electromagnetic pulse weapons (EMPs) to disrupt their enemy's technology. Most technology with a computer chip is now completely useless. In recent years horse ownership has risen as a primary form of transportation, as vehicles manufactured after 1975 are non-operational due to their electronic parts and computer chips. Consequently, motor vehicles are awfully expensive to purchase, run and maintain. To the best of my knowledge, modern vehicles are no longer even being manufactured, and if they are, they are definitely not being imported to the land of Oz. Roger is not just my mate, he's my sole method of transportation. Walking is not an option over the vast dry plains of the Eastern Goldfields. You'll shrivel up like a grape left in the sun on a forty-five degree day.

The citizens of Kalgoorlie kept to themselves as I moseyed down the dusty sidewalk to my current place of abode. My palm pushed open the hand carved saloon doors of the Exchange Hotel. It wasn't much cooler inside the venue than out. It may be grimy and full of cheesy neon signs and memorabilia, but this is my favourite watering hole. Drinking, fighting, and furphies have taken place within these walls since the early 1900s. Not much has changed in that regard.

The cloakroom attendant made small talk as I checked-in my rifle. When I'm in the presence of strangers, or those that I do not trust, my revolver and knife never leave my side. However, it's a strict rule to hand over your longarms upon entry to a licensed establishment. Longarms include firearms such as assault rifles, shotguns, lever action rifles, and bolt action rifles. Publicans, owners, and staff want to avoid patrons settling arguments with an assault rifle that can fire 600 rounds a minute, or a shotgun that can separate a man's head from his neck before he can shout '*Don't Shoot*!'. Aside from the necessary clean-up after a shoot-out, it's also considered bad for business. No one wants to spill their drinks as they're ducking and diving behind furniture.

The haze of the unfiltered tobacco smoke wafted throughout the venue. The bar was full of miners; tough resilient men and women who worked hard and played even harder. The jukebox was thumping out a heavy metal tune as the skimpy barmaids delivered jugs of beer to the tables. I scanned the room and noticed that sections of the crowd were intoxicated and rowdy, with everyone appearing to be in good spirits. The young men at the dart board were mucking around, grabbing each other in headlocks and slap-fighting. There was no sign of the colossal bouncer with the broad shoulders of a silverback gorilla.

The publican is a red head in her early sixties named Jules. She has a tiny waist with impressive mammary glands; with a blonde wig she could win first place in a Dolly Parton lookalike competition. Jules came around the counter, gave me a big hug and then pinched my backside. She may be twenty-five years older than me, but she can still make me feel mighty uncomfortable. I could feel the heat rising to my cheeks and I was worried it would match the pigment of her hair. As she returned to the other side of the bar, she shouted above the sound of AC/DC's, '*Highway to Hell*,' "What are you having cutie?"

"I'll have a pint of Hannans thanks. And Jules, I'm planning to fix up my account this arvo."

Jules smiled as she poured the beer from the bar tap. "No worries luv, I know you're good for it. You're not planning to stick around?"

I'd been lodging at the hotel for the past three months while searching for Billy and was hoping that another contract presented itself in the interim. "I'll be staying put for another week or so. You know how it is, I'll have to follow the gold."

Jules passed me the pint and looked up at my bandage, which was beginning to unravel. "You be careful luv."

Acknowledging her advice with a nod, I took a swig of my beer and turned towards the sound of a ruckus. A skinny blonde skimpy in her early twenties had a young wiry looking bloke pressed hard up against the dart board. She had both her hands wrapped around his throat. She spat in his face and shouted, "Don't you ever grab me like that ever again, you got that you filthy fucker?"

Unless there's a transaction of value, or I'm drunk, I'm hesitant to become involved in any type of physical confrontation. Otherwise, it's high risk for no reward. The young fella wouldn't have been more than twenty-one years old, but he looked like he worked on the tools or some other form of hard labour. He appeared to have recovered from the initial onslaught. He picked up the bare-chested blonde from beneath her armpits and threw her against the side of the jukebox, which was still screaming out *'Highway to Hell.'*

Jules darted around the counter with a concerned look on her face. The blonde was one of her barmaids and she wanted to protect her asset. There was still no sign of the bouncer. *Where the hell was he?* The barmaid was sitting on the floor leaning against the jukebox with her palms defensively raised above her head, while the young bloke stood over her with his fists clenched.

I looked over at Jules and gave her a wink as I approached the young fella. "Hey mate, I think you've made your point, time to move on."

He turned to face me with a thousand-yard stare. "Who the fuck are you and what makes you think you can get involved in my business?"

I placed my open palms up in the age-old gesture of peace. As I tried reasoning with the young bloke, the barmaid rose to her feet and launched the toe of her high heeled foot right between his legs, in a kicking action that would have made an Aussie Rules footballer as proud as punch. For a split second the young man had a look of shock on his face, before wincing in pain and toppling over into a foetal position and dry retching as he cupped his hands between his legs.

The 150-kilogram plus bouncer suddenly bounded forward from behind the bar. He made his appearance known by grunting expletives at anyone in the crowd who got in his way and pushed and shoved those that failed to heed his warning. When he arrived at the scene of the disturbance, he bent down and picked up the bloke by the back of his jeans and dragged him out the saloon doors to the curb. The no-nonsense bouncer gave him a solid kick to the ribs just for good measure, leaving him groaning in the dirt clutching his groin with one hand and his stomach with the other. I considered the turn of events and hoped for the young fella's sake that the outcome would be an important lesson – *'Don't ever hit women.'*

Now that the situation had calmed, I sculled the remnants of my pint and made my way up the spiralling staircase to my room. Once inside, I carefully locked the door and placed my travel pack on the table. The room was spartan, with a single bed, bedside table and draws, and a door to the balcony.

The floorboards creaked as I trudged to the bathroom. I was keen to wash the four days of grime from my hair and skin. I turned the cold tap and lukewarm water dribbled from the rusted shower head. As water soaked the blood-stained bandage, I looked down between my feet to see the red liquid trickle down the drain. It's amazing how a little blood mixed with water can turn into rivers of red. The heat of the day was still stifling, so much so that when the cool water eventually flowed freely, steam rose from the top of my shoulders and neck. I stepped out of the shower and wrapped a salmon-coloured towel around my waist. Before I had a chance to get dressed, there were three sharp knocks on the door.

Retrieving my revolver from my holster, I pointed it towards the door and pressed my shoulder against the sidewall. I unlocked and slowly turned the door handle. The blonde skimpy involved in the fracas was now fully clothed, wearing tracksuit pants and a white t-shirt with a diagram of a red drum kit printed on the chest. Before I could ask what she wanted, she barged her way into the room and stood with her back to the wardrobe. Not for the first time I noticed that she had an athletic runner's body with narrow hips and small breasts.

I was both surprised and mildly irritated by her presence. I stood awkwardly and all I could manage to splutter was, "Can I help you with something?"

She gave me a cheeky smile. "Probably not with what you have in mind. Don't get me wrong, you have the chiselled six pack and the exotic looks, I'm sure you make all the girls swoon, but I happen to be batting for the other team."

Fatigue started to set in and I suddenly had little patience for games. "Okaaay, look, I'm not sure what you want but I'm shattered, so please cut to the chase."

"Jules asked me to come up and have a look at your cut," she explained.

After re-holstering my revolver, I sat down on the edge of the bed, self-consciously keeping my legs together. The barmaid held a white metal container with a red cross stencilled on the side. She stood next to me and examined my cut. "This won't need stitches, but I'll apply a fresh gauze and bandage."

It took considerable self-control not to flinch as she applied antiseptic from an aged brown medicine bottle. As she applied the bandage she spoke quickly, "Short story, my name is Fiona, I arrived in Kal a week ago thinking I could pick up work. I started working as a skimpy when I got desperate. But as you witnessed downstairs, I'm not exactly cut out for it. What I was thinking was..."

My patience was wearing thin, so I cut her off, "Look, I appreciate you helping me out with the cut, but what's your situation got to do with me?"

She finished securing the fresh bandage and stood in front of me. "Well, Jules tells me you're quite the bounty hunter and she seems to think quite highly of you, which is saying something. What I want is a job as your assistant to get some experience. I learned some advanced first aid on a farm and I'm a fast learner, so I can be useful."

I was a bit taken aback to say the least, but I told her straight, "The answer is no thank you, no way, not on your life."

She looked exasperated and dug her heals in. "Come on, you've seen what I can do, I can handle myself. Why not give me a shot? What have you got to lose? Just pay me enough so I can afford food and my room."

I was sore, tired, and grumpy. I'd had enough of her nonsense. I pointed towards the door and in a firm tone I told her louder than I had intended, "You need to leave now!"

She must have seen the look in my eye because she seemed to bite down any further argument, and walked out with a straight back, slamming the door behind her.

I locked the door the moment she left, swallowed my second oxy for the day and face planted onto the bed.

I embraced the numbness that has become my loving mistress, and finally fell asleep.

Chapter Two

Wednesday January 16, 2041 – Archie

CAW, CAW, CAW. I woke just after dawn to a couple of crows sitting on the balcony balustrade. I wondered whether they were discussing the politics of the day, or maybe what they planned to steal for lunch.

The towel was still wrapped around my waist from the night before. I slid on my jeans, grabbed a clean shirt, and started cleaning my revolver. My former army drill sergeant would turn in his grave if he knew my choice of handgun is a revolver. Most people shake their head in astonishment when they discover that I prefer revolvers over semi-automatic pistols. My Smith and Wesson .38 special doesn't pack much of a punch compared to most semi-autos, and you only have six rounds in the cylinder, but they have fewer parts and are almost indestructible.

When a bounty hunter regularly resorts to using a firearm, they are either unprepared, unprofessional, or one sick puppy. The use of firearms is generally my last option, but one that I'm more than prepared to use if I have to defend myself.

My three main weapons consist of my revolver, rifle, and a F-S fighting knife which I inherited from my father. My old man inherited the knife from Grandad, who served in the Royal Australian Regiment during the Vietnam War. Grandad described Vietnam as a fucked-up War that served no purpose. That may be the case, but at least the combatants didn't use NUKES and almost destroy civilisation. In 2025, when I returned from backpacking through Vietnam, I told Grandad that the locals referred to the war as the American War. He mumbled '*What would they know?*' as he shuffled towards the fridge to grab a beer. As I cleaned the seven inch acutely tapered pointed blade, I reflected on how it had been quite useful in getting me out of some sticky situations.

I re-holstered my revolver and returned the knife to the leather sheath. I'm right-handed, so both weapons are positioned on the master-side of my belt. On the left-hand side I have two speed loaders clipped near my belt buckle. These provide me ready access to twelve additional rounds during a gun fight. My drill sergeant would claim that I wouldn't need the extra rounds if I used a semi-automatic pistol, '*blah blah blah,*' I've heard it all before.

Out in the bush my life depends on having a sufficient supply of perishables and serviceable equipment. I removed all of the items from my pack and placed them on the bed. The survival items and necessities include – dehydrated meals, flint, Leatherman multitool, map book, journal, lock pick set, compass, night vision goggles, duct tape, rope, torch, batteries, folding spade, extensive first aid kit, water purification tablets, and two pairs of merino wool socks. The army taught me to be prepared and keep my feet healthy and dry, so I can run, fight, and survive. You can't travel far if your feet are blistered and sore.

I retrieved my journal from the side pocket of my trusty pack and recorded the date of capture alongside Billy Spratt's entry. This was my first completed bounty contract for the year. I reviewed last year's results; I had successfully captured eleven felons and earned sixteen ounces of gold. I also took on other jobs to supplement my earnings, such as private contracts and security work.

Issued	Fugitive	Capture	Reward
31/1/40	Tony Adams	8/3/40	2 ounces
7/2/40	Daniel Shahwani	8/4/40	2 ounces
18/2/40	Urs Keusen		
5/3/40	Sun Jin-Song	7/4/40	2 ounces
6/5/40	Water Train	6/5/40	½ ounce
9/5/40	Alex Stathopoulos	12/4/41	3 ounces
12/4/40	Elsie Findlay		
17/6/40	Edgar Eisen	21/10/40	1 ounce
14/5/40	Water Train	14/5/40	½ ounce
13/8/40	Joel Cooper		
19/9/40	Debt collect - Kroy	23/9/41	½ ounce
24/9/40	Erin Clarke	25/9/40	1 ounce
18/10/40	Water Train	18/10/40	½ ounce
19/10/40	Yasuda Takao	8/11/40	3 ounces
24/10/40	Drago Simic	27/10/40	2 ounces
1/11/40	Billy Spratt	15/1/41	2 ounces

I checked my jeans pocket to ensure I had Billy's handover document, before attending the bondsman's office to collect what I was owed. In most large towns the bondsman's office is located next to the police station, and it's no different in Kalgoorlie. I stepped into the office and greeted Henry. Henry Jenkins was a morbidly obese man who struggled to tie his shoelaces, which is why he chooses to wear thongs. He also likes a tipple during the day, his favourite being vodka from a gold flask that he keeps under the counter.

As the town's bondsman I have to keep Henry on side, which is why I ignore his racist jibes. You see, my mum was Korean and my father's ancestry is Irish and Jamaican. I've been told that I look like an Islander - Samoan, Māori, Tongan, take your pick. At the end of the day, I'm Australian - I was born here and like my old man and grandad, I fought under the national flag. I even eat bloody Vegemite.

Henry belched, and with a slightly slurred speech he inquired, "How are you going coconut?"

As I sighed, I took out the paperwork and handed it to Henry.

Attempting to hide my irritated tone I snapped, "I'm here to pick up the reward."

Henry leaned on the counter and lifted his turkey neck to look me in the eye, "Okay, hold your horses' coco."

In frustration, I took a deep breath, and watched Henry waddle to the back office and remove two ounces of gold from the safe. He placed the gold in a leather satchel and waddled back to the counter. He handed me the receipt and I counter-signed the contract. Henry knew of my prior occupation, which is why he crossed his t's and dotted his i's. Cheating me was not an option. I secured the satchel in my pack and asked him if there were any outstanding bounties. As a bounty hunter it's important to look for the next payday. You can't afford to rest on your laurels.

Henry paused and tapped his fingers on the counter as he looked down at the carpet with a furrowed brown. As I looked on, I was concerned that he'd forgotten my original question. He then suddenly came alive, "That's right, Brad Hill from Esperance called me this morning. They have an escapee that's been seen in the area. Brad is acting as bondsman until Charlotte returns from a funeral up north."

I was pleased, as this may be an option if something local didn't suddenly come to fruition. "Cheers. Have you heard of any other upcoming trials or escapees in the region?" I asked more as wishful thinking than a realistic prospect.

Henry chuckled with exuberance - his neck wobbled in cadence with his shoulders as they moved up and down. "Ha ha, you are a greedy monkey, aren't you? Don't you think I'd have told you?"

There is only so much a man can take. This time he'd taken the racist remarks one step too far. I leaned over the counter and launched a short right cross, slamming my knuckles into the bridge of his nose. There was a loud crunch and his eyes started to water. Blood instantly dripped down from both his nostrils. I grabbed him by his tie just below the knot and pulled him towards me.

I calmly and slowly explained, "Henry, listen carefully. In the future, please don't refer to me as monkey, coconut, or any other racist name. Just call me Archie. Do you understand Henry?"

Henry quickly nodded his head as he was wincing and pressing the sides of his nose with his fingertips, the blood pooling on the countertop.

As the local work had dried up, it was time to leave town. I used the public telephone located at the front of the convenience store to call Esperance's acting-bondsman. He confirmed the details of the outstanding bounty and provided me some brief facts. Before I proceeded to search for the escapee, I needed to attend the Esperance office and pick up the contract. It's not legal for bounty hunters to capture a fugitive without being issued a contract by the bondsman. A bondsman can issue copies of the contract to multiple bounty hunters, so it's important to visit the office as soon as possible - 'first come, first served.'

On my way back to the hotel I visited a local store and purchased an adequate supply of water and food for the twelve-day ride to Esperance. I dropped by the stables to have a quick word with the stable boy, asking him to prepare Roger for our departure. Roger is a well-muscled Australian Stock Horse, bred for their courage, intelligence, toughness, and stamina. My best mate is a good-looking fella - with large eyes, long arched neck, deep chest, and a strong broad back.

The stable boy stuck out his chest. "I've given him a wash and a good rub down sir."

He's a good boy who treats Roger like a treasured pet. I presented him with a chocolate bar that was almost worth its weight in gold. The boy's grin spread from ear to ear as he grabbed the bar out of my grasp with the speed of a chameleon's tongue capturing its prey. The cost to manufacture, distribute, and refrigerate dairy products, make items such as chocolate an extravagant culinary treat.

The bar at the Exchange Hotel was busy for this time of the day, with patrons shouting over the sound of the jukebox. While I was clearing my debts with Jules, I noticed Fiona, the feisty young lady that burst into my room the night before. She was bare chested serving some boisterous miners who were attempting to grab her around the waist and pinch her backside.

"SORRY JULES," I shouted across the bar.

She leaned over the bar. "What do you have to be sorry for luv?"

"I'm taking your skimpy with me," I replied with an apologetic tone.

Jules laughed. "She's not interested in men luv, not even good-lookers like you. You know you can always come to old Jules for some loving."

The heat returned to my cheeks. "Thanks Jules, but I love you like a sister." I was careful not to say mother, as I'm rather fond of my front teeth. "I'm taking her on as an apprentice."

It's a rare occurrence indeed for Jules to be lost for words.

While trouncing up the staircase to my room I yelled out, "FIONA, be out the front in an hour, we're leaving Town."

I didn't turn to look in her direction, but after a slight pause I heard a "FUCK YEAH!"

My left hand shook slightly as I swallowed an oxy. Placing my hands on the edge of the bathroom basin, I examined myself in the mirror. With four days of stubble and dark circles under my eyes, I was looking and feeling a bit rough. It was important that I demonstrate at least a modicum of professionalism to my new apprentice, so I decided to shave and freshen up a bit before the long ride.

As I used the cut-throat to shave the remaining stubble from under my chin, a familiar feeling of fatigue was suddenly upon me. Next came a pressing weight on my chest, followed by a repressive feeling of losing control. You can never outrun the '*black dog*,' but that doesn't stop me from trying. This is one of the reasons I take as many challenging and risky contracts as possible. In fact, the greater the risk, the better the job. It keeps my mind focused and the black dog at bay. I enjoy the challenge and the subsequent endorphin rush when I finally close in on the prey. It helps take my mind off Janet, the lost love of my life. Even if it only relieves the pain for a brief moment, it's well worth it.

While I wiped the shaving cream from my cheeks, I thought of Janet, holding her and doing my darndest to make her smile and laugh. My state of mind can change in an instant and without much of a warning. I slammed my fist into the mirror, watching it spread like a spider's web. My middle knuckle split, and blood began to flow. Breathing deep from the pit of my stomach, I held my breath after a long inhale, and then counted down as I slowly exhaled, and then rinsed and repeated, each cycle lasting for fifteen seconds.

It took twenty minutes for the oxy and deep breathing cycles to finally take effect. My mind started to clear as I lay on the bed gazing at the water stains on the ceiling, letting my imaginings run wild, finding the face of an old man, a dolphin, and a truck. I shook my head and glanced at my watch. Time to get moving. Once I'd packed my belongings and supplies, I said my farewell to Jules before exiting the hotel's swinging saloon doors.

Fiona was patiently waiting for me out front. She was dressed in jeans, a long-sleeved denim shirt, and was wearing an Akubra hat. It was pleasing to see that she also had a desert toned camouflaged pack on her back.

"Alright, let's get a coffee and I'll lay down the rules and how this is going to work."

She looked at me defiantly. "This is not my first rodeo cowboy."

I stepped towards her and looked down into her eyes and stated with a firm tone, "First rule, don't talk back, just listen. If you want to be my apprentice, you will listen to what I say and do what I ask. Or else this won't work. Do you understand?"

Fiona looked like she was about to argue the point, but wisely decided to bite down on her bottom lip and nod. Good, a little humility goes a long a way in learning this trade, not to mention staying alive.

We walked two doors down to a café and sat outside under the tin roof. The welcome shade provided an escape from the scorching sun.

After I ordered two long blacks I returned to our table. "Look, I don't want to know your story right now, there'll be plenty of time for that on the trail to Esperance. For now, I just want you to answer some simple questions. Do you know how to use a firearm?"

"We're riding to Esperance?"

I tried not to sound frustrated and repeated my question, "Do you know how to use a firearm?"

She paused for a second. "I've used a shotgun when I had to shoot some wild dogs attacking a calf."

Second question, "Do you know how to ride a horse?"

"I rode quite often when I was working on a farm," she replied confidently.

"Do you own a horse?"

She laughed as if the premise of the question was completely ridiculous. "Ha, are you serious? How could I afford a horse working as a barmaid?"

The long blacks arrived in chipped ceramic mugs. As Fiona sipped her coffee, careful not to place her mouth over any jagged edges, I took a tattered notebook and pen from the front pocket of my pack and placed it in front of her. "Write down your next of kin's contact details, your blood type and any allergies."

Fiona held my gaze for a moment and then began writing. It didn't take her long to scribble my request and place the notebook in front of me on the plastic table.

I retrieved an unused notebook from my pack and handed it to her. "This is your notebook. I want you to record important learnings and intel we receive during an operation. I also want you to repeat what you wrote in my pad in the inside front cover of your notebook. Also write my name down. If the authorities or another hunter finds your body, they'll know who to notify."

She lost the colour in her cheeks as she opened her notebook and recorded the details on the inside cover.

"Okay, your turn, any questions?" I asked.

She paused and then asked, "How long is the apprenticeship and what's my pay?"

I had expected this to be the first of many questions. "The apprenticeship is as long as it takes for you to learn the business. You will commence on a basic stipend for the first two contracts, and if you learn fast, I'll give you a 25% cut of subsequent bounties. Of course, you can leave at any time. When you feel like you're ready to go it alone, go for it, you won't hurt my feelings, trust me."

"Have you killed anyone?" she asked quickly with wide eyes.

Most people have a romantic notion of the life and work of a bounty hunter. When meeting people for the first time, I actually get asked this question more often than not. Give or take a few words, I answer with the same response, "You don't ask a bounty hunter, soldier or police officer that question. Killing someone is my last option, and one that I tend to avoid."

Before she could retort, I asked, "What's your surname?"

"Katsaros, K-A-T-S-A-R-O-S," which I scribbled in my notebook. She must have been asked a thousand times to spell her surname.

I returned the notebook to Fiona. "Have a read of my one and only condition of employment, and if you agree, scribble your moniker and today's date."

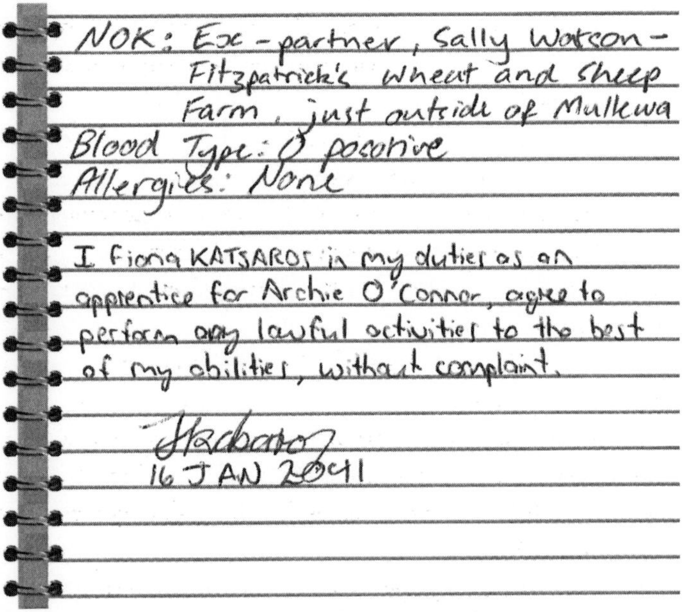

She looked at me with a quizzical expression. "It means your signature," I explained.

"I know that. I'm not stupid. What's the date?" she replied sarcastically.

I gave a deep sigh and wondered for the first time but certainly not the last - *What have I got myself into?*

We walked to the stables and asked the boy to grab Heidrick, the stable boss. Heidrick was a short heavy-set man with massive forearms that would make Popeye jealous. "Hey Heidrick, how you going mate?"

He replied in his usual friendly manner. "Not bad Archie, not bad at all, what can I do you for?"

I tilted my head towards Fiona. "Mate, this is Fiona. She'll be working as my apprentice. I need to purchase her a mount and all the necessary kit."

Heidrick couldn't hide his smirk. "Didn't take you for a man that had the patience to teach Archie."

I gave him a look of mock offence. "I've been watching you train the apprentices over the years mate, and I've picked up a bit. I'm sure we'll be just fine."

Heidrick opened the stable doors. "Oki dokie, come inside and have a gander at what we have in stock."

Just after walking through the stable doors, Roger stamped his left front hoof and made a soft low whinny. He gave me a look that meant something like, *"Where the hell have you been? By the way I'm excited to see you. Hey, let's get out of here."*

I placed my palm on his forehead. "It's good to see you too mate, we'll be taking off soon."

Heidrick was standing in front of a stocky and compact dark brown Brumby – he had a long thick neck and large elongated head. "This is Jasper, he's seven years old and he has a fine temperament. Don't you matey?"

Fiona walked up to Jasper and stroked his forehead, who in turn lowered his head and nuzzled his nose into her shoulder. They appeared to have made an instant connection. "We'll take him," I announced.

We saddled up and rode down the main street of town. I

explained to Fiona that if we rode thirty kilometres a day, we'd arrive in Esperance in about twelve days.

As we trotted past the Town Hall, I was surprised to see a growing tumultuous crowd. Being on horseback enabled us to see over the heads of the crowd. The hangman was leading Billy Spratt up the steps to the gallows platform.

I have no idea why Samuel Jones, a local baker and part-time executioner, wears a black hood over his head. Everyone knows that he's the hangman. Samuel has luscious curly locks that he swears are natural. The rumour-mill has formed a different opinion, speculating he has a secret monthly perm at the ladies salon. I'm willing to give him the benefit of the doubt, not that there's anything wrong with desiring curls.

Billy shouted profanities at the crowd as they spat, cheered, and jeered. I pondered that Samuel may wear the hood to protect his precious curls from the crowd's spittle.

Samuel expertly placed the noose around Billy's neck, ensuring the knot was positioned under his jaw on the left-hand side of his neck. If Billy were fortunate, the jolt to his neck at the end of the six-foot drop would be enough to cause his axis bone to break, which in turn would sever his spinal cord - *A quick and painless death!* If he were unfortunate and his neck failed to break, he'd experience a painful strangulation for up to twenty minutes - *A slow and tortuous death!*

We continued to trot down the dusty main street. The sudden roar of the crowd erupted, followed by an accompanying ovation. Fiona swung around in her saddle towards the cheering. I'd be lying if I said I wasn't tempted to look back to determine whether it was quick or slow. However, one thing's for certain, Billy has definitely had better days.

Chapter Three

Wednesday January 23, 2041 – Fiona

For seven days we'd travelled through a landscape that most city dwellers would describe as both beautiful and desolate. So far, distractions were few and far between, and Archie was not much of a talker, he mostly kept to himself.

On the morning of the second day of our journey, I asked Archie about the ring on his wedding finger. He told me snippets about his late wife and was then deathly silent for the remainder of the day. The only time he showed any interest in interacting was just after dinner, when he taught me skills such as finding and purifying water, orienteering, lighting a fire, hunting, and foraging. He told me that it was a priority to learn survival skills before shifting to the tactical aspects of the job. I had no idea what he meant by 'tactical aspects,' but I wasn't game to look foolish and ask him to elaborate. He must have misinterpreted my confused look, as he asked in a stern manner, "If you can't travel and survive in the bush, how do you expect to locate and capture a fugitive?" *Well, all righty then.*

Archie explained that prior to learning how to shoot, it was necessary to first identify and describe the basic parts and functions of the bolt-action rifle - *muzzle, sights, barrel, chamber, forestock, magazine, bolt, bolt handle, trigger, trigger guard, safety, stock, butt, bore, breech, firing pin, and receiver.* Once I could reel them off to his satisfaction, he then taught me how to conduct a weapon serviceability. This involved stripping, cleaning, re-assembling, and dry firing the rifle to ensure it was functioning correctly. It wasn't any harder than assembling the Meccano building set my parents bought me for my eighth birthday, but I kept this to myself as I didn't want to sound like a smartass, which I've been told is one of my most annoying traits.

At school I displayed a real aptitude for learning and received straight A's up until the nuns drained the fun out of the classroom. When I stripped the firearm and reassembled it with ease, I think I surprised him, as he commented that I was a 'natural.' However, that didn't stop him from insisting that I perform the repetitive tasks at the start and end of each day.

Archie explained, "Your firearm is a tool that you may require at a moment's notice to save your life. If you don't look after your tools, then they won't look after you. If it goes *Click* instead of *Boom*, you're dead."

Archie was turning out to be a real fun guy!

A mixture of boredom and desire to form some type of connection, encouraged me to tell Archie my story, at least the parts I was comfortable for him to know. I was ten-years-old when the War started. Few people at the time believed Perth, the capital city of Western Australia, was at risk of being attacked. People reassured themselves by reminding others that the city had escaped attention during World War Two. The fact it's a little known place and one of the most isolated cities in the world, fuelled the belief that it wouldn't be targeted. There were still those that chose to be cautious. Parents that could afford the fees, sent their children to the outer regions to attend boarding school. I happened to be one of those scared and confused kids.

My parents were considered upper middle class, both working in the Perth central business district (CBD) in managerial positions. I first heard about the nuclear missiles striking Perth from Natalie, one of my besties. Natalie lived in Mandurah, a town seventy-two kilometres south of the city. Before I was sent to boarding school, we'd spend almost every afternoon chatting about boys, the latest bands, and TikTok stars. The first letter I had ever received was from a friend who informed me that Natalie had been killed during the initial evacuation. Natalie was one of 1.5 million people who died as a result of the attack; at the time this represented more than half of the State's population. Entire suburbs were decimated, families were torn apart, and society was thrown back into the Dark Ages. Darwin and Hobart were the only Australian capital cities to be spared the devastating effects of nuclear strikes.

The boarding school was closed two weeks from the day Perth was attacked. Scared and confused, we awoke to find our teachers missing. Years later I assumed that they left to find their friends and family members, but at the time we felt abandoned and unloved. Like many of the orphans, I was taken in by nuns from a nearby Christian college. We could all relate with the children of the early 1920s who were sent to orphanages during the First World War – there was not enough food, and emotional, physical, and sexual abuse was tolerated by those in charge.

Early on I felt a sense of isolation and guilt, constantly reminded that we were the lucky ones. By fifteen years of age, I was distrustful of adults and had an inability to maintain friendships. What is the point of making friends when they can be taken away at a moment's notice? I decided to start afresh and ran away from the orphanage on my sixteenth birthday.

Over the previous six years I had moved from one local town to the next, working as a maid, nanny, and fruit picker, before taking on work as a barmaid in the Eastern Goldfields. I'd resisted the encouragement of publicans to work as a skimpy, until I ran out of coin and found myself destitute.

We had ridden hard all day and I was beginning to suffer from saddle sores. I sighed with relief when Archie decided to set up camp at the Mount Thirsty rest area, which was situated on the banks of Lake Cowan, nineteen kilometres north of a town called Norseman. The name of the area was true to form, as Lake Cowan was a saltwater lake which was utterly dry for most of the year. I asked Archie why we weren't stopping off at Norseman. I was beginning to fantasise about having a bath and sleep in a soft bed. He explained that he'd been provided intel that the town had been taken over by a murderous outlaw gang. It had been reported that this gang had crossed the South Australian border and was wreaking havoc throughout the region. I decided that I was able to do without the creature comforts after all.

We watered, fed, and gave Roger and Jasper a good rub down. Our food supplies had dwindled, and we were left with a measly two dehydrated packs of mushroom soup. Archie commented that he couldn't believe how much I ate for a person of my size, before confessing that he'd failed to take into consideration the amount of food required for a party of two. I bit my tongue and thought – "And this is my teacher?"

We headed out from camp to hunt for our dinner. My stomach was rumbling and growling, begging to be fed. It was predusk, with enough light in the sky to witness a mob of kangaroos chewing on grass about one hundred metres from where we stood. A big grey's ears twitched, he extended his hind legs and stood six-foot-five, sticking out his powerful chest. I'd been practicing with the rifle over the previous four afternoons. We propped near a gum tree where I had a clear shot through the clearing. Archie gently held my shoulder and pointed to the ground. I knelt, ensuring I made as little noise as possible, and rested the meaty part of my tricep on my front knee.

Archie whispered in my ear, "Take out the young buck to the left of the big boy, and make sure it's a head shot."

I peered through the scope and exhaled, holding my breath as I squeezed the trigger. Just as he had taught me. The mob scattered as the shot echoed through the bush. I felt instant relief when Archie acknowledged the clean shot. The last thing I wanted was to cause a slow and agonising death. We returned to the gum tree and butchered the buck, while brushing the bush flies from the carcass.

The stars stood bright in the night sky. We sat by the campfire, with bowls in hand slurping roo stew with gusto. Archie was outlining our route to Esperance when I was alerted to the rumble of vehicles in the distance. "Do you hear that?" I asked.

Archie quickly rose from the log he was sitting on and kicked dirt onto the fire as he spoke in a faint voice, "You grab Roger and Jasper and I'll pack up our gear."

We headed deep into the scrub, waiting, and listening. Archie grabbed a pair of night vision goggles from his pack and then held his rifle in a ready position. I could clearly hear movement – van doors being slammed, equipment being pulled and dragged, and boisterous voices - the singing and laughter of numerous men and women.

Archie turned towards me. "Come on, let's go back. It's all good, they're just a travelling carnival."

Five colourful bongo vans were parked alongside our smouldering fire. *The Marvellous & Exotic Carnival* was painted on the side of each vehicle. Men, women, and people of indeterminate sex - various ages, shapes, and sizes exited the vans.

A pair of identical twins in their mid-thirties, dressed in navy blue dapper suits approached us with surprising swiftness. Give-or-take a couple of centimetres, they stood four-foot tall, with one wearing a red cravat and the other a purple tie. One twin held onto my left hand while the other reached for my right; they simultaneously bowed and kissed the top of my hands, asking in chorus, "How can we be of service miss?"

Having no clue on how to reply and not wanting to offend them, I turned to Archie to rescue me from a case of '*foot in mouth*'. Before I could mumble a response, Archie smiled and asked, "Where are you all headed?"

Both twins started to speak at once, before the gentleman with the purple tie looked up at Archie and took the lead, "We are taking our Marvellous and Exotic Carnival to the good people of Kalgoorlie. I'm Jesse and this is my brother James."

"Good to meet you both. My name's Archie and this young lady is Fiona. Jesse and James, hey. Your parents must have been fans of American Westerns."

"Nah, they're stage names. Where are you travelling to Archie?"

"We'll be heading to Norseman in the morning," Archie replied.

The twins looked concerned. The twin with the cravat spoke in a muffled voice while cupping a hand to his mouth, "We left Norseman this morning. We had few issues, however you both may wish to change your plans based on the new occupants of the town. I will say no more on the matter. Best you do not mention it either."

The twins spun on their heels and walked off towards the nearest van, and then after a couple of steps they asked simultaneously, "I hope you don't mind us sharing your campsite for the night?"

When the twins were no longer within earshot, I asked, "Weren't we planning to avoid Norseman?"

"We were and we still are. Didn't anyone teach you not to trust strangers?"

While trying not to stare at our visitors, I placed some logs on the fire pit and used my flint to generate a spark. Liquid suddenly passed over my shoulder and a blaze erupted towards my face, almost singeing my fringe. In shock I stood up. "What the fuck?"

A handsome man in his late- twenties stood with his hands on his hips belly laughing. "Ha ha ha. Settle down sweetheart. Just a little diesel to help you earn your girl guide badge."

I clenched my fist. I was about to take a swing to wipe the smug look off his face, when the most beautiful woman I have ever seen pushed the arrogant bloke in the chest. "Don't be an asshole Blane." She turned towards me, I was instantly smitten, emotions switching from anger to desire. "Blane is our resident fire-breather, he gets jealous when others play with fire."

She extended her hand. "Hi, I'm Evelyn."

Regaining my composure, I shook her hand. "Fiona."

Evelyn was about six-foot tall, with hourglass curves and long black hair that fell to her waist. "So, what's your role in the carnival Evelyn?"

Evelyn replied with a question, "Can I please hold your hand Fiona?"

She sat down on a log beside me and held my wrist while examining my left palm. Blane stoked the fire, seemingly losing interest in our conversation. She traced her index finger along a line near the centre of my palm. "You will have a long and exciting life. You have found and lost love. Don't worry, love will come again. Just don't expect it in the near future."

I consider myself quite sceptical, however there's a small part of me that wants to believe in the fortuity of life, even if it's through fortune telling.

Archie and the carnies joined us by the fire. A jolly enormous bowling ball of a man handed us a hot dog and beer. He wore a purple robe and sported a magnificent handlebar moustache.

We were sitting in a circle with the blazing fire as the centrepiece, telling wild and fanciful furphies and lewd jokes. This was the most visually interesting group of people that I'd ever had the pleasure to feast my eyes on. There was a pencil thin man that would have been at least seven-foot tall, a woman that was the size of a three-year-old child (a head shorter than the twins), a man who manoeuvred his body like it was made of rubber, a woman whose bulging rippling muscles would make almost any man feel inadequate, and a middle-aged man whose entire body was inked with exotic art.

Just as I had thought I'd seen it all, a monkey dressed in blue denim overalls and a red felt bowler hat, approached me riding a black Labrador and presented me with a beautiful white rose. Evelyn couldn't help but giggle when she saw the astonished expression plastered on my face.

The contortionist and the extremely tall man set up a poker table surrounded by outdoor folding chairs. They politely invited me to play. The human artwork dealt the cards to the muscular woman, the twins, the contortionist, and then finally to me. While I examined my hand, one of the twins asked, "If I can be so bold, what's your story lass?"

While presenting my best poker face, I replied, "I'm just a girl making my way through life, trying not to lose my hard-earned coin at cards."

The muscular woman laughed. "Be careful boys, we may have a shark here."

As one of the twins was considering his hand, I noticed Evelyn and Archie sitting by the fire. They were speaking in hushed tones, while Evelyn held Archie's wrist and pointed to his palm.

We played late into the night until yawning became contagious.

I had broken even, winning a few hands here and there but also losing when it counted. The carnies trundled off to their bongo vans, hollering out good night as they disappeared into the darkness.

Archie and I laid out our sleeping bags near to the extinguished fire. As the van lights were switched off, I gazed at the stars dancing high in the night sky. Not long after settling down, I heard a rustling and opened my tired eyes. Evelyn walked past what must have appeared to be my sleeping form. With her back to me she knelt down towards Archie, placing her index finger to his lips. She then adjusted her knee length skirt before straddling his face. She bent down towards his crotch, unzipped his jeans, and placed his member into her mouth. I could hear a barely audible moan as she gently and rhythmically moved her hips back and forth, and her head up and down. Soon after I heard her gasp, Archie released a rasping moan. I quickly closed my eyes as Evelyn rose to return to her van.

Once she'd departed, I whispered to Archie, "You lucky bastard!"

He turned his back without acknowledging my tongue-in-cheek remark. I fell asleep whispering the parts and functions of a rifle.

~

Archie gently shook my shoulder, waking me from my deep slumber. "Wakey wakey, hands of snakey. It's time to get up."

"I know I'm a tomboy, but I don't have a snakey," I said while yawning.

I felt like I'd just fallen asleep. It was the crack of dawn; a black and white magpie was singing his beautiful tune. I groaned and squirmed out of my sleeping bag, stretching my back and neck. There was movement around the carnival vans in preparation for the start of the day.

"What's for breakfast?" I murmured.

"It's time to go, we'll sort out brekky on the road," Archie responded hastily.

By now I knew what that meant, it was code for '*no breakfast*'.

"What's the rush?" I asked.

"It's too early for questions. Now get a move on," he replied cryptically.

As we left camp, Blane the fire breather gave me a smile and a wave as he was relieving himself by the trunk of a gum tree. In reply, I scowled and presented him with my middle finger.

Chapter Four

Tuesday January 29, 2041 – Archie

We arrived in Esperance on the afternoon of our thirteenth day on the trail. Over the previous three days Fiona had been complaining of saddle soreness, which I know from experience is not fun at all. In sympathy, instead of visiting the bondsman's office and picking up supplies, I decided to ride directly to our lodging to give Fiona a much-needed break from the saddle.

I planned to bunk with my best (human) mate, Clarry. *Just don't tell Roger!* Clarence Ugle is an Indigenous bloke from Fremantle, a proud Whadjuk man from the Noongar nation. Clarry and I have been through thick and thin and up to mischief since the beginning of high school. He's saved me from certain death on more than one occasion, and I in turn have returned the favour.

Like Perth, Fremantle is contaminated from the nukes, and hence Clarence cannot return to the home he had lived in since he was a boy. Clarence also lost his mum and dad during the War, but he's fortunate to have a brother living in Alice Springs and extended family throughout the South West and Eastern Goldfield regions of the state.

Clarry lives on the outskirts of Esperance and is working as an abalone diver; a dangerous occupation when great white sharks are patrolling the waters. Abalone is a marine snail that has a low open spiral structure to their shell, a mouth-watering delicacy throughout the world. Forget about prawns, my mouth waters just thinking about abalone on a barbie with a beer in hand.

Clarry is one of the most intelligent men I have ever met. Prior to the War, he was a scientist working at the Commonwealth Scientific and Industrial Research Organisation (CSIRO), which was an Australian Government agency responsible for scientific research, such as astronomy and space, biosecurity, information technology, health, and climate. The lack of qualified personnel, government financial support, and functional equipment, forced the CSIRO to close its doors just after the War.

Within moments of arriving at Clarry's home, Fiona gingerly dismounted Jasper. "No offence Jasper, I love you, but I need some time out of the saddle, preferably sitting on a couch or lying on a bed."

Clarry's double brick four-bedroom home is typical of your average Australian dwelling. However, his backyard is anything but typical, with stables, a mechanical workshop, greenhouse, and expansive gym.

I knocked loudly on the security screen and bellowed, "Clarry, are you in mate?"

I heard the scuttle of paws on a hard wood floor, and then BANG!, two paws pounded onto the screen followed by a menacing growl and thundering repetitive barks. I instinctively took a large step back.

"Zeus, settle down boy!" Clarry grabbed the enormous Rottweiler's silver studded collar and gave him a pat to his muscular chest. "Good boy, you're a good boy, yes you are." Zeus returned the compliment by licking Clarry under his neck and then obediently sat, paying particular attention to our presence, with a low but unmistakable rumbling growl.

Clarence opened the security screen, rushed forward, and gave me a forceful man hug. I managed to escape his grasp and made the necessary introductions, "Clarry, this is Fiona, my new apprentice. Fiona, this is Clarry, my no-good mate."

They both shook hands and sized each other up.

"How do you put up with him?" Clarry asked.

"I'm beginning to get used to him," she laughed.

"Bring the horses to the stables and we'll get them all sorted with feed and water," offered Clarry.

"I was just wondering how Zeus is with horses?" asked Fiona. I was pleased that she's shown an affinity with animals and had the initiative to ask.

"He's all good with other animals, he just has a problem with people." Clarry must have noticed Fiona's concerned expression. "Don't worry, he knows you now and thinks you're a member of the pack. He's all good."

After we settled Roger and Jasper, Clarry led us to the front lounge area of the premises and handed us both a bottle of home brewed beer. We both greedily guzzled the beverage, finishing them off in seconds, our excuse being that it had been a long time between drinks.

Zeus took up an entire three-seater couch, which he appeared to have claimed as his own, with bite and claw marks throughout the upholstery. Clarry explained how he had found Zeus in an abandoned drug lab, malnourished, and abused. He instantly fell in love with the big lug and brought him home.

It has been too long between visits. I hadn't had the opportunity to catch up with Clarry for almost eight months. Clarry is of average height and is whippet thin, he wears grandiose tortoise shell glasses, which I don't have the heart to mention do not suit him at all. Clarry and I engaged in banter and discussed the latest trials and tribulations, within our personal lives and throughout the community. One such story involved an attempt by a South Australian (S.A.) outlaw bikie gang to take over the Esperance Town Centre. I had heard the story of the battle on the grapevine, but I was interested to hear the details straight from the horse's mouth.

The military was disbanded after the fall of the Federal Government, while the State Police consisted of under-resourced localised hubs that were struggling to maintain law and order. Think Mad Max and you'd be close to understanding the lay of the land. In partnership with the local sergeant and his two constables, Clarry organised a home-grown militia to crush the attempted take-over. People from all over the surrounding area joined the militia to fight the scum that were threatening their town. Just your normal everyday civilian stepped-up to do their part – farmers, miners, shopkeepers, labourers, truckies, bakers, and alike. After the dust had settled, the town held a funeral for eight of their residents, before marching the captured outlaws to the town centre and hanging them by their necks. The bikies that managed to escape by the skin of their teeth, retreated over the S.A. border with their tails between their legs.

Zeus gave an expansive yawn before rolling onto his side and falling into a deep slumber.

"So, enough about me. What are your plans Archie?"

"Mate, I'd appreciate it if you could put us up for a couple of days. We're going after a bounty in the area. We'll get out of your hair once we've prepped."

Clarry nodded. "Anything for you brother. And let me know if you need any help."

True to his word, Clarry led us to guest bedrooms with fresh linen and a comfortable bed.

~

The next morning, I found Fiona sitting at the dining table chewing on a piece of Vegemite toast while stroking the nape of Zeus's expansive neck.

"I'm going to visit the bondsman's office," I advised her. "You stay put and rest up. Fingers crossed the bounty contract is still open."

With her mouth half full, Fiona replied, "Okay, good luck."

Clarry was in the driver's seat of his bright green 1971 Volkswagen Beetle with the window wound down. "Do you need a lift brother? I'm just heading down to the harbour."

Grateful for the offer, I walked to the passenger side door and hopped in. There was a crumpled Science Illustrated magazine dated June 2031 lying at the footwell. I picked it up and threw it onto the back seat. Clarry chuckled, "I actually wrote an article in that mag."

I was impressed. "Yeah, what was the subject?"

"I was speculating on Australia's involvement in the race to colonise Mars. It now sounds ridiculous to even contemplate any type of space exploration. Not for the next fifty years anyway."

Clarry drove the Beetle into the main part of town, which you couldn't be blamed for mistaking as a ghost town. A disheveled old man pushed a bulldog in a pram. He appeared to be enjoying the ride, while his owner dodged the scattered litter and thick weeds poking out from every crack in the path.

Clarry kept his eyes on the road. "Soooo, what's with Fiona?"

"Let's just say that she's had some challenges, so I'm helping her out. I've taken her under my wing so to speak. I'll just see how she goes."

Clarry gave me a sideways glance. "Fair enough brother, just make sure you know what you're doing. Sounds like a big responsibility."

"Ye of little faith," I said while looking out the passenger window.

"I don't want to give you a hard time. It's just that she seems like a nice kid, and your occupation is dangerous to the mind, body, and spirit."

I pondered which spirit he referred to, but kept my mouth firmly shut. Clarry wore the Christian cross and also believed in the Noongar spirits.

Clarry dropped me at the bondsman office, which was situated beside the police station. As soon as I entered the doorway I was greeted with an uninviting musty odour.

I approached the coffee-stained laminated bench top and tapped the counter bell. A tall thin man with a thick black lumberjack beard, approached the counter from the office hallway. "How can I help you?"

"Brad Hill, is it?" I asked.

He replied with his hands up walking towards the counter, "Guilty as charged partner."

"My name's Archie O'Connor, I spoke to you on the phone almost a couple of weeks ago about an outstanding contract. I believe it was a bail jumper named Lewis. Has he been brought in yet?" I asked apprehensively, fearing that I'd travelled all this way for a lost cause.

"No offence, but can I see your hunter's ID?" Brad asked with an apologetic expression.

It's legislated that every bounty hunter must carry official identification. The laminated piece of cardboard with my photo in the corner wouldn't be too difficult to forge, but I guess what's left of the State Government believe it's better than nothing. I took out my ID from my back pocket and presented it to Brad. He in turn examined the ID and then looked up at me, before handing it back.

Brad reached under the counter and handed me the paperwork. "It's still active, but I had another hunter pick up the contract three days ago."

It's common for more than one bounty hunter to be chasing the same contract. Which doesn't bother me in the slightest as I'm good at my job, and most of the time I'm first to find the fugitive. However, it can be challenging when the competitor has a considerable jump on you.

"Who's the hunter that picked up the contract?" I asked tentatively.

"You know I can't tell you that," Brad replied with mock surprise.

Noticing Brad's nicotine-stained fingers, I pulled out a packet of cigarettes from my pack and placed them on the counter. "In this part of the world it has to be either Sal Willis, Jess Oh, or Ronnie Coleman."

Brad picked up the packet and gave me a conspiratory wink. "It isn't Jess or Ronnie."

Well, that certainly put a damper on things I thought. Sal Willis is an old-timer who happened to be a highly competent and experience hunter. He was a member of the Second Commando Regiment, a special forces unit of the Australian Army. Their motto was Foras Admonitio, which is Latin for 'Without Warning.' He is known to have claimed more contracts than any two bounty hunters combined.

I was both genuinely surprised and a little dismayed that Sal had picked up the contract. I'd heard through the grapevine that he'd retired from hunting and was working as a debt collector. It's not as lucrative as hunting, but involves considerably less risk. It may have been wishful thinking on my part, but as Sal is almost sixty years old, I thought it was a perfect transition to a safer vocation, and hence believed the rumour to be true. If one thing is for sure, with Sal on the trail, time is against us.

Sal and I had crossed paths on numerous occasions, and he became somewhat of a mentor to me. Our first job together occurred eighteen months after I started hunting. Two crooks had killed a farming family of five in Salmon Gums, which is located one hundred kilometres north of Esperance. After ransacking the property, they set it on fire, which spread to a nearby farm causing considerable damage. The *'Dead or Alive'* bounty was substantial. Four or more hunters were searching throughout the state in the hope of claiming the four ounces of gold.

After Sal had tracked the fugitives to the south western tip of state, to a fishing village near Peaceful Bay, he suggested that we work together and split the bounty. Even after he proposed a sixty-forty split, I wholeheartedly agreed. Why would I haggle? The split was fair; he had located the fugitives and I thought it was an excellent opportunity to learn from a legend. And boy, did I learn.

We propped in an abandoned cabin seventy metres from their hideout. When I asked Sal, "What time are we going in?" He replied, "Soon enough." Three hours went by, and I was getting a little impatient. Sal used the time to talk about his favourite subject, Australian Rules football. He was describing a memorable goal scored by the West Coast Eagles in the dying minutes of the match which won them the 2018 premiership, when two men walked out the front door holding assault rifles. In mid-sentence Sal shot them both through their foreheads with his Tikka M55 Sniper Rifle.

After we had dragged the bodies to the backyard, I asked him, "What did you need me for?"

He handed me a saw from his pack. "For the good conversation and your assistance in removing their heads. I'm not ashamed to admit that I'm a bit squeamish when it comes to dismembering bodies."

Snapping out of my reverie, I reviewed the bounty paperwork. Two months prior, Lewis Hutchins had skipped bail on armed robbery charges and two counts of murder. Lewis had used a sawn-off shotgun to rob the pharmacy just down the road, killing the manager and a young employee as he left the building. He had what he came for – drugs, silver, and gold – he just wanted to permanently silence the witnesses.

It came as no surprise that the contract stipulated his capture as '*Dead or Alive*.' What did come as a surprise was the decision to release him on bail.

"How did he get bail on these charges?" I asked Brad in disbelief.

"You're going to have to give me a lot more than a packet of ciggies for me to spill the beans on that one. Let's just say that his family has done well in the mining game and leave it that."

As the government structures crumbled, corruption became rife throughout the community, which can both aid and obstruct me in performing my job.

"What is the latest intel on Lewis's whereabouts?" I asked in anticipation.

Brad lit up a cigarette and took a long drag before turning his head, blowing out a cloud of smoke over his shoulder. "He was last seen near Merivale. There are rumours around town that he's cooking meth somewhere out there."

After I said my farewell, I stopped by the convenience store and pharmacy to pick up supplies - food, medication, and three packets of cigarettes. Smoking is a dirty habit that I don't partake in, but the cancer stick can be very useful when bartering, or as in Brad's case, for the purpose of *bribery*.

A taxi stopped by the curb and dropped off an elderly lady. I stepped into the taxi's front passenger seat. "How many ciggies to take me to the boat harbour?"

The middle-aged female driver looked me up and down. "Five ciggies will get you there."

She released the 68 Toyota Corolla's handbrake and stepped on the gas. "You don't look local, how long you in town?"

"What does local look like?" I asked in an irritated tone.

The driver sneered. "Don't get your panties in a knot, I just mean I haven't seen you around the traps."

After an uncomfortable pause, I added, "I'll be sticking around for as long as I need to."

With a huff the driver turned up the AM radio which was playing an old Beatles song.

On arrival at the harbour, I handed the driver six cigarettes, an extra fag because I felt guilty about being an ass. As I inspected the jetty, I filled my lungs with the fresh breeze blowing from the southern seas of the Great Australian Bight.

Clarry was standing on a ten-metre aluminium boat with the name Mother Teresa painted on the side. Seagulls were gliding in the breeze as a gentleman in his early-seventies with a long white beard, stood with his hands on his hips watching Clarry scrutinising a compressor.

"Permission to come aboard Captain?" I hollered.

The old salt looked down in my direction. "Permission granted young fella."

As soon as I stepped on board, the Captain rushed forward and grabbed me in a bear hug that almost knocked the wind out of me. About five years ago I performed a private job for Captain Ross, which involved extracting his fifteen-year-old granddaughter from an insidious cult. When I was cornered by members of the group and almost beaten to death, Clarry came to my rescue in his Beetle and almost ran over my attackers. This wasn't the first time he'd saved my bacon.

"Perfect timing son, as I'm a man down. My decky has come down with the flu," the Captain explained.

Clarry chuckled. "Likely story. Scotty probably had a hard night out and woke up feeling like crap."

"Can you help us out for the day?" asked the Captain.

Even though I have a contract in the works, it'd be impolite to drop by for two minutes and then take off. And besides, a day out on the water would do me some good.

"It'd be my pleasure, Captain."

"Good man," he beamed.

My duties as deckhand were mainly watching out for sharks and shucking and putting the catch on ice. The Captain believes that the decrease in the human population and the demise of the monster fishing trawlers has increased the fish stocks, including the biggest and baddest fish of all, the great white shark. The Captain took us out one kilometre from shore to one of his favourite spots. It was a beautiful day; the water was postcard calm and clear.

Clarry dives without a shark-proof cage, arguing that he can bag more abalone minus the restrictions of the steel framed refuge. The Captain dropped anchor and checked the hookah air-line and compressor, which Clarry relied on to supply oxygen during a dive.

Clarry squeezed into his tight-fitting wet suit and secured his fins and mask before plunging into the clear blue water. He would be diving at a depth of between fifteen to twenty metres, not only searching the reefs for abalone, but also remaining vigilant for shapes that resembled any relatives of *Jaws.*

Captain Ross stood beside me as I scanned the waters, watching a pair of majestic dolphins break the surface, before returning to the deep. The Captain's leather tanned skin failed to hide the forty-five centimetre scar that trailed from the middle of his forearm to the tip of his shoulder. A couple of years ago he told me the story behind the scar. In his younger years, he was spearfishing alone near our current location. The clouds were dark, and the water was choppy. The conditions were not ideal for diving, but like many a young man, he had a feeling of invincibility. Just after he speared his first fish of the day, a great white shark struck him from behind and took an exploratory bite. He said that he felt like he'd been hit by a truck. When the predator returned to finish the job, he launched the point of his steel spear into the shark's nose, before extricating himself from the water. He was a lucky man that day, he should have bought a lotto ticket. Once he'd returned to the beach, a local ranger who just happened to be patrolling the area, rushed him to a nearby hospital, where he received a blood transfusion and 163 stitches.

"How you going son?"

I kept my eyes on the water. "I'm doing okay in the scheme of things."

He grabbed me by the side of my jaw and looked me directly in the eyes. "You don't look well. I'm worried about you." He let go of my jaw and stared out over the ocean. "I'll never be able to pay you back for saving Rosa."

"Captain, I don't expect, or want you to pay me back."

He shook his head. "Being a hunter will be the death of you. Why don't you come and work for me? The wind turbines are at eighty-five percent capacity, giving most households six hours of electricity a day. Our militia could use a man with your skills. And a handful of attractive ladies are new to town. Elizabeth could introduce you to the right one."

I raised my hands and laughed. "I appreciate the offer, but I'm not ready to settle down just yet. Besides, I enjoy my job."

The captain muttered something indecipherable under his breath as he sauntered back towards the helm.

The Captain returned with a wetsuit, goggles, snorkel, fins, and speargun. "I'll lend you my suit. It won't be the best fit, but it'll have to do the job. Hopefully, you'll catch something before you freeze your balls off."

Over the last three years my busy work schedule had prevented me from spearfishing, which was why I was eager to get back in the water. I slipped on the one-piece neoprene wetsuit, which was two sizes too big in width and two sizes too small in length. The Captain chuckled when he saw me in the ill-fitting suit.

He was unimpressed when I pulled on the neoprene around the waist and teased, "You may have to lay off the burgers and beer."

Quick as lightning the Captain retorted, "You're just too skinny string bean. Now stop flapping your gums and go catch us some supper."

Upon entering the water, I peered down to see Clarry searching the sea floor for the tasty molluscs. I was impressed to discover that his catch bag was already half full. Spotting a large blue grouper swimming below me, I extended my arm aiming for the base of its skull and pressed the trigger. The spear moved at lightning speed and hit the target. In its death throes the fish frantically flapped its tail fin. And that's when I saw movement from the corner of my eye.

Something large, grey, and fast. My pulse quickened as I turned towards the shape. I was relieved to discover that it was an inquisitive seal. She came within arm's reach and then swam away presenting the underside of her belly before swimming back to me. Even though she was behaving like her Labrador retriever cousins, I was careful to keep my hands from straying too close to her powerful jaws, aware that although cute and playful, she was still a wild and unpredictable animal. After the seal lost interest in me and moved on, I continued to fish, catching a queen snapper, harlequin cod, and boarfish. The Captain gave me the thumbs-up after I exited the water and presented him with my catch.

Clarry also had a successful day, bagging almost 600 molluscs over a six-hour stretch. Working in such a pristine and stress-free environment, allowed me to clear my head while spearfishing and shucking the abalone. Not once did I think of reaching for an oxy. The Captain may be right, this may be a better lifestyle, but within a week I'd get itchy feet and long for the hunt.

I know the pills are a problem, but it's a problem that I'll deal with when I have the time.

By the time we returned to the jetty I was itching to start prepping for the contract. I'd had enough relaxing and it was time to get paid. But first things first, I needed to ensure that Fiona was kitted up for the operation. Clarry drove me to the town's most reputable firearm and ammo supplier - Mitt's Gun Store.

Mitt was a grizzled character in his early-seventies who did not suffer fools. He has such a wealth of knowledgeable and experience, that most firearm enthusiasts would concede 'he's forgotten more about firearms than they'll ever know.'

Naturally, I asked for his opinion. "I'm looking for a reliable handgun for a petite lady and I'd be grateful for some advice."

"What's her experience level with a pistol?"

"Minimal," I admitted.

Mitt peered through the glass counter cabinet and considered his wares while keeping an eye on the front door. A gun store was a high value target for any would-be gangster. Mitt wore a Browning pistol with a mahogany grip positioned in a quick draw holster on his right hip. He had the firearm cocked and ready to repel any crim that wanted to test their mettle.

"I have a pre-owned Glock 19 in stock, it takes nine-millimetre rounds with a fifteen-round mag. It has a smaller grip for a smaller hand. I haven't been able to get rid of her. I'll throw in a cleaning kit, two extra mags, and fifty rounds if you take her. I've stripped it, cleaned it, and put a hundred rounds down range. The weapon is functional, and the sights are true."

Mitt and I put on our game faces and haggled over the price. He was a tougher negotiator than many of the top-level executives I dealt with in the old world. As we finalised the agreement, I felt a bead of perspiration running down the back of my neck. As a contract lawyer I'd negotiate multi-million dollar deals without breaking a sweat. I ended up purchasing more than I'd originally planned. Along with the Glock 19, I also bought a .223 Ruger Rifle and a Ka-Bar 1256 short fighting knife. After taking me to the cleaners, I suspect that he threw in a Glock Armourers Handbook to massage my ego. The book provided detailed instructions on the assembly, disassembly, and cleaning of the pistol's thirty-four main parts.

During the drive back home, Clarry explained that Mitt had dispatched two outlaws during the recent town raid. Both outlaws had the jump on him, with their firearms pointed at his chest. Mitt drew his Browning pistol from the holster, shooting one of the men in the forehead and the other through his mouth. It was reported that one of the outlaws managed to fire a shot, but missed his target, most likely jerking the trigger in panic. I whispered under my breath – *'slow is smooth, smooth is fast.'* Community members recalled seeing Mitt moments after the shooting, acting as cool as a cucumber, scanning for threats, and giving instructions to fellow militia members. I took a mental note - *Do not upset Mitt!*

Chapter Five

Thursday January 31, 2041 – Fiona

Waking earlier than I was accustomed to, I ambled out to the kitchen to make breakfast. Archie was standing over a large map laid out over Clarry's dining table. He was using a pencil and ruler to draw straight horizontal and vertical lines over the surrounding area of Merivale.

"Good morning," I said, before grabbing the kettle and making myself a coffee.

"Good afternoon you mean. You slept in," he said in an accusatorial tone.

"It's not even 7 a.m.," I said, rubbing the sleep out of my eyes.

"When we're on a job, we start no later than five. Before you start the day, you must prep for the day. We have a lot to do."

"Good to know," I said, stifling a yawn. *He's obviously not a morning person.* "Sooo, what are you up to?"

"I'm outlining a grid search to locate Lewis."

I picked up the bounty contract from the table and examined Lewis's mug shot; he's a white male in his late twenties, with sleepy eyes, a know-it-all grin, and a mullet hairstyle that you would be excused for thinking had never been washed.

"Do you reckon we'll find him?" I asked.

"Who knows? There's a lot of skill involved in hunting, but there's also a lot of luck involved. One thing's for certain, we'll give it our best shot." Archie pointed to the map. "Merivale is only twenty-five kilometres east of here, so we'll leave *early* tomorrow and scout the outskirts of the town," he explained, with an emphasis on early.

He had cigars, jars of honey, packets of painkillers, and three bottles of hooch stacked together beside the map.

I picked up a cigar and placed it under my nose, smelling the rich earthy aroma of the tobacco. "Who's this all for?" I asked.

"Goodies to aid in loosening the locals' lips."

~

The saddle soreness that had plagued me during the final days of the ride had almost disappeared. With the help of a eucalyptus salve that Clarry gave me, both the bruising and skin abrasions had receded to the point that I was looking forward to getting back on the horse, so to speak. I'd spent the whole of yesterday preparing for my first bounty operation. I'd cleaned and lubricated Archie's rifle, revised the orienteering learnings, and prepared Roger and Jasper for the trip. I was determined to demonstrate to Archie that I was treating this job seriously and appreciated the opportunity. There was no way I was going back to dead end jobs so I can be used and abused. I'd be lying if I said that I wasn't excited, but I hid my enthusiasm to play it cool.

Archie asked me to fill my water bottle and meet him in Clarry's backyard gym. Under a pergola with polycarbonate roofing, he had a boxing ring, six-foot boxing bag, padded dummy, free weights, and an assortment of exercise equipment. As he stretched on the jigsaw mats he beckoned me over by placing his hand on top of his head. During the final days of the ride he taught me hand signals that he learned in the Army. He explained that 'nonverbal communication is necessary when speaking may alert people to our presence and position'. So I wouldn't forget them, I drew diagrams of the signals in my notebook.

As I sat on the mats facing him, he confessed, "Over the last couple of weeks I've taught you as much as I can in the limited time we've had. Your accuracy with the rifle and orienteering skills have exceeded my expectations. There's no doubt you're a quick learner, which is good, because we don't have a lot of time to train before your first job."

I was a bit taken aback. This was the first time I'd received a compliment for as long as I could remember, other than patrons' commenting on my ass.

His expression suddenly became stern. "It's important that you understand and abide by my hunter's code, ah, I mean *our* hunter's code. I want you to write the four rules in your notebook." I grabbed my notebook and pen from my pack and returned to the mat. "Rule one is always go home at the end of the operation. No reward is worth giving our lives away, and this is why we always plan our operations to mitigate the foreseeable risks. Rule two is we never intentionally cause physical harm to an innocent person. That rule is self-explanatory, and one that I know you understand full well. Rule three, we never steal another hunter's bounty. Admittedly this is a bit of a grey area, as two or more hunters may be chasing the same fugitive. But when a hunter steps over the line and steals another hunter's gold from right under their nose, it's obvious to all involved that they've broken a cardinal rule. Admittedly, the final rule is one that most hunters don't abide by. But it's important to me. We always attempt to capture and transport the fugitive alive. I'm not an executioner and I don't plan to take up the vocation. In saying that, and this is an important point Fiona, this rule is not always achievable, especially when they're trying to kill you. That's why we revert back to rule one, and if need be, we defend ourselves with lethal force. I sleep well at night knowing that I do my best to abide by these four rules. Do you have any questions in relation to the code?"

I shook my head. They seemed pretty clear cut to me.

"Moving on to more practical matters, I have the rest of the day to teach you the very basics of weapons and tactics. In normal circumstances this would be mission impossible, however we have little choice in the matter as there's a competitor in the field, and we need this job."

Archie reached into his pack and presented me with a black gun and knife. Archie removed the magazine and locked open the slide of the gun, pointing the muzzle slightly forward so I could confirm that the chamber was empty.

"This is your pistol, it's a Glock 19. I've taught you the four firearm safety rules. What are they?"

When he handed me the pistol, I immediately pointed it towards the padded dummy, before reeling off the four rules that I had memorised using the acronym TAKI. "Treat all firearms as loaded, always point the firearm in a safe direction, keep your finger off the trigger until you are ready to shoot, identify your target and surroundings."

Archie nodded. "Excellent. Now if you break any of these rules during training, you owe me a ten-kilometre run or one thousand push-ups, your choice. Do you understand?"

I looked him in the eye and responded earnestly, "Crystal clear Boss."

I was truly gobsmacked when Archie presented me with the weapons. They fit so perfectly in my hand. It's as if they were made specifically for me. I was beginning to really respect him as a teacher and mentor. And it wasn't just about the gifts, I feel like he's interested in my learning and trusts me not to fuck up.

Archie had me perform close quarter fighting (CQF) drills will my knife and pistol. He taught me to bend my knees for balance and stand in a bladed stance to present a smaller target to my opponent.

He reiterated that I must keep the weapons close to my body. "Don't let your enemy take your weapon and use it against you," he instructed.

Archie taught me how to correctly hold the knife and where to strike. I practiced slashing and stabbing the six-foot padded dummy that was tied to a metal pole, aiming for vital areas – throat, back of the neck, armpit, and groin.

Archie had me repeatedly drawing, loading, and unloading the Glock without looking directly at the pistol, which I found difficult at first, but after being given fifty push-ups for each infraction, I quickly learned to focus on the target. He told me to relax my hand, breath normally, and focus on the movement of the task itself, rather than how quickly I was performing the task. Before each firearm draw, he had me repeat the mantra, over and over and over, '*slow is smooth, smooth is fast*.'

We drove to the gun range and practiced firing at paper targets with my new Glock. I don't know if it was all in my head, but for some reason I found it much harder to shoot with the pistol than the rifle. I wasn't expecting to be Deadeye Dick, but nonetheless my shooting left much to be desired. I was aiming for the centre of the target, but continually hit low and to the left. Archie mentioned something about anticipation and jerking the trigger. He said that instructors use a variety of terminology for squeezing the trigger, but whether you refer to it as a trigger squeeze, press or even pull, the most important thing is to focus on the front sight and apply pressure to the trigger in a smooth continuous motion. I became so focused on my sight picture that I was actually surprised when the gun fired, and even more astonished when my rounds hit the centre of the target.

We returned to Clarry's and completed tactical drills late into the afternoon. Archie stated that we'd be using plastic dummy rounds rather than live rounds until he thought I was proficient. He taught me how to tactically enter through doorways and scan my area of responsibility (AOR) while being constantly aware of the pistol's muzzle direction. We divided the rooms of Clarry's home into sections. As we entered the room, I would be responsible for engaging threats on my side of the room and he would be responsible for his side. Archie explained that the only time I should cross shoot into his sector is when I had cleared my area and he needed support due to a weapon malfunction or is facing an '*imminent threat*'. During the water breaks I took notes of everything he taught me, including the jargon, which was like learning a new language.

As the day wore on, my concentration and focus began to fade. There was just one occasion that I failed a safety rule, and even though it was only for a split second, it was enough to make me feel like a failure. I broke rule two when I accidentally pointed my muzzle at Archie as we entered a doorway. He didn't shout, jump up and down, or threaten to sack me, he just shook his head in disappointment and instructed me to re-holster my pistol. After I silently chastised myself, I promised him that it would never happen again. As punishment I chose to complete the ten-kilometre run. My shoulders were still sore from the morning activities, and the mere thought of completing 1000 push-ups made me want to vomit.

By dusk I was soaked with perspiration and smelt worse than a shearer covered in sheep shit at the end of a hectic day in the sheds. We both sat on the jigsaw mats greedily gulping down water from our stainless-steel bottles.

"I know that was a lot to take in. Over time, with extensive practice, your knife and firearm will feel as if they're an extension of your arm. Right now, I just want you to focus on the fundamentals."

"Slow is smooth, smooth is fast," I said for the hundredth time that day.

"Spot-on," Archie said with a smile.

Now that all the noise had subsided, Zeus wandered over and sat beside me, looking up at me with puppy dog eyes. He panted with delight as I scratched his back. "I won't let you down Boss. I'm going to get better, and I want you to know that I'm taking this job seriously."

Archie scooted his butt over the mats so he sat directly opposite me. He scratched Zeus behind his left ear. "I'm glad to hear it. I need to reiterate rule one. You must go home at the end of the day. To do that, you must look after number one." He pointed to my chest. "Yourself! Do you understand what I'm saying?"

I nodded, even though I had no idea where he was going with this.

He continued, "If we're in a situation where I've been captured, seriously injured, or killed, YOU RUN! and never look back. Do you understand?"

Zeus looked at me and tilted his head, as if he was waiting for my answer.

Chapter Six

Friday February 1, 2041 – Archie

I woke Fiona at the crack of dawn so we could get on the move. We had a quick breakfast with Clarry and Zeus before we packed our gear. As we left the stables, Clarry as thoughtful as ever handed us both a packed lunch of dried salted herring and oranges for the trip. And that's why the silly bugger is my best mate.

Prior to riding out of town, I stopped by the bondsman's office to ensure that Lewis hadn't been apprehended since our last conversation. I knocked on the side door where Brad's sleeping quarters were located. Brad made it known in no uncertain terms that he wasn't impressed with being woken at this '*godforsaken hour*'. I handed him five cigarettes after thanking him for his time and apologising for the early call.

This was my first trip to Merivale, which made me a little anxious as I had limited knowledge of the area or residents - not something that I'd readily admit to my new apprentice. I used the time on the road to explain the plan, pointing out the need to tread carefully while scouting the area and gathering information. The last thing we needed was to create angst and mistrust with the locals. Going into town all guns blazing was an amateur move which would at best scare your quarry from the area, and at worst get you killed. To the best of my knowledge, over the last two years there's been eleven hunters killed in Western Australia. I don't plan to add Fiona and myself to the statistician's ledger.

We trotted down Merivale Road keeping our eyes peeled. Cows were munching in a green pasture near a full-sized replica of Stonehenge: a tourist attraction that must have been popular before the War. The surroundings were idyllic - blue sky, green hills, and wildflowers. In a different time, I'd be relaxing, looking for the perfect spot to stop for a picnic and drink a bottle of Shiraz and devour a slab of cheddar. Instead, I'm scanning the environment for threats and looking for the perfect spot to seek cover or concealment.

We passed a number of small farms, observing cattle and sheep grazing in the paddocks, but failed to spot their owners. Where were they? I didn't anticipate a hive of activity, but I expected to see at least one farmer on a tractor or horse. It was probably a case of residents not wanting to be seen. It wasn't just the outlaw gangs that caused their shyness, it was also the actions of hungry individuals taking desperate measures. A majority of citizens who survived the War are unable to find work and lack the knowledge to live off the land. It's no wonder that violent crime has drastically risen, when the order of the day is *survival of the fittest.*

After riding for another three hours or so, I noticed movement behind a large gum tree in the front yard of a heavily fortified property. Something buzzed past my head at high velocity. "SEEK COVER!" I shouted.

Wasting no time I dismounted Roger, drew my rifle from the scabbard and scanned for threats. As I firmly held Roger's reins, I noticed Fiona mirroring my actions, drawing her Glock and using Jasper as cover.

I saw movement from my periphery and was relieved to see a small boy grasping a slingshot, giggling, and running towards a nearby shed. "Stand down, it was just a boy slinging a rock," I said with a tone of embarrassment.

Just as I was getting my breath back, a man yelled in a serious tone, "PUT your weapons down and move in front of your horses. Do it now, or we'll fire."

I paused for a moment before peering under Roger's belly, failing to locate the owner of the voice. "What's in it for us?" I shouted in reply.

"You have four rifles aimed at you. If you do what I say we won't shoot. I have a fondness for horses, so don't make me kill yours."

I scanned my surroundings for cover from fire, but just saw a whole lot of scrub. Great for concealment but useless in preventing us from being used as target practice. The nearest cover was a paperbark tree that was at least eighty metres away. We were running out of options.

I raised my voice to be heard, while trying to speak in a calm and friendly tone, "We're licensed bounty hunters on a contract. We were just startled by your boy, there's no harm done. We'll just be on our way."

"With your right hand, slowly raise your ID above the saddle," he shouted like a drill sergeant.

Damn I thought, he must have a scope. I was praying that this bloke was a reasonable man. I did as he instructed, facing my ID towards the sound of his voice.

After what felt like an eternity, I heard boots on a gravel road. I looked at Fiona and cupped my hand to my ear and then raised my palm towards her - signalling her to listen and stay put.

I then heard the familiar sound of a creaky gate opening. "I've put my gun away, but I still have rifles on you. Either re-holster your weapons, or if you must have them drawn, point them towards the ground. You can bring your horses as well."

As I peered around Roger's neck, I saw a middle-aged man of Chinese descent standing by an eight-foot high opened gate. True to his word, his revolver was holstered. I returned my rifle to the scabbard secured to the saddle on Roger's side and advised Fiona to re-holster her pistol, ensuring I was loud enough for the property owner to hear my instructions.

We both led the horses towards the man standing by the gate. He held his right hand in front of him, first shaking my hand with a crushing calloused grip and then shaking Fiona's. He introduced himself as Charlie Wong. I later learned that Charlie was a third-generation farmer from these parts. After the introductions had concluded, we were both invited onto his property.

As we were led by Charlie up a blue metal gravelled driveway,

I could see glimpses of a limestone ranch house between the thick branches of pine trees. I glanced at a young man standing near a tree trunk, pointing a bolt action rifle towards the ground, and then noticed a young lady in her mid-teens on the opposite side of the driveway doing the same. They both appeared attentive and ready to act. Given a signal from Charlie, I had no doubt they'd attack our flanks in unison.

The cause of this drama came darting towards Charlie. A six-year-old boy with a cheeky grin jumped into Charlie's arms, wrapping his little arms around the man's neck. Charlie pulled a slingshot from the boy's back pocket. When I was a young boy, I tormented the kids down the street with a similar toy. The Y-shaped wooden frame had two rubber tubes attached to the upper two ends.

Charlie gave us an apologetic look, "Boys will be boys."

I had a slightly different perspective; *boys will be little shits.*

As we approached the ranch's veranda, the young man who now had the rifle strapped to his back, stepped forward and introduced himself as Sonny, Charlie's eldest. He kindly offered to take Roger and Jasper to the stables.

We were invited to sit on a leather couch in the sunken lounge room. Charlie introduced his family, to our left, his father sat in a settee with his bare feet up, wearing a blue singlet and stubbie shorts. Beside him stood Charlie's wife Sonja, an athletic middle-aged woman who he candidly introduced as his childhood sweetheart.

Before sitting down, I paid my respects by shaking their hands and complimenting them on their beautiful home. Charlie's sixteen-year-old daughter, Jillian, who was moments earlier pointing a rifle at our chests, graciously served us freshly squeezed orange juice.

When I asked Charlie about his farm, he spoke proudly about their achievements. The farm is 200 hectares, with four 45,000 litre water tanks, a windmill, three bores, a dam and soak. They have an extensive solar system that powers water pumps, milking machines, lighting, refrigeration, a security system, electric fencing, and tools. They farm cattle, sheep, pigs, chickens, and citrus trees. He has four workers and an extended family of six adults and four children, along with three working dogs. The Wong's are a fine example of a self-sustaining family that has thrived post-war, in contrast to most, who have struggled to survive.

"We thank you for your service, Archie. We need a hell of a lot more hunters."

Charlie complained about the lack of police. There are three coppers to patrol the entire Shire, which is an area of 42,000 square kilometres with a population of 14,000 souls. I was absolutely positive that Charlie would not be impressed with Senior Constables Atkins's fondness for sitting on his ass and completing crossword puzzles. I wisely kept this fun fact to myself.

The conversation moved on to the difficulties he faced in hiring experienced workers, which I found bewildering when you consider the number of people needing a job. I wanted to ask, 'why not train people?', but I decided to keep my opinions to myself, reminding myself that: '*Opinions are like assholes, Everyone's got one*'.

He expressed his regret in losing a worker during the Esperance raid. Charlie and two of his workers joined Clarry's militia to defeat the outlaws. They did their bit for the community but lost a valued member of the farm in the process. When he heard that I was mates with Clarry, he offered me two fingers of his finest single malt whisky, which I politely declined.

Charlie was fuming as he informed us of his constant problems with relentless thieves. Just last week they were forced to shoot and wound two members of an armed gang who were attempting to steal two lambs. I chose not to fan the flames by explaining that bounties were issued for offenders that commit the most heinous of crimes - murder, armed robbery, and kidnapping - and we don't concern ourselves with livestock thieves and trespassers.

Charlie took a sip of his juice. "So, who are you looking for?"

I took Lewis's mug shot from my pocket and handed it to him. After taking a good look at the photo, he showed it to his family.

"What's he wanted for?" he asked with interest.

"Murder and armed robbery."

The members of the family were visibly concerned as they took turns to gaze at the mug shot.

It was difficult to hide my disappointment when they failed to recognise Lewis.

Charlie stood from the couch. "Come out to the shed and we'll show the photo to Smithy. He's regularly out and about."

Smithy was a mechanic, shearer, fence repairer, and general roustabout, who Charlie had employed just after the end of the War. He had seen action in Darwin when serving as a mechanic in the Australian Navy. As we strolled into the large aluminium shed, Smithy had his head down with a spanner in hand examining a tractor engine.

Charlie introduced us to Smithy and explained the purpose of our visit. He was an Irishman who looked like your typical grease monkey; face and arms covered in grease, with band-aids taped around fingers that have been banged and jammed against machinery.

I found it odd that he was unaware of the circumstances surrounding our arrival. I handed him the mug shot, which he took in one hand as he reached for reading glasses hanging from his neck.

"Have you seen this man?" Charlie asked him.

"I'm not sure," Smithy replied softly while staring at his tools.

"Cut the shit Smithy. If he's hanging around the area, I want him gone. He's bad news. Now let the man do his job," Charlie ordered angrily.

"Sure Boss, I've seen this bloke," he admitted.

Charlie didn't look surprised. "Where?"

"I've seen him at the fights," he replied shamefully.

Charlie explained that a South West gambling ring organised caged fights, where both human and animal contestants fought for supremacy and survival. Charlie had never attended the fights himself and appeared visibly disappointed that Smithy would frequent such an event.

Charlie encouraged me to give Smithy the third degree. With Charlie looking on with an irate expression, he wasn't exactly a hard nut to crack. We learned that the event occurred every Friday night at 7 p.m. on a farmstead ten-kilometres south east of Charlie's property. The fights took place in a chain linked cage situated in a large shed at the back of the forty-hectare property. Lewis was one of a hundred or so men that attended last week to gamble on the fights.

Charlie graciously agreed to allow Smithy to escort us to tonight's event, under the proviso that he was to return to the farm shortly after our arrival and was not to engage in our business in any shape or form. I would not have had it any other way.

We planned to attend the event at 9 p.m., which was two hours after opening. Smithy explained that most punters have usually arrived by this time, as the dog and cock fights conclude, and the main card begins. The main card consists of local and interstate brawlers who fight in vicious no holds barred contests, with the only rules being no eye gouging or biting.

Once we arrived, we'd act like punters – gamble, drink, cheer, and get upset when we lose our coin. During this schtick we'll be on the lookout for Lewis. Once identified, I'll keep an eye on him without giving away our true intentions. I plan to discreetly follow him to his place of abode, or if the opportunity presents itself, detain him during the journey. Any attempt to apprehend him at the event would likely get us killed. The punters that attend these types of events don't typically support the law and wouldn't act kindly to one of their brethren being detained by bounty hunters. It's especially dangerous when a majority of them are armed, full of piss or drugs, and amped-up from watching the fights.

We'd both wear our sidearms overtly, which was the common practice when attending these types of events. It was my experience that it actually reduced the number of brawls, as most men didn't want to take the risk of a fistfight suddenly escalating into a gunfight. My plan was to secure our rifles in a nearby location, as longarms would not be allowed on the premises. Shortly after our arrival, Smithy will return to the farm with Jasper and Roger. Charlie was happy to look after the horses. However, he made it crystal clear that if we captured Lewis, he didn't want him anywhere near his property, which I could fully appreciate. I wouldn't want that psycho anywhere near my family either.

We sat around the outdoor table with plates in hand, eating lamb kebabs and drinking apple cider. Sonja treated us to a lemon meringue pie. I didn't have to be asked twice to grab seconds. I noticed that Fiona had barely touched her kebab and wasn't even keen to try the delicious pie.

I thought it'd be a good idea to give her a pep talk. "We'll be leaving in two hours."

She looked down at her plate of food. "I know, I'll be ready."

"It's natural to be nervous on your first job. Just follow my lead and everything'll be fine."

She didn't look convinced. Mental note - *I may need to work on my pep talks.*

Chapter Seven

Friday February 1, 2041 from 8:30 p.m. - Archie

Smithy led us to a small dirt track that was effectively hidden when viewed from the main road. I pondered how new punters found the place. It then became apparent when I observed a scarecrow standing in a nearby field, wearing a tattered Everlast singlet and boxing gloves tied to his broom handle arms.

We led the horses about 200 metres to a large, gravelled carpark, which provided an area to secure the horses on one side, and a designated space to park vehicles on the other. There were thirty or so mounts already tied to hitching posts; they appeared to be getting along just fine. I heard a loud BANG! and drew my revolver. The horses whinnied in panic. I scanned across the way to see an old green bus backfiring, with black smoke blowing out of the exhaust pipe. Just after I re-holstered my revolver, twenty or so inebriated punters exited the bus's side door.

While I tied Roger to a post, I noticed the outline of a blue drum standing five metres from the curb in thick bush. I looked around to ensure no one was watching and walked into the scrub. I placed our rifles and packs behind the drum, ensuring they could not be seen from the carpark.

After securing the horses, we followed Smithy to a large steel shed that was originally designed to house tractors, trucks, and farm machinery. As we entered the enormous doorway, I steered clear of a young man vomiting on the gravel.

My ears were immediately tuned in to the rumble of the crowd. There were approximately 150 men and women of various ages, standing around a thirty square metre cage, cheering, and yelling at the fighters. The two bare chested gentlemen wearing small fingerless gloves and shorts, were grappling with each other on the canvas floor. The fighter on top was butting his opponent's nose with his forehead.

The shed's aroma consisted of a concoction of stale beer, bootleg whisky, tobacco, marijuana, and putrid body odour. I could feel the electricity in the air as the crowd was baying for blood. I was trying not to look anyone in the eye, as the scene could get ugly very quickly if I were recognised by a relative or friend of a felon I had caught.

I glanced over at Fiona, observing her body-language and demeanour. She wore an irritable scowl with her arms crossed over her chest. I speculated whether she was reassessing her career choice. I wouldn't blame her if she were.

Whilst feigning interest in the fight I covertly observed the crowd. Trying to appear nonchalant, I placed my arm around Fiona's shoulder and whispered in her ear, "I hope you're a decent actor." Anyone watching would view my behaviour as a tipsy bloke sweet talking his lady.

"I'll just have to try really really hard," she replied with a big cheesy grin that failed to reach her eyes.

Displaying my full repertoire of acting skills, I laughed boisterously as I shook my fist towards the centre of the cage. The fighter with the badly broken nose was hammering his fist into his opponent's groin.

Just after I noticed that Smithy had disappeared, I turned to see my mark. He was casually walking towards a makeshift bar, comprising of a large plank of wood atop of two columns of stacked wheel rims.

Playing my part to a T, I squeezed Fiona's shoulder and hollered, "I'll buy ya a drink sweetie." Our code for – *'I have Lewis in sight.'*

Leaving Fiona where she stood, I threaded my way through the crowd to the bar. Upon joining the group of punters lining up to be served, Lewis picked up three bottles of beer from the bar and sauntered towards the far side of the cage.

Now that I was in the line, it'd look mighty suspicious if I just suddenly walked off, so I purchased two bottles of lager to look the part before returning to Fiona. "I'm struggling to see the fight, let's go to the other side to get a better view," I hollered over the noise of the crowd.

While grasping Fiona's hand I led her through the dense crowd, trying my utmost to avoid knocking a punter's beer and risk starting a fight.

We stood about five metres behind and to the right of Lewis. He was still sporting the mullet hairdo from the day of the mug shot, but he appeared to have gained weight in all the wrong places. He was conversing with two men who bore a strong familial resemblance. I wouldn't be surprised if they were his brothers or cousins. What appeared to be the eldest brother wore a black beanie, and the other wore a red and white baseball cap. The brother with the cap apparently enjoyed his booze, as his t-shirt failed to cover his protruding basketball sized beer-belly. They were all about the same height, and all three wore filthy, unkempt, and ill-fitting clothing. The brothers were highly engaged in the fights - shadow sparring, yelling out abuse, and offering the fighters unsolicited advice.

For the next two hours we slowly and methodically sipped our beers. Even though we continued with the pretence of being absorbed in the fights, I'd lost count of the number of bouts that had been fought. After placing a couple of bets and losing miserably, it didn't require an Oscars performance to feign my disgust at the results, not naive to the fact that most were fixed. Each fight lasted for no more than twenty minutes, and usually ended with both men being severely disfigured. I was relieved that we were spared the discomfort of witnessing the earlier proceedings, when dogs and roosters were forced to fight to the death.

Chapter Eight

Friday February 1, 2041 from 11:30 p.m. – Archie

When the announcer introduced the last two fighters of the night, the crowd erupted with a cheer as the men ran towards the cage. The first man to enter was of medium height and grossly obese, while his opponent stood at six-foot-eight and was stick thin. I squeezed Fiona's shoulder and dipped my head towards the brothers, who were making their way towards the exit. They were obviously not interested in the spectacle of a fight between an elephant and a giraffe.

The brothers left through the enormous shed door and moseyed towards the horses. As planned, Smithy had taken Roger and Jasper back to Charlie's farm.

I had wrongly assumed that Lewis would one, leave with the crowd at the end of the night, and two, show greater signs of intoxication. All three gentleman mounted their horses and ambled down the path towards the main road. We picked up our rifles and packs from behind the blue drum and skirted into the bush.

When the brothers arrived at the main road they headed in an easterly direction. While keeping a sufficient distance to remain unseen and unheard, we stalked quietly through the bush adjacent to the road. It helped our cause that the brothers maintained the pace of a slow trot as they laughed loudly and ridiculed each other. Just after they rode over a crest, they turned onto a narrow sandy track, where they were forced to enter single file.

We waited thirty seconds before following them down the side of the track. The full moon enabled me to see the outline of the brother traveling at the rear. As the brothers slowed to a walk, we adjusted our pace accordingly. When the brothers suddenly stopped and dismounted, I gave Fiona the signal to stop - opening my palm at shoulder height, and knelt by the side of the trail, where we were concealed by thick shrub. Fiona quietly knelt behind me. I could just see the frame of a building sitting under the foliage of a mature gum tree.

They tied their horses to a tree on the western side of the building and entered through the front door of the premises. I cupped my hand and whispered into Fiona's ear, "We're going to head half a click to the east through the bush. We'll find a spot to prop so we can see the front eastern side of the building. Do you understand?"

After Fiona signalled a thumbs-up, I slowly crossed the track in a low crouch and proceeded into the bush. As she followed closely behind, I silently prayed that they didn't own any dogs. Dogs could devastate an operation by alerting their owners to your presence, not to mention taking chunks of flesh from one or more of your limbs. I touched the handle of my knife and the rubber grip of my revolver - an idiosyncrasy that I perform during the pointy end of an operation. Even though I know the weapons are attached to my belt, I just can't help but double-check.

Chapter Nine

Friday February 1, 2041 from 11:50 p.m. – Archie

We knelt behind a eucalyptus stump that was about two-feet in height and as wide as a V12 engine. We were about forty metres from the property, so without spotlights and knowledge of our presence, they were highly unlikely to detect us.

The derelict fibro house sat on stumps at a slight angle. Considering the condition of the premises, it had likely been abandoned prior to the brothers moving in. After hearing the front door open, I witnessed a man walk to the rear of the house, bend down, and inspect a piece of equipment that I was unable to identify in the poor light. This could be the perfect time to grab him I pondered. However, from our location, I was unable to confirm that it was Lewis.

As I reached into my pack for the night vision goggles, I was alerted to the sound of a generator starting. When lights from inside the property suddenly beamed through the two windows facing us, I could see movement from within.

As the man did an about turn and returned to the front of the premises, I was able to identify him as the brother with the beanie.

I was contemplating our options when I was startled by the sound of heavy metal music. I immediately recognised the tune as '*Bullet in the Head*' by Rage Against the Machine. De la Rocha's razor-sharp vocals were booming out from an impressive sound system. I couldn't help but grin when I considered how fitting the song was given our current predicament.

Fiona looked like she was about to vomit. Upon reflecting on my first operation, I concluded that the poor girl's heart must be thumping against her chest. I recalled being inches from an Akita's jaws as the fugitive ran for a shotgun in the kitchen. I regretted killing the dog, but not his owner.

"I'm going to move closer to the house and do a recce. You cover me with the rifle and stay put. After I'm finished, I'll come back, and we'll make a plan."

Fiona rested her rifle on the stump and peered through the scope.

It was not my intention to stress her out any more than she already was, but I had to make sure she remembered the most important rule. "If something serious happens to me, what do you do?"

She paused for a second, "Run."

Out of habit I covertly rubbed my fingers over the stump to ward off bad luck. After I gave her the thumbs-up, I crept ten metres north of the stump, before making my way back towards the house.

With the music blaring, I took solace in the fact that the twigs snapping under my boots would not be heard. I was also grateful that I couldn't hear or see any dogs. All I had to worry about was being spotted by one of the men.

I gripped my revolver at chest level, elbows bent, muzzle pointing parallel to the ground in the direction of my line of sight.

As I crouched under one of the side windows, I peered through the bottom of the glass and noticed the window frame rattling from the volume of the music.

JESUS! I could see my old mentor, Sal Willis, hanging from a thick rope that was tied around his wrists and secured to an exposed support beam in the roof. He'd been beaten to a pulp, with blood oozing from his nose, mouth, and ears. With his eyelids twitching and his legs limp, the poor bloke looked barely conscious.

Lewis was dancing around Sal, throwing punches and kicks into his face, ribs, and groin. In his sick and demented mind, he was likely reliving the fights that he'd watched earlier in the night.

I stopped peering through the window and knelt on one knee. The rage I felt was almost overwhelming. I inhaled, held my breath, and slowly exhaled for fifteen seconds. It was critical that I composed myself before making a tactical entry. It was only yesterday that I was telling Fiona about body alarm response and how it can negatively affect your fine motor skills and critical thinking. Time was of the essence, so I repeated one last breathing cycle before making my move.

I reflected on the instructions I gave Fiona – *'I'll come back and we'll make a plan'.* Two weeks is not enough time to train and prepare anyone for this kind of op. She's just not ready!

I crouched low and crawled under the window, slowly making my way to the front of the premises. When I peeked around the corner, I immediately saw that the front door was wide open. It was simply good luck that the outward facing door was concealing my presence.

It was now or never I whispered to myself. With my firearm still raised, I entered through the doorway and was confronted with an open space that in the past would have been used as a lounge, kitchen, and dining room. Past the kitchen was a hallway leading to the back of the house. There were empty beakers, pipes, and chemicals lying all over the place. Unmistakable evidence that they'd been cooking meth.

The muzzle of my Smith and Wesson followed my eyes as I scanned for threats. Sensing movement to my right, I turned to see Lewis standing about eight metres away. He had an expression of shock plastered on his face, eyes widened like saucers and mouth agape. In his right hand he was gripping a butcher's meat cleaver. I presumed that he'd planned to use it on poor Sal. He suddenly snapped out of his trance and sprinted towards me with the cleaver raised above his head. It takes less than two and a half seconds for the average man to run eight meters. I shot him once in the centre of his chest and put a round in his forehead. Lewis and his cleaver fell to the ground in a heap, landing less than a metre from my feet. Four live rounds remaining in the cylinder.

It was a matter of life and death that I maintain discipline and stay focused. Taking a glance at Sal risked breaking my concentration and tempting fate. Where are Lewis's brothers?

The brother wearing the beanie ran screaming through the

hallway holding a spiked baseball bat at shoulder height. I may have aimed for his chest, but I shot him through the side of his neck. It's not like the old movies, a moving target is not easy to hit, especially when he's armed and running at you with the intent to bludgeon you to death.

The round didn't stop him, or even slow him down for that matter. He was almost upon me when I instinctively stepped back and to my right, pivoting on the balls of my feet as I shot him a second time, this time shooting him through his wide-open mouth. He dropped dead like a bag of potatoes, landing alongside his brother. Two live rounds remaining in the cylinder.

As I scanned for further threats, I suddenly felt a stinging sensation in my upper back. When I turned to face my attacker, a rusted machete blade slashed downs and across my chest, soaking my shirt in blood. Just after I yelled out in pain and dropped to my knees in agony, my revolver fell from my grasp.

Chapter Ten

Friday February 1, 2041 from 11:50 p.m. – Fiona

Archie motioned for me to kneel behind a large tree stump. We had followed the brothers to a house that was well hidden from the main road.

As soon as he told me to cover him, I leaned the barrel of my rifle over the stump and peered through the scope. I could see a bloke mosey to the rear of the property. He was wearing a beanie, so he must have been one of Lewis's brothers.

He was carrying a can which he used to fill a generator. Just after I heard the rumble of the generator, the house lights suddenly switched on. I gazed through the windows using my scope, but I couldn't spot the other brothers.

They were playing a song that my grandfather had on his playlist. I think it was a rap-metal band from the late 1900s. I eyeballed Archie for the purpose of seeking reassurance or some form of guidance. He seemed to be enjoying himself, obviously finding something amusing. Whatever it was, it was beyond me. I'm glad that he was having a great time, because I was trying not to piss myself, both figuratively and literally. I desperately needed to pee - it was a mixture of both nerves and that I hadn't had the chance to go to the loo since leaving Charlie's farm.

"I'm going to do a recce. You cover me and stay here. I'll come back and get you," said Archie.

I looked through the scope to make sure the area was all clear. "If something serious happens to me, what do you do?"

I told him what he wanted to hear. "Run."

Archie gave me the thumbs-up and crept towards the house. He crouched under a window and stuck his head up to have a gander inside.

He then knelt back down and was looking towards the front of the house. I thought he may have seen something. I scanned the area with the scope but couldn't see anyone. He then knelt motionless. Why is he just sitting there?

Taking me by surprise, he suddenly crept to the front of the house. What is he doing? I thought he said he was going to have a quick look and then come back to the stump.

Archie walked around the corner towards the front door. *WHAT THE FUCK IS HE DOING?*

I heard two pops over the music. Gunfire.

Another two shots then rang out.

They mustn't have securely tied their horses as they bolted down the track.

I started to step forwards with the rifle and saw the brother with the baseball cap step through the front doorway with some type of sword. Shit, he must have come from the western side of the house. I didn't have time to even consider aiming, let alone take a shot.

After the brother entered the house, I didn't hear anything other than the stupid song about eating a bullet. *FUCK! FUCK! FUCK!*

I turned towards the tree stump, stopped, and then looked back at the house. Archie had told me to *RUN!* I considered running back to Charlie's farm to get help.

In an absolute daze I placed my rifle on the ground alongside Archie's pack. Everything was starting to slow down. I could feel my heart thumping hard and fast against my chest. The house appeared to be closer than it was just minutes ago, and the music was just a dull background noise.

Archie advised me during training that it was common for people in life threatening situations to experience something called body alarm response. The stress was triggering my brain to activate my adrenal gland and release the hormones epinephrine and cortisol. This was causing me to experience tunnel vision, auditory exclusion, and time and distance distortion. I shook my head, took one deep breath, and steadied myself.

I drew my Glock pistol and walked towards the front of the property. After I stepped through the front doorway, I immediately scanned the room like Archie had taught me. There were three bodies on the ground, blood splattered everywhere, and a tortured man hanging from a rope. The scene looked like something from a slasher movie, which is probably why I started to feel lightheaded.

Archie was crawling along the lino floor towards his revolver, leaving a trail of blood in his wake. When it was almost within his reach, the brother with the baseball cap kicked the revolver towards the side wall. He then lifted a blood-stained sword above Archie's head. They both had their backs turned to me. Neither of them acted like they knew that I was in the room.

I pulled the trigger, once, twice, pulled it again, and again and again. Each time I pulled the trigger the man barely moved. He just stood their motionless with his back turned. *How could I have missed him?* I must have hit him, as I see blood soaking through his shirt. When I pulled the trigger again, it went *click* - the pistol's slide locked open. *FUCK! I need to reload.* As my hands shook, I ejected the empty mag and inserted a full one. Just as I racked the slide, Lewis's brother finally fell to the ground with a thud! Just like a bag of sheep shit.

I had fired sixteen rounds. I reckon at least four of them hit the sword wielder in the back. The rest went flying wide into the fibro wall, hallway, and ceiling. Thank God I didn't hit Archie or the poor sod hanging by the rope.

Archie was still lying face down. I noticed a deep cut along his upper back, not far from his neck. After I rolled him onto his back, I was shocked to see another wound across his chest. Almost his entire shirt was covered in his blood.

He looked up at me with glassy eyes and gasped, "Pass me my revolver."

Immediately after I placed the revolver in his bloodied right hand, he pointed the muzzle at the brother with the cap and fired two rounds into his face.

He spoke through gritted teeth, "Clear the rest of the house, turn the music off and come back to me with my pack. In that order. Do you understand?"

"No problem Boss, I'll take care of it," I replied with false bravado.

A new song started blasting from the speakers, with the singer advising the necessity to '*know your enemy*.' That would have been helpful for this operation I reflected.

I left Archie on the floor and stalked towards the rear of the property. There was a bedroom to the left and right of the hallway. After clearing both bedrooms, I searched the sole bathroom at the back of the house.

I was startled to see three women of various ages chained to a V6 engine block that was sitting where a bath once stood. I could see drag marks on the wood floor where they had attempted to move the engine towards the bathroom door. Their wrists were torn, and bleeding and their faces were bruised. One of the women who looked at least twice the age of her fellow captives, was just staring out into the distance, while the younger ladies were screaming at me to help them.

The music was still blaring, and I could feel a migraine coming on.

I looked them each in the eye and shouted above the music, "I'll be back to help you. I promise!"

I moved to the very back of the house and cleared the laundry room. I checked that the back door was locked and ran back to Archie who was now lying on his back. "The house is clear, I'm off to get your pack. I'll be right back," I yelled.

I sprinted to the stump, almost tripping over a fallen branch. When I bent down to pick up the pack, I noticed my left hand was shaking violently. "Come on Fiona. Get it together," I said to myself.

When I returned to Archie, I placed his pack on the floor and knelt beside him. "Please turn that bloody music off," he gasped.

Before opening his pack, I marched over to the stereo and pressed stop on the tape deck. Silence at last.

"Grab the first aid kit and take out the surgical glue, scissors, stapler, bandages, and bottle of antiseptic," he instructed.

I retrieved the items and placed them on the floor alongside him. "Use the scissors to cut my shirt off."

I cut his shirt down the middle and then along the shoulders, throwing the remnants to the side.

"First we'll take care of the stomach wound," Archie imparted with laboured breath.

The wound was about thirty centimetres long and ran diagonally from just below his left pec to his lower ribs on the right side. I had treated workers on the farm and even stitched a bloke up. But I'd never seen a wound this long and deep.

"Pour the antiseptic on the wound. Don't be frugal but leave enough for the back wound."

As I poured antiseptic on the wound, he scowled in pain while holding his breath. He was losing a hell of a lot of blood. Too much!

He looked me in the eye with increased intensity, "Okay, I'm going to press the wound together, you apply the glue. Don't glue my fingers to my chest because that'll be very bad." He gave me a wink as he grinned.

I can't believe he's smiling, even if it quickly contorted into a grimace. His light-heartedness was helping me to keep it together. I glued the wound together, carefully avoiding the tips of his fingers.

"You're doing great Fiona. Now I want you to staple the wound with a two-centimetre spacing."

Archie continued to press the wound together as I pushed the staple gun into his skin. Click, click, click. Having never gripped a staple gun, I was surprised how easy it was to use.

The cut to Archie's upper back was slightly more challenging as he was unable to assist in holding it closed. After applying the antiseptic, I surprised myself by managing to press, glue, and staple the wound without much trouble. It was all a bit of a blur really. After I'd placed gauze and bandages over the wounds, the bleeding had almost stopped. *I did it. Thank God!*

My next mission was to get him off the dirty floor. We both

grunted, him in pain and me with exertion, as I held his arm around my shoulder and staggered to a shabby couch in the loungeroom.

Archie lifted his head. “You need to cut Sal down and look after him.” He then closed his eyes and scowled in pain.

“Are you going to be, okay?” I asked.

“I’ll be fine, just take care of Sal,” he replied unconvincingly.

This was the first time I had the chance to examine the man that was tied to a rafter in the kitchen. He was in his late-fifties, balding, and had a slight paunch. He was dressed in his underwear and a singlet. The poor man looked terrible. He was black and blue around his ribs and chest, with split lips, a broken nose, and both eyes swollen shut. He was unconscious but still breathing. I could see his chest slowly rising and heard gurgling noises coming from his throat.

I grabbed an old dining chair to stand on and cut him down as carefully as I could manage. His weight made it impossible to lower him gently, but I made sure I supported his neck in the crook of my arm as he fell to the floor.

I took my jumper off and placed it under his head. “Water,” he mumbled.

I grabbed a bottle of water from the kitchen sink and brought it to his bloodied lips. He took small sips and then asked, “Who are you?”

“I’m Fiona, I’m Archie O’Connor’s apprentice.”

The corners of his cracked lips raised up, smiling through the pain, “You tell that boy that I’m willing to split......sixty-forty.”

“You can tell him yourself after we get you both out of here.”

“I’m in a bad way luv. On the kitchen counter there’s an envelope in my pack. You give that to Archie........you hear?” he said with laboured breath.

I glanced over at the counter and saw an orange backpack with items scattered around it. When I returned my attention to the man, he had a fixed stare with mouth agape. With the tips of my fingers, I closed his eyelids and let out a deep sigh.

Chapter Eleven

Saturday February 2, 2041 from 1:15 a.m. – Fiona

The night sky was pitch black due to the heavy thick clouds drifting across the full moon and concealing the stars. There was a chill in the air with a strong north-westerly breeze. As soon as I started jogging down the main road towards Charlie's farm, I felt a dampness in the lining of my knickers. How embarrassing, I can't believe I'd wet myself. My best guess is it occurred when I shot Lewis's brother. I put the humiliation to the back of my mind and focused on the task at hand. I wanted to sprint but knew that the smart move was to set a steady pace that would not only take me to the finish line, but also leave me enough breath to ask for help.

Before setting off on the ten-kilometre journey, I freed the three women that I later learned had been abducted, raped, and beaten by the brothers. Sandra, the woman in her mid-fifties, was completely unresponsive until I asked her if she could look after Archie while I ran for help. Surprisingly, she immediately became focused. It was as if someone had flicked a switch in her brain. She examined his wounds, checked his vitals, and asked him a series of health-related questions before inspecting the first aid kit.

"You seem to know what you're doing. Are you going to be all good?" I asked her.

She looked at me as if I'd asked her a stupid question. "Of course I know what I'm doing child, I'm a nurse for Christ's sake." *Well, all righty then* I thought as she placed one hand over her mouth and the other on her forehead. "Oh, I'm so sorry, I must be in deep shock."

"No need to apologise, I'm just glad you're here. I mean, not here in these circumstances, but you know what I mean." I was experiencing a familiar case of '*foot in mouth*,' with no one to rescue me on this occasion.

The other two women weren't much older than me. They told me their story as I struck their chains with a meat cleaver I found near Lewis's body. They'd become close friends as they backpacked through the south-west, working as fruit pickers, cooks, and cleaners. A couple of days ago they were walking to a nearby river to have a swim and cool off during their lunch break. This is when the brothers came across them and their nightmare began. As I left for my run it was pleasing to see them assisting Sandra to keep Archie alive.

I checked the luminous dials on my wristwatch. I had covered the first five kilometres in just over twenty-five minutes. My legs still felt strong, and I had complete control of my breathing.

I kept running the operation through my mind……I had killed a man……. I don't feel guilty, it was him or Archie……. Is it wrong to think that way?…….What could have I done differently?………… Why did Archie rush into the house without me?………Didn't he trust me?

Archie had been visibly distressed when I told him of Sal's passing. This was the first time I'd seen Archie express raw emotion. It was hard to stay angry at him when he was both physically and mentally hurting.

I ran the final five kilometres even faster than the first. My plan to pace myself went right out the window when I sprinted the last 400 metres. By the time I arrived at the Wong's front gate, my lungs were burning, and I was struggling to breathe. I took a deep breath and shouted, "CHARLIE…. SONJA…. SMITHY!" A horrible metallic taste lingered at the back of my throat. I was desperate for water.

I was greatly relieved when the flood lights were switched on and I could see Charlie running down the path with a rifle in his hand, with Smithy following closely behind carrying a shotgun. As Charlie opened the gate, I was bent over with my hands on my knees trying not to vomit.

"Archie…needs…help," I gasped.

As Charlie pointed to my shirt, he asked, "Whoa, slow down. Is that your blood?"

I looked down and was shocked to see my shirt covered in Archie's and Sal's blood.

I took a deep breath and spoke in breathless spurts, "No……I'm okay……Listen." I concentrated on my breathing, cleared my mind and continued, "You have to come right now. Help Archie. He's on a farm. Ten kays away. Come on, let's go."

Charlie asked Smithy to grab Ben and drive the Ford ute to the front gate. I assumed Ben was another one of Charlie's workers.

Charlie led me by my shoulders to a tap and hose. I held the hose to my mouth and greedily gulped down the water. As I washed my hands and face, I intentionally sprayed water over my shirt and pants in an effort to wash away the stench of blood and urine.

Charlie spoke softly and slowly, "Are there any bad people with Archie?"

I had just started to recover my breath. "They're all dead," I explained.

"Is Archie or anyone else badly hurt?"

"No, I mean, yes. I bandaged him up, but he's lost a lot of blood. A nurse is looking after him."

Charlie looked confused. Smithy drove the ute to the gate. Ben jumped out of the passenger seat and climbed into the tray with a rifle in his grasp.

"Where exactly is this property?" Charlie queried.

I explained that the property was only a couple of kilometres east of the shed holding the fights. Charlie retrieved a pen and paper from the ute's glove box and asked me to sketch a mud map. Smithy examined my map and confirmed that he knew of the property, describing the layout to Charlie. Sonja walked up beside me holding a blanket and wrapped it around my shoulders.

Charlie spoke softly to his wife, "Sonja, please take Fiona inside, we'll be back in less than an hour."

I looked at Charlie in disbelief. "I'm coming with you. I'm not just waiting here."

"You've done your part Fiona, and you've been very brave, but there is only so much room in the tray."

"That's bullshit, there's plenty of room for me," I said pointing to the tray.

Charlie gave Sonja a look that only a long-lived couple would understand. A look that spoke a thousand words.

Sonja grasped me by the shoulders. "It's time that you let someone look after you, trust me, this is for the best." Her eyes expressed a care and concern that broke something from within. I instantly felt exhausted - physically and emotionally. As Smithy drove down the main road, Sonja held me as I sobbed into her shoulder.

Sonja took good care of me, running me a bath, giving me pyjamas, and making me a hot tea. She then led me to a bedroom at the back of the house. Before she shut the door, I pleaded, "Can you please let me know when they get back?"

Sonja nodded. "I'll be waiting in the loungeroom until they return. Just call out if you needed anything."

Unbeknownst to me at the time, Sonja had placed a strong sedative in my tea. She may have had good intentions, but she'd broken my trust. I was pissed at her for weeks.

Chapter Twelve

Sunday February 3, 2041 from 10:30 a.m. – Fiona

I woke in a confused state and looked around the room, momentarily unaware of where I was. As I rubbed sleep from my eyes it all came rushing back. "ARCHIE!" I jumped out of bed and raced to the kitchen to find Sonja and her daughter making breakfast. It looked like a professional spread - with eggs, bacon, mushrooms, tomatoes, and toast. Still dressed in pink flowery pyjamas, I spread out my hands and asked frantically in a raised voice, "Where's Archie?" I must have looked like a mad woman.

Sonja paused for a split second, and then pointed down the hallway from which I'd just sprinted from. "He's in the bedroom opposite yours. Hey, are you alright?"

Disregarding Sonja's question I marched straight down the hallway to the bedroom, swiftly opening the closed door with more gusto than I'd intended. Sandra, the nurse whom I'd rescued, was examining a thermometer alongside Archie, who was lying bare-chested in bed propped up by several pillows. Bloodied bandages lying on a nearby dresser looked out of place in a room decorated for a child, with its bright blue walls, and balloon and animal stickers.

"Good Morning. Say, you did a wonderful job closing his wounds. Have you had medical experience?" Sandra inquired with a chirpy tone.

I wasn't in the mood to play questions and answers with the nurse. "Are you okay?" I asked Archie.

"I'll survive, thanks to you, Charlie and Sandra," he answered softly.

"We need to talk about what happened last night," I insisted.

"There'll be plenty of time to debrief later. Sandra here has warned me that my injuries will take at least a month to heal. Look, I don't want us to wear out our welcome. I want you to take the horses to Clarry's. Ask Clarry if you can borrow the Beetle so you can return and pick me up."

"When do you want me to leave?" I asked.

"After breakfast. Oh, before you return, I want you to drop by the police station, pick up the handover documentation and go next door to settle the bounty. Use some of the proceeds to pay for Clarry's fuel."

"What if they don't believe me? How do I prove that we have him?"

"Take Lewis of course," he replied, grinning from ear to ear.

"What do you mean take Lewis? Did Charlie bring his body back to the farm? How do I even carry him on Roger?"

Archie raised his palm. "No need to worry, you're just taking his head."

"That's bloody gross!" I said in disgust.

Archie held his stomach in response, trying not to laugh at my repulsion.

"It's not funny," I grumbled.

When I turned to exit the room, Archie said, "One last thing Fiona. Thank you. You did great!"

I had breakfast sitting under the backyard pergola over-looking the garden. I hadn't eaten since last night, but I wasn't that hungry. Whilst contemplating the previous night's events, I pushed my food from one side of the plate to the other. My stomach was clenched tight. I felt frustrated by my earlier conversation with Archie. I know he's injured, but he didn't want to give me the time of day. I think I deserve some answers.

I watched Charlie's youngest sling rocks at old beer cans that he had lined up on top of a forty-gallon drum. Each time he knocked over a can he cheered with bravado and looked around to see who was watching. His siblings were kicking a football from one side of the garden to the next. Charlie had his arm wrapped around Sonja's waist as they watched the kids and sipped coffee from their mugs.

Memories of mum and dad came flooding back when I saw the love in Charlie's and Sonja's eyes. I thought of the times I was such a bitch; whining about going on family outings and screaming when Mum took my H-phone away. I'd rather chat about nonsense with holographic composites of my friends than spend time with my family. I'd move heaven and earth to spend just one more minute with them. I choked back tears as I covertly scraped my leftovers into the garden. I didn't want Sonja to think I was ungrateful. Spoiling the dogs with affection when they came sniffing around my leftovers lifted my spirits somewhat.

Charlie promised me that they'd take good care of Archie. He handed me a hessian bag that contained Lewis's head wrapped in plastic. Sonja had graciously placed potpourri in the bag to help hide the smell. I'm sure the coppers will get a kick out of that. She also packed me some lunch for the trip. I gave her my best wan smile. I was still upset at her for giving me a Mickey Finn.

I rode Jasper with Roger following from the rear, secured by a long rope. Poor Roger had Lewis's head strapped to his saddle. Archie's absence visibly upset Roger. His ears, neck, and head were rigid, and he had wide open eyes. I spoke soothingly, attempting to pacify him and improve his mood. It didn't appear to make a difference. I know how he feels. Anger, disappointment, and loss are emotions that animals share with their human owners.

The twenty-five-kilometre ride provided me with time to reflect on my first operation. I replayed my future conversation with Archie like a pre-war television sit-com, each time altering my statements and questions, along with his predicted responses. Other episodes focused on imagining myself chastising him and letting him know how upset I was of his mistrust and subsequent bravado. Other times I envisaged Archie explaining how disappointed he was in my performance, with the final scene ending with my employment contract being terminated – '*YOU'RE FIRED!*'

Just as the sun was fading over the horizon, I trudged up Clarry's winding driveway, exhausted more from the events over the previous twenty-four hours than the ride itself. The journey had provided me the time to digest and analyse the recent events. But I still needed answers. And some closure.

I wearily led Roger and Jasper to the stables. Clarry assisted me to feed and water the horses while Zeus rolled around on the grass. He must have seen how tired I was as he only asked me one question, "Is Archie Okay?"

I followed Clarry into the kitchen and told him the condensed version of events as he made me tea. During the story, Clarry shook his head in amazement and concern, at times making comments such as, "No bloody way!... Stupid bastard!.... You're shitting me!.... What the fuck?"

Clarry agreed that first thing in the morning we'd visit both the police station and the bondsman's office, before driving to Charlie's farm to pick up Archie. I didn't even have the energy to have a shower, I just collapsed into bed and was comatose within seconds.

Chapter Thirteen

February 4 - 5, 2041 – Fiona

I had nightmare after nightmare, waking numerous times throughout the night. Zeus slept on the floor beside me, snoring like an old drunkard. He was jerking his front paws as he slept, probably dreaming of chasing down an intruder, or maybe a rabbit. I woke early to find Clarry working on his Beetle's rear engine. I assumed he wanted to ensure it would make the journey. He must have seen the urgency on my face, as he slammed the rear bonnet and said, "Let's get a move on, shall we?"

Like a driving instructor showing off his skills, Clarry parallel parked the Beetle into a tight space between two cars in front of the cop shop. He advised me that he had a few errands to attend to and would meet me back at the car in half an hour. I entered the station to find Senior Constable Atkins playing cards with the admin officer. He certainly didn't look like a copper. I cleared my throat and introduced myself, explaining that I was Archie O'Connor's apprentice.

He didn't batter an eyelid and scoffed in a sarcastic tone, "I feel for you. Now, what do you want?"

What an asshole!

I placed the hessian bag on the counter. He looked down at the bag, "What's in there?"

"Archie mentioned you fancied puzzles and quizzes. Multiple choice question, is it A) a bush melon, B) a bowling ball or C) Lewis Hutchins's head."

"Ah shit!" he groaned.

I was quietly proud of my witty remark. Atkins carefully grabbed the bag by the top knot, and while holding it out at arm's length he carried it to the back of the station.

Atkins returned shortly after and handed me a document. "Is this the paperwork I need to collect the reward?" I asked.

Atkins raised an eyebrow. "What do you think it is?" He sighed and added, "I forgot you're an apprentice. It's the handover document to prove you've delivered the shithead. Just take it next door to Brad and he'll sort you out."

As I was leaving Atkins taunted, "I love the potpourri, is that your touch?"

I mumbled under my breath, "Dickhead," and proceeded to walk next door.

I greeted Brad, signed for the reward, and collected the gold. It felt gratifying to be paid, even though Archie had made it clear on day one that I wouldn't be receiving a cut for my first two jobs.

Before we left town Clarry pulled up to the petrol station and filled up the Beetle. He not only refused to take payment for the fuel, but also bought me an egg sandwich and coffee. "You don't take coin from family," he muttered. I was quickly growing to like this man.

During the drive back to Charlie's farm I asked Clarry to tell me about Archie. I wanted to learn what makes him tick, but he skirted around any serious topics and focused on funny anecdotes of their adventures together. The central theme consisted of Archie performing some foolish act that caused Clarry to cry from laughter.

One of the more humorous stories involved rescuing one of his cousins who'd been caught by the father of a young lady he'd been shagging in the farmer's barn. The father chained the boy to the barn door and was threatening to blow his balls off. Archie had successfully negotiated his release, but only after agreeing to stay for dinner to meet his spinster sister, who happened to be desperate to find a husband. The sister was as wide as Archie was tall. Before he could leave for the night, she'd insisted on taking him for a tour of the barn. By the end of the story, I had to grab the steering wheel as

Clarry's raucous laughter was causing the Beetle to swerve all over the road.

Upon arrival to the farm, we were both relieved to find Archie looking well considering his injuries. We thanked the Wong family and their workers for their hospitality. Archie made it clear in no uncertain terms that he was keen to leave. Clarry gave him a disapproving look that could not be mistaken for meaning anything but '*Stop being a rude and ungrateful bastard!*' I pondered, *what's gotten into him?*

It was pleasing to discover that Sandra and the two rescued girls had been offered employment and lodging at the farm. Sandra's nursing skills were invaluable, and Charlie was impressed by the girls' willingness to muck in. All three accepted Charlie's proposal after they inspected the farm's security and experienced the family's compassion.

We fully extended the back rest of the front passenger seat to enable Archie to lie flat. He groaned in pain as Smithy and Clarry assisted him into the Beetle.

Sandra handed me a bottle of antibiotics from Charlie's medical supplies and explained that Archie needed to take two a day, morning and night. She also clarified when to change his bandages and how to identify signs of infection. Sandra once again stated that I did a wonderful job with the glue and stapling, but explained she took the staples out and stitched the wound, as it was likely to heal faster.

Sandra turned her back to the passenger side of the Beetle and placed four bottles of oxycodone in Clarry's hands. Three of the bottles were empty. Archie was resting his eyes as Sandra confided in a soft voice, "I found these in Archie's pack after he asked me to find his pills. I think he has a big problem. These are highly addictive and can be harmful if taken over extended periods. With his injury, he only needs codeine for pain management, but convincing him to wean off oxy in the first week of his recovery is likely to be counterproductive. By the way, he only has four tablets left and he's been munching on them like Tic Tacs."

I gave Clarry a worried look. He sighed, "Thanks for everything you've done Sandra, you've been a godsend. Don't you worry, I'll look after my brother from another mother."

We said our goodbyes and returned to Clarry's house, the second time I'd completed the journey in thirty-six hours. At least this time it was a lot faster and in comfort. Even though I sat behind Clarry in the rear passenger seat, I was able to look Archie in the eye as he turned his head.

"So, where's my revolver and knife?" he asked.

Clarry piped up before I could answer. "You don't need weapons when you're travelling in the green machine, it's faster than lightning and as strong as a tank."

Archie replied in amusement, "This looks like the inside of your Beetle, sounds like your Beetle, and even has the fishy smell of your Beetle. Am I mistaken mate?"

Clarry reached for the volume of the vehicle's tape deck and turned up the sweet music of Bob Marley singing 'Buffalo Soldier.' He swayed his head and sung to the chorus with exuberance.

Upon arrival home, I helped Clarry set up his spare room to transform it into Archie's recovery room. We placed fresh sheets on the bed, vacuumed the old carpet, decluttered, jemmy opened the jammed window frames and dusted the furniture. Zeus kept Archie company in the front lounge while we prepared his room.

This was our first opportunity to chat in private since learning about the oxy. "What are we going to do about the oxy situation?" I asked.

"I'm going to deal with it. You don't need to concern yourself," he said abruptly

I was about to counter that opinion when he marched from the room. "Well, okaaay then," I murmured to myself, feeling disappointed about being so easily dismissed.

Clarry won a short-lived debate, convincing Archie to have his chicken soup in bed. Before falling into a deep slumber, he'd swallowed the antibiotics and two oxys, leaving just two of the addictive pills remaining.

While Archie slept, we slurped the remaining soup in the small dining room. Clarry cleared his throat, "I have a proposal for you."

"I'm listening."

"Do you get seasick?" Clarry asked.

"I've been on a few boats and have never felt sick. Why?"

"My employer needs the assistance of a deckhand for a week, no experience required. I'm planning on helping Archie with his little problem, so he'll be a man down. I thought it'd be a perfect time for you to learn some new skills while Archie's recovering."

"I'm not okay with it. I need some answers and I'm his God damn apprentice. I should be here, with him," I said angrily.

"Fiona, you're not going to get answers from him in his current condition. He's an addict, and we're not going to supply him oxys when he runs out. This is for the best as it's going to get messy," he retorted in a frustrated tone.

I was annoyed at being treated like a child. "I'm sick of people telling me what's for the best. I'm young, but I'm not stupid."

Attempting a different tact, Clarry stated with diplomacy, "I didn't say you were. I'm not going to say trust me, because you hardly know me. What I'm going to ask you to do is think with your head, not your heart. What do you think is the best thing to do?"

We sat in silence while we finished our meals. I looked deep into Clarry's eyes, "Only seven days and then I'm coming back."

"Seven days and I'll come and collect you myself. I promise," he said in earnest.

The following morning, I farewelled Archie, advising him that I'd be working with Captain Ross as a deckhand. He appeared both surprised and confused. Before Archie could question the plan, Clarry stated that we needed to get on the road and hurried me out the door.

As I grabbed my pack in the loungeroom, I saw Sal's orange backpack leaning against Zeus's couch. I thought no one would miss it, so I heaved the heavy pack over my shoulder and shuffled outside to the Beetle.

Clarry dropped me off at Captain Ross's house, which was located opposite the boat harbour. The Captain's wife, Elizabeth, was a portly woman that was very welcoming and eager to show off her kitchen. She had hundreds of potted plants that filled almost every nook and cranny in the house. A pink and grey cockatoo flew past my head chirping, "*Cocky wants a cracker.*"

Before Clarry left, I stepped to within a bee's dick from him and whispered, "Seven days. Not a day longer."

He nodded, "Seven days," and walked down the Captain's driveway.

I watched him drive off at speed in his green machine, wondering if Archie was going to beat his addiction. And would I have a job to go back to?

Chapter Fourteen

February 5 – 6, 2041 – Archie

I was initially taken aback to hear that Fiona would be working as a decky. After giving it some time to sink in, I could see merit in the idea. Clarry had obviously asked the Captain to take her under his wing to keep her busy while I recuperated. Not only was I incapable of conducting hands-on training in my current condition, but I also needed time to clear my head before I debriefed her.

With a methodical approach, I moved onto my side before bringing my knees slowly to my chest. I then used my elbow and hands to push myself to a sitting position on the edge of the bed. The pain in my stomach was intense throughout the movement. I gradually managed to stand and stagger to the dresser table. I found an oxy bottle and emptied the contents into my palm, stunned to see only two tablets remaining. I swallowed the tablets and then slowly and painfully dragged my pack towards the bed, careful not to strain my wounds and tear open the stitches. I conducted a thorough search by first removing the larger items and then gingerly tipping the remaining kit onto the floor. Frustratingly, I failed to locate any other bottles.

Clarry knocked and then opened the door while I was searching through the side pockets of my pack. He stood with his hands on his hips and regarded the equipment and supplies strewn all over the floor. He shook his head and claimed with vexation, "Brother, I just vacuumed and cleaned this room."

I was a little embarrassed by the mess I'd made and the circumstances behind my erratic behaviour. "It's all good. I'm just looking for, ah, Sal's compass."

Clarry didn't even look slightly convinced by my white lie. To his dismay he said, "I'm guessing you're now out of oxy's."

"What are you talking about?" I asked.

"Let's cut the shit brother. You're an addict. You know it and I know it."

"Jesus Clarry, settle down. Look, forget that nonsense, I need to go to town," I responded desperately, sounding weak even to my own ears.

"If you try to ride Roger, you're going to split those wounds wide open. And then you'll be stuffed."

"Then do me a favour and drive me," I said, annoyed by his insinuation that he wouldn't give me a lift.

"I'm going to do you one better. I'm going to help you get clean for your own sake, and Fiona's sake for that matter."

I angrily shouted at him, spittle spraying from my mouth, "What's with you? Why are you all of a sudden on my case?"

Clarry held one of the empty bottles inches from my face and insisted in an exasperated tone, "The oxys will kill you brother, maybe not tomorrow or the next day, but THEY WILL KILL YOU! Now, you may want that, but you've taken responsibility for Fiona. She told me about what went down. This shit obviously affects your decision making, which will get you BOTH KILLED!"

I sat back down on the bed with my face in my hands. Clarry was telling me some hard truths that I didn't want to hear, especially from a mate who I greatly respected. I'd finally been called out. Thoughts of doubt and failure came rushing into my mind - 'Was it time to give the pills up? Am I a coward? Am I strong enough?'

Clarry sat on the edge of the bed and placed his arm around my shoulders, "Listen brother, it takes at least seventy-two hours to get this shit out of your system. You can do this. Zeus and I'll be here the entire time. We won't leave you."

I'm not sure if it was Clarry's words, or the fact that I almost got Fiona killed. Maybe I was just sick of being dependent on opiates. Whichever it was, the decision to get clean made me feel a sense of relief. I wiped my eyes with the back of my hand and held out a science magazine, "Do you at least have some decent reading material?"

Clarry laughed. "I think I have some comics in the shed somewhere."

"Let me guess, your Archie collection?" I asked facetiously.

"How did you know? Don't worry, I've got you covered. I'll find my brother's Sharpe novels. I think they're in the shed somewhere."

Once Clarry had left the room, I laid back down on the bed and contemplated my situation. What would Janet think if she could see me now? She wouldn't be able to hide her disappointment, that's for sure. I knew this day was coming. I convinced myself - I'll do another job and then I'll take care of it. The problem is - there was always another job.

An hour later, Clarry returned with a cardboard box containing five bottles of water, a thick blanket, three towels, a large bowl, and three Sharpe novels.

Clarry handed me a book. "You don't have to read these in chronological order, but I know you're a pedantic bugger, so here's the first three of the series."

The front cover had a picture of a flash looking musket. "Thanks mate, and not just for the book."

Clarry went to leave the room, and then paused before saying, "I'll be in the loungeroom. Brother, if you change your mind halfway through and try to leave the house, I'm going to have to stop you. I know you're stronger than me and you know all that Bruce Lee shit, but Zeus gets very agitated if members of his pack are angry with each other. It's not a pretty sight, let me tell you."

"I read you loud and clear Clarry. I plan to suffer in silence."

~

I read the first novel in just under six hours – it's a series written by Bernard Cornwall about a British soldier in the early 1800s, who begins his career as a down and out private and rises in the ranks through great risk and adversity. I love to support the underdog. I was an avid reader of fiction as a young man. I completed a speed-reading course during my first year in law school. The facilitator would play Mozart and Bach while we completed timed comprehension exercises. My newfound abilities came in handy when required to read copious books on case law. However, whenever I read fiction, I'd have to remind myself to slow down and enjoy the plot rather than rushing through the story.

The sun was setting as I commenced the second novel. The two oxys were now out of my system, leaving me to feel irritable and agitated. It didn't help that I also had a splitting headache. Clarry checked up on me on the hour, sometimes giving me paracetamol and water and other times just popping his head into the room. Zeus placed his huge head on the edge of the bed, whimpering with sad eyes. He knew something was wrong. When I rubbed him behind his ears, he wagged his tail and nuzzled his wet nose against my neck and licked my cheek. Clarry made me leek and potato soup for dinner and reminded me to drink copious amounts of water to stay hydrated.

During the first half of the night, I experienced constant stomach pain and diarrhea. The regular trips to the toilet frustrated me to the nth degree. Each time I got out of bed, the pain to my back and stomach was excruciating. I could feel the stitches pull the skin at the edges of my chest wound and the constant crapping was making my ass red raw. It's safe to say that I was feeling sorry for myself.

Clarry came to my rescue. He gave me a doxylamine tablet, an antihistamine that helps treat insomnia, and two paracetamol tablets for the pain. With great relief I began to feel drowsy and closed my eyes. He wiped my forehead with a wet cloth and mentioned something about having to change my wet sheets in the morning. I hope he was referring to the perspiration soaking the sheets, because I wouldn't live it down if I'd pissed the bed.

Chapter Fifteen

Archie

Smithy had his back turned - he was lifting a British calvary sword and striking it downwards and then repeating the action. Blood was flying in all directions, splattering the ceiling, floor, and walls. He then stood motionless before turning towards me, holding Lewis's head by his fringe.

I was in a sitting position with my back against a fibro wall. Smithy placed Lewis on my lap facing me. Lewis glared and challenged, "I reckon I could beat you in a fight, you druggie prick. Come on, stand up and put your dukes up."

Charlie stood in front of me and asked me to follow him. I placed Lewis on the lino floor and walked outside. We were standing in a clearing, surrounded by an abundant forest. Janet, the Captain, and Senior Constable Atkins were standing around a barbecue cooking abalone and chicken. They all glared at me and replied in unison, "What's wrong with you Archie?" They were each holding kebabs, chewing the meat off the sticks.

"I have your kebab here Archie," claimed Charlie. He handed me a six-foot stick with Lewis's head spiked at the top.

After I walked through the forest I was suddenly standing in a desert; the red sand blew into twisters that reached far into the clear blue sky.

"Where are my brothers Archie?" Lewis screamed.

I threw the stick down and sprinted across the desert sand; my bare feet were burning and blistering in the searing heat.

When the desert abruptly dissolved beneath my feet, I was relieved to be standing at the base of a steep muddy mountain. I gripped a thick green vine that was hanging from a rocky precipice and climbed up the mountain, grasping the vine hand over hand until I reached the summit. I tripped as I ran down the other side, rolling head over heels until I landed in a small pond. At the edge of the pond stood a five-foot Venus flytrap that was chomping on thousands of blow flies. I sat in the pond and felt my right foot being pulled. A gigantic black eel wrapped its cold wicked jaws around my ankle. I held my knife and struck it to the top of its head. It flinched and released its grip, providing me an opportunity to jump out of the pond.

I raced along a gravel road, looking over my shoulder in fear of being chased. Suddenly I no longer felt the ground beneath my feet. I was falling down a mine shaft, hurtling down a dark abyss, screaming for Janet to help me. Each time I reached for a crevice to slow my descent, my fingers would break, and my fall would continue. I looked down, waiting to strike the unseen ground below, waiting for the inevitable.

I woke startled with my head racing. I was drenched in sweat and was suffering a severe migraine. I had vomited all over my pillow and sheets. Like an angel that I didn't deserve, Clarry was standing above me with a glass of water and two paracetamol tablets in his palm.

Chapter Sixteen

Saturday February 9, 2041 – Fiona

The Captain was stern but fair. He assigned me work on the boat by first demonstrating and then watching me perform a task until he was confident that I could complete it to his satisfaction. As Scotty, the abalone diver, fished on the seabed, I learned the duties of a deckhand - shucking the abalone, cleaning the deck, cooking lunch, and making coffee.

The Captain encouraged me to snorkel during breaks, which was great fun until the crew told me countless horror stories of sighting great whites, tiger sharks and bull sharks. The Captain took great delight in explaining in graphic detail how he was savaged by the enormous jaws of one of these ocean predators.

During the afternoons I worked with Elizabeth in their fish 'n' chips shop. She taught me how to batter the snapper and deep fry the chips. She was a complete motor mouth, but in between breaths she'd stop to ask me questions about my past life, dreams, and ambitions. She made me feel like I was the most important person in the world. Something I hadn't felt for a long time.

To my surprise, I actually enjoyed having a chit-chat and a laugh with the customers. However, some of the conversations became sombre when they spoke of their day-to-day challenges. Recurring concerns included power shortages, a lack of supplies and amenities, and avoiding gangs when traveling between towns. I discovered that many of the residents were petrified that the gangs will return to town. After seeing what Lewis and his brothers were capable of, I don't blame them in the slightest for being fearful.

After eating a delicious meal of fried pepper squid with a wonderful fresh salad, which Elizabeth grew in her garden, I excused myself to return to my room. The bedroom belonged to their daughter who was currently working on a sheep farm in Lake Grace, located 375 kilometres north east of Esperance.

I dragged Sal's orange pack to the edge of my bed. It felt as heavy as Archie's, so it must have weighed at least thirty kilos. My pack is only about half that weight. When I asked Archie why this was the case, he explained that we don't require two of everything. I doubt he's being chivalrous, so I'm guessing he thinks I can't carry a heavier pack. It shits me to tears that he's probably right. I opened Sal's pack and emptied the contents onto the carpet. It contained similar items to Archie's and was packed using an almost identical method. I wondered if there was a bounty hunter training academy, or whether Archie apprenticed under Sal. I decided that it was fanciful thinking. It was more likely that they sat around a fire drinking beer, talking shit, and learning from past experiences. They probably droned on about their pack's weight and balance, being prepared and alike... blah...blah....blah.

I found a letter sized envelope in the front pocket of his pack. I held it in my hands, suddenly recalling Sal's plea to give the envelope to Archie. It was literally his last words. After the stomach-turning action and stress of the night, I completely forgot about his request.

I opened the envelope and found a folded contract inside. It was a civilian contract between Sal and a gentleman named Kadesh Singh.

Wow! Fifty ounces of gold was an absolute fortune. I held the contract in my grasp and let my imagination run wild. You could purchase a house and car with fifty ounces and still have enough left over to hold one hell of a party. When I signed up for the apprenticeship, I had no idea you could work on contracts worth this much coin.

I wonder why Sal was hunting Lewis when he had a contract worth a gazillion in his mitts?

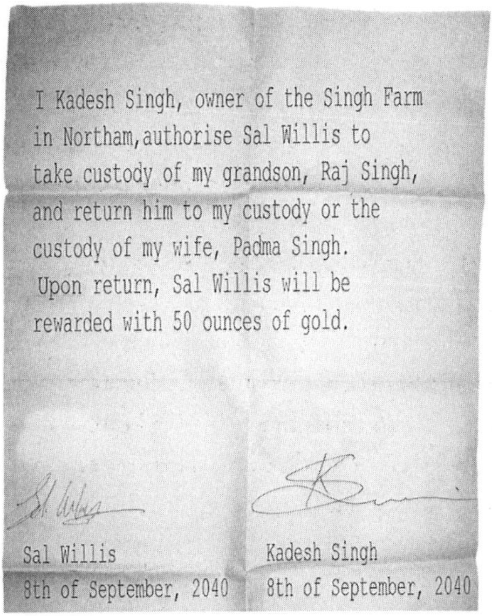

I Kadesh Singh, owner of the Singh Farm
in Northam, authorise Sal Willis to
take custody of my grandson, Raj Singh,
and return him to my custody or the
custody of my wife, Padma Singh.
Upon return, Sal Willis will be
rewarded with 50 ounces of gold.

Sal Willis
8th of September, 2040

Kadesh Singh
8th of September, 2040

I folded the contract and returned it to its envelope. In the left-hand side pocket I found Sal's notebook, which was protected by a beautiful brown leather cover. He had meticulously recorded the dates and times at the top of each page. On the last fifteen or so pages, he had scribbled and underlined the words Op Singh or Op Hutchins beneath the dates.

I paused before reading the notebook, pondering whether I was peeping into Sal's private thoughts; like reading a personal journal. After thirty seconds of deliberation, I reasoned that since Sal wanted Archie to read the contract, he'd obviously want him to learn more from his notebook. And as I'm Archie's apprentice, he'd also give his blessing for me to do the same. I might be drawing a long bow, but I couldn't wait to learn more.

I focused on Operation Hutchins as it was relevant to my first bounty job. I pieced together an order of events that led to Sal's rendezvous with Lewis and his brothers. Sal had received information from a postal worker that a man fitting Lewis's description was working at a nearby sheep station fixing fences. This is where the operation must have gone awry; he may not have realised that Lewis had his brothers close by.

The notes concerning the Singh job were pretty comprehensive. Ten-year-old Raj was taken from his family farm by his stepfather, Noel Patterson, on the 27 of August, 2040. Raj's mum had died from cancer a month prior. There seemed to be a disagreement in regard to the custody of Raj. Sal had received information from a miner in Kalgoorlie that Patterson was headed to Perth. The miner must be an award-winning bullshit artist. You would have to be crazy to enter the fifty-kilometre exclusion zone and risk being contaminated. The Government reckons it could be a thousand years before people can once again reside in Perth.

Chapter Seventeen

Tuesday February 12, 2041 – Archie

As I sat at the kitchen table and chewed a mouthful of scrambled eggs, I was relieved that the withdrawal symptoms had diminished in duration and intensity. In fact, I was feeling pretty good. Even the wounds to my stomach and back were beginning to heal. Clarry mentioned that he'd remove the stitches in the next couple of days.

Clarry was returning to work this morning and planned to bring Fiona home in the afternoon. I was looking forward to setting things straight with her. I owed her an explanation and an apology. I had failed to prepare her for her first job, placed her in a perilous situation and gave her poor instructions. There is no doubt that I had failed in the seven Ps; proper planning and preparation prevents piss poor performance. And to her credit, she still managed to save my ass. I was fortunate to hire an apprentice that could not only use her intuition but determine when her boss was wrong and act on it. A rare attribute indeed.

I spent the remainder of the morning with Roger and Jasper, sweeping the stables and giving them a rub down; while being careful not to strain my injuries and impede my recovery. Zeus was curled up in the corner of the barn, not a care in the world. Boy, I was envious!

After lunch I documented an initial four-week training plan for Fiona, detailing the knowledge, skills, and performance outcomes that I wanted her to achieve. The plan aimed at revising the previous learnings and scaffolding new knowledge and skills in tactics – door entries, room clearances, movement drills, marksmanship, and close quarter fighting. I was pre-empting her decision to continue with the apprenticeship, even though I wouldn't blame her in the slightest if she decided to wave me goodbye.

Clarry and Fiona arrived with fish and chips from the Captain's shop. Most shops use too much batter and not enough fish. This was not an issue at the Captain's shop; his wife covered the snapper with the perfect amount of batter. It smelt and tasted delicious. Clarry placed the food and two bottles of his home brew on the kitchen table, and said he was off to have a shower and then drive to a friend's house for dinner. When I inquired if this happened to be a lady friend, he instantly informed me to mind my own business. A touchy subject indeed I thought. A subject that I will scrutinise at a later date. We enjoyed teasing each other – it was like a sport - competitive and relentless.

Fiona and I sat at the dining table and started to dig into the meal. We both steered clear of the elephant in the room, instead discussing Fiona's time with the Captain - her duties, his idiosyncrasies, and superstitions. We both laughed and started to relax in each other's presence.

I inadvertently burped and proclaimed, "Elizabeth went above and beyond once again."

Fiona smiled. "I actually cooked this."

"Wow, I'm impressed."

"Well, admittedly Elizabeth is a great teacher."

Fiona cleared the table while I made tea. After we both sat back down at the kitchen table I said with sincerity, "Fiona, I want to say sorry and thank you."

She looked down at her coffee, "You don't have to apologise."

"Yeah, I do. This is not easy for me to say, but I need to get it out in the open. I owe you at least that." I let out a deep sigh before continuing. "Look, I'm an addict running from guilt and grief. That's not an excuse, that's just the state of things."

Fiona looked uncomfortable as she continued to stare at her coffee, as if answers would materialise from the cup.

"I failed to prepare you for the job, and when it counted, I went in like a bull in a china shop, because I didn't want to carry the guilt of you getting hurt. That's on me. I'm hoping that you want to continue working with me, but I don't blame you if you tell me to bugger off."

She looked up from her cup and declared, "Of course I want to continue. I've had time over the last week to think about my options, and if there's one thing I know, it's that I want to be a bounty hunter. I have no doubts about that."

"Can I ask why?"

"I um, I think I'm good at it. I mean it's the first time I've really ever conquered my fears. And yeah, you have issues, everyone does, but I was able to walk through that door because of what you taught me."

"I'm bloody glad you did, because I like the way my head sticks to my neck."

We both laughed, only stopping when I grabbed my chest in reaction to the pain. I waved her off when she expressed concern. As we sipped our tea, we discussed the four-week training course I had developed. I was pleased with her eagerness to continue the learning journey. Fiona provided input regarding her lack of accuracy and awareness when shooting under pressure. In response to her concerns, I adjusted the training plan to include pressure shooting activities and desensitisation drills.

I was beginning to feel the onset of fatigue, and was about to say goodnight, when Fiona reached into her pack and handed me an envelope and a notebook.

"Sal asked me to give this to you. They were actually his last words. I hope you don't mind, but I had a quick look through them."

I was more than a little intrigued at the prospect of learning how Sal ended up in such a precarious situation, one that ended up getting him killed. I opened the envelope and took out a letter from within. "What's this?"

"It's a contract between Sal and a guy called Kadesh Singh, to find and return his grandson."

I whistled. "Fifty ounces of gold. Bloody hell!"

I could start my brewery with that much coin. I'd have enough to buy the equipment, supplies, and pay two years of rent. It was a tantalising prospect.

I held Sal's notebook in my hand. "So, what did you learn from this?"

"Sal spoke to a miner in Kalgoorlie, who said the stepdad took the kid to Perth."

I shook my head, "That's impossible, unless he was on a suicide mission. Poor kid."

I suddenly felt drained. I lethargically raised myself up, placing my hands on the kitchen table for support. I saw the concern on Fiona's face. "I'm fine, I just need a good night's sleep. I'm going to think on this Singh job. Hey, we had a good talk tonight, and I'm glad you're sticking around."

As I ambled down the hallway to my room I revealed, "Oh, your training begins tomorrow morning after brekky. Good night, Fiona."

Chapter Eighteen

Wednesday February 13, 2041 – Archie

After breakfast we conducted an operational debrief in the gym, - focusing on what went well, what didn't go so well, and how we can improve for the next op. Fiona's skills development and my piss-poor tactical decisions were not the sole issues. To be an effective team, we needed to learn how to work together.

We spent just over an hour stating our perceptions of the night's events, our actions, and omissions. I admitted that I should have returned to the stump to develop a contingency plan to rescue Sal. I didn't disclose the heightened anger I felt witnessing Sal used as a punching bag, and there was no point in mentioning my concern that Fiona was not prepared for the tactical entry. I didn't want to begin the training amid an air of distrust.

Fiona explained the physiological effects she felt during the operation - the shaking, auditory exclusion, tunnel vision, and time and distance distortion. She was concerned with her placement of rounds, adamant that she only hit Lewis's brother four times, meaning that twelve shots were wide of the target. I reiterated the theory of body alarm response and emphasised that her reactions to the stress was natural. After I reassured her that the intensity of the reactions would lessen with experience and further training, she appeared quite upbeat. And to my surprise, she wasn't in the slightest concerned about killing Lewis's brother. I reflected at the time that the debrief was going smoother than I'd expected. If I had an inkling of the looming complications, I would have taken greater care in exploring her mindset.

During the following four weeks, Fiona trained for twelve hours a day, with a fifteen-minute morning tea, thirty-minute lunch and fifteen-minute afternoon tea. The first week of training involved countless dry-fire drills using plastic dummy rounds – drawing her pistol, reacting to stoppages, and re-holstering. I interspersed these drills with close quarter fighting, door entries, and room clearances.

Clarry did me a favour and dropped by Mitt's Gun Store and purchased two thousand reload rounds for the pistol and rifle. The extra ammo came in useful for the second week of training, which took place at the Esperance Gun Range. We practiced marksmanship and live fire movement drills. At the conclusion of each session, we collected the empty casings for Mitt, as he promised to provide a discount on future purchases of reload rounds. Call me a miser, but I was constantly looking at options to save my coin, especially now that I have an apprentice.

During the third week of training, we performed tactical live fire drills using a derelict brick dwelling just outside of town – our kill house. I positioned cardboard targets against tyres and heavy bags of sand. Fiona and I drilled tactical entries, room clearances, and close contact engagements. Each subsequent entry, I re-positioned the targets and marked them with a red cross to represent an attacking fugitive, and a blue cross to represent a captive. Fiona's identification of the threats and shooting accuracy improved considerably.

The fourth week involved duress and desensitisation training. The aim of these activities was to raise her heart rate and place her under physical stress, before evaluating her fine motor skills and shooting accuracy. I instructed Fiona to sprint forty metres, perform thirty push-ups and then draw her firearm to engage the targets. I placed dummy rounds in the firearm's magazine to assess her ability to clear the stoppage and re-engage the target. At first her precision declined, but after repetitive drills, she controlled her breathing and improved her shooting accuracy. I was impressed that she focused on the mantra- '*slow is smooth, smooth is fast*.'

I was still recovering from my injuries, so I asked Clarry to spar with Fiona. Both wore sixteen-ounce boxing gloves and beat the hell out of each other for two minutes. Clarry would be the first to admit that he's a lover, not a fighter, but he did his best to give Fiona a decent work-out. As soon as the timer buzzed, I ripped off her gloves and we entered the kill house to engage the targets. The four weeks passed swiftly, and by the end of the training we were both satisfied with the results.

After dinner, I examined Sal's notes connected to the kidnapping of Raj Sing and considered whether to contact the grandfather. Sal had specifically wanted me to take this job. Why else would he use his last breath to instruct Fiona to give me the contract? It was obviously important to him. Did he want me to claim the reward, or was he primarily concerned with locating the child? My curiosity was certainly piqued. I decided to write Mr Singh a letter to request a meeting. The demise of the Internet has resulted in a renaissance in writing letters and postcards. The State Postal Service may travel at a snail's pace, but it's remarkably reliable given the challengers the posties' face. Transporting valuable packages around the state all by your lonesome, while dodging gangs and violent criminals, is not my idea of a safe and rewarding career. They're a brave bunch those posties.

Chapter Nineteen

Friday March 15, 2041 – Archie

Six weeks had passed since Lewis's brother sliced me open with a machete. I was shirtless in front of my bedroom mirror, examining the raised pale scar running down my stomach. I turned my back to inspect the jagged edges of the smaller but wider scar across my upper back, when I was interrupted by my nosey apprentice.

Fiona stood at the doorway with her hands on her hips. "The ladies are going to luuuv those."

I waved her away. "Leave it be would ya."

She obviously wasn't done teasing. "You never know, we may see the travelling carnival again on the road. You can show those bad boys off to that palm reader. What was her name? Evelyn, wasn't it?"

I grabbed my t-shirt and turned my back as I slipped it on, hoping to hide the inevitable redness on my cheeks. Fiona had worked out how to push my buttons like an annoying little sister, but I had to admit that I was getting used to having her around.

Late in the afternoon I received a response letter from Mr Singh. He accepted my request to meet at his Northam farm, which is located 650 kilometres northwest of Esperance. Given that I was not yet one hundred percent fit, it was far too great of a journey to ride Roger. I decided that it was time to invest in a motor vehicle. Western Australia is the country's largest state; with an area of about 2,500,000 square kilometres, it's more than three times the size of Texas. Travelling by motor vehicle from the town of Kununurra at the top of the state to Esperance at the bottom of the state, takes thirty-eight hours if you drive the 3,700 kilometres non-stop. With the number of pre-1975 vehicles being few and far between, the old law of supply and demand becomes a major factor in being able to afford a decent set of wheels. Fortunately, my work ethic and frugal endeavours have amounted to a tidy sum of coins, so I was confident that I could enter the market for a *very used* car.

After expressing my interest around town, Captain Ross introduced me to one of his customers who was selling a 1971 Chrysler VH Valiant Charger 770SE. The vehicle was a beautiful machine in marvellous condition; a two-door hardtop coupe with a short-wheelbase and a V8 5.6 litre engine. The midnight black beast had an aggressive wedge-like stance and sharp lines that give the effect of speed, even when she's standing still.

The seller's emotional attachment to the vehicle made it near on impossible to haggle. In fact, after thirty minutes of negotiating a price, I ended up paying more than he was originally asking for. My ill ease at paying such an exorbitant price in gold coin, vanished into the stratosphere when I witnessed Clarry's envious stare as I pulled up into his driveway. "You bastard, she's a bloody beauty!" he exclaimed.

We said our goodbyes to Roger and Jasper, promising that we'll return as soon as we can. Clarry cheekily agreed to take care of the horses in exchange for letting him have a drive of the Charger upon our return. Roger would sulk during my departure, but I was grateful that he had Clarry, Jasper and Zeus to keep him company.

When Clarry gave me a farewell hug, I was pleasantly surprised to be free of pain. "I'm proud of you brother," he whispered as Fiona waited in the car.

We packed the basics for the trip (food, water, fuel), but were also prepared for any eventuality by ensuring our weapons were always within reach (handguns, knives, rifles). It pays to be vigilant - mindful of gangs patrolling the highways and scavenging in packs like hyenas.

I turned the ignition and the V8 5.6 litre engine rumbled alive. Zeus gave a savage bark, as if he were competing with the growl of the Charger. I restrained myself from putting the pedal to the metal and summoning Clarry's green-eyed monster. I drove down the driveway and yelled out the window, "Maaate, I'll let you drive her when we get back."

The seven-hour non-stop journey to Northam was both scenic and deserted, which made it challenging to stay alert. During the entire trip we only observed three vehicles travelling in the opposite direction. As we approached the front gates of the Singh Farm, two gentlemen pointing pump-action shotguns approached our vehicle.

The gentleman on my right shouted, "Driver, keep your hands on the wheel. Passenger, slowly place your hands out your window."

I kept my hands positioned on the wheel at nine and three o'clock. The guard stood behind the driver's side door at a slight angle. "State your business and don't move your hands."

"My name's Archie O'Connor. I have a meeting with Mr Singh concerning his missing grandson."

"Don't move! Just tell me where your identification is situated."

"It's in my front shirt pocket, left-hand side," I replied.

"Slowly use you left hand to remove your ID and then hand it to me."

I complied with his instructions, passing him my bounty hunter identification. I noticed that his colleague had Fiona and me covered. They were both well trained, most likely former military or police.

The guard shouted to his colleague, "It's all good Jamie, open up the gates."

The guard lowered his shotgun to a ready position. "Thank you for your cooperation sir, it's much appreciated. Please follow my colleague to the homestead."

I drove down the red gravel driveway, maintaining a substantial gap between us and the guard on his quad bike.

"Why are you driving so slow?" Fiona asked.

"Just giving the bloke some room," I explained.

She laughed. "Bullshit! You don't want loose gravel chipping the paint job."

I was embarrassed to admit that she was right on the money.

The tall wheatgrass pastures provided a tranquil backdrop to an expansive red brick two-storey home. The guard led us to a white gazebo at the rear of the home, where a gentleman in his early-eighties wearing denim jeans and a navy-blue satin shirt was sitting behind a jarrah table. I suspected that the guard at the gate must have used a two-way radio to inform Mr Singh of our arrival. Apparently, he didn't want to invite the help into his home.

As we approached, Mr Singh stood from his chair, introduced himself and asked us to take a seat. I introduced Fiona and thanked him for taking the time to speak with us. He spoke with a posh English accent, providing a clear pronunciation of the letter 'H' at the beginning of words and making his 'Rs' inaudible.

"Mr O'Connor, may I ask how you are associated with Mr Willis?"

"He was my mentor and a good friend."

"What do you mean, WAS?" he asked with a concerned tone.

"I didn't want to inform you by mail sir, but Sal is dead," I replied solemnly.

The truth of the matter is, I omitted Sal's death from my letter for no other reason than I didn't want to give Mr Singh time to hire a new hunter before I had the opportunity to speak with him.

He looked gravely disappointed. "How did he die?"

"He was killed by an offender during an operation. Just before he died he asked me look into your contract."

"Why do you think he wanted *you* to look into the contract?" he asked inquisitively.

"I can only guess that he wanted me to find your grandson."

Mr Singh leaned forward. "Did he have any idea where Raj is?"

It's all about timing - every good salesman needs to know when to throw his pitch. "He spoke to a witness that had dealings with the kidnapper, Noel Patterson, but he didn't record a specific location in his notebook. I propose that you draw up a new contract and we'll track down the witness and follow Sal's leads."

I decided to omit the intel concerning the Perth lead, as I thought that it was unlikely to be true and I didn't want to cause him and his wife any unnecessary concern and false hope.

Looking disappointed, Mr Singh sighed before continuing. "Mr Willis was highly recommended. I don't wish to offend you Mr O'Connor, but this all seems very convenient. May I ask, are you and Miss Katsaros well regarded in your profession?"

Is he accusing me of killing my old mentor to acquire the contract? I hid my irritation at his insinuation and stayed on point. "Not to blow my own trumpet, but I have one of the highest capture rates in the State. If required, there are a number of bondsmen that can provide me a reference."

Mr Singh waved his hand in a gesture of dismissal. "References are not required, I have already looked into you, and as you say, Mr Willis must have had faith in your skills. Wait here please while I type up a new contract. I would invite you into the house, but you must understand that this whole matter has greatly upset Mrs Singh."

As computers were no longer functioning, he would use an old school typewriter to draw up a new contract.

Mr Singh returned a short time later with a new contract. After he sat down and handed me the paperwork, I had to ask, "Sir, I hope you don't mind me asking, and there is no intent of disrespect on my part, but what is the situation with custody of your grandson?"

Mr Singh raised an eyebrow before answering. "That is a fair question, and one that I should expect from a former lawyer." He wasn't kidding about the background checks. Mr Singh relaxed in his chair and rested his hands in his lap. "Let me explain. My daughter passed away earlier this year. Her husband, Raj's dad, died in an accident two years prior. Chandra fell for a horrible man that has no legal custodial rights. However, as you are aware, the police are too busy and under-resourced to deal with such family matters. Hence the reason for a private contract."

Not for one moment did I believe that was the half of it. "Perfectly understood sir, thank you for clearing that up. I have Sal's notes and they're quite detailed, but for my benefit, do you mind if I go over some old ground?"

"Of course, go ahead and ask away. Anything to assist you in locating Raj."

I took out my notebook and gestured for Fiona to do the same. "What do you know of Patterson's background?"

A young lady arrived with a tray of ornate glasses, which she deftly placed in the centre of the table. Before picking up a glass, Mr Singh said, "Please help yourself to a glass of homemade lemonade." We each took a sip of our beverage before he continued. "I believe that before the War he was engaged in health research. Some big wig that sat on this and that board. When he started dating Chandra, he appeared to be quite the gentleman, purchasing her jewellery and taking us all out to lavish dinners. When he asked me for a loan, it became apparent that he had financial problems, not unlike many businessmen post-war. I wanted to do the right thing by Chandra, so I lent him a substantial amount of coin at a very low interest rate. I became concerned when he defaulted on the loan repayments. And then my suspicions were raised when one of my men saw him chatting to a local ruffian in town. It wouldn't surprise me to learn that he's mixed up in some form of illicit activity. When I spoke to my daughter about my concerns, she dismissed them out of hand. Chandra was smitten with the awful man."

"Do you have a photo of Raj and Patterson that I could borrow?"

Mr Singh turned to a nearby guard and asked him to retrieve his brown leather satchel from his study desk.

I continued my questioning. "Does Patterson have any family or friends that you know of?"

Mr Singh huffed. "He was not forthcoming with information concerning his personal life, or work affairs. I found this quite troubling in the circumstances."

Understanding Patterson's motive may assist me in understanding the man himself. "Why do you think he kidnapped Raj?"

Mr Singh appeared visibly upset. "This question keeps me up at night. Why? He didn't appear attached to the boy. He has not asked for a ransom. I just do not understand his intentions."

"I'm sorry to upset you sir, but I have to ask, do you have any idea where they could be?"

He looked away and wiped a tear from his eye. "Unfortunately, no. I only wish I did."

Upon the guard's return, Mr Singh handed me a family photo of Patterson, Raj and Chandra, all smiling dressed in formal wear, standing in the foreground of a horse and carriage. Patterson was a good-looking man with a square jaw, perfect teeth, and a stylish haircut.

I assured Mr Singh that we'd make every effort to locate his grandson and thanked him for his confidence in our abilities. The guard on the quad bike kindly escorted us to the main gate. Just as the Charger's radial tyres hit the bitumen of the main road, I put my foot down hard on the accelerator pedal and sped off towards Northam's town centre.

Fiona held the contract in both hands as she read it aloud. "Why did you ask him to put my name on it?" she asked in a bewildered tone.

"You deserve it and we're a team. I was going to tell you later, but now is as good a time as any. Fifty-fifty split from now on."

Fiona was silent to the point where I started to feel worried. "What's wrong?"

"I just...it's just a lot of pressure. I didn't think we'd be equal partners so soon."

"Fiona, you're my first apprentice. I think you've known for a while now, that I'm sort of making it up as I go along. I mean, I'm teaching you from my experience, and what I've been taught in the army and by pros like Sal, but in terms of a real apprenticeship, I'm just doing my best. But that doesn't change the facts, you're taking just as much risk as I am, and therefore it's not right for you to earn less. Do you get me?"

Fiona smiled, still gazing at the contract. "I get you."

"And don't you worry, I'll be taking fifty percent of the expenses from your cut, including the cost of the fuel to satiate this thirsty lady," I explained while patting the Charger's dash.

Before travelling to Kalgoorlie to locate one of Sal's informants, a miner named Paddy Doherty, I thought it wise to stop by Northam's Bondsman's office to check if there were any outstanding contracts.

The payday on Singh's contract was enticing to say the least – A *fifty* ounce reward is life changing - but from what I've discovered from the intel gathered thus far, it was most likely a long-term job with little prospect of success. After spending considerable coin on the Charger, I needed to boost our funds. I was also keen on providing Fiona an opportunity to put her training into practice. And the best way to achieve these outcomes is to collect '*Dead or Alive*' bounties.

We entered the bondsman's office just before closing. Cathy Ward had been in the position for the past five years. Just after she commenced the role, I assisted her in a family matter involving her son's gambling debts to a criminal gang. They'd already broken his hand and were threatening to take an appendage every Monday he failed to pay, starting with his right thumb. I successfully negotiated a favourable outcome; the gang took possession of her son's motorcycle and he was indentured to work as a fruit picker for six months. Cathy was so appreciative of my intervention, that she'd occasionally give me the heads-up on new bounties, and leak intel on the whereabouts of fugitives.

"Cathy, this is Fiona, my new partner."

After they shook hands, Cathy stated, "It's good to meet you Fiona. We're always in need of new hunters." She gestured towards me, before adding, "Smart move in picking this one as your partner. He's a good sort, and he's smarter than most. Not to mention, easy on the eyes."

Before Fiona felt obliged to respond, I cut in on the conversation. "Thanks Cathy, I appreciate the kind words. But I'd really like to know if you've got any new bounties."

Cathy sighed. "You're all business Archie O'Connor, no fun! How bad do you need the coin?" she asked.

"I could use the funds, if it's worth my while."

"I have a small bounty in Coolgardie. It's not worth much, but it's easy-peasy."

"Okaaay. Who and what is it?"

"It's an Alive contract for an offender named Curtis Gates. He robbed a young couple at gun point. No one was injured. No shots fired. He got twenty-five years hard labour after being tried in absentia."

When the accused cannot be located, it's now common practice to conduct a trial without their presence. Trials are conducted before a Judge alone, with the local police sergeant performing the role of prosecutor.

"How reliable is the intel about his whereabouts?" I asked with trepidation.

"Very," she replied. "The contract arrived yesterday, and less than an hour later a bloke phoned up claiming to be the father of a lass Curtis is bedding. Understandably he wants him gone, ASAP!"

"How much?" I asked, getting to the crux of the matter.

"Half an ounce," she replied sheepishly.

"You know it's not worth our time Cathy," I stated incredulously.

She put her palms up. "Hey, don't shoot the messenger."

I looked over at Fiona to gauge her thoughts on the matter. Her blank expression and shrug did little to assist me in making a decision.

Cathy leaned over the counter and disclosed, "I do have something else that you may be interested in. Sort of kill two birds with one stone."

"I'm listening."

"They're three guards short for the water train on tomorrow's run. You could pick up the security work, grab Curtis and get a lift back on the return trip. Simple, for a capable man like yourself."

I superstitiously touched the timber counter. "Yeah, simple. How much is the train manager paying?"

"I've heard they're desperate. One ounce."

I found that hard to believe. "What, each?"

"Yep, I did tell ya they're desperate."

Kalgoorlie is a desert community that can no longer rely on water being transported by O'Connor's pipeline. The water source, Perth's Mundaring Weir, was contaminated by the nukes. The water train transports a vital and extremely valuable commodity that must be protected from foul play. The water is pumped from a section of the Avon River called the Burlong Pool, which was known to the Indigenous Noongars as a place where the Wagyl - *a snakelike creature responsible for the creation of local rivers and waterways* - would rest in the summer. I have guarded the water train on occasions when I've been low on funds and bounties were scarce.

Cathy handed me the Curtis bounty and we took notes concerning the intel of his whereabouts.

We moseyed to a nearby coffee shop to discuss our plans. I carried the two long blacks to Fiona's table and we both took out our notebooks.

"After we finish our coffee, we'll head straight to the train station and speak with Jack. He's one of the train managers who's hired me in the past. Once we arrive in Kal, we'll find a driver to take us to Coolgardie, apprehend Curtis and then drop him off at the police station. If we have time, we'll locate the miner and find out what he knows about Noel Patterson and Raj Singh, and then catch the train back to Northam."

"You did a Cathy," Fiona scoffed.

'What do you mean?"

"You know, making it sound like a walk in the park," she said.

"Well, it's about time I have an easy one." I swallowed the remnants of my coffee and got up from my chair. "Anyway, shake a leg, it's time to book our train ticket."

Jack was standing in the train station's front carpark, pointing his finger at a train driver's chest, and yelling abuse. The driver looked utterly defeated - he turned on his heals and slumped away.

As we walked towards Jack, he was glaring at the driver's back and screaming, "You make sure you're here first thing in the morning and do what you're bloody told!"

Jack wore the strain of the job all over his exhausted face. He was of average height and weight; with his only distinguishable feature being waist-length hair that he tied into a top knot. His primary responsibility as a train manager was ensuring that the passenger, supply, and water trains were running on schedule. His ass was on the line if the train ran late. Time is coin.

"Hey Jack, I hear that you're short on guards for the water run tomorrow. Fiona and I are free to help you out."

"That's what I like about you Archie, you're a straight shooter. Can you vouch for the sheila?"

Before Fiona's hackles started rising, I said, "She's also a straight shooter, both with her mouth and rifle."

Jack laughed. "Point taken Archie, you're both hired. A bloody life saver mate. I've got issues with belligerent drivers, and until now I was two guards down. I'm paying one ounce. Be here at 6 a.m. on the dot."

"No problem, we'll be here. By the way, why are you paying so much?"

"I've never heard someone complain about high pay. You know how it is, we're low on guards and we need an enticement to ensure we keep on schedule."

Something didn't feel right. My intuition was screaming at me to question him further, but I didn't want to take him to task and risk losing the job. I pointed at the Charger. "Can I park her out the back?"

Jack whistled and nodded. "I'm in love. If you ever need to sell her, come and see me first."

"Join the line, Jack."

I've become somewhat attached to the car, so much so, that I've decided to nickname her the 'Beast.' It may sound corny, but it suits her to a T.

We hired rooms at the Riverside Hotel in the centre of town, within walking distance of the Avon River. We sat at a table on the second-floor balcony, pouring the first drink from a jug of lager. To my palate it tasted like piss, but I regard myself as bit of a beer connoisseur. Most people would just call me fussy.

"So Boss, what's the deal with tomorrow?" Fiona asked.

"Two guards are usually positioned in the cab with the driver, and then there's a guard located on top of every third tank. Because this is your first run, they'll probably put you with the driver."

"Why is that?"

"The guards on the tanks need to know what to look out for, and the more experienced guards are less likely to lose their balance and take a tumble. The company doesn't give a shit about the guard's welfare, they just don't want to be a guard short."

Chapter Twenty

Saturday March 16, 2041 from 5:45 a.m. – Archie

I parked the Beast in the train station staff carpark at a quarter to six in the morning. Jack was walking towards the briefing area, which was situated on the platform alongside the NR Class Diesel Train. The thick steel that encloses the V16 engine functioned as a Faraday cage, preventing the enemies EMPs from damaging the locomotive's electronics. The twenty-two metre General Electric freight train was purchased over forty years ago, and on the day of her arrival she had a maximum speed of 115 kilometres per hour. On today's run she'd be pulling thirty tanks, a total of 725,000 litres of water, at a maximum speed of ninety-five kilometres per hour. A perfect run from Norseman to Kalgoorlie with no mishaps would take just over thirteen hours. You get the occasional lunatic taking potshots at the train and the odd wreckage that requires clearing from the tracks, but aside from that, it's easy coin.

The train's livery displayed a Wagyl; the serpent-like creature's head started at the engine and its body stretched down all thirty tanks, painted in all seven colours of the rainbow. I'd heard through the grapevine that as the water was being pumped from one of its resting places, the owners were hoping that the Aboriginal Dreamtime creature would protect the train and its valuable cargo. I don't consider myself a spiritual man, but similar to my stance on Christianity, I'm not going to dismiss what I don't understand.

The unhappy driver from the day before was busy in the train's cab preparing for the trip. As we stood on the platform trading small talk with Jack, guards were arriving with coffee and newspaper in hand. By 6 a.m. there were a total of twelve guards including Fiona and me waiting to be briefed. The professional guards take their role of protecting the train and its cargo as a serious undertaking. Kalgoorlie would turn into a ghost town without the water – the residents couldn't survive the harsh environment and the Super Pit gold mine (the second largest in the country) would be forced to close.

Jack blew a whistle hanging from a chain around his neck. He hollered, "Okay, can I have your attention ladies and gentlemen. We are on a tight schedule. Our mission today is to deliver the 725,000 litres of water to Kalgoorlie safely and on time. I repeat, our mission today is to deliver the 725,000 litres of water to Kalgoorlie safely and on time. Katsaros and Lau, you'll be riding in the cab. The rest of you have the privilege of taking the scenic tour, Sayer – tank three, Bull – tank six, O'Connor – tank nine, Dimoska – tank twelve, Goddard – tank fifteen, Gizzarelli – tank eighteen, Harper – tank twenty-one, Samdup – tank twenty-four, Geeves – tank twenty-seven, Kettle – tank thirty. Any questions? No? Good. Grab a walkie-talkie, you're on channel twelve. Get in position, we leave in fifteen minutes. Don't be late boys and girls, as she'll leave without you."

Each guard selected a two-way radio from a crate at Jack's feet and moved in all directions - some headed towards their assigned tank, others were checking their firearms and two guards were saying their goodbyes to loved ones. I noticed that one of them was Lau, the guard selected to ride in the cab with Fiona. He was passionately locking lips with an attractive young lady on the platform.

Fiona was gazing at the length of the train in a trance when I grabbed her attention by snapping my fingers. "Make sure you stay focused. I'll see you in about thirteen hours. Any issues, don't hesitate to call me on the radio."

Fiona gave me the thumbs-up before grasping the handrails with both hands and climbing the ladder to the cab door. I walked down the length of the platform to tank nine. Sayer and Bull were already in position on top of their assigned tanks. They stood on a steel mesh platform that ran down the length and width of the tank, surrounded by a waist level railing. Before climbing the ladder, I checked my revolver and rifle and felt for the handle of my knife.

I stood on an identical platform and peered down my rifle scope to see the last of the guards settling at their post. The driver gave two short blasts of the air horn to signal that we were beginning the journey.

I whispered to myself, "Let this be a nice quiet run," and out of habit glanced in all directions for a piece of wood to touch.

I performed a radio check once I'd ensured that my pack was tied securely to the base of the handrail. The pack makes for a great seat during short rest breaks throughout the thirteen-hour trip. I had packed lunch, water, and an empty bottle to use when I needed to relieve myself. It was too risky to stop the train for scheduled rest breaks and depending on the direction of the wind, urinating off the side of the tank would likely blow back, or may even hit the guard on the next tank. I had never met Dimoska who was stationed at tank twelve, but peeing on her was definitely not a good way to make friends.

Peering down my scope, I'd describe Dimoska as a no-nonsense, broad-shouldered middle-aged lady with short cropped black hair. I was surprised to see her holding a Blaser R96 Tactical 3 Sniper rifle. You'd have to part with at least nine ounces of gold to purchase such a weapon. While I watched Dimoska adjust her scope, I pondered if she'd served as a sniper in the army. The armour piercing .338 calibre rifle has an effective range of 1500 metres and was used by Australian snipers during the War. I made a mental note to introduce myself to her upon our arrival. It pays to make professional acquaintances as you never know when you may need backup for a challenging job.

It was a beautiful twenty-five-degree day, with a clear blue sky and a slight north westerly breeze. My mind was clear and for the first time in eight years I was feeling optimistic. The first four hours of the journey was thankfully uneventful - the only activity I'd witnessed was a distant tractor in a wheat field and a couple of kangaroos bounding alongside the train.

As we passed through the small wheatbelt town of Kellerberrin, a bunch of children standing at a crossing were waving enthusiastically at the train. The driver reciprocated with a long blast of the air horn. I was not the only guard to wave to them as we flew past.

We were just over halfway to our destination. As we travelled through the town of Southern Cross, I heard the distant sounds of *pop pop pop pop*. Shots being fired! The driver then gave three successive long blasts of the air horn. The signal for danger! I felt the train slowing but dismissed it as my mind playing tricks on me.

I performed a 180 degree scan, searching the highway crossing and dirt tracks for threats. Dimoska was in a firing position engaging a target and then actioning her rifle's bolt to chamber the next round. I peered down my scope in the direction of her muzzle. I observed a dirt bike in the distance, followed by a two-seater off-road buggy skirting on the dirt alongside the rear tank. Guards along the train were actively engaging threats at the rear of the train.

The radio attached to my belt started to erupt. Guards were yelling and talking over each other. And with the sound of gunfire in the background, it made it impossible to discern any meaning from the transmissions.

I turned to look in the direction of the engine and saw an old beaten-up Land Rover pulling up alongside the cab. From tank six, Bull was firing his AR-15 rifle at the rear of the four-wheel drive (4WD) vehicle.

Frustratingly, I was unable to obtain a target from my current position. I considered moving up the line to assist Fiona, but quickly dismissed the idea as being tactically unwise. There were already four guards who had sights on the Land Rover, and it would be Murphy's law that as soon as I moved, I'd be needed back here. As if on cue, I turned to the rear of the train and saw the buggy speeding towards the front of the train. I instantly fired at the driver, missing as the vehicle accelerated alongside Dimoska's tank.

Dimoska drew her pistol from her holster and fired multiple rounds at the driver and passenger. I took another shot at the driver, missing once again. CHRIST! Sal would have been looking down from above and shaking his head in disappointment. I was so focused on the buggy that I wasn't watching my six. Unbeknownst to me at the time, a four-door jeep was traveling on the other side of the train - level with my tank.

Gunfire erupted - It was close - Real close. I spun to my rear to see a man with a shaved head and goatee standing on tank eight pointing a double barrel shotgun in my direction. Someone up there must be looking out for me because he missed me with both rounds. A nonbeliever would put it down to the difficulty in taking aim on a moving train. Whatever the case, I was going to take advantage of my fortune. As he was reloading his shottie, I dropped my rifle to my feet, drew my revolver and put three rounds into his chest.

I recovered my rifle, actioned the bolt and fired at the driver of the jeep. The jeep's steel plating soldered over the doors and windows prevented my rounds from penetrating. I pondered - if only I had Dimoska's rifle and armour piercing rounds. Sal would preach, '*Don't blame your tools O'Connor.*' I wish my subconscious projection of Sal would give me a break - I was a bit too busy to handle criticism right now.

The driver of the jeep must have given up on capturing my position, as he drove forward towards the engine. As I scanned for new threats, I saw Dimoska wrestling an enormous outlaw. He had the mass required to compete in a sumo wrestling tournament. With his arms wrapped around her upper torso, she was getting the life squeezed out of her. I didn't want to risk taking a shot in fear of hitting her. I quickly scaled the waist high railing at the end of my platform and jumped to the railing on platform ten, quickly running down the platform to land on platform eleven and then twelve.

By the time I arrived, Dimoska was on her back with the sumo stomping his size sixteen Dr Martens boots down onto her hip and ribs. Dimoska must have landed a few good hits, as he had a badly broken and bloodied nose, and half his ear was torn and hanging.

Just as I fired the first of three rounds from my revolver, there was a loud crash, metal hitting metal as the train shuddered. The movement of the train affected my accuracy. I fired another three rounds - managing to hit the sumo twice - one round in his belly and one in his shoulder. He didn't go down. He was like a bloody rhinoceros on steroids.

The platform shook as he sprinted towards me. I was in the process of reloading my revolver when he struck me to my solar plexus with his shoulder - knocking the wind out of me as I flew backwards. I grasped the side railing to prevent my fall but dropped my revolver in the process. As I was recovering from the shock to my diaphragm, the sumo grabbed me in a bear hug, lifting me off the ground and squeezing me like a boa constrictor. This was obviously his go-to move.

I arched my head back and rapidly brought my forehead forward, smashing his broken nose. It was disconcerting when he started to laugh wildly while he continued to squeeze the life out of me. I forced myself to relax, taking small breaths, closing my eyes, and lulling my head forward. Just like a possum in imminent danger, I was 'playing dead.' As soon as he relaxed his grip to throw me to the ground, I swiftly drew my knife and slashed his larynx. Blood seeped out of the horizontal cut, resembling a thin-lipped smile.

He placed his meaty hands over the wound in a futile attempt to stem the flow of blood. Without hesitation I stabbed him hard and deep under his armpit. He gasped in agony before falling back onto the platform.

I stepped over the sumo's carcass to check on Dimoska, reaching down to assess her vital signs. She wasn't breathing and she had no pulse.

After I recovered Dimoska's rifle, pistol, and spare mags, I stood to search for the jeep. I witnessed the vehicle spectacularly swerve and crash into an old wreck at the side of the track and then flip onto its roof.

Chapter Twenty-One

Saturday March 16, 2041 from 6:15 a.m. – Fiona

I was ten years of age the last time I had the pleasure of travelling by train. My mother took me to Her Majesty's Theatre to watch the West Australian Ballet. I almost fell asleep during the performance, but I couldn't wait to jump back on the train for the return journey.

I inspected the interior of the cab, trying to hide my delight as I gazed at all the buttons, levers, and switches. Growing up, I was hands-down one of the biggest tomboys. I left Barbie in the sand pit because I was too busy smashing my Tonka truck into my train set.

The driver was a stern looking man who was mumbling under his breath in the corridor behind the cab. He was flicking switches on a panel and cursing management for not providing him an offsider. I had no idea what he was doing, but he looked extremely busy as he prepared the train for the journey. When he marched swiftly to the front of the cab, Lau and I were forced to skip out of his way.

"Okay, I'm in charge of the train. Do not touch anything unless I ask you to. If you listen to my instructions, we'll get on fine. Understood?"

We both quickly nodded.

I held out my hand. "Hi, I'm Fiona." He just glanced down at my hand before continuing to scuttle around the cab pressing buttons and flicking switches. Lau, who looked thoroughly intimidated, didn't even attempt to introduce himself.

"Get out of my way," the driver snapped at Lau. Poor Lau didn't know what to say and where to stand. "Both of you just stand here," he said in a harsh tone as he pointed behind and to the right of his chair.

"I've heard that we may receive some attention from some gang. So you two make sure you're switched on," the driver revealed.

"What gang? Have the other guards been advised?" I asked.

The rude prick ignored my question, turned his back, and sat down in the driver's seat. I peered through the cab windscreen and saw the signals turn to yellow. He engaged the bell and then manipulated the throttle lever, one, two, then three notches. The train's engine rumbled as he gave the air horn two quick blasts. The train picked up speed as the driver continued to manipulate the lever up to eight notches. I glanced out the side cab window to watch the station disappear from view.

Lau and I were standing shoulder to shoulder. He asked, "So have you done this run before? This is my first time. I've been working with my girlfriend's dad hauling farm machinery all the way from Broome to Esperance. It can be as boring as batshit but it's pretty good pay. That's a nice rifle you have there, I'm a pretty good shot. My girlfriend and I are saving up for our first home, that's why I'm picking up extra work. You know, it's......"

I quickly butted in before he could continue on his train of thought. "I think I should go outside and have a look down train."

I stepped outside the cab door to get some respite from Lau and the arrogant driver. I carried my rifle over my left shoulder by the strap and my pistol and knife were secured to my belt. As the train followed a slight bend in the tracks, I could see the guards at the rear of the train as I dangled out from the side railing.

I checked that my radio was switched to channel twelve and weighed up whether to give Archie the heads-up about the driver's comments. On the one hand it's probably just a rumour, and if it was important, they would have said something during the briefing. But on the other hand, it's intel that may interest Archie. I decided to play it safe and not embarrass myself over the radio. The guards would get a major kick out of me transmitting, '*The driver said there may be some gangs providing us attention.*' It's not hard to envisage their response, '*The new girl wants to be in charge.... Be careful fellas, Fiona wants us to look out for gangs.... She's been here two seconds and she already thinks she knows it all.*' Yeah nah, I'm not falling into that trap.

It was a real struggle to stay attentive as the journey progressed. It didn't help having Mr Morose and Mr Verbose as company. To stay awake I made regular trips outside and even read the 'Glock Armourers Handbook.' It has a terrible plot, but the pictures are detailed. While I was daydreaming, I heard a garbled noise over the radio. It sounded like someone was yelling. I then heard the distinct *crack*, *thump*, and *pop* of gunfire.

I looked over at the driver who was manipulating the throttle lever down. The train started to slow.

"What the *fuck* are you doing?" I shouted in disbelief

"I've been instructed to slow the train if we're being attacked," he grumbled.

"You make this bitch go full-speed or we're all dead!" I screamed.

The driver looked undecided for a split second and then operated the throttle, willing the sixteen cylinders to increase the speed of the train.

Lau looked absolutely petrified, so I spoke to him as calmly as I could muster, "You go out the driver's side railing and I'll go out this side. If you see a shithead, shoot them. And don't forget your rifle." When I opened the door, Lau's feet were still cemented to the floor of the cab.

Exiting the cab was like entering another version of reality. My senses were immediately overloaded. I had walked from the safety of the enclosed soundproof cab to the scene from a dystopian horror film. A dark green 4WD vehicle that looked like it had been driven from a demolition derby was racing alongside the cab. A young woman with long bright red hair was leaning out the rear passenger side window firing a revolver at the cab windows. I drew my Glock and returned fire. The redhead disappeared from view. The rear window of the 4WD shattered. The guards were firing from the tanks.

The 4WD suddenly veered within spitting distance of the cab. I saw a shotgun muzzle protrude from the front passenger side window. *BOOM!* I felt a stinging sensation to my left shoulder and breast. As I lifted my arms to return fire, my left shoulder felt like it was being stabbed with the tip of a samurai sword.

I fired one handed in the direction of the shotgun - pop, pop, pop - before being lifted off my feet and thrown down onto the steel platform. After shaking my head, I looked up to see a powerfully built man standing above me. I pushed myself up to my knees, but before I could stand, he wrapped his muscular arm around my neck and began crushing my windpipe. His garlic breath invaded my nostrils as I experienced double vision and dizziness - my brain started to shut down from lack of oxygen. '*What a fucked way to die!*' I thought.

A loud bang penetrated my ear drums. The arm around my throat vanished. I turned to see Lau pointing his rifle in my direction. Motormouth Lau had shot Mr Bad Breath point-blank to the back of his skull. He's the last person I thought I'd refer to as 'my hero!'

Breathlessly I spluttered, "Thanks Lau, you're a life saver, literally."

BOOM! BOOM! In one breath Lau was smiling after receiving my gratitude, and by the next breath his face was torn in half by a shotgun slug.

I fired my semi-automatic pistol though the open windows of the four-wheeler until the mag was empty and the slide locked open. I instantly grabbed a new mag and reloaded while I kept eyes on the threat, and then fired another sixteen rounds at the occupants. Just like I was trained. The driver lost control and drove into the path of the train, causing the cab to tremor as the vehicle was smashed to the side of the track.

I was careful not to tread on poor Lau's brain matter as I stepped over his body to re-enter the cab. I found the driver on his knees behind his seat as the gunfire pinged off the cab's external steel panels.

"Where the fuck have you been?" he bellowed.

"Oh, I've just been relaxing and enjoying the ride," I replied sarcastically.

I walked to the other side of the cab and looked down at the driver. "FUCKWIT!" I shouted.

I opened the cab door and used the side panel as cover. I took a deep breath and released it while peering through the scope. I aimed for a slit in the window of the homemade armour and took the shot as rounds ricocheted off the train. The jeep swerved and crashed into the carcass of an abandoned truck, flipping once and then twice in a monumental movie-like fashion.

"See ya later motherfucker!" I yelled with glee.

Chapter Twenty-Two

Saturday March 16, 2041 – Archie

Pressing the radio transmitter I asked, "Fiona, are you okay up there?" Static erupted through the radio speakers before I received Fiona's reply, "Ccrrsssshh good Boss. Are you okay?"

I was relieved to hear that she'd survived the attack. "Roger. Stay frosty, there may be more of them."

In the distance I could see Gizzarelli - the guard that was issued tank eighteen - pummelling a prone figure on tank twelve. There were no other vehicles or outlaws within sight. I hastily walked and climbed to tank twelve. Goddard was lying on his back gazing at the sky. The poor bloke had bled out after receiving multiple rounds to his groin and chest. Gizzarelli had his knee on a semi-conscious outlaw's throat while pointing a pistol at his face.

I closed Goddard's eyes and approached Gizzarelli, "Do you have any cable ties mate?"

He looked up at me with a confused expression. "What the fuck for?"

"We need him for intel," I explained wearily as I pointed at the beaten man.

Gizzarelli spat at the dazed outlaw, pressing the muzzle into the middle of his forehead. "That's not happening. He killed my mate."

Gizzarelli is a middle-aged grizzled veteran who has the body of a man that had been working on the tools for most of his life, and the mindset of a man unwilling to consider others' perspective. He'd be hard to convince.

"I know mate, but we have to give Kal's sergeant a chance to interview him. You'll get to see him hang, there's no doubt about it," I suggested in the calmest tone I could summon.

Gizzarelli's gun hand shook as he yelled, "FUCK!" before standing and lumbering to Goddard's pack. Once he'd returned with the cable ties, I rolled the outlaw onto his side and secured his wrists.

Revenge has a powerful appetite that is rarely sated. The outlaw had severe injuries to his face – broken nose, missing teeth, and swollen eyes. Each time he took a breath I could hear gurgling emanating from his throat and wheezing in his chest. After examining Gizzarelli's handiwork, I concluded that he'd be lucky to survive the journey. But I knew that if I left him alone with Gizzarelli, *luck* would most certainly be removed from the equation.

"I'll look after this tank mate. You go back down the line to look after the rear."

"I don't report to you O'Connor," he said gruffly.

"I just thought you'd like to get involved in the action if they return."

Gizzarelli stomped off mumbling obscenities under his breath. He was not a happy chappy. The outlaw convulsed for a minute or two before lying still. I pondered that it may have been merciful to let fate take its course by allowing Gizzarelli to put him out of his misery.

Blood was oozing down the condemned man's leather jacket. This was the first moment I'd been given to examine their gang patch. In thick block letters the name 'Norse Men' was stitched above a skull with a long wispy beard floating above a double-bladed fighting axe. How original, a skull with a play on words from the town they now occupied - 'Norseman.' I was once told by a drinking buddy that a prospector in the late 1800s named the town after his horse – 'Hardy Norseman'. Now that's a man that loved his horse. I placed myself in the prospector's position – would I have named the town Rogersville? Rogerstone? Much to Roger's dismay, I don't think I would have been so presumptuous to name the town after him. I much prefer the Aboriginal name for the area – 'Jimberlana.' My reverie was interrupted by my grumbling stomach.

We still had at least five hours remaining until we arrived in Kalgoorlie. I searched through Goddard's pack for a bite to eat, not having the energy or desire to walk back to my pack. And I wouldn't put it past Gizzarelli returning to blow the Norse Men's head from his neck.

It was good business to maintain positive relations with the constabulary. They will be appreciative of a live felon - for the intel they'll extract and for the public spectacle they'll exhibit. From their perspective, there's nothing better than a hanging, to demonstrate to the populous that justice has been served.

In the side pocket of Goddard's pack, I located a plentiful supply of roo jerky and a flask of whisky. I sat on the pack, indulging in the rich salty flavours of the dried meat. Feeling grateful to be alive, I took a couple of swigs from the flask and appreciated the serenity.

Chapter Twenty-Three

Saturday March 16, 2041 – Fiona

The sun was disappearing over the horizon as the diesel locomotive arrived at the Kalgoorlie Train Station. I was surprised by the lack of blood from the wounds to my shoulder and breast. But it still fucking hurt! Applying the gauze and bandaging was challenging, not only because the area was tender to touch, but the driver was next to useless in giving me a hand. I found the one straight man that when provided the opportunity to look at a bare-chested woman, was forced to look away. “Blood makes me squeamish,” he whined. *What a wimp!*

After I stepped off the train, I examined the damage to machine and flesh. The cab was riddled with dents from gunfire and the front right-hand corner was caved in from the collision with the 4WD. Lau was not alone in losing his life while protecting his colleagues and the train. I was shocked to see the bodies of the unfortunate guards who zigged when they should have zagged. Goddard, Dimoska, Geeves and Kettle were lying motionless on the platform, waiting to be transported to the morgue. Samdup and Bull were more fortunate, although wounded and needing to be stretchered to an awaiting ambulance, they were expected to survive.

Sayer, the guard positioned on tank 3, approached me as I watched the ambulance leave the station. “The company will ensure their families are compensated,” he stated confidently.

“What makes you so sure?” I asked in cynical tone.

“A failure to do so would cause a strike, which the companies cannot afford. Without the water, there’s no mine or town. No gold!"

I considered the man and his words. During the assault he continually engaged the attackers, forcing them to seek cover, which gave me the time to reload and return fire.

"Thanks for covering my ass back there," I said.

Sayer nodded before turning his attention to the men lifting the guards' bodies into the tray of an awaiting ute. "Sorry about Lau mate. From where I was, it looked real nasty."

"I didn't know him before today," I admitted. "But he bloody saved my hide back there."

Sayer shook his head solemnly. "We lost too many today, that's for sure. The only silver lining is we killed fifteen of the scum."

Remarkably we lost just two of the thirty water tanks; both were at the rear of the line where poor Geeves and Kettle were gunned down. With 48,000 litres lost, I wondered who'd be missing out on their baths and coffees tonight. It won't be the mining bosses and public officials, that's for certain.

Sayer grinned from ear to ear and waved eagerly to an attractive woman. "Look, I've gotta go. I might catch you up later."

He ran to the lady, lifted her off her feet and spun her around 360-degrees. They laughed, kissed, and hugged with joy. While I watched them like a shameless voyeur, I thought of Sally and felt sudden and unexpected envy. It's not that I wanted to be back with Sally, I just missed that tingly feeling of yearning for a lover and then finally holding them. As they walked towards the carpark hand in hand, I snapped out of my daydream and began searching for Archie.

I found him on the platform handing over a bloodied outlaw to the local sergeant. He then started to chat to the Kalgoorlie station manager. By the look of Archie's body language, he seemed to be having a heated discussion.

Guards were assisting to load the body bags onto the tray of an old ute. Members of the public were gawking and pointing at the carnage, making me feel angry at their lack of empathy.

I looked over at Archie and saw him shaking the station manager's hand. He noticed me and walked over to where I was standing,

"What happened to your shoulder?" he asked.

I looked down and saw blood seeping through my t-shirt. "I think I got hit by some shrapnel from a ricochet."

Archie placed a small leather satchel in my palm. "That should make you feel a bit better."

I opened the satchel to reveal my pay; a one ounce bar of the seductive yellow metal. Some companies pay you in silver or gold coins, while others pay in bars.

Archie pointed to my shoulder. "Come on, we'll grab a taxi to the hospital and get that looked at."

"Really, do you think it's necessary?"

Archie crossed his arms over his chest. "Lift your left arm above your head for me." With considerable effort I managed to lift my arm above shoulder height. By the look on his face, I had failed his test. "I reckon you have some shrapnel embedded in the muscle. You need to have it looked at," he said emphatically.

After waiting twenty minutes for a taxi, the driver literally spun around the bend to arrive at the hospital carpark. "We could have walked," I claimed.

"You're injured and I couldn't be stuffed walking," he explained.

We plodded into the waiting room and approached the counter. The hospital clerk was an elderly lady with a kind face, who moved her head as slow and purposeful as a tortoise. She handed me a three-page patient information form and asked me to take a seat. I filled in the form while sitting in an uncomfortable plastic chair; the type that you tend to find in backyards and hospital waiting rooms. When I returned to the counter to submit the form, it was as if the clerk had not moved a centimetre during the time it took me to complete the form.

Archie and I read crumpled magazines from the late 2020s while we patiently waited. I flicked through a gossip magazine while Archie perused a fishing mag. I was only thirteen years old when the War ended, so I find it hard to remember why I was so fascinated with the lives of celebrities and influencers. Especially those that didn't appear to have any skills or talent.

The old lady called out, "Come through dear, the nurse is ready for you."

Archie remained in the waiting room while I walked through the emergency room door. He was completely engrossed in the world of fishing, so I doubt that he even noticed that I had left.

I was met by a middle-aged woman dressed in crisp white pants and a red blouse. "Come and have a seat luv."

I obeyed and sat down on the gurney.

"So, what's happened?"

"I think I have some shrapnel in my left shoulder and boob."

The nurse didn't miss a beat, "Okay, I'm going to take your t-shirt off. Can you lift your arms?"

I attempted to lift my arms but almost cried out in pain. "Sorry, it feels like it's gotten worse."

The nurse nodded and reached for a pair of silver scissors and cut my shirt straight up the middle from the front and then the back. She then cut the bandages and carefully removed the gauze.

She looked closely at the wound. "I've seen similar wounds in dogs that have been brought into the surgery. It's definitely birdshot or buckshot."

"Excuse me?"

"You know, triple A pellets from a shotgun," the nurse explained.

"I know what pellets are, but what do you mean by dogs being brought into the surgery?"

"Oh, I was trained as a vet nurse, but don't you be concerned, animals are a lot more complicated to deal with than most humans. If I can take birdshot out of a conscious pit bull, then your wound is a walk in the park."

People with medical experience are few and far between, with most losing their lives when the missiles struck the cities. Beggars can't be choosers.

The nurse cleaned my wound and injected a local anaesthetic. She grasped a scalpel and spoke as she worked. "I just have to make an elliptical incision around the entry wound."

Blood doesn't scare me. I've received advanced first aid training while I was working on a farm, and I've treated workers after all sorts of accidents. I've even stitched someone up.

The nurse placed the scalpel on the tray and picked up another instrument that looked like a pair of scissors with blunt ends. "What are those?" I asked.

"These are called Allis forceps. I'm going to use them to grasp the elliptical area of your skin."

I closely watched her technique, her process, and her manner during the procedure, as I may need to perform a similar surgery in the future. She incised downwards from the edges on both sides towards the centre and used the forceps to grasp and remove the small pellet. The pellet was only four millimetres in diameter. She removed a further three pellets before stitching me up with expert precision.

"You were lucky luv, they were small lead pellets, and they weren't too deep. There doesn't appear to be any damage to tendons or nerves."

As I slowly rotated my shoulder forwards and then backwards, I was astonished to discover that it felt a lot better already. "Thank you for all your help, I really appreciate it."

"No worries luv. You will need to purchase some clean gauze, bandages, and antibiotics. I'd give you some supplies, but we're almost out with all the traffic we've had over the last twenty-four hours. I can however find you a shirt."

"No problem, I've got some medical supplies. A shirt would be good. My colleague is prone to embarrassment." She laughed and returned with a red flannelette shirt that was at least three sizes too big for me.

I returned to the waiting room in my oversized shirt and found Archie dozing. He was leaning back in the chair with his legs stretched out, using his pack as a pouffe. If he can sleep in these chairs, he can sleep anywhere. "Wake up old man."

He woke after I nudged his shoulder. He wiped his eyes with the back of his hand, yawned and commented, "I like your shirt."

"Good, because you can have it when we get back to the hotel."

He asked me about the specifics of the injury and how I was feeling. After he was satisfied with my response, we hailed a taxi.

It felt a little peculiar returning to the Exchange Hotel. It's only been seven weeks, but I had changed since I walked out those hotel doors. I had my rifle over my left shoulder and my Glock on my hip. I was wearing bloodied jeans and the manky red flannelette shirt. The miners that I served as a skimpy barmaid were staring wide-eyed as I walked past their tables to the bar. I could see it in their eyes and posture - they no longer viewed me as a barmaid to use and abuse - they recognised what I had become - *a hunter!*

Jules rushed around the counter to hug us both. She couldn't help herself and grabbed a handful of Archie's ass. With embarrassment written all over his face, he quickly explained that we were checking in for at least two nights.

Archie carried my pack into my room and plonked it on the ground. "I'll see you downstairs for a late dinner in an hour or so. We'll have a debrief and go over the plan for the next two days."

As soon as Archie closed the door, I tore off the filthy shirt and almost ran to the shower. The water pressure may have been weak, but it still felt heavenly, especially knowing that I was one of the twelve guards responsible for delivering the water to town.

Chapter Twenty-Four

Saturday March 16, 2041 – Archie

After freshening up I met Fiona downstairs at the bar. I ordered a steak burger, chips, and a jug of lager. Fiona ordered a fried cricket sandwich. The expense of beef and pork culminated in the culinary demand for insects. Like most youngsters, Fiona would have grown up eating all sorts of creepy-crawlies. As my palate is yet to diversify, I am left with expensive tastes.

We explained our experience of the attack in detail – what went well, what didn't go so well and how we fared overall. I confessed my tactical errors while engaging the off-road buggy; my lack of awareness of my surroundings would have got me killed had it not been for the outlaw missing me with his shotgun.

I was impressed with Fiona's account of the events; not only did she have to fight through the adversity of losing Lau and being wounded, but she also fought a battle on two fronts while maintaining a clear head. She confirmed her ability to control her reactions to the physiological stress of a gunfight.

I swallowed a mouthful of beef and leaned across the table. "I spoke to the local sergeant when I handed over the outlaw. They're members of a gang called the Norse Men, the same gang that currently occupy Norseman. Go figure. The sergeant has intel that their plan was to capture the train and extort a heavy price from the companies to return her. I'm guessing that's why they didn't target the tanks."

Fiona replied with her mouth full of crickets and bread, "Just as we began our journey, the train driver mentioned something about a gang that may target us."

I glared at her aghast. "Why didn't you say something?"

"I thought he was just talking shit," she answered sheepishly.

"Lesson learned. Always pass on intel, even if you don't believe it to be credible."

"Crystal clear Boss," she replied earnestly.

"Good. Don't forget it."

I pondered what Jack, Northam's train station manager, knew about the attack. My intuition was setting off alarm bells when he offered us the job. Now with the benefit of hindsight, I have a strong suspicion that he screwed us. One ounce pay for a standard trip was unheard of, even if they were short on guards.

"Remember when we met Jack in the carpark, and he was having a heated argument with the driver. I wonder if that had something to do with the attack."

I drained half my beer and then it dawned on me to ask, "Did you feel the train slow down just after the shit hit the fan?"

Fiona's eyes widened. "Fuck, I forgot about that with everything that happened. It was really weird! Larry actually started to slow the train. When I asked him what he was doing, he said something about being instructed to slow down if we were attacked. You can imagine what my response was."

I filed a mental note to have a quiet word with Jack and Larry. There were some irregularities that needed to be cleared up. The jukebox started to play David Bowie's song - *Let's Dance*. As I was a fan of Bowie, I could clearly recall watching the music clip on YouTube. It was filmed in a New South Wales rural pub, which didn't look much different from a majority of the pubs I frequent. I regularly listen to music on AM radio and receive news from around W.A. and other parts of the country. However, it's often amateur hour, with information being almost impossible to verify. It's disconcerting to think that we are all but cut off from the rest of the country.

I poured myself another glass of lager and ordered another jug. "The station manager reckons the train won't return for another three to four days. It's going to take that long to patch her up and find some more guards for the return trip. I let him know that we'll be returning on her."

Fiona took out her notebook and after flicking through the pages she asked, "What's the plan for the next three days? Are we going searching for Curtis tomorrow, or are we going to try to find the miner who has info on Patterson and the kidnapped boy?"

I didn't tell her, but I was impressed that she was referring to her notebook and thinking ahead. Cathy Ward, Northam's bondsman, stated that Curtis's Alive bounty for armed robbery was a walk in the park. I decided that we should cash in on the bounty before looking into the Patterson contract.

"We're going to find Curtis first. We'll get a ride out to the informant's address tomorrow morning. Curtis is not known for violence, but that doesn't mean he won't shoot at us to escape."

The informant is the father of a lass dating Curtis, who is obviously keen to split the two up. He's a prospector named Greg Nguyen, who resides in Coolgardie, a mining ghost town forty kilometres south-west of Kal. Sometimes the simplest plan is the most effective plan. Sal would regularly refer to the acronym KISS, '*Keep It Simple Stupid*.' We'll knock on Nguyen's door. If Curtis is home, we'll apprehend him and if he's already decamped, we'll identify ourselves and seek information about his whereabouts.

I heard a ruckus and turned around to see the hotel's enormous bouncer escorting two intoxicated gentlemen from the premises, each arm the size of a leg of ham wrapped around a patron's neck. Fiona ignored the commotion and queried, "I forgot to ask you, where did you get that fancy looking rifle? It looks badass."

"You mean the Blaser Sniper rifle with armour piercing rounds," I chuckled, before pausing and suddenly looking solemn. "It was Dimoska's. When we get back to Northam I'll inquire if she has any next of kin and offer to buy it from them. If there's no kin, then it's mine. Of course, I'll let you play with it."

The hotel was busy for a Thursday night - the bar was packed and the music was thumping. After finishing my fourth pint I was beginning to mellow. I wasn't a teetotaller, but I wasn't a big drinker either. "So, you enjoying the job Fiona?"

She leaned back in her chair. "I'm enjoying it more than any other job I've had. It's exciting and challenging, and of course the gold is REAL good. Lau having his head blown off was fucked up. But, I guess the risk is worth the reward."

After sculling my fifth glass I transitioned from mellow to tipsy. "Yep, be careful Fiona. It can be a slippery slope. You know the action can be real addictive. All those endor....endor....what's the word I'm looking for? Endorphins, that's it. And before you know it, you're de...de...desensitised to violence. You know what I mean, numb! I grabbed all that pain from losing Janet and buried it down real deep. I thought the action would keep it buried, but it didn't work. And that's where the oxys came in. Not good mate, not good."

"How you going with that?"

I was conscience that I was starting to slur my words. "What, the oxys? I'm done with that sshhit!"

"That's great Boss, I'm happy to hear it. Anyway, I'm shattered, I'm going to hit the hay."

I rose from the table and accidentally knocked the chair over. "Yep, me too."

As I stumbled to my room, I turned to see Fiona unlocking her door. "Good night matey. Oh, don't forget to give me that flanno in the morning."

She smiled. "Don't you worry, I can't wait to get rid of it. Good night, Boss."

I sat on the edge of my bed and searched through my pack. I located my brown leather wallet sitting at the very bottom. I opened the wallet and gazed at the photo of Janet and myself, dressed to impress at her university graduation. We were grinning like Cheshire cats. I had booked a room at the Ritz, where I got down on one knee and asked her to marry me.

I fell asleep with the photo resting on my chest and a tear running down my cheek.

Chapter Twenty-Five

Sunday March 17, 2041 – Fiona

I left the flanno shirt on Archie's door handle with a note to meet me for breakfast, before walking across the road to a cafe where I purchased bacon and egg burgers and two long blacks. Archie and I sat on a bench at the front of the hotel and devoured the burgers. I wore a scruffy t-shirt and jeans, and Archie wore the horrible flanno. We both had our shirts hanging over our holstered handguns. Archie handed me some cable ties which I placed in my jeans pocket and we discussed the plan for the day.

Archie had a file in his hands. He took out Curtis's mug shot and handed it to me. Before the War, Curtis could have played a role in a TV soap opera. "He's a good-looking fella. If I were straight, I'd give him a second look."

Archie wiped his mouth with the back of his sleeve. "I'll take the lead when we arrive at Nguyen's. If I grab the back of my neck, that's my signal that I want you to go around the back and have a look around. Remember, this is an Alive contract, unless he draws a firearm or blade, don't shoot him. Any question?"

"What if his girlfriend interferes?"

Archie went blank for a moment and then replied, "Mmmm, good question. Play it by ear, but if you have to use force, so be it, just make sure it's reasonable. We don't want to upset her old man."

I thought to myself, what the hell does '*play it by ear*' mean? But like a lot of questions I have, I kept it to myself.

We hailed a taxi at the front of the cafe. "Mate, can you please take us to Coolgardie, 5 Lindsay Street. We're visiting a relative who's been ill. We're only dropping by for half an hour. Can you keep the meter running and drop us back?" Archie spun a story about the sick rellie, as he was worried that the driver would knock back the return fare for fear of damage to his vehicle or reputation.

"No problem. That'll be five coins."

It took just thirty minutes to arrive at Lindsay Street. "Mate, can you drop us off at the end of the street. We want to surprise them."

The house was a cream brick dwelling with orange roof tiles. Archie knocked on the security screen. When no one answered, he knocked again, but louder. I heard an agitated man's voice from inside, "Hold your horses would ya."

A short wiry man in his mid-fifties wearing a white singlet opened the security screen door. "I'm not buying what you're selling. And no, you can't come inside for a glass of water."

Archie who towered over Mr Nguyen's thin five-foot-five frame was rubbernecking through the doorway in an effort to get eyes on Curtis. While displaying his bounty hunter license, Archie said softly, "Mr Nguyen, my name is Archie O'Connor, and this is Fiona Katsaros. We're bounty hunters and we're here to apprehend Curtis. Is he home?"

Mr Nguyen's eyes widened, "Finally, about time. He's in the back granny flat, go get him."

"Is your daughter with him?" asked Archie.

He looked worried. "Yes, why? Caroyln's done nothing wrong."

"We're not concerned with your daughter sir. We just want to make sure she doesn't get hurt. Can you call her to come inside the house and keep her occupied while we apprehend Curtis?"

"Okay, okay, no problem."

"Do you have any dogs?" I asked.

Mr Nguyen shook his head. Archie whispered, "We'll wait around the side of the house until your daughter comes inside. Please make sure she doesn't come out the back until we've left with Curtis. Okay?"

Mr Nguyen gave the thumbs-up sign and walked back inside the house. He shouted, "Carolyn, can you please help me feed the cat?

I've lost my glasses again and I can't find the can opener or the cat."

We snuck around the side of the home and peered into the backyard. We saw a pretty young woman with long black hair to her waist, leave a fibro granny flat and enter the back door of Mr Nguyen's home. Archie signalled for me to follow him. I noticed the hinges of the front door of the granny flat, noting that it was an outward opening door. Archie drew his revolver and positioned himself at a 45-degree angle nearside to the door handle. I stood at the opposite side of the door and drew my pistol, holding it to my chest with the muzzle pointing downward. I twisted the door handle and rapidly opened it towards me. Archie advanced through the doorway, and I followed closely behind. We both scanned our area of responsibility and approached Curtis with our firearms pointed towards his centre of scene mass – at his chest, just like Archie had taught me.

Curtis was lying in bed glaring at an old dirty magazine, with his hand on his erect penis. Archie momentarily paused and then instructed, "Get your hand off your weapon and lay on your front."

I suppressed a giggle as I covered Archie while he re-holstered his revolver and took cable ties out of his back pocket. He approached the bed yelling, "Don't move!"

Curtis shouted, "What the fuck dude? I have rights you know. Who are you people?"

Archie had just secured the cable ties around Curtis's wrists, when his girlfriend burst through the granny flat door and jumped onto Archie's back. She was screaming obscenities as she clawed at his face like a deranged wildcat. He in turn was spinning around and grabbing her arms in what I assumed was a desperate attempt to dislodge her from his back. Mr Nguyen suddenly entered the flat in a panic. He was holding a black cat that jumped out of his arms and scampered under the bed. Mr Nguyen then waved his arms and jumped around like a mad ferret on a hot tin roof, yelling at his daughter, "Get off him Carolyn."

During all of this chaos Curtis was sobbing into his pillow. I was forced to bite my lip so I wouldn't start cackling at the ridiculousness of the situation. I re-holstered my pistol and stepped forward to bring some sanity into this crazy situation. I grabbed Carolyn's luscious long black hair in a firm grip and yanked downwards with considerable force. As her backside hit the ground, I rolled her over to her front and secured her wrists with cable ties. She was screaming like an absolute lunatic. I didn't attempt to calm her as she was crazy in love, with an emphasis on the *crazy*.

We left Mr Nguyen comforting his distraught daughter and led Curtis outside and down the street to our awaiting taxi. Curtis was wearing purple boxers that Archie had graciously pulled up from around his ankles to his waist. Archie placed Curtis in the rear passenger side seat and slid in beside him, while I rode shotgun.

Curtis yelled to the driver, "Please help me, these people have abducted me, I need....."

Curtis didn't have an opportunity to complete his sentence as Archie's arm moved forwards and then back with incredible speed, striking Curtis's chest with the tip of his elbow. Curtis shrieked in agony.

I said to the taxi driver, "Take us to Kalgoorlie Police Station. Our cousin has lost the plot and we need to have him committed."

"I like it, good imagination," said Archie. He showed the driver his bounty hunter ID and explained, "We've apprehended an offender and need to drop him off at the police station."

The driver nodded. "Why didn't you just say so in the first place. A fare's a fare, it doesn't bother me either way. I get paid the same whether you're bounty hunting or visiting family."

Curtis sobbed the entire thirty-minute journey. He was trying everything to convince us to let him go, from begging to bribery. Archie ignored his whinging and asked the driver to turn up the volume of the radio.

The view of the police station from my taxi window couldn't have come any sooner. I felt a mixture of frustration and repugnance after having to listen to Curtis's constant whining.

I grabbed Curtis's elbow and pulled him from the cab, dragging him into the police station. Archie paid the driver and then quick marched to catch up to me. The driver bellowed from his vehicle, "If you need another ride, ask for Clint."

"Thanks Clint, we'll keep you in mind," I shouted while I manhandled Curtis towards the front door of the station.

Senior Constable Atkins was reading a Footrot Flats comic as we approached the counter.

"Good plot mate?" Archie teased.

"Don't be a smart-ass Archie," he retorted.

"No offence mate, everyone likes a good comic. I'm partial to The Punisher or Judge Dredd myself. Anyway, we have another one for you, this is Curtis Gates."

Archie handed Atkins the contract. Atkins sighed, "Bring him through Archie."

I have the distinct feeling that Atkins is not that keen on working for a living.

Archie dragged the hysterical Curtis around the side of the counter to the cells.

Upon their return, Atkins pointed to Archie while saying to me, "I'm surprised you're still his apprentice. I thought he would've scared you off by now."

"I don't scare that easy. And besides, I'm a full partner now," I replied proudly.

Atkins raised an eyebrow. "Good luck in keeping him out of trouble," he said with a sneer in Archie's direction. "So, are you two joining the militia? I've heard they're recruiting guns for hire."

"What militia and what are they hiring for?" I asked with interest.

He looked surprised. "You haven't heard? The news is all-around town. The Kalgoorlie and Esperance militia are combining to attack the Norse Men Gang in an attempt re-take Norseman. Ha ha, a bit of a tongue twister hey. The whole thing's a bit foolhardy if you ask me. I hope they come to their senses."

"Why do you say that?" Archie asked.

"I'm just saying that it's a big risk. A lot of lives could be lost. Let them have the shitty town and leave them be as long as they don't journey south."

Archie's eyes narrowed and his lip curled in contempt. Atkins either didn't seem to notice or didn't care. He handed me the completed handover documentation and returned to his chair. He put his feet up and opened his comic. As we were leaving Archie taunted, "Enjoy your comic Atkins and don't work too hard!"

Just before the door shut, I heard Atkins mutter, "Fuck off Archie."

We both moseyed next door to the bondsman's office. Henry Jenkin's resembled a bowling ball, which was an oddity, as a majority of the pre-war processed junk food was no longer produced. Chocolate, toffee and boiled lollies were still available, but they were exorbitantly expensive. With his nose severely bent at the bridge, he looked like a retired pugilist that rarely had his hands raised - during or after the fight.

Archie placed the handover document on the counter and stated, "We need to collect this massive reward mate."

Jenkins raised his hands and squeaked, "Don't blame me Archie, I don't set the rewards."

Archie's eyes narrowed. "I'm not blaming you, Henry. By the way, are there any new bounties?"

Jenkins looked scared shitless for some reason. "No, and I'm not just saying that. It's been quiet. Although, I have heard that the militia is hiring pros to assist in attacking that Norse Gang."

"Yeah, we've heard," I said.

Henry placed a half ounce of gold on the counter. Archie picked it up and handed it to me. "I also need you to prepare a bounty hunter identification for Fiona. She's completed her apprenticeship and is ready to be issued a license."

Henry opened a counter draw and handed me a triplicate carbon form, which only took me a couple of minutes to complete. He then signed it and presented me a copy.

Henry pointed to the side wall. "Please stand in front of the wall. I just need to take your photo."

He took the photo with an old canon camera. "I'll develop the film this arvo. Come by the office tomorrow morning and your ID will be ready. Until then, the form you have their proves you're a licensed bounty hunter."

"Cheers Henry," I said.

I inspected the document with a feeling of pride. I had a new career and over two ounces in my pocket. More gold than I've ever had. For the first time in my life, I felt wealthy and independent.

After we stepped out of the office I turned to Archie and said, "I'm a bit overwhelmed. It sort of doesn't feel deserved."

"Like I told you before, you've earned it. Let's go and grab lunch."

"What's wrong with Henry? He seemed a bit skittish," I asked.

"Let's just say that the last time we spoke, we had a bit of a disagreement."

We returned to the café we frequented earlier, and I ordered a beetle sandwich. Archie was chewing on a meat pie that had likely been sitting in the bain-marie for the last four days. I don't know why he eats that shit; bugs are a lot healthier and it's rare to get food poisoning from fried insects.

Archie wiped a piece of mince from his chin. "Once we've finished lunch, we'll visit the local council office and see if we can discover where our miner lives."

When the waitress handed me my sandwich, I couldn't wait to get stuck into the fried beetle yumminess. After I took my first bite I asked, "Are we going to join the militia? I'll be honest with you, I'd like some pay back, and if we're going to get paid for it, then bonus." I couldn't get poor Lau out of my mind. He saved my life and lost his in the process.

"I know what happened to Lau is bugging you. I feel a similar way about Dimoska and Goddard. It's just that it's a risky business for little reward. In saying that, if Clarry is joining up, then I guess I'll be in for the ride."

He paused before continuing, "You need to think about it carefully and make your own decision. Don't get me wrong, the brothers and the train were hectic, but Norseman will be a real bloody battle."

I took what Archie said for granted, automatically dismissing his words as an exaggeration. I mean, how much worse could it possibly get? It can't be any different to the blood, guts, and carnage I've seen over the last couple of months.

It was a beautiful thirty-degree day, so we decided to walk the three kilometres down Hannan street to the council building.

Archie warned, "The council is no longer the bureaucratic behemoth it was pre-war. It now consists of just a mayor and a couple of administrative staff. I don't have my hopes up that they'll be able to assist us. But you never know."

A thin Aboriginal lady of indeterminate age, wearing large dark rimmed glasses and a beautiful silk scarf, welcomed us and introduced herself as Miriam.

"Howdy Miriam, I'm Archie and this is Fiona. We're both bounty hunters that are trying to locate a witness that will hopefully help us find a kidnapped child. I was hoping you could give us his contact details. By the way, I love your scarf."

I love your scarf? If this was Archie's idea of flirting, then I need to give him some pointers.

"Thank you, it was my mothers. I can help you. But first, can I please see your bounty hunter identification. I also need the name of the witness?" she replied in a succinct manner.

Archie presented his identification. "He's a miner named Paddy Doherty."

Miriam walked brusquely to the rear of the office and opened a large grey metal cabinet. She flicked though the index cards under D and selected a card. Before reading it, she blew the dust from the cardboard surface. "I don't have a current residential address for Mr Doherty, but I have him recorded as being employed at the Super Pit."

We both thanked Miriam for her assistance. The Super Pit is the second largest open cut gold mine in the country and is located just eight kilometres from where we were standing. If you've frequented the town's pubs, it's impossible not to know the ins and outs of the mine, as the miners' brag about it every chance they get. I could have been one of those tourist guides they employed before the War, you know, when there were actual tourists. I could see myself standing at the front of the tourist bus as it approached the mine: '*The mine is approximately 3.5 kilometres long, 1.5 kilometres wide and over 600 metres deep. The operation employs 1100 workers and moves about fifteen million tonnes of rock, to produce 425,000 ounces of gold annually.*'

We hailed a taxi and were surprised to see Clint, the bloke that drove us to and from Mr Nguyen's house. He must be the hardest working driver in town. After we haggled back and forth on the price, we agreed to hire him for the day. The grateful driver took us to the Super Pit's main office, which was located just outside the mine entry.

We jumped out of the taxi and approached the twelve-foot high reinforced steel gate. The place reminded me of a prison, with thick concrete bollards and barbed wire fences enclosing the mine. We were greeted by four guards armed with steely expressions and glistening assault rifles.

Archie flashed his bounty hunter ID. "Hey guys, we're just here to speak to one of your employees, a fella by the name of Paddy Doherty. Can we come inside to have a quick word with him?"

A guard with a pencil thin moustache and bulging biceps stepped forwards. "No, you can't. That is contrary to company regulations."

"Okay, Understood. Can you see if he's in and ask him to meet us out here?"

"No, we can't its cont......"

"Contrary to company regulations," Archie said, finishing his sentence for him. When Archie reached into his pack, the four guards levelled their muzzles at his chest. Archie raised a palm in the air. "Settle down fellas. I'm just reaching for some ciggies and hooch."

"Save it. If you're not out of here in the next sixty seconds I'm calling the police," threatened the impatient guard.

During the journey back to the hotel, Archie lamented, "I guess we'll have to do this the hard way. How old are you?"

"Why?" I asked suspiciously.

"Come on, just answer the question."

"I turned twenty-one last November."

"Did you have a party?" he asked with a cheeky smile.

"What do you think?" I replied sarcastically.

Archie laughed. "Well, we're belatedly celebrating your twenty-first tonight by going on a pub crawl. Being a miner, Paddy's likely to hit the town."

I groaned inwardly. I was actually looking forward to an early night of curling up in bed with a sci-fi book that the previous occupant of my room had left in the bedside draw.

"Do you know how many pubs are in this town? Because I do," I said, trying to hide my dismay.

Archie smirked. "Oh, I reckon about twenty-one. Look, it's going to be a cracking birthday party. And the good news is, I'm buying. What are you doing tonight, Clint?"

Clint raised an eyebrow. "I guess I'm driving you two around town."

Archie was enjoying himself. "Spot on Clint, spot on."

Chapter Twenty-Six

Sunday March 17, 2041 from 7 p.m. – Archie

I put on a fresh pair of jeans and my good shirt, which I covered over my revolver. I wasn't planning on getting into any trouble, but I always carried no matter what the occasion. I hadn't partaken in a pub crawl since my Buck's party in 2027. My new philosophy was to embrace the good moments in life, and this was one of them. Sure, I was still on the clock, but I had gold in my pocket and something to celebrate.

I was having a good chat to Jules at the bar, when Fiona sidled onto the stool beside me. Jules walked off to sort out an issue with her cook; apparently, like all masters of the kitchen, he was a little temperamental.

"Jules hasn't heard of a Paddy Doherty, but she asked around the bar for us, and a bloke who used to work with him says he's a regular down the road at the York Hotel. This might turn out to be the shortest pub crawl in history."

"Oh well," she replied with an amused expression.

"You don't look or sound too disappointed," I said in an accusatorial tone.

Fiona yawned. "I'm just a bit tired Boss. That's all."

I didn't hide my disappointment. "Okay party pooper. Come on, let's go to the York. I'll ask Clint to hang around in case Paddy's not there."

We moseyed down the Hannan Street sidewalk to the York Hotel. The York was built in 1901 and is located just down the road from the Paddy Hannan Statue. Paddy Hannan was a prospector, who in

1893 found over one hundred ounces of alluvial gold. Within three days, 700 prospectors had arrived in Coolgardie, and the Gold Rush was set in motion. The irony that we're searching for a miner named Paddy, is not lost on me.

We ambled through the front doors of the Hotel. I ordered a couple of pints and said to the barman over the music, "G'day champ. I'm trying to locate a mate of a mate named Paddy Doherty."

The young barman looked at me suspiciously. "I've never met a Paddy Doherty."

I placed a packet of cigarettes on the bar. "I don't smoke. You wouldn't be able to use these would you?"

The barman placed a hand over the packet. "See the bloke in the black t-shirt playing pool, I believe he may be the fella you're looking for."

I grabbed the two glasses and walked over to sit at the table alongside Fiona. "There's two blokes playing pool. The one in the black t-shirt is the man we want to speak to. While I have a word with him, I want you to distract the young bloke he's playing with."

We left our drinks and moseyed on over to the pool table. Fiona didn't need to make much of an effort to distract the young man. He acted as if he'd won the lottery and was more than eager to perform like a peacock - all charm and charisma.

While the young bloke was fanning his tail feathers, I approached the so-called Paddy. He was in his mid-sixties and had the lean athletic frame of a long-distance runner. "Mate, if you're Paddy Doherty, I just need a quick word with you."

He immediately raised his pool cue and quickly swung it towards my head. I blocked the shaft not far from the tip with the outside of my forearm and launched an uppercut into his lower abdomen. His knees instantly buckled, and he gasped for air as he fell to the ground. I was gratefully amazed that his buddy hadn't seem to notice. I shouldn't have been surprised, as the young fella appeared totally captivated with Fiona. I lifted the bloke to his feet, placed his arm around my neck and assisted him to our table. Once he'd recovered and appeared settled, I passed him a pint of beer.

"Mate, I just want to ask you a couple of questions about a bloke named Noel Patterson and a young boy he kidnapped named Raj. I believe you spoke to a former colleague of mine, Sal Willis."

I took out my hunter ID and covertly displayed it to him, without attracting attention from any of the patrons.

He'd recovered his breath but was still clutching his stomach. "Why didn't you just say so?"

"Maaate, you didn't give me a chance."

"Sorry about that. I thought you'd be sent by Noel."

"Why would he send someone?" I asked.

"Look, I don't know anything about the lad, but I can tell you everything I know about Noel."

I removed my notebook and pen from my jeans pocket. Fiona had started to play pool with the young bloke, who had eyes on the prize.

"Tell me everything you know about Patterson, and I'll keep buying the drinks."

I grabbed the barmaid's attention and ordered two more jugs of lager. I learned a long time ago that if you want information - just shut your trap and let the person talk – and then drill down to specifics. I should also add that alcohol is the human equivalent of WD-40; it's a handy lubricant to loosen lips.

Paddy took a sip of his beer before leaning forwards in a conspiratory manner. "I've known Noel for over twenty-five years. We both worked for a biomedical company that spent billions of dollars researching human longevity. In layman's terms, Noel and I were specifically working on increasing the production of an enzyme called telomerase. We hoped that it would result in maintaining the length of one's telomeres. This would greatly increase life spans and possibly reduce the risk of diseases such as cancer. But we had significant hurdles. Each occasion we thought we made a breakthrough, we found that all our efforts actually stimulated cancer. Noel became desperate and proposed a madcap idea of using radiation as a countermeasure. We both ended up being sacked because he had a crazy plan of using criminals as lab rats. Anyway, I thought it was all water under the bridge."

This was an interesting story, and even though my plan was to let him talk, we were getting way off track. "Okay, but how does this help me find him?"

I poured him another drink to the rim of his glass. "Don't worry, I'm getting there. You just have to be patient," he assured me.

I apologised for interrupting and urged him to continue.

"After we were sacked, I heard through the grapevine that he was working for the military. This rumour was confirmed when he requested my assistance just after the War started. I wasn't given much of a choice, either head to the front and prepare for the invasion with a rifle in hand or assist my psychotic former colleague within the safety of a military laboratory. You can guess which door I selected. Unfortunately, Noel's sinister methodology had transitioned into insanity. He was conducting inhumane experiments on criminals and POWs. It was horrifying! He was conducting surgery without anaesthetic and injecting them with harmful drugs. I frequently have nightmares about those experiments, waking breathless in the middle of the night dripping with sweat."

Paddy wiped his brow. Visibly shaken he continued, "Anyway, after the war I scampered at the first opportunity I got. I made my way here and Bob's your uncle, I was hired at the Super Pit as a metallurgist."

"How did you survive the missiles?" I asked.

"Oh, we weren't based in Perth, our lab was situated at the Yongah Hills Immigration Detention Centre in Northam. That's where the POWs were being kept. Noel was using the unfortunate souls as guinea pigs. I tell you, if I were a believer of Hinduism, I reckon I could easily be convinced that he's Josef Mengele reincarnated."

I recalled reading about Josef Mengele's murders when I completed a history unit as a part of my Bachelor of Laws. Mengele, also known as the Angel of Death, was a Nazi physician during World War Two, and the chief medical officer at the Auschwitz concentration camp, where he conducted research on heritability and anthropology. He demonstrated particular interest in dwarfs, pregnant women, identical twins, and people with physical abnormalities. One of his many atrocities included personally killing fourteen twins in one night by injecting their hearts with chloroform. He also performed numerous surgical experiments - removing his victims' hearts, stomachs, and kidneys without anaesthesia.

I was stunned and a little shaken by Paddy's account. "After hearing your tale, it's paramount that we locate Raj as soon as possible. Have you seen Noel since you left the lab?"

Paddy nodded, "He tracked me down in early February. He had this lunatic plan of re-populating Perth under his so-called leadership. He said he had a group of followers that he'd injected with his longevity drug, and he wanted me to be a part of it. He's stark raving mad I tell you!"

I really needed another drink. I topped up both our glasses. "So, do you believe he travelled to Perth?"

"Look, I can't be certain. But he had two of his thugs take me to a house on Butler Street. He made me sit through a presentation. It was like sitting through a time-share sales pitch on acid. He had posters on the wall, numerous reports, even bloody white boards. I was that bloody nervous that I can't recall all of the detail, but I remember the gist of it. His plan was to occupy the Blue Opal Resort and branch out to various properties based on strategic significance. He mentioned raiding the Perth Mint and the Campbell Barracks in an effort to build a private army. Look, I can't remember much more. I mean, it was just so bat-shit crazy, and I had a real concern that he was going to do me in."

"How'd you manage to get away?" I asked with interest.

"I told him I needed to go to the loo and slipped out through the bathroom window. I ran all the way to the Super Pit and told the guards I needed to enter my office to complete some urgent work. I didn't leave the Pit for more than a week."

"Think carefully Paddy, did he mention anything about a kid?"

"No, sorry. Definitely not."

I leaned towards him. "Can you take me to this house on Butler Street?"

"No, I'm not going anywhere near that place," Paddy replied

defiantly.

"Do you have kids Paddy?"

When Paddy gazed down at the table with anguish in his eyes, I knew I'd hit him where it hurts and instantly regretted asking the question. One in two parents alive today lost children during the War.

"Listen Paddy, I'm sorry mate, but Raj is only ten years old and if Noel is only half as bat-shit crazy as you described, then he's in real danger. The boy's parents are both dead and his grandfather and grandmother are worried sick. Come with us in a taxi, point out the house and then the driver will immediately drop you back here. You won't even get out of the car."

Paddy contemplated my request and sighed. "Okay, but like you said, I'm not getting out of the car and I'm coming straight back here."

I nodded and handed Paddy my notebook, asking him to sketch the layout of the property, both the yard and premises. He had a remarkable recollection given the stress he was under on the night in question. He described two-bedrooms and one bathroom situated at the rear of the premises, with one living area at the front alongside the kitchen.

I called Fiona over to the table. She sat down and handed me three packets of cigarettes. I must have looked perplexed, because she explained, "I won them playing pool against Craig, who happens to be Paddy's nephew."

After ordering Craig and Paddy another jug, I took Fiona aside and briefed her on what I had discovered. We agreed to conduct a tactical entry of the premises in the hope of locating Raj. The reward was well worth the risk, from a financial and moral perspective.

I hailed Clint and asked him to drive us to Butler Street. I squeezed into the back seats with Fiona and Craig. When we arrived at the eastern end of Butler Street, I asked Clint to slow down so Paddy could identify the house. To save power, street lighting is non-existent in the suburbs. I dared not use a torch in fear of Patterson or one of his goons being alerted to our presence. Fortunately, the moon was almost full, providing Paddy enough light to see the features of the homes and fences.

We had just driven past a white fibro home with a blue picket fence when Paddy piped up, "That was it, the one on my side with the blue fence."

I instructed Clint to make a left turn at the end of the street and park fifty metres from the corner. As Fiona and I exited the vehicle I thanked Paddy, and asked Clint to drive them back to the York Hotel before returning and waiting for us at the end of the street.

Fiona and I held hands as we strolled around the corner towards Patterson's premises, acting like lovers out for a walk. As we approached, I listened carefully for any noise emanating from the property. The house was in complete darkness with heavy curtains drawn across the front windows. After failing to hear or see the presence of any occupants, we climbed over the waist high fence.

I signalled Fiona to follow me to the rear of the premises. As I stepped under the thick foliage of a peppermint tree, I was alerted to the ghoulish green glow of canine eyes. I placed my left palm up at shoulder height - signalling for Fiona to stop. A tingle ran down my spine as I heard a deep guttural growl. A black Doberman stalked forward baring her incisors and fangs. As the dog bounded forward and leapt, I crouched low and drove my knee up, striking it clean under its muzzle. Before it could recover and continue its attack, I wrapped my right arm around its neck in a bulldog choke, driving it to the ground and squeezing with all my might until it was limp.

After applying cable ties to her legs, I was relieved to see her diaphragm contract and relax rhythmically. The last thing I wanted to do was kill a dog. Especially when it was just doing its job.

We drew our handguns and crept to the rear of the property. I motioned towards the rear door. We stood on opposite sides of the door frame. Fiona covered me as I delicately twisted the door handle, confirming that it was locked. I swiftly re-holstered my revolver and retrieved a leather pouch from my back pocket that contained my lock pick set. The lock was a common tumbler. I first inserted the tension wrench and then my rake, manipulating it back and forth until I managed to unlock the door.

We entered the property with guns drawn and cleared the two

rear bedrooms, before advancing down the narrow hallway towards the bathroom. There was a strong scent of curry that I assumed was wafting from the kitchen.

Just as I approached the bathroom door, a naked muscular man charged at me, grabbing me by my throat with both hands and throwing me against the hallway wall with unnerving ease. As I flew through the air I jerked the trigger in panic, causing my shot to miss the enormous target and hit the ceiling.

Two events occurred almost simultaneously – the hulk of a man tore my revolver from my grasp as Fiona fired her Glock pistol. She must have missed as he didn't even flinch. He mechanically removed one of his hands from my throat and reached for Fiona's gun arm. I heard another shot ring out as the steroid freak threw Fiona's pistol down the hallway and grabbed her by her wrist. As I took deep breaths, I pressed my thumbs into his eye sockets with as much force as I could muster. Fiona seized the moment, jumping into the air and stabbing downwards with her Ka-Bar knife, embedding the 129-millimetre blade into the base of his neck. He looked up at the ceiling and roared like a grizzly bear, before charging Fiona with shocking speed for a man his size.

In great haste I picked up my revolver from the floor and from a distance of two metres I shot him in his upper back five times. While I released the rounds from my speedloader into the cylinder of my revolver, he was throttling and throwing Fiona from one side of the hallway wall to the other. I snapped the cylinder shut, stepped forwards and fired all six rounds into the side of his skull from point-blank range. The hulk dropped to the ground in a heap at our feet, his body jerking on five or six occasions before finally lying motionless.

Fiona switched on the hallway light and retrieved her pistol from the floor. We both took deep breaths before clearing the remaining rooms of the premises. Once we were satisfied that we were alone, Fiona gaped at me in disbelief and asked, "WHAT the FUCK was THAT?"

"I know, I've never seen anything like it," I replied in astonishment.

I've witnessed extraordinary human strength from steroid and methamphetamine abusers in the past. However, the only word I could use to describe this man's extreme power, pain threshold and ability to absorb physical punishment - is '*supernatural*.'

The massive man lay in the hallway stark naked and covered in a dark green fluid. The fluid was splattered all over the walls, floor, and ceiling. Until Fiona wiped my cheek with her fingers, I hadn't even realised that the green gunk was all over me. I gripped Fiona's knife and pulled it from his neck. After I examined the blade and wound, I scrutinised the 38-calibre bullet holes in his upper back, face, and skull. I couldn't quite believe what I was seeing - his blood was a dark artichoke green. I sauntered to the kitchen and wiped Fiona's blade with a white tea towel.

"Are you seeing what I'm seeing? Or have I taken a hit to the head on one too many occasions?"

She stared at the towel and then at the monstrous man that not more than five minutes ago was attempting to slaughter us, "Fuck me! His blood is fucking green."

With Fiona's help I rolled him onto his back so I could examine his features. His extreme muscular proportions would have forced him to turn sideways when walking through a standard doorway. And he was excessively vascular, with enlarged varicose veins protruding like a spider's web over his entire body. His muscularity may have been commonplace in the upper echelon of the competitive bodybuilding community, but I also noticed other physical oddities - his entire body was hairless, with no eyebrows or pubic hair - and his pupils were bright red.

One of the two bedrooms appeared occupied, with a foam mattress and sleeping bag situated in the back corner of the room and a Samsonite suitcase sitting opened on a glass coffee table. Fiona rummaged through the suitcase, finding extra-large shirts, pants, and underwear. The bathroom contained an abundant supply of syringes, unmarked vials and pill containers dispersed on the vanity. It appeared that my past reliance on pharmacology was a mere drop in the ocean in comparison to this bloke's dependence.

The loungeroom set-up was almost identical to Paddy's description.

Two whiteboards stood against the living room windows, crammed with posters and maps of Perth's CBD and inner suburbs. Reports and lever arch files were scattered all over the dining table.

We located an F92 Austeyr assault rifle with a grenade launcher attachment sitting on the kitchen bench, alongside spare magazines, two hundred rounds of ammunition, and several grenades. This was an Australian Army issued firearm that was now as rare as hens' teeth. As I checked the weapon, I wondered how he managed to get his mitts on one.

The aroma of curry was arising from a pot sitting on the stove. After I turned the stove off and inspected the contents of the pot, I found a clean bowl and a couple of spoons in the sink and scooped a generous portion of chicken curry into the bowl. Fiona was examining the whiteboards when I handed her the bowl. I was absolutely starving, so I stirred the pot and chowed down as I read the posters.

"Instead of working for Patterson, the big bastard should have opened a restaurant. This curry is bloody fantastic," I asserted, licking my lips.

Fiona was too busy eating to talk. She was making appreciative noises as she churned through the bowl like a pig at a trough.

"Easy tiger, you'll get indigestion," I joked.

She belched before replying, "You weren't kidding, this is fucking delicious!"

I closely examined the documents and maps, taking notes of my observations. A black marker was used to circle the Blue Opal Resort. The resort was built in 2031 on the grounds of the old WACA cricket ground. I remember the disappointment on my father's face when the demolition of the ground was announced, having watched his cherished Australian Cricket Team hit the winning runs against the English from the stands, first as a child sitting with my grandfather and then as a father sitting with me on his knee. At 1000 metres and eighty-five floors, the resort was the third tallest building in Australia. The building encompasses two towers with an impressive oval structure encased in blue glass resting on top of the two structures. I checked my notes and read that Paddy had mentioned Noel's desire to occupy the resort.

The Perth Mint and the Campbell Barracks were also marked on the maps. The Perth Mint was a government owned bullion mint which refined approximately seventy-nine percent of the Australasian gold production, and thirty percent of the silver. In 2030 it sold about twenty-eight billion dollars' worth of pure gold, silver, and platinum bullion bars and coins. There were rumours after the War that the Mint's vaults still contain a fortune in gold and silver; enough to buy a private army.

Campbell Barracks was an army base which was home to the Special Air Services Regiment, a special forces unit of the Australian Army. It's possible that the army left weapons on-site in their rush to evacuate when the missiles started falling. The military weapons such as assault rifles and machine guns would provide any private army a distinct advantage over the authorities and militias.

I scrutinised the whiteboards as I gobbled down the curry. There were individuals names, addresses and occupations listed with either a cross or tick beside their entry. The posters appeared to be propaganda, with the heading "The New World Order Party" inscribed in large thick bold letters above a list of promises to be had for those that joined.

THE NEW WORLD ORDER PARTY

Be part of a new order and receive

ONE ounce of gold per day for your service
Three quality meals a day prepared by our trained chefs
Accommodation at pre-war standards
Electricity & Hot Water 24/7
And Respect from an organisation that cares!

The reports appeared to be scientific research papers that I couldn't make heads or tails of. The last time I studied science was twenty years ago as a fifteen-year-old in high school. I made a mental note to ask Clarry to peruse and explain the contents of the reports. It would be interesting to explore if they had any relevance to our operation. They may even assist in explaining the hulk that attacked us. The man of many talents – chef, bodybuilder, and private army recruiter.

Fiona gathered the reports, maps and posters and placed them in Hulk's suitcase, while I copied the details from the whiteboard into my notebook. Our search of the house convinced me that the corpse in the hallway was the sole resident of the premises.

I took some leftover chicken from an esky that I found resting on the kitchen bench and strode to the backyard. I knelt beside the whimpering Doberman who was still lying on her side. "Now girl, you and I got off on the wrong foot. I want to make it up to you and be friends. Okay?" I placed a chicken thigh near the dog's nose, and she immediately scoffed it down. I put the rest of the chicken on the ground and cut the cable ties securing her legs. She immediately gulped down the rest of the chicken and then darted around the yard wanting to play. After we jumped the front fence, she started to whine.

Fiona pointed at the Doberman. "What about her?"

"What about her? No doubt one of the neighbours will take care of her."

Fiona crossed her arms and with a furrowed brow she asked, "You sure about that?"

Fiona's presumption was spot-on; in this day and age a stray dog was more likely to be eaten for dinner than to be taken in. After a long sigh, I jumped back over the fence, found the dog's lead and knelt down. "Come here girl if you want to be friends." The dog came running towards me with her tongue out, and when she was within reach, I attached the lead to her collar.

The three of us walked to Clint's awaiting taxi. Fiona jumped in the front passenger seat, and I entered the back seats with the Doberman and the Samsonite suitcase. Clint noticed the assault rifle between Fiona's legs and then saw the dog through the rear vision mirror. "You two look like you've been busy."

"It's been an interesting night. Full of surprises," said Fiona.

"That's the biggest understatement of the year," I chuckled as I rubbed my sore throat.

I stretched wide and stifled a yawn before asking Clint to return to the Exchange Hotel.

It was just after midnight when we approached the well-worn steps leading to our rooms. Gizzarelli staggered up to me in an alcohol-induced stupor and grabbed my shoulder with one hand and the back of my neck with the other, "You know that cunt, the one that killed Dimoska?"

The Doberman by my side stepped forwards and lifted her head with a snarl. As she exhibited the protective behaviours, I was pleasantly surprised that she already considered me a member of her pack. Gizzarelli hadn't yet dulled all of his brain cells, as he released me from his grip and shuffled back a step. He pointed his finger at my chest as he slurred, "He's hanging tomorrow, make sure you're there O'Connor."

I shortened the dog's lead and turned to walk up the stairs. "Get some sleep Gizza. I may see you on the train for the return trip, I've heard it's leaving at 7a.m."

I said goodnight to Fiona as we passed her room. "Come on Xena, it's time we get some rest. It's been a big night for the both of us."

"Xena. Where did you get that name from? It sounds Greek."

I patted Xena on the back of her neck. "I think it was a TV show from the 90s, something about a warrior princess. I don't know, it just sort of suits her."

Fiona unlocked and opened her room door. "Cool, I like it. Good night, Boss. Good night, Xena."

Chapter Twenty-Seven

Monday March 18, 2041 – Archie

I packed all of the documents, posters, and maps from the night before, and met Fiona downstairs at 6 a.m. We settled our tab with the assistant manager and walked out onto the busy street to witness an excited crowd. As I gripped Xena's lead, I noticed that her ears were pricked and her body was tense. On a purely instinctual level, she was likely sensing the tension in the mob and their anticipation of a violent death.

Samuel, the part-time executioner and full-time baker, was forcing the unwilling participant up the gallows stairs with the assistance of Senior Constable Atkins. The bruised and battered man who had his wrists tied together, was bucking left and right trying to break free as the two men lifted him onto the platform.

There was a larger security presence than normal. Armed police and hired guards anxiously observed the crowd. There must have been a concern that the Norse Men Gang would attempt a rescue.

Gizzarelli was standing at the front of the crowd, vigorously yelling obscenities at the condemned man. "Dead man fucking walking," he yelled.

I was momentarily taken aback after Fiona remarked, "I'm going to stay and watch the hanging."

With my eyebrows raised I asked, "Are you sure?" She nodded and stood on her toes to see over the heads of crowd. "Okay, I'll meet you at the train station. Just make sure you're there before a quarter to seven, or the train will leave you behind," I cautioned.

As I walked to the station, I contemplated whether I should

have tried to convince Fiona to forego the execution. I understand that she's no snowflake. Over the past eight weeks she's witnessed and participated in violent confrontations that have resulted in destruction and death. It's true that killing an unarmed man troubles me. As I'm rewarded for capturing the condemned men, I know full well that I could be considered a hypocrite. Nevertheless, I choose not to watch the man's neck break on the drop, or when the fortune of a quick death is absent, his asphyxiation as his body twitches and his bowels release.

My professor for legal ethics used a metaphor to discuss and debate the ramifications of mental health in the community. He asked students to envisage a glass jar sitting beside a bag of marbles. The jar represents our conscience and state of well-being, while the marbles represents loss, regret, and guilt. We are born with an empty jar, as we are innocent and free of negative emotions. As life delivers adverse and painful challenges, we are forced to deal with these negative emotions. Marbles are dropped into the jar as a consequence of failing to acknowledge, process and manage loss, regret, and guilt. As the jar fills, our mental well-being and ability to contribute to the community is diminished. If the jar overflows, individuals cease to function in a healthy manner, causing some to behave in harmful or violent ways, either towards themselves or others.

I've known for a while that my jar had been overflowing for years. But I'm working on returning some of those marbles to the bag. I just hope that watching the execution doesn't add another marble to Fiona's jar.

The locomotive engineers were busy completing last minute tasks before the old Diesel Train commenced her return journey to Northam. Steel plates of various shapes and sizes had been welded over bullet holes in a haphazard manner. Larry the train driver, exited the cab and walked down the steps to speak with the Kalgoorlie station manager. I stood within earshot in an attempt to overhear any concerns they may have for the return trip. The driver's biggest concern was being paid on-time, while the manager countered by reiterating the necessity of remaining on-schedule.

I approached and greeted them both, "Morning gentlemen." They acknowledged my salutation with a simple nod and then continued their debate. I interrupted, "So, do you have any concerns about the return trip?"

The station manager replied irritably, "No, we don't Archie, but if anything comes up you'll be the first person we speak to. Satisfied?"

He was very touchy this morning. I stepped forward with Xena and looked him dead in the eyes, "I currently have some trust issues concerning intel being passed on to me and the other guards. If either of you know anything that you're not telling me, and I find out, I'm going to visit you, and I won't be so polite."

The station manager instinctively took half a step back with eyes wide, "I think I know what your concerns are Archie, but I don't operate like that. What I know, you'll know."

"We won't have an issue then."

I noticed a group of guards milling around outside the station café.

The station manager grabbed my attention by raising his voice, "Oh, by the way Archie, you and Fiona will be riding in the cab today."

"Why is that?" I queried.

"Larry here has requested for experienced guards to ride in the cab," he disclosed. He glanced in Larry's direction. "You're a bit jittery, aren't you?"

Larry looked offended. "Can you blame me?" he retorted.

I remarked, "No problem, I was actually going to suggest it. And you get three for the price of two." I looked down and scratched Xena behind her ears as she wagged her tail.

"He's not going to shit in my cab, is he?" asked the driver.

My eyes narrowed. "She's not a *he*. And mate, that's the last thing you need to worry about."

As I turned my back and walked towards the café, I could hear him ask, "What is that supposed to mean?"

"You'll know soon enough," I whispered to myself.

I moseyed to the café and purchased a coffee and a carton of water.

I knelt and poured the water into a metal bowl that was secured by a chain to a metal post. I patted Xena and sipped my coffee as she greedily slurped the water. Fiona approached as the station manager blew his whistle to gather the guards for the briefing. As he stated the mission and assigned the positions, I glanced over at Fiona. She looked ashen and withdrawn. *I wondered, was that another marble in the jar?*

Chapter Twenty-Eight

Tuesday March 19, 2041 – Fiona

The thirteen-hour return journey was fortuitously uneventful. Thankfully, outlaws were not trying to kill us and capture the train on this occasion. The action inside the cab turned out to be far more interesting. Archie spent the first hour of the trip interrogating Larry about what he and Jack knew about the recent attack ahead of time. I had to hand it to Larry, Archie was verbally tightening the thumbscrews, but he didn't fold. It was not hard to see that Larry's obstinance was beginning to frustrate Archie. When Xena squatted and peed near the driver's chair, Archie went out of his way to congratulate her.

After his initial failure to loosen Larry's lips, Archie tried a more direct tack. As Larry sat in the driver's seat and looked out the windscreen, Archie invaded his personal space and warned, "Larry, listen to me very carefully. You know I'm a hunter and you know I'll get Jack to cough. He's going to throw you under the bus, or in this instance, the train. He's going to say you did a deal with the gang. Then you're up for MURDER mate. Who's going to believe different? You slowed the train, not him. You're going to hang in the main street in front of the mob."

Larry stammered, "I.... I.... I didn't know a gang was going to try and take the train. I mean, I heard rumours from other drivers that they were worried about gang activity, but I had no idea. I swear!"

Archie leaned back as Larry sat nervously in his chair. "Then why did you slow the train?" he rebuked.

He bleated, "The day before the trip Jack told me there was a new procedure in place. If we're under threat, we're to slow the train so the guards can respond. I told him that it didn't make sense and I hadn't heard anything about it from the other drivers. He then threatened me. He told me to do what I was told, or he'd fire me. I need this job. I've got five kids!"

"You keep this between you and me. If I find out you've lied to me, I'll drag you into the cop shop myself and march you to the gallows," Archie warned in a menacing tone.

For the remainder of the trip, Archie and I took turns scanning for threats in the distance, while examining the material we attained from the premises the night before. I gave up attempting to decipher the meaning of the scientific reports, but Archie continued to pore over the pages. We also discussed our next steps in locating Raj. For now, it appeared we'd hit a dead end. We agreed that our only option was to look for a new contract and keep moving.

Upon arrival at the Northam train station, Archie told me that he needed to have a quick word with Jack. He knocked on the Northam station manager's office door. As soon as Jack opened the door, Archie swiftly stepped in and grabbed him by his jacket lapels and slammed him against a six-foot tall metal cabinet. Archie lifted Jack's thin five-foot-eight frame off the ground, so they were at eye level.

"You sold us out and now you're going to pay for it," Archie snarled.

Jack stuttered, "W.... W.... What, what are you talking about?"

When Archie let go of his lapels, his back slid down the cabinet until his ass hit the ground. Archie grabbed Jack by his top knot and pressed the muzzle of his revolver against his forehead. "Five guards are dead because you did a DEAL!" Archie roared.

Jack let out a high-pitched squeal, "It's not my fault! They weren't supposed to hurt anyone! I didn't have a choice, I owe them gambling debts and they said if I didn't help them, they'd kill me."

I closed the office door to prevent any unnecessary interruptions. Interrogation was a part of the job that I definitely wanted to learn more about. Archie mentioned in passing that he was a contract lawyer before the War. Not knowing much about pre-War corporate life, I speculated whether he used similar techniques in gathering information from competitors.

Archie grabbed a chair and sat opposite Jack with Xena sitting beside him. "You still a single man Jack?"

Jack looked confused. "Ah, yes. Yes, I am."

Archie leaned forward so their noses were almost touching. "This is what you're going to do. You're going to empty your savings account, divvy it up and send it anonymously to the five guards' families. You are then going to resign from the locomotive industry and piss off up north. If you don't do what I ask by the end of next week, then I'll contact the police and the guards' families and friends and tell them what you did. I'll make sure I tell Gizzarelli in person. I'd rather hang any day than have that brutal bastard knocking on my door."

We left the office leaving Jack weeping on the floor with his head in his hands. Archie had a spring in his step as we strolled towards the train station carpark. He was looking forward to driving the Charger, which he'd nicknamed the 'Beast.' I feel sympathy for any girl that fancies him - she could never compete with his car or his horse. And now he has a dog.

Archie drove out from the carpark onto the bitumen of the main road. He couldn't help himself - he put the transmission in drive, firmly pressed down on the brake and revved the engine until the tyres spun and the rubber was smoking. Archie would have been a blast to hang around with as a teenager; someone I would have definitely got up to mischief with.

Chapter Twenty-Nine

Wednesday March 20, 2041 – Archie

We drove most of the night, arriving in Esperance at about 3 a.m. Upon parking the Beast at the top of Clarry's driveway, I said a quick hello to Clarry before introducing Xena to Zeus. Being dog-tired from the long trip, I was silently praying that the meeting between the two tough pooches would go smoothly. They began their greeting by touching noses, then sniffing the anogenital regions before investigating the back end. The big Rottweiler then emitted a series of deep throaty barks, making it clear that he was the boss of this territory. Xena appeared to accept the verdict and followed her new pal to the loungeroom. I wearily ambled to the stables and gave Roger a big hug before heading straight to bed.

Waking just before midday, it felt great to sleep in for once. When I sauntered out to the backyard, I was pleased to find the dogs playing as if they were old mates. Clarry was sitting on a garden chair under the pergola cleaning his pump-action shotgun. He had his Browning Lever Action .223 Rifle and Browning nine-millimetre pistol placed on the jigsaw mats alongside his cleaning kit.

I grabbed a chair and sat down beside him. "Morning mate," I said cheerfully.

"Hey," responded Clarry in a voice barely louder than a whisper.

I yawned loudly, stretching my arms out wide before relaxing back in my chair. "Fiona and I are fortunate that we're still alive and kicking. That Norse Men gang attempted to capture the train we were guarding. It's not good mate, they're buying informants."

When Clarry failed to respond, I asked, "You're not working

today?"

Clarry shook his head as he methodically picked up his rifle and commenced cleaning the sleek weapon. Clarry wasn't acting like his normal cheery self – his shoulders were slumped, and he wouldn't meet my eyes.

"Mate, what's wrong?"

He sniffed and wiped his eyes with the back of his hand before responding, "They killed my two cousins Archie. The two young brothers who'd kick the footy with you. After my mob arrives, we'll have our sorry business and then decide if we should join the militia when we seek our payback."

It's traditional Aboriginal law across Australia not to speak the dead family member's name, as they believe it will recall and disturb their spirit. Clarry was referring to Jeff and Pete. They were both fit young men who had a cheeky nature. Clarry made a habit of keeping the inseparable brothers out of mischief by finding them work and giving them advice when it was needed. When I was in town, I'd have a beer with them at the pub and then walk to the oval to have a kick of the footy. I found them to be good natured blokes who worked hard and played even harder.

"What happened Clarry? Who killed them?"

Clarry's mood changed like the flick of a switch. He was incensed. "They were dancing with some of their women at the pub, so they beat them and then lynched them in the main street."

"Whose women Clarry?"

"Those Norse Men fuckers you were just talking about. I'll kill them all Archie, every last one of them. My cousins must be avenged so their spirits can rest."

"I'll help you brother," I pledged.

I picked up Clarry's pistol and sat with him cleaning the weapons in silence.

By mid-afternoon, Clarry was cooking a barbeque as I rubbed down the horses. Clarry had butchered two roos and three pigs. I was forced to multi-task when Xena and Zeus conscripted me to throw the tennis ball around the yard.

Fiona walked from the house and greeted us all. She looked embarrassed when I teased her, "Good afternoon sleepy head."

She ambled over to Clarry. "Something smells real good. Wow, you cooking for an army?"

"Yep, I'm cooking for a Noongar and Wongutha Army," declared Clarry. He grinned before adding, "Of course, I'm also cooking up a storm for my pale sister and my mongrel brother over there."

"It's appreciated Clarry, let me know if you need any help," Fiona offered.

Fiona picked up the ball that Xena dropped at my feet and ditched it towards the side fence. Both dogs chased it down enthusiastically, with Xena getting to the ball first, but swiftly backing away when Zeus came barrelling forward.

"Archie, what does he mean by army?" Fiona murmured.

"He's talking about his extended family. Two of his cousins were murdered by the NMG, so they'll be seeking payback."

"NMG?" she quizzed.

"Norse Men Gang. NMG is easier to pronounce, especially when using it in a sentence with Norseman."

"What does payback involve?" she asked.

"That depends on what the family decides. But they believe a man's death has to be avenged before his spirit can rest. They may go it alone or they may join the militia. That is, if the town agrees to raise the militia."

She placed her hands on her hips. "Well, I guess we'll be joining his family, no matter what. And before you say anything, you know I want revenge for Lau, so yes, I'll be coming."

I pondered, how many marbles is this going to add to the jar?

Clarry's extended family arrived in small groups, with members travelling from all parts of the South-western corner and Eastern Goldfields of Western Australia. The proud men and women belong to what is considered as one of the oldest living cultures in the world, which is both rich in respect for the land and spiritual beliefs in the Dreamtime. Clarry explained that all life - human, animal, bird, and fish - is a part of a vast enduring network of relationships which can be traced back to the great spirit ancestors of the Dreamtime. At the time of creation these ancestor beings broke through the crust of the earth with tumultuous force, creating all that we see today, including the sun, moon, and stars. Wearied from their exertion, they descended back into the earth, returning to their state of sleep.

I mingled with the family members as we ate the roo burgers and pork kebabs, many of whom I had already met during happier times. Once everyone looked satisfied from chowing down on Clarry's bush tucker, the Elders moved under the pergola and sat on the jigsaw mats to discuss the murder of the brothers. I stood with Fiona and watched the proceedings from afar. Clarry respectfully waited for his Elders to be seated before entering the pergola and taking his place in the circle.

Almost two hours later, Clarry and the Elders exited the gym and sat on the grassed area near the barbecue. Two of the Elders moved between the family and spoke softly. They all sat on the grass. Members of the group started to cry and share their grief. Clarry invited Fiona and I to sit and mourn with the family, which we were both honoured to do.

~

As the sun went down, Clarry asked Fiona and me to speak with him in private. The three of us sat at the kitchen table, with both Zeus and Xena resting at our feet, worn out from chasing after the ball for most of the afternoon.

Clarry cleared his throat, "The Elders have made a decision to invoke payback. They have given me the responsibility of representing the mob at tomorrow's council meeting."

Clarry explained that the Esperance Council was holding a community meeting to decide whether they should invoke the Militia and rescue the residents of Norseman. We both agreed to attend the meeting with Clarry.

As per my normal practice I woke for an early start – what my grandfather would refer to as 'at a sparrow-fart.' After giving my room to the Elders I had bedded down on the couch. I carefully extracted my feet from under Xena's body, not wanting to wake her unnecessarily. Fiona was making breakfast and handed me a much-needed coffee. My morning plan was to take Roger out for a ride on the beach and run the dogs. As I smeared Vegemite on my toast, I asked Fiona if she'd like to join me. She declined as she'd been invited by the female Elders to participate in Women's Business. Women Elders play a pivotal part in the family, nurturing the emotional and spiritual wellbeing of the young ladies. These events can involve ceremonies and rituals that are both colourful and socially significant. I knew better than to ask about the day's activities, as Women's Business was gender-specific practices that encompass strict rules.

I rode Roger on the shoreline with Jasper following closely behind. The seventy-metre cliffs of the cove provided an awe-inspiring backdrop. The dogs ran in and out of the water as the waves crashed onto the sand. I saw kids laughing and throwing a ball to each other, while another group were climbing into a cave hollowed from an enormous rock. When I was a kid, I'd climb into that very cave and pretend to be a pirate or soldier. I would then dry off by running along the wide sweeping beach, crushing the white sand and tiny shells underfoot. Watching the kids run and play without a care in the world made me feel hopeful for the future. One of the boys picked up a curved stick, pretending to shoot his mate as he ducked and dived over the sand dunes. My mind instantly switched to the upcoming battle and my mood darkened.

~

I threw the Beast's keys to Clarry. "As promised mate, you can drive."

Clarry drove us to the Esperance Council substantially quicker than we needed to travel. He whooped all the way there like a kid in a candy store, taking the corners hard and fast and opening her up as she entered the straight.

The façade of the council building was curved, with large dark glass windowpanes reflecting the Australian, Torres Strait Islander and Aboriginal flags that were hanging from poles at the front of the building.

Clarry parked the Beast in one of the last available spaces in the packed Council carpark. Inside the Council chambers were men and women of all ages, cultures and backgrounds talking amongst themselves, some standing, and others seated, but all eagerly waiting for the start of the proceedings. A grey-haired lady was serving coffee and biscuits behind a large plastic table. A rotund mother gave her mischievous son a smack on the backside for grabbing a handful of Anzac biscuits when he thought she wasn't looking. These men and women were not soldiers - they were farmers, miners, store owners, butchers, transport workers and a myriad of other occupations.

Sergeant Lee, the most senior Esperance police officer, stood behind a long oak desk with the Esperance Mayor standing beside him. Mayor Jason was a fit and sturdy man who worked part-time as a plumber. He had once held the State record for running four marathons in a week, all completed in under two and a half hours. He motioned for Clarry to come to the front of the room and join them. Clarry had worked with Sergeant Lee to rid the Town of a S.A. bikie gang that had attempted to take over the town centre. Sergeant Lee was a short Scotsman with a shiny bald head, who was known for his no-nonsense nature and expertise in Kung Fu. It was no surprise to those that met him that his nickname was Bruce after the famous martial-art actor of the 1970s.

I noticed Senior Constable Atkins leaning against the side wall in an attempt to distance himself from the crowd. Curious to find out why he was here, I weaved my way through the crowd. "I didn't think I'd see you making the trip from Kal," I stated facetiously.

"My Sergeant volunteered me due to the number of local residents that are joining this crazy undertaking," Atkins replied glumly.

I'm sure Kalgoorlie's Sergeant wasn't going to miss him I pondered.

Having known him for many years, I wasn't at all surprised by his poor attitude. "What, you don't think we should free Norseman?" I asked with eyebrows raised.

Atkins looked at me disapprovingly. "Talk it up Archie, the gun for hire lecturing me? Why risk our lives? Let Norseman look after themselves. Most of the people here are going to get themselves killed, and most likely me along with them. Anyway, how much are you getting paid to join up?"

"I'm not doing this for coin," I refuted.

It was not unheard of for Militias to employ guns for hire to assist in protecting a town from gangs. Fiona and I agreed that we 'd provide our assistance at no charge. It didn't feel right to take coin from the community. Besides, it was personal for the both of us, with what happened to Lau still fresh in Fiona's mind, and my determination to support Clarry revenge his cousins' murder.

The sharp thud of the wood gavel striking the sound block three times echoed through the chambers. The crowd came to attention and the mayor asked everyone to take a seat so the meeting could commence. With a coffee and biscuit in our grasp, Fiona and I found a seat in the row second from the back.

The mayor started the proceeding. "I'd like to thank you all for attending tonight's meeting and want to especially acknowledge those that have made the journey from Kalgoorlie. I'd like to start by making the purpose of this gathering crystal clear. As you'd be aware, Norseman was ambushed and is currently occupied by an outlaw gang who refer to themselves as the Norse Men Gang. We must decide tonight whether we're going to form a militia to rescue the Norseman residents and rid the town of these depraved degenerates."

A diminutive middle-aged man sitting three rows from the front, stood from his chair and with a confident voice stated, "With all due respect mayor, I've heard from a reliable source that this gang is heavily armed and well organised. Even if we succeed in freeing the town, many of the people in this room may not survive. Should we not err on the side of caution and protect our northern border?"

There was a murmur from within the crowd, with pockets of citizens supporting his position. I couldn't help but notice Atkins nodding his head in agreement.

Sergeant Lee cleared his throat, "If you don't mind mayor, I'd like to address this statement. You make a good point sir, but our concern is that Norseman is the NMG's first conquest, and Esperance or even Kalgoorlie will be next. If we don't take the opportunity to stand up now and purge the State of this gang, they may grow too large for us to deal with in the future. We don't have the resources to fortify a border, and do you all want to live in fear for the unforeseeable future?"

An elderly woman stood, resting her arthritic hands on the back rest of the chair in front. "I agree with Sergeant Lee, but what do we know about this gang? How many are there? What weapons do they have? Do they have hostages? We need these questions answered before we drive into Norseman all willy-nilly."

The sergeant looked at Clarry who nodded and stood to face the crowd. "My name is Clarence, I'm here today representing my mob. I fought with many of you last year when we chased the bikie gang from our town. I've felt great shame since hearing what has occurred in Norseman, as I haven't lifted a finger to help them. I wish I could tell you that I'm here today to right a wrong for the sake of our brothers and sisters in Norseman, but the truth is, this has become very personal for me. These animals lynched two of my cousins for chatting up a couple of ladies in a pub, right here is Esperance. Twenty-three of my mob have arrived in town to mourn our loss. They've decided to seek payback with the intention of joining the militia. They hope to join all of you. Now, I understand that many of you are concerned about the gang's resources. That's why I'd like to nominate Archie O'Connor to plan the rescue mission. Please stand-up Archie and say hello."

Everyone in the room turned around to pinpoint the man he was speaking of – I just wish that it didn't happen to be me. I thought, *you bastard Clarry*, it would have been nice if you had asked me first before putting me on the spot. I reluctantly stood from my seat and comfortable anonymity.

Clarry boomed, "My friend here has military experience. He was a corporal who served in Darwin when the enemy was on our doorstep. You may have heard of the soldiers who rescued twelve nurses captured by the enemy. This man was one of those soldiers. He's a hero."

I could feel the heat rising in my cheeks, suspecting they were as red as a beetroot. Fiona lifted her chin and looked up at me with a surprised expression. When the War commenced, I was a corporal in the Army Reserves serving with the Eleventh Battalion. We were sent to Darwin to join the First Battalion; our mission was to repel the invading force. It was a messy bloody battle, with both sides fighting to a stalemate. During the final days of the campaign my team rescued a group of civilian nurses who were being held captive on an enemy frigate. I don't consider myself a hero. I was just a soldier doing my duty like every other man and woman that served.

The mayor stepped forward. "Thank you, Clarence, for your honesty and recommendation. I'd like to put forward a motion. I propose that we provide Archie O'Connor three days to prepare a plan of action and present it to the Town Committee. Raise your hand if you say *yay* to this proposal."

All but a select few of staunch residents surveyed the crowd before making their decision. About two thirds of the crowd raised their hand to support the motion. As I raised my hand I had already started to strategise and consider my options.

After the meeting was closed, Clarry stayed to mingle with select members of the crowd - those who he believed would be crucial in supporting the raising of the militia. As I sipped on a coffee, residents patiently waited their turn to approach me; some were probing for answers to their concerns, while others didn't hesitate to provide unsolicited advice. One particular lady wanted to know if I was free for dinner. I was non-committal to all of their queries, including the dinner date.

We were almost the last to leave the Council carpark. I drove at a snail's pace so as to give me time to berate him without the presence of his family. "What the hell Clarry? Talk about dobbing me in!" I exclaimed with a furrowed brow.

"What do you mean?" he replied with an angelic expression.

"You know what I mean," I responded in frustration.

Clarry turned in his seat towards Archie and raised his palms. "Okay, in all seriousness, I should have talked to you first. And I'm sorry about that, but in truth I didn't even come up with the idea until I saw the reluctance of the crowd. And answer me this, who's the best person to develop the plan? Who lives by the motto, proper planning and preparation prevents piss poor performance? And Archie, who do you trust to do it better?" he asked in earnest.

Fiona chimed in, "Shit Clarry, you sure you weren't a lawyer?"

Clarry smiled. "Nah, I was far too smart to be a lawyer. Fiona, what do you call a lawyer with an above average IQ?"

Fiona leaned forward, "What?"

Clarry chuckled before answering, "Your honour."

I rolled my eyes and put the pedal to the metal. I was keen on being alone with my thoughts.

Chapter Thirty

March 21 – 22, 2041 – Archie

From 10 p.m. to 3 a.m. in the morning, I laid on Clarry's couch staring up at the ceiling and contemplating how we could achieve the mission. The mission was clear: To free Norseman and rescue the residents. However, the objectives, strategies, and tactics to achieve the mission alluded me for one simple reason – *our woeful intel.* The wise old lady with the gnarled hands was dead on; we have no idea about the specifics of when, where, who, how, what, and why? I had made my decision. It was the only plausible course of action that would provide us the intelligence required to develop a plan that had any chance of avoiding mass casualties and succeeding in the mission. From 3 a.m. to sunrise I deliberated on how I could convince Clarry and Fiona that my idea, however crazy it sounded, was our best and only option.

As the sunlight streamed through the side of the blinds, I could hear Clarry bellowing, "Play outside!" The kids playfully darted through the kitchen, chasing the dogs to the backyard as they screamed with delight. As soon as I sauntered into the kitchen, Clarry's auntie wished me a good morning and handed me a plate of bacon and scrambled eggs and a mug of coffee. I planted a kiss on her cheek and sat down at the dining table. Clarry was swallowing the last bite of his breakfast and gazed fixedly at my plate.

"Don't even think about it mate," I warned jokingly.

I decided that now was as good a time as any to enlighten Clarry of my plan. To his credit, he didn't interrupt me while I delivered my spiel, but I could tell by his expression that he wasn't keen on the idea.

After I'd concluded my closing argument, he shook his head while I reached for my coffee. "It's too risky Archie. Going into the belly of the beast unarmed without backup, is without doubt, utterly insane! Does Fiona know about this barmy idea?"

I took another sip and then explained, "I wanted to talk to you first. Look, the old lady last night was spot-on, going into battle with untrained butchers and bakers with next to no intel is far too risky. My strategy risks one life. Going in blind risks hundreds."

Fiona walked into the kitchen rubbing her eyes and yawning. "Why do you both look so serious?"

"Archie, tell Fiona your *not* so bright idea," Clarry said in exasperation.

I sighed and pushed my plate of bacon and eggs to the centre of the table. Clarry's refusal to support my plan had caused my loss of appetite. Fiona grabbed the plate as Clarry's fingers were centimetres from the edge of the porcelain.

"Clarry is going to drop me off ten kays out of Norseman, so I can walk into town and gather some intel. That way I can develop a plan that won't get us all killed! I've thought about this all night, it's the only way."

Fiona's jaw dropped. I was about to tell her to eat with her mouth closed when she spluttered egg and bacon all over the table. "Is this some sort of weird joke?"

Clarry shook his head. "Nope, and he forgot to add the kicker. He wants to be dropped off unarmed in the middle of the goddamn day!"

Fiona glared at me with a confused expression. "Sorry, have I missed the punchline? No disrespect Boss, but this just sounds bloody crazy."

There was no point in going around in circles and I wanted to cease the discussion before I became frustrated and angry. "This is happening, there's nothing more to discuss. We're all going to be tooled up in case we come across any outlaws on the way to the drop-off. Be ready in three hours," I stated brusquely, leaving no room for debate.

I stood up from the table and marched to the gym to stretch and perform my breathing exercises. It was important to clear my mind for the trials and tribulations that I was about to face.

~

I was sitting in the back seat of the Beast, dressed in a worn pair of black denim jeans, a ripped muscle top and some old black Dunlop sneakers. For almost the entire two-hour journey we were as quiet as church mice; Clarry and Fiona were understandably worried about me, and I was deep in thought.

Clarry pulled over to the side of the road about ten kilometres from the edge of town. I swiftly exited the vehicle with my sole possession - a bottle of bootleg whisky. Admittedly, I was feeling a little naked without my revolver and knife.

I bent down to meet their eyes through the opened driver's side window, "Meet me back here tomorrow night at 9 p.m. If I'm not here, don't wait around, I'll make my own way back."

Clarry clasped my hand with a firm grip. "Good luck mate. If the shit hits the fan you hightail it out of town. No one's going to think any worse of you. You hear me brother?"

"Understood mate, now get going."

Fiona hollered, "Good luck Boss!" as the Beast accelerated down the highway, the heat shimmering off the bitumen.

After I stepped over the train tracks, I had a good look around to gain my bearings before heading directly into the bush. I opened the bottle of whisky and poured half the contents over my shirt and jeans. As I walked through the scrub I stepped on twigs, dry grass, and leaves, mindful that arriving clandestinely was not an objective.

I was being watched with curiosity by an emu that stood at least six-foot tall with his long neck extended. "How you going old man emu?" I asked him as he gave me a puzzled look before darting into the bush. I trekked at a steady pace for about forty-five minutes, only stopping when I saw the outline of homes through the gaps in the scrub and eucalyptus trunks. My mind was racing as I took a large swig of whisky and then poured the brown liquid into the cup of my hand. I rubbed the spirit into my hair and scalp. It was time to put this crazy plan into action. "I hope this pays off," I whispered to myself. I took a deep breath and transformed into my character, Junior Tilo, a drunkard brawler searching for his runaway wife.

As I staggered down the suburban street, I held the whisky bottle by its neck, slack jawed and acting barely conscious. Stumbling from one street to the next, I observed and made mental notes - counting every man, woman, and firearm. One of my best attributes when I practiced law was my keen memory. I could cite legislation by rote and recall obscure case law when addressing a Magistrate or rebutting a colleague off-the-cuff. I rarely needed to refer to a legal text.

The NMG were easy to identify; they were either wearing their leather jackets with patches or exhibited their gang tattoo of a bearded skull on their right forearm. Each time I turned a street corner I mentally calculated the numbers - 15 NMGs, 8 rifles, 2 shotguns, 12 pistols, 8 assault rifles.

Before the gang captured the town, there were about 250 residents doing their best to survive and eke out a living. Being the closest major town to the S.A. border is a double-edged sword; there are advantages in trade, but there are also greater risks of crime and gang violence. The S.A. Government lost control of their jurisdiction in the late-thirties, with the decimation of their police force and local councils. This structural collapse resulted in the surge of gangs crossing the border and behaving like Vikings in Europe during the tenth century - with raids, theft, rape, and slavery becoming a common occurrence.

The odd NMG thug would yell or jeer at me as I shuffled down the streets, but I was yet to be physically accosted. I noticed men and women in neck-irons, either chained to metal posts in front yards or being dragged by their enslavers. It was fair to assume that all of the residents had been enslaved. Faced with the reality of the situation, it was shockingly worse than I had imagined. A majority of the residents I came across had been viciously beaten, with bruising, cuts, and swelling apparent on their faces, arms, and legs. My heart broke when I saw a young girl being dragged by a neck chain to a nearby house by an NMG soldier. It took every ounce of my willpower to stop myself from running over to the house and freeing her. My mind was reeling with *outrage* - that an innocent kid would be forced to endure such an ordeal, and *shame* - that I chose to keep walking and ignore her torment. The overwhelming feeling of impotence and anger induced me to bite down hard on my tongue, splitting the flesh so the metallic taste of blood swirled down my throat. As I maintained my drunken façade, I took note of the home's unusual post box, a converted wine barrel, and peered up at the street sign – '*Fuller Street*'.

After ambling for about twenty minutes, I came to a roundabout that had a large town clock sitting in the centre of an island - it was 3:30 p.m. A large black and white picture of Sinclair and his horse, '*Hardy Norseman*,' was fastened to the exterior second level wall of the town's hotel. I felt a sense of relief that Roger was not walking alongside me and exposed to the danger I was confronted with.

An old white school bus was parked opposite the hotel. NMG guards pushed and shoved a line of male and female residents through the side door of the bus. There was misery etched on their wretched faces. One of the guards pointed and shouted at me. In haste I entered the front door of the hotel. A mixture of stale beer, body odour and blood filled my nostrils. The hotel was packed to the brim with armed outlaws. I quickly performed my mental arithmetic before the curtains parted and the show commenced.

Slouching near the pool table in the centre of the hotel I yelled in a slurred speech, "Where's my CUNT OF A WIFE? She's a runaway, *BURP*.........I want her back, NOOOWW!"

For a split second there was silence, then laughter, and then violence, brutal and unabated violence. The first blow to the back of my head shouldn't have come as a surprise, but it's the punch that you don't see coming that hurts you the most. The impact caused me to fall forwards and stagger, but somehow, I managed to regain my balance and remain standing. Just as I started to recover my faculties I felt the second blow to my temple. I wish I could say that the sensation of dizziness, nausea and ringing in the ears was not a familiar one. As soon as I hit the ground I rolled up into a ball, covering my ribs and kidneys with my knees and elbows, while protecting my face, neck, and solar plexus with my forearms.

Fortunately, a majority of the kicks and stomps were striking my arms and legs. Throughout the ordeal I tensed my abdominal muscles and focused on staying conscious, silently repeating – 42 NMGs, 25 rifles, 8 shotguns, 21 pistols, 12 assault rifles.

I heard a deep gravelly voice with a Samoan accent yell, "The young blood's had enough." I felt another two or three blows before I heard, "Did you FUCKEN not hear me BRUVVERS?"

A giant Samoan in his mid-fifties stepped forward and gazed down at me, "Hey bro, do you come from the islands?"

I gingerly removed my forearms from my face and performed my best attempt at a Māori accent, "I'm from Tonga, but grew up in New Zealand."

"What's your name?" he asked.

"Junior Tilo. Thanks for helping me Uncle."

"You want to join a gang bro?"

"Yes Uncle."

"Then stop cowering on the ground like some pussy and stand-up like a man. Let the brothers see you."

While attempting to clear the fog from my brain, I rose gingerly from the sticky floorboards and rested my elbows on the green felt of the pool table. The Samoan turned to face the men in the bar and raised his hands in the air, "Who here wants to initiate this man into our club?"

I very much doubted that the initiation ritual involved a civil vote, with each member deciding whether to raise their hands to vote Yay or Nay. "If nobody steps forward, then I'll do it," the giant Samoan bellowed.

A muscular man in his mid-thirties with a shaved head and swastika tattoo on his neck stepped forward, "I'll gladly do it Iokua. I wouldn't want anyone accusing you of going easy on him because he's a bro."

In response, the big Samoan glared at the agitator, as if goading him to say more. He then suddenly turned his back to the man, leaned in close to my ear and spoke in a low tone, "I've thrown you the rope cuz, it's up to you to pull yourself to safety. Fuck him up good and I'll buy ya a beer."

The NMG moved bar tables, stools and even the pool table, clearing a five square meter area. They then formed a human circular barrier with Skinhead and me standing at the centre. Sadly, the initiation was not a game of darts or snooker, but a bare-knuckle no-holds barred contest. *A fight with no rules.*

Five hundred years before Christ, Sun Tzu, the Chinese General who wrote the *Art of War*, preached '*Know the enemy and know yourself.*' As I stretched my neck muscles and cleared my head, I analysed my opponent - critiquing his body type, height, reach, size, features, and the way he moved and stood. I noted the knotted scar tissue above his eyebrows and across his forehead, and his thickly calloused knuckles. He may look like an experienced fighter, but I could take advantage of his scarring by striking and cutting the tissue to encourage blood to flow into his eyes. I was still feeling a little unsteady from the solid punch to my temple, so I was hoping that his previous fights had made him vulnerable to head strikes.

Even though I had beaten all but two of the opponents I'd faced, a majority of them were untrained fighters. Once I'd weathered my opponent's initial storm of punches and kicks, their adrenalin spike would inevitably dip, leaving them fatigued and exposed to my attack. My experience in the cage is what gave me the real advantage, not my skill or cardio. It was my ability to control my breathing and adjust my tactics to take advantage of my opponent's weaknesses and avoid their strengths. I was under no illusion that Skinhead would follow the script and throw caution to the wind until he tires.

Skinhead probably outweighed me by at least fifteen kilos, but I had a height and reach advantage. He brought his fists to his jaw, raised his shoulders, slightly dipped his chin, and stood with his feet shoulder width apart in an orthodox stance. As I stretched my arms and rolled my shoulders, I was relieved that although the bashing had left me bruised, battered and a little woozy, I'd escaped any serious injuries such as broken bones or torn tendons.

The crowd roared and cheered for Skinhead. Surprisingly, a small group in the crowd were actually cheering for me. Either they were partial to supporting the underdog or had a beef with their comrade and wanted him to lose. Men started to place bets as Skinhead threw a jab, corkscrewing his knuckles towards my face. I reacted swiftly by darting back beyond his reach. He followed up by stepping forward and throwing an overhand right, which I desperately managed to block with my lead forearm.

I felt hands in my back violently push me towards my opponent, who took advantage of the crowd's involvement by delivering a right hook that careened into my jaw. My vision blurred as I was knocked off balance. I chastised myself – '*Come on, switch on, it's time to get to work.*'

I stepped slightly forward and launched a traditional Muay Thai kick, striking him to the outside of his lead thigh with the middle of my shin.

He grimaced in pain and shouted, "I'm going to fucking stomp your monkey brain."

It was just the reaction for which I was hoping for. Angry fighters are foolish fighters, who focus on their rage instead of their breathing and tactics.

Skinhead threw a jab-cross combination which I countered with a front kick - raising my front leg and kicking him to his lower abdominal muscles with the sole of my Dunlops and driving him back two steps. Taking advantage of my momentum, I stepped forwards and slightly to the right, kicking him with my left shin to his lower ribs. Just after my toes returned to the floor, I followed up with a right cross to his jaw. He almost crumbled to the ground as I circled to his left. A glass or bottle bounced off my back and I heard men in the crowd shouting abuse. The crowd roared with encouragement, baying for violence and blood.

The fascist shit was persistent and tough, I'll give him that. My kick-punch combination would have dropped most men to their knees. Spittle flew from his mouth as he screamed an indecipherable slur and swung a right fisted haymaker towards my temple. I bobbed and weaved under his punch and threw an uppercut to his jaw, rocking his head violently back. I looked on in shock when he shook his head, snarled, and stepped towards me. *What do I have to do to put this bloke's lights out?*

Skinhead had obviously decided that he no longer wanted to box, as he rushed forward to tackle me to the ground. This was to my advantage as I could tell by his technique that he was anything but a wrestler. And with my black belt in Brazilian Jiu-jitsu (BJJ) and years of grappling experience, I'd have a distinct advantage on the ground. Unbeknownst to Skinhead, he was stepping into my world. I surprised him by pulling him into my guard, placing my foot on his hip, grabbing the back of his neck and arm, and controlling our descent to the ground.

My back was on the ground with Skinhead on top looking down on me. I had wrapped my legs around his waist, holding his hips and torso so close that it would appear almost intimate. Those in the crowd unfamiliar with grappling would view the position as some form of homoerotic posture, while their counterparts would cotton on to my game plan. Skinhead grinned with confidence, clearly unaware that this is where I chose to be. He threw a punch downwards towards my face. His knuckles glanced off my forearm. As he brought his fist back, I slipped my leg over his neck and locked his head and arm between my inner thighs. I performed a triangle choke – squeezing the arteries in his neck so tight that I blocked the blood flow to his brain. As his eyes flickered and he was about to lose consciousness, I whispered in his ear, "You've lost, now go to sleep, you Nazi piece of crap!"

The small group of men that had wagered on my win cheered boisterously and gloated animatedly when collecting their winnings. Iokua helped me to my feet and escorted me to the bar, ordering me a pint of lager.

He laughed, "You've got some skills cuz." He raised his glass and bellowed, "Welcome to the Norse Men." I guzzled the beer and pretended to be pleased about my newfound membership. "I'll take you over to the clubhouse where they'll organise your quarters and give you a gun and jacket." Iokua looked over at Skinhead who was still comatose on the floor. "We best get going before Gilly wakes up. I've never seen him lose a fight, but I've seen him lose at darts and he's a fucken sore loser!"

We walked some 200 metres to the former Council office, where I was introduced to a well-groomed young man with thick dark rimmed glasses. He looked more like a librarian than a member of an outlaw gang. The big Samoan introduced me, "This is Jarrad, he'll get you all sorted. We'll catch up later and talk some more. I've got some shit to do."

As soon as Iokua left the building, Jarrad handed me a set of keys and two documents. "This is your key to eighty Talbot Street. Please fill in this form. As you can see, I've also given you a map of the town." The document resembled a gym membership form. I scrawled Junior Tilo in the first box and completed the document.

"So Jarrad, how long have you been in the gang?" I asked inquisitively.

"I'm not a member of the gang sir. I am still one of the lucky ones though," he explained.

"What do you mean by that?" I asked. When I observed that the young man was reluctant to answer, I said, "Hey Jarrad, I'm not one to Judge. I've just joined up, so tell it to me straight."

Jarrad looked down at his feet solemnly. "Most of my friends are either working in the mines or are sex slaves. Three of them died during the first night. I'm just grateful that my younger brother is working in the kitchen, and I've got this job."

"Well, Jarrad, keep working hard and before you know it, you'll be patched up," I told him, regretful that I had to maintain my deception.

I handed him back the form. "What now?"

Jarrad reached under the table and issued me an old nine-millimetre Beretta pistol, a leather jacket, and a red card. "The red card is both your meal and ammo pass. The address of the canteen and armoury is typed on the back of the card. Would you like a lady for the night?"

"No, I'll be right."

Jarrad coughed. "Um, I could also send you a boy or a girl. I mean, you might need work done around the house."

Rather than feeling angry and disgusted by his proposal, I just felt sorry for the kid. I noticed severe bruising around his neck and pushed the horrible thoughts to the back of my mind. "I'm exhausted Jarrad, and I've only just been initiated into the club as you can see by my face. I'll pass on the lady tonight and I'll never need any help around the house. I'm quite handy."

Jarrad nodded his understanding before continuing. "You'll be working as a guard at the mine. The bus leaves outside the hotel at 6:30 a.m. and returns at 9 p.m."

I slipped on the leather jacket and sauntered towards the armoury with the empty pistol secured in the back of my jeans. I found it somewhat ironic that the gang had selected the police station to store their weapons, but I guess it was the most practical location. As I passed outlaws in the street, I continued my mental arithmetic. Now that I had the luxury of observing facial and body features, I could avoid doubling up on my count.

A severely thin man with sunken eyes, shallow cheeks and a long wispy beard was sitting behind a desk completing a crossword puzzle with his feet up. I pondered whether he was the inspiration for the NMG patch. I handed him my red card and placed my pistol on the counter. "Mate, I'm newly initiated and I need some nine-millimetre ammo."

He acted as if I'd just asked him to build the Sydney Harbour Bridge. He lethargically pushed his chair back from the desk and approached the counter. "Come on then, I'll take you out the back so you can fill your pockets," he explained irritably.

The skeleton led me to an office at the rear of the station that was previously used by constables to complete their paperwork. The gang possessed a considerable number of rifles and pistols laid out on the office desks. About 200 boxes of various calibres of ammunition were piled up on the floor. I couldn't see any assault rifles or shotguns. Either they'd all been issued, or they were short of longarms. I promptly continued my mental count as I reached for two boxes of nine-millimetre rounds.

There was no hurt in asking, "Are there any shotguns or assault rifles you can issue me?"

The skeleton chuckled. "You've only been here two minutes fella. Only senior members are given high powered weapons."

"Duly noted, but if you can requisition me a rifle it would be much appreciated," I replied.

He stroked his wispy beard with a puzzled look. "That's fancy pantsy talking. What did you do before the War?"

I internally chastised myself for acting out of character. "I worked in an abattoir. But I'm pretty good with big words as my mum made me attend Sunday School *religiously* each week. Excuse the pun."

As he cackled, I noticed he had only three remaining teeth. "I see what you did there. Very clever. When I'm stuck on my crossword, I'm gonna seek you out."

"No problem, you do that Skel.....I mean mate."

I left the skeleton musing over his crossword puzzle and continued on my journey to the canteen, which was situated at the Railway Motel. As I moseyed through the hotel doors, I nodded a greeting to the outlaw standing guard. I added one NMG and a shotgun to my count. The residents working in the canteen were free of chains so they could move freely and serve their masters. The guard with the shotgun was enough of a deterrent for residents with ideas of escape to think otherwise.

Within sixty seconds of sitting down at a table, I was served a plate of chicken and rice by a poor dishevelled girl who moved and looked like a zombie – cold, vacant, and soulless. I stopped myself from reaching out and giving her hope, immediately recognising the feeling for what it was - *a foolish sentiment that would achieve nothing but get us both killed.*

I ate quickly and then used the map to locate the premises Jarrad had issued me – 80 Talbot Street. My ribs ached when I opened the fridge door. I couldn't believe my good luck. A bucket of ice was sitting in the freezer compartment. I wondered if Jarrad had anything to do with this. I wrapped the ice in a tea towel I found in the kitchen and rested it on my forearms and ribs. Before drifting off to sleep in a rickety old bed, I recited – '51 NMGs, 32 rifles, 12 shotguns, 32 pistols, 15 assault rifles'.

~

I woke with a throbbing headache and aches in muscles I didn't even know I had. I glanced at my watch - 5:30 a.m. Sitting on the floor in the loungeroom, I stretched my hamstrings and performed my breathing exercise to prepare for the day ahead. After I had a quick shower, I left the house and walked to the Norseman hotel, arriving just before 6:30 a.m. Two lines of residents were waiting on the side of the road with neck-irons securing them to the person in front and behind them.

An NMG guard wearing blue overalls under his bomber jacket sauntered over to me, "Are you the new guard?"

I nodded an affirmative. "I've been told I'm working at the mine."

"Good, because I need to get some breakfast. When the bus arrives, load the cattle on and I'll be back before you can say, 'I'm an ugly fucker'." Mr Overalls gave me a wink before marching towards the direction of the canteen.

There were twenty-four chained residents waiting to be transported to the mine. As I waited for the bus to arrive, I speculated where they kept the residents at night. I couldn't risk talking to the residents, so I spent my time silently repeating my guard and weapons count. The sudden arrival of the bus broke my reverie.

The bus door opened. "Come on, get them on the bus, we don't have all bloody day," grumbled the driver.

I gained eye-contact with the middle-aged resident standing at the front of the line. "On you get," I ordered dispassionately. He didn't move. He just gazed into the distance. When I reached for his upper-arm to guide him onto the bus, he flinched backwards and almost stumbled into the woman behind him. I hated myself for it, but I had no choice, I grabbed his neck chain and forced him up the steps. I had to push him down into the rear seat. Fortunately, the other residents automatically sat in the seats leading to the front of the vehicle.

I was about to exit the bus to grab the second line of residents, when Mr Overalls with a muffin in his mouth roughly dragged the unfortunate people up the steps. Once they were all seated, the driver honked the horn and drove us down the main road to the underground gold mine - situated just outside the townsite. The slavery of the residents shouldn't have shocked me. Humans had practiced slavery since the proliferation of agriculture 11,000 years ago. Even in the modern era prior to World War Three, forty million people a year were sold across the globe; bought through sex trafficking, forced labour, child soldiers and forced marriages.

The driver parked the bus near the mine administration building. We escorted the line of captives from the bus to the awaiting guards, who issued them their work tasks. A group of adults and male teenagers were separated from the two lines.

A filthy young NMG guard with a toothless grin pointed at me, "You're new, so you're gonna go down the tunnel wiv em," he barked.

Three guards joined me in escorting the chained residents to the tunnel; a decline mine dug into the side of the rock-face to allow workers and machinery to reach the ore. One of the guards unlocked their neck-chains and pushed them into the mine, yelling at them to start working.

The underground gold mine had been bought and sold on numerous occasions since the operation commenced in 1936. In 2015, a mine worker was buried alive after the floor of an open pit collapsed into a massive void caused by old underground workings. Accidents from rockfalls and plant malfunctions had caused a number of injuries and deaths, until its closure in 2029. A year later the firm I worked for consulted with a potential buyer, but it ended in tears when their partners had a falling out over ownership rights. The NMG reopened the mine by enslaving the residents of Norseman, forcing them to carry out the high-risk duties for which they had no experience or ability to perform. Work health and safety was clearly not one of the NMG's priorities.

A majority of the guards were carrying either shotguns or rifles. A perverse few held bull whips, which they used with delight to force the residents to work harder and faster. They were working malnourished in harsh conditions – hauling, digging, and drilling – with no form of training or safety equipment. I stood fifteen metres from the tunnel entrance, not game to travel any further underground.

About six hours into my shift, an older gentleman and middle-aged woman holding hands shuffled towards me asking for water. As I considered my reply, I heard a thunderous rumble from deep inside the mine. In a heartbeat a cloud of dust chased me as I sprinted towards the tunnel entrance. I felt a hand grab my arm and I in turn gripped their wrist and pulled the person behind me as I ran for my life. As I exited the mouth of the mine, I fell to my knees coughing and spluttering.

I rubbed my eyes and gazed back towards the tunnel entrance. All I could see was darkness and rubble. The woman who had grabbed my wrist was now dry retching beside me, trying to remove the dust from the back of her throat. She placed her hand over her mouth and looked around franticly. "Where is he?" she asked. She turned to face the tunnel entrance and screamed, "Dad. Oh my God. Dad." It didn't take long for my addled brain to realise she was calling for the old bloke who just moments before stood alongside her, who without doubt had been crushed by a ton of rock and debris.

Acting like he didn't have a care in the world, the leader of the mine operation decided that work would stop for the day and ordered us to take the 'slaves' back into town. No attempt was made to rescue survivors or inspect the tunnel. Sixteen residents were working deep in the mine at the time of the rock collapse. It was not easy, but I remained stone-faced as I witnessed the residents' anguish at losing their friends and loved ones. I knew just how they felt, but I couldn't afford to show any emotion and draw attention to myself.

We escorted the dust covered survivors to the mine administration building where the bus was waiting to transport us back to town. We left town with twenty-four residents. We were returning with just eight.

After I ensured the residents were all seated, the driver sneered, "Great results on your first day. You are a lucky charm aren't ya cobber." He chuckled at his own gibe, before yelling, "I hope you've purchased ya tickets. Off to town we go."

Three of the residents were sobbing, while the remainder just stared vacantly out the bus window as we travelled back to town. The driver stopped at the high school, parking near two NMG guards. The shorter of the two guards asked, "Where are the others?"

I shrugged my shoulders. "There was a rock collapse," I replied nonchalantly.

The guard snorted and led the residents off the bus. As the driver accelerated down the street, I looked through the rear window and observed the guards leading the residents to the school gym. That's where they bunk at night I noted.

Mr Overalls moved from the back of the bus and sat on the seat in front of me. He turned around and asked, "You going to the pub?"

"Yeah, of course," I lied.

"Good, you're buying the first round."

He maintained eye contact and smiled. He was one creepy bastard. The silence was beginning to make me feel uncomfortable, so I asked, "So you been with this crew for long?"

"Nah. Just three months. I was running with some blokes out of Coober Pedy, but they got greedy and got themselves killed," he said, cackling like Heath Ledger's portrayal of the Joker.

After he finally stopped laughing, he added, "So, it's a bummer we lost so much cattle today. But don't concern yourself, some more S.A.S. are arriving in the morrow."

"S.A.S.?" I asked.

"I forgot you're a newbie. Stands for South Australian Slaves. Fresh meat for the mine."

"Okay, that's good to hear. For a moment there I thought I might be out of a job."

He continued to stare at me. I wished he would just turn around and mind his own bloody business. He pointed at me, "Hey, do I know you? I mean, did we meet in the old world?"

He meant before the War, but I was worried that he had seen me guarding the train or bringing in a felon. I shrugged, "Who knows, anything's possible. Did you live in Dumbleyung?" I chose Dumbleyung as it has a tiny population and is not well known.

He shook his head. "Nah, I've never heard of it."

Thank God the bus pulled up at the pub before he could continue his yapping. "I'm getting something to eat, see ya at the pub," I lied, before swiftly exiting the bus.

As I strolled down the road to my quarters, I added another two outlaws to my count. I sat at the kitchen table impatiently waiting for the sun to go down. It was clear that I was pressing my luck and it was time to leave town.

So far, this risky operation had paid off. I had pretty much formulated my battle plan and had a good estimate of the force we were up against. I glanced at my watch - 7 p.m. - time to get moving. I had agreed to be at the pick-up point at 9 p.m. (ten kilometres out of town), and I needed to do something important before I left. Something that had been weighing on my conscience. Peering out the window I saw a cat jump over the front fence. Just my luck; it was almost a full bloody moon.

Holding my favourite prop, I staggered down Fuller Street guzzling from the bottle, again acting like I'd had one too many. The tortured sounds of a woman screaming reverberated down the long narrow street. I found what I was looking for - a wine barrel post box.

I sauntered up to the front door. A muscular man of a similar height to myself responded to my knock on the door. As soon as he opened the door, I barged my way in shoulder first. "What are you doing in my quarters mate?" I slurred.

My aggressive entry and question had caught him off guard. The young girl I noticed the day before was whimpering in the corner of the loungeroom. She was just skin and bones. The chain attached to her neck iron was secured to a table leg.

The bloke regained his wits. "This is not your place, go fu......" I punched him in the stomach and then followed up with a hook to his chin, knocking him to his backside. As he was endeavouring to stand, I kicked him behind his knee and encircled my right arm around his neck. I felt no remorse as I tightly squeezed the life out of him.

I approached the young girl and knelt in front of her. "My name's Archie. I'm not going to hurt you. I'm here to take you away from here to somewhere safe."

I turned the dining table on its side and slid the chain from the leg. The girl was understandably petrified. I've never been great with kids. I was trying to think of a way to gain her trust and I didn't have a lot of time. Noticing a Ruger pistol on the table, I picked it up and placed it in her hands. "This is your gun. If anyone tries to hurt you, aim the muzzle in the centre of their chest and press the trigger."

"What's your name?" I asked.

"Helen," she replied quietly.

"Listen to me carefully Helen. We need to leave town. I can't remove that neck-iron right now, but I promise I'll take it off as soon as possible. Okay? Now, please come with me real quiet."

We both exited the front door and walked to the edge of town. Helen carried the chain in her spindly arms like she was cradling a doll. We were only fifty metres from the edge of the bush when I heard a familiar voice shout out, "HEY, I do remember you!"

Groaning inwardly, I did an about turn to find Overalls standing in the middle of the street with a pistol wedged down the front of his jeans.

"Were you a carnival fighter? You were, weren't you?"

Just after the War I had a gig as a tent fighter. *What can I say? I needed the coin.* We travelled throughout the State, exhibiting bare knuckle boxing and mixed martial arts (MMA) fights to entertain the locals. The talent would be matched by weight with young bucks (usually shearers, butchers, labourers and alike). Unless my opponent was a trained fighter, I'd pull my punches and dance around the ring until they wore themselves out. It was important to put on a good show, and besides, most of the young men only stepped between the ropes to show-off to their mates and impress their girlfriends.

I hesitantly grabbed Helen by the neck chain and whispered in her ear, "Sorry luv." Her eyes widened in fear as I strolled towards Overalls with her chain in my grasp.

Just as I came within reach of Overalls, two things occurred almost simultaneously – Helen pointed her Ruger at me and pressed the trigger while I shot Overalls right between the eyes. He didn't even have a chance to blink, let alone reach for his pistol.

Fortunately, Helen didn't know how to disengage the pistol's manual safety lever. If she had, I'd be dead in the street!

I grabbed the Ruger from her tiny hand, picked her up by the waist and placed her over my shoulder in one fell swoop. Without a moment's hesitation, I legged it towards the bush like our lives depended on it. She wouldn't have weighed more than thirty-five kilograms - about the same weight as my pack. With the assistance of the full moon lighting my path, I ran swiftly through the scrub. I needed to make as much distance from the town as possible before the guards' bodies were discovered. My heart was pounding, my lungs were on fire, and my lower back and knees were aching. The last two days had taken its toll, but I was still appalled by my lack of stamina. I had to remind myself that I was no longer in my twenties, but it wasn't great for the ego to feel a notable decline in your physical performance. I made a mental note – *start pack running twice a week*.

After running for about two kilometres, I stopped and put Helen down. After taking three deep breaths I tried to reassure her by explaining my motives. "I'm sorry Helen, but I had to act like I was a member of the gang so I could get the jump on that guard."

Helen gazed at her feet. "I understand now. I'm sorry for trying to shoot you. I thought you were taking me back. I'll never go back, I'd rather die!"

"There's no harm done. And if it makes you feel better, lots of people want to shoot me. Now jump on my back and hold on. I have friends waiting for us."

I knelt down and Helen placed her arms around my neck. It was now 8.20 p.m. My task was to run eight kilometres in forty minutes with a thirty-five-kilo load. This was going to be tough ask. I attempted to control my breathing and pace myself, knowing that if I didn't make it to the pick-up point on time, we were going to have an awfully long walk ahead of us.

By the end of the run I was absolutely shattered. Sweat dripped from my brow as I peered down at the phosphorescent hands of my watch. DAMN! It was 9:15 p.m. I didn't make it in time. As soon as I put Helen down, I sighed with relief. With the weight off my back, *I felt as light as a feather* as I skipped over the train tracks – in more than one respect. I'd collected the intel that I required and managed to rescue Helen; I couldn't have lived with myself if I'd left her behind.

Thank God Clarry's a stubborn bastard! My beautiful Beast was waiting for me on the side of the road.

Chapter Thirty-One

March 22 – 23, 2041 – Fiona

I whispered to Clarry, "I can see two people walking on the other side of the tracks. One large, one small. I can't make out if it's Archie." Clarry grabbed his shotgun from the backseat and slipped out the driver's side door. He had already disabled the vehicle's interior light. He motioned for me to do the same. I slipped on the night vision goggles and rested my elbows on the bonnet with the rifle in my grip.

I sighed with relief. "It's all good Clarry, it's Archie and some kid."

I removed the goggles and ran over to Archie. In an attempt to hide my shock, I planted my best wan smile and slapped his shoulder. He was busted up pretty bad - with a swollen jaw and dark nasty bruises running down the entire length of his arms, from the tip of his shoulders to his fingertips. The dark circles under his eyes, hanging eyelids and drooping corners of his mouth, made him look like death warmed up.

Archie gestured towards me. "Helen, this is Fiona and that ugly old dude over by the car is Clarry."

Helen was a skinny twelve-year old with a ghastly metal ring and chain hanging from her neck. The poor girl looked pale and sickly. I could only imagine the evil that she had endured.

Clarry pointed his finger at Archie. "Helen, don't listen to Archie, he's just jealous of my good looks and charm."

Helen flinched away from my hand when I attempted to guide her to the car. "We're riding in the back Helen. You're safe now, we won't let anything bad happen to you," I vowed in a soothing tone.

Archie collapsed in the front passenger seat and rolled his head listlessly towards the window. He must be exhausted!

Clarry glanced at his mate, his expression one of concern. "You must be pretty stuffed brother to let me drive your baby back."

Archie gave Clarry a weary smile. "I had a bad sleep mate. The bed they gave me was horrible. Lumpy mattress and crappy springs." He craned his neck to face me. "Fiona, have you got a pen and paper?"

"Of course," I replied, grabbing my notebook and pen from my pocket.

"Write this down. 55 NMGs, 34 rifles, 13 shotguns, 32 pistols, 15 assault rifles. Got it?"

"No problem, Boss, 55 NMGs, 34 rifles, 13 shotguns, 32 pistols, 15 assault rifles."

Archie yawned like a tired lion in the Savannah. "Thanks for waiting guys. I was dreading a walk back to Esperance." He leaned back into the seat and was comatose within seconds.

Helen avoided eye contact and just stared out of the window in silence.

Clarry drove the Beast hard and made it back home in just over an hour and a half.

Archie groaned like an old man with a bad back as he exited the vehicle. "Can you and Clarry get that thing off her neck and take care of her?"

"Consider it done. You get some sleep. You look dead tired."

He smirked. "Rather that, than being just plain dead."

Archie shuffled to the couch and collapsed. He was snoring like a trooper within sixty seconds. Xena patiently waited until I placed a woollen blanket over him, before jumping on the couch and lying by his feet.

The Aboriginal women roused from their sleep as I made Helen a chicken sandwich on the kitchen benchtop. Clarry retrieved bolt cutters from the shed and severed the padlock that was securing her neck-iron in place. I noticed red swollen welts lining her neck. The exhausted girl stood in the middle of the kitchen and watched me in silence as I cut her sandwich into four squares and placed them on a plate. Two women Elders entered the kitchen and approached her, whispering private messages close to her ear. Helen broke down and wept convulsively, the women crying with her in empathy. I held the plate with one hand and wiped the tears from my face with the other.

After Helen finished her sandwich, I led her to the shower. The Elders raided their children's suitcases and presented her clothes to replace her tattered t-shirt and skirt. I promised her that I'd purchase her a whole new wardrobe first thing in the morning. When I heard her sobbing through the bathroom door, my resolve to make these NMG bastards pay was strengthened. She slept in my bed as I settled on the floor and fell into a restless sleep.

It was 9 a.m. and Archie was yet to waken from his slumber. It was apparent that Helen had been informally adopted by Clarry's family. I was pleasantly surprised to see her laughing as the kids played with the dogs and kicked the football around the yard. Considering my own circumstances, I shouldn't need to be reminded of how resilient kids are.

"Dorinda and Dale are going to the beach. Can I go with them?" she asked.

"Ah, yeah, why not? Of course you can. Go and have some fun."

I'm not sure why, but I was a little unnerved when she asked for my permission. I guess, I'm comfortable taking on the role of a big sister, but I have no desire to be a mother.

Archie rolled out of the couch just after midday and made himself a strong brew and Vegemite toast. His eyes were clear, and he had a spring in his step. Wonders will never cease what a good night's sleep and a coffee can do for your general disposition.

"Mate, can you find your old typewriter? I need to type out my plan," he said with a piece of toast in one hand and his coffee mug in the other.

Clarry raised his eyebrows, "I heard your numbers last night brother. You're confident we can defeat them?"

"It's not going to be a walk in the park by any stretch of the imagination, and no doubt there'll be casualties, but I'm convinced we can defeat them with a good plan. And I have a good plan mate."

"My family will be pleased."

"Can you tell the mayor that I want to meet with him an hour before tonight's meeting. I don't want to go over the details with you both until I finalise my operational plan and order. Are you cool with that?"

"Well, we'll just have to be, won't we Fiona?"

I nodded while thinking - *I don't care what the plan is*, as long as we make these NMG fuckers pay for what they've done to Helen, Lau and all the others they've hurt.

~

For the rest of the day Archie furiously typed page after page on the Vintage Lemair typewriter, only breaking to stretch his neck and sip from his coffee mug. I could hear him talking to himself each time he hit the wrong key, cursing in his Boy Scout manner while reminiscing about photocopiers and printers. He completed the last of the six copies of his order just before we needed to leave for the meeting.

As I waited in the Council chamber while Archie met with the mayor in his office, I watched the residents of Esperance and Kalgoorlie file into the building. It was packed, with almost double the number of attendees than the previous meeting. I scanned the crowd and noticed Charlie Wong and Smithy from the Merivale farm sitting in the front row. Senior Asshole Atkins was leaning against the back wall chatting up some lady with a big ass wedding ring on her finger. I laughed my tits off when her broad-shouldered husband tapped her on the shoulder while Atkins ashamedly slinked away.

I turned my attention to the front of the chamber when the sergeant hushed the crowd – "Quieten down please, the mayor is about to speak. DON'T make me blow my whistle!" The crowd laughed at his corny joke as the mayor stood and walked towards the podium. Clarry and Archie sat beside the sergeant, busily whispering to each other as the mayor welcomed everyone.

The mayor coughed into his fist. "Welcome ladies and gentlemen, thank you for your attendance. I've received a compelling and disturbing briefing by Mr O'Connor, which you must all hear. Without further ado, I'd like to hand the floor to Mr Archie O'Connor."

Archie stood to a lacklustre applause. I was surprised to see him holding Helen's neck-iron and chain by his side. "Thank you, mayor. I know you're all busy people, so I'll get straight to the crux of the matter. I've received explicit intelligence that the Norseman residents – men, women, and children, have been enslaved and as we speak are experiencing torture, rape, and hard labour." After a short pause for dramatic effect, he lifted the neck-iron by the chain at shoulder height. "I recently met a sweet young girl who was chained like a dog and forced to perform unspeakable acts. Residents are dying daily from the dangerous work and inhumane conditions. The fact is, they need more workers, so it won't be long before they travel further afield to enslave people like YOU! I have a plan and it's a good plan. But I'll tell you what I told the good men sitting behind me. There are likely to be casualties amongst you. However, if you don't act and take the fight to these VERMIN, they'll be bringing violence to your doorstep. That, I have no doubt."

Archie spoke with intensity and passion, with a pinch of theatrics to ram home his message. I pondered whether he used to perform like this in court. When he concluded his speech and sat down, there was a dead silence in the chamber. There were a wide range of emotions in the crowd, but most were either visibly shaken or outraged.

The mayor rose from his seat. "Thank you Mr O'Connor for your candid update. It's now time to vote." The crowd were on the edge of their seats. The mayor raised his voice and in an emphatic tone he said, "For the sake of the Norseman residents and to prevent these animals from enslaving our sons, daughters, brothers, and sisters, I propose that we take the fight to the NMG and rid them from our State. Raise your hand if you say YAY to this proposal."

There were so many raised hands that it was difficult to ascertain if anyone intended to vote nay. Gizzarelli turned in his chair and gave me a wicked smile as his arm shot high into the air.

For a brief moment the mayor appeared relieved. "I would like it recorded that a vast majority of attendees have voted for the affirmative. For those that are not registered with the militia and would like to do so, please write your details in the register before you leave. Your designated team leader will contact you with further information. Please do not leave the Esperance area within the next five days. Team leaders, please come to the front. Thank you all."

After the residents had left the building, the militia team leaders, consisting of Mayor Jason, Sergeant Lee, Clarry, Archie, Senior Constable Atkins and Charlie Wong met in the mayor's office. It was a tight squeeze, but we all managed to find a seat around the meeting table. Archie saved me a seat between Charlie and himself.

I felt like a bit of a third wheel until Archie spoke up. "Gentleman, for those who don't know, Fiona here has been promoted to team leader. Congratulations Fiona."

I've come to realise that Archie and Clarry aren't the best communicators. This was the first time I'd been told of this appointment. Charlie Wong patted me on the shoulder while the others smiled or gave me a nod. Atkins just looked totally disinterested.

Archie addressed the group, "First of all, thank you for taking the responsibility to lead this battle. I kept it short and sweet out there because there's always a possibility that an NMG mole was sitting in the crowd. That's why it's critical that you discuss what is mentioned in this room on a need-to-know basis with those that you completely trust. Is that understood?" Archie looked at each person, ensuring they understood his meaning. "Some of you would be unaware, but I went for a recce in Norseman and had eyes on the ground before developing this plan."

Charlie Wong whistled. "Man, you've got big balls."

The mayor and sergeant chuckled in unison while Atkins' mouth twisted in a contemptuous sneer.

"Thank you, Charlie, but others may disagree and counter that I'm a bit soft in the head," Archie replied while looking in Clarry's direction. "Nevertheless, this gave me the ability to formulate a plan that I truly believe will succeed."

Archie outlined his plan in a manner that the mayor referred to as both 'logical and comprehensive.' Not even Atkins could find fault in the proposal. Archie explained that the plan centred on actioning a 'five-pronged assault' on key strategic locations. This was all new language for me, and I'd be lying if I said I understood all of it. But I was taking it all in like a sponge. I've been told since I was six years old that I'm a fast learner. And I have an excellent memory.

Phase One involved simultaneously assaulting the Gold Mine, School Gym, Hotel, Canteen, and Armoury. Archie determined that 8.45 p.m. was the most 'opportune time to commence the assault,' with a majority of the men either drinking in the hotel or shutting down the mine for the night.

Archie stated that his knowledge of the operation made him the ideal person to lead eighteen people to assault the mine. Clarry was selected to lead fifteen of his family members to assault the hotel. Archie didn't need to provide his reasoning for this decision. It was obvious. A majority of the NMG should be at the hotel, giving Clarry and his family the ultimate opportunity for payback. Archie determined that Sergeant Lee's and Senior Constable Atkin's familiarity with the police station would be invaluable when capturing the armoury with six men. Mayor Jason was tasked with leading eight team members to secure the canteen. Charlie and I were chosen to lead a team of twelve and rescue the residents at the high school gym. I had a sneaking suspicion that even though Archie was giving me a leadership role, he'd placed Charlie in my team to hold my hand. I didn't know whether I should feel pissed off or relieved.

Once Phase One is complete, a core group of militia members will meet at the gym and execute Phase Two. Assault teams will then be formed for the purpose of clearing each and every street, house, public building, and business in the town.

Archie placed his twenty-page Operational Plan on the table and handed us each a copy of the Operational Order. The Op Order contained essential information and directions required to carry out the operation. It was broken into five key elements - the Situation, Mission, Execution, Administration and Logistics and Command and Signals (SMEAC).

Archie read the order and then said, "Please review this Op Order over the next half hour so we can discuss any concerns you may have. I will then meet with you individually and assist you to develop a specific plan and order for your team. The mayor will develop and coordinate the Recovery Plan to restore the town. A priority will be the re-opening of the town hospital to treat our wounded."

When Archie spoke of 'our wounded,' the situation suddenly became real. We were actually doing this. I'm responsible and accountable for a group of people and the success of my team's mission. My stomach tightened as I carefully read through the Op Order.

****** OPERATION FRELSI ******

SITUATION:

The Norse Men Gang (NMG) have captured the town of Norseman and have re-opened the Gold Mine, using residents as slave labour. There are 55 known NMG members in the town. Their known arsenal includes: 34 rifles, 13 shotguns, 32 pistols and 15 assault rifles. Total ammunition is unknown, but a minimum of 200 boxes of ammunition of various calibres are known to be stored in the police station. The Hotel is used by the NMGs as a common meeting and drinking establishment. The residents are imprisoned at the Norseman High School. Total number of residents are unknown. The Railway Motel is used as a canteen where residents are forced to cook and serve the NMGs.

MISSION:

To free Norseman and rescue all residents on Wednesday 27 of March 2041.

EXECUTION:

Phase 1: Simultaneously assaulting the Gold Mine, School Gym, Hotel, Canteen and Armoury.

Alpha Team: At 8:45pm Archie O'Connor will lead 18 militia to eliminate or capture all NMG guards and free all residents at the Norseman Gold Mine.

Bravo Team: At 8:45pm Clarence Ugle will lead 18 militia to eliminate or capture all NMG members at the Norseman Hotel.

Charlie Team: At 8:45pm Sergeant Brian Lee and Senior Constable Sean Atkin's will lead 6 militia to capture the armoury at the police station and eliminate or capture all NMG members. Once captured, the armoury is to be defended.

Delta Team: At 8:45pm Mayor Jason Bridle will lead 8 militia to the Canteen Railway Motel and eliminate or capture NMG guards and free residents.

Echo Team: At 8:45pm Fiona Katsaros and Charlie Wong will lead 12 militia to rescue the residents from the School Gym and eliminate or capture all NMGs.

Phase 2: Transport all residents to the School Gym. Form assault teams and clear all houses, public buildings, and businesses in the Town.

Once Team Leaders have completed their missions, they will transport all residents and rendezvous at the School Gym. Sergeant Lee will leave a nominal force to guard the armoury.

Team Leaders will form four assault teams and clear the town from the North, East, South, and West.

A Team will remain at the gym and protect the residents.

Phase 3: Implement the Recovery Plan.

Mayor Jason will coordinate and implement the Town's Recovery.

ADMINISTRATION & LOGISTICS:

A Walkie talkie will be issued to each militia member. Team Leaders and their number two ICs will be issued 2 x walkie talkies

Each militia member to be armed with a handgun and longarm (rifle or shotgun).

Alpha team to be armed with 5 x sniper rifles.

Each member to carry a map of the town and Militia Aide-mémoire.

Torches to be issued to each militia member.

Each team to carry door breaching tools (ram, jimmy bar, hinge puller, bolt cutter).

A medic and supplies to support each team will be provided.

Vehicles:

Alpha Team: Victor 1, 2, 3, 4, 5
Bravo Team: Victor 6, 7, 8, 9
Charlie Team: Victor 10, 11
Delta Team: Victor 12, 13
Echo Team: Victor 14, 15

COMMAND & SIGNALS:

Team Leaders will be on Command Channel 4 and their designated Team Channel.

Alpha Team: Channel 5
Bravo Team: Channel 6
Charlie Team: Channel 7
Delta Team: Channel 8
Echo Team: Channel 9

After reading the Op Order, Archie asked if we would like to add, delete, or alter any part of the plan.

"Why are we giving ourselves only four days to prepare for this?" asked Charlie.

"Fair question Charlie. There's a couple of reasons why. We appreciate that those from Kal can't wait around forever. And that's also the case with Clarry's family. I'm also concerned that the NMG will receive intel the longer we leave it. And from a personal perspective, having seen the pain and suffering in the town, I'd prefer we move sooner than later."

"Understood, thanks Archie," replied Charlie.

The sergeant piped up. "I'm worried we won't have enough ammo. I'll meet with you later Archie to discuss what we can do about it."

Clarry leaned forward. "I think there's an opportunity for the gang to be given advanced warning during our approach."

"Please elaborate mate," said Archie.

"If we all leave at the same time and head to our positions, some of us will arrive before others and then POOF!, we've lost our element of surprise."

"Good point. We'll meet at an assembly point outside of town and stagger the teams' departure so we're all in position as close to go time as possible."

There were nods all around the table aside from Atkins, who just frowned.

"Is there something wrong Atkins?" asked Archie.

"You've named the operation Frelsi. I've never heard of the word. What does it mean?"

"I'm glad you asked. I borrowed Clarry's Norse dictionary to come up with it. I believe it describes the aim of this operation. It means freedom!" explained Archie.

"Perfect Archie. Absolutely perfect," beamed the mayor.

"Good. Now if there's no other input or questions, please develop your team plan over the next twenty-four hours and I'll organise a time to meet with you individually. You can then organise training with your team. Remember, we only have four days."

Atkins scowled, "Training?"

"Apologies if I'm being blunt, but running training exercises that are directly aligned to your team's plan is paramount, not only for the success of the mission, but also to ensure that the number of body bags required are kept to a minimum."

The sergeant glared at Atkins while he said, "I completely agree. The more training the better."

The mayor opened a manila folder and handed us each a list of names. "This is a list of your team members' contact details. I encourage you to contact them ASAP to discuss their role and organise training sessions."

After the meeting had concluded and the team leaders left their seats, I took a deep breath to compose myself as I stared at the Op Order. I couldn't help but feel a bit anxious about having a leadership role. Doubts started to creep into my mind. I was so self-absorbed that I almost jumped out of my seat with fright when Charlie put his hand on my shoulder.

Charlie returned with us to Clarry's to discuss our team plan - *Echo Team's Plan*. Archie encouraged me to voice my ideas and concerns. He only chimed in to make suggestions when Charlie and I drew a blank, which wasn't often. I was actually surprised by how much I contributed - providing input on the type of weapons and equipment we should use, door entry strategies and training requirements. I'd learned more than I'd given myself credit for. With Echo Team's plan in my grasp, my stomach loosened, and I started to feel like I could do this.

Chapter Thirty-Two

March 25 – 26, 2041 – Archie

Over the previous twenty-four hours I had met with all of the team leaders to revise their plans and provide strategic input. The seven team leaders will command a total of sixty-two militia, a comparable size to the NMG. Even though the NMG are sadistic killers with greater firepower, we have the advantage of surprise and discipline. I'm confident that we can succeed in our mission. However, in battle anything could happen, with mass casualties a real possibility. Sal used to preach, "*All plans are great until the first shot's fired.*"

The team leaders developed a training plan aligned to their team's mission, concentrating on marksmanship and tactics such as door entries, room clearances and movement drills. I made it clear that they needed to reinforce firearm safety rules, as the last thing we needed were casualties from friendly fire. A majority of the volunteers participated in last year's action to crush the attempted take-over of the Esperance Town Centre. However, they were by no means experienced operators. The following three days involved drilling their respective teams at the gun range and kill house.

I strategically asked Mitt (the gun store owner) to perform the dual role of second in-charge of Alpha Team and Logistics Officer for the entire operation. This was to my advantage on two levels. Firstly, Mitt is more than capable of leading Alpha team if I get taken out, and secondly, he may feel duty-bound to assist with arming the militia.

My strategy worked like a charm. Mitt was so chuffed at being assigned the roles of Alpha's Number Two and Logistics Officer, that he not only offered the use of his cache of weapons, but was also generous in supplying ammunition at cost. He had just one condition - all weapons must be cleaned prior to their return. Mitt was meticulous in obtaining and maintaining the equipment. He mitigated the risk of vehicle breakdowns by organising two of his mechanic mates to service all operational vehicles, tasked a team with cleaning and conducting a serviceability check of every firearm, ensured we had backup batteries for the radios and torches, and the list goes on. A true professional in every sense of the word.

I was definitely burning the candle at both ends, but I had set this tight time frame, so I intended to sprint to the finish. When I wasn't preparing my team or assisting Fiona, I was checking up on Clarry. Bravo team have without doubt the toughest assignment, but they have a unique leg-up on the other teams. They're a family on a 'personal mission' who know each other's strengths and weaknesses inside and out. And they drilled like it. They appeared to almost read each other's minds as they performed movement drills in an abandoned hotel that was irreparably damaged during last year's raid. Clarry had spray painted sandbags with black stripes to represent the NMG's leather jackets, placing the bags throughout the hotel – behind doors, in corners, and in and around furniture. They entered smoothly through the hotel doorways, exercising their areas of responsibility and accurately engaging the targets. They were ready!

Mitt wasn't the only senior citizen that was keen to assist. Captain Ross told Clarry in no uncertain terms that he'd be joining Clarry and his family – '*So help me God I will do my part. You will need an army to stop me from missing out on the action*.' He demonstrated his conviction by attending each and every Bravo Team training session.

After the first day of training, the Captain's wife arrived at Clarry's doorstep. She requested a private meeting with Clarry, but was happy for me to be present as they spoke at the dining table.

"I know he's a stubborn man. He was like that when I married him. But Clarry, you can't let him go to Norseman, he'll just get in the way. He has a dicky heart for God's sake. Please tell him he can't join you," pleaded Elizabeth.

Clarry placed his hand over Elizabeth's. "If I thought it'd make a difference, I'd tell him to stay behind. But you know he'll just make he's own way there. Look, he'll be with me, so I can promise you that I'll keep him out of harm's way."

"You promise?"

"I give you my word Elizabeth."

I felt bad for Elizabeth, but Clarry didn't have the heart or courage to kick the Captain off the team. And to be honest, I couldn't do it either. But it was unwise to appease her by promising to keep him safe. I kept this opinion to myself. What good would it do to do otherwise?

Late in the afternoon before the day of the operation, I rode Roger along the eastern side of a salt lake known as 'Pink Lake.' Clarry mentioned that after thirty years of exodus, the lake had reclaimed its pink hue from just the right amount of salt concentration and green algae. Three men were working up a sweat as they crushed and bagged salt at the edge of shore, which they'd later sell for food preservation.

As I cantered along the shoreline, I contemplated the operation and all the possible things that could go wrong. Responsibility weighed heavy, not only for the success of the mission, but also for the safety of the people under my charge. I think I'm ready to lead this mission. Not that I had any other choice in the matter. We'd all come too far to back out now. I put the butterflies that were madly fluttering in my stomach to the back of mind as I raised myself up from the saddle and leaned forward. I said excitedly, "Come on boy, show me that you've still got it." Roger's ears pricked up and he picked up speed, his hooves crushing the salt underneath as he galloped along the shoreline. His cheerful mood was infectious, and I felt my spirits lift. By the time we returned to Clarry's, I'd cleared my mind and felt reinvigorated - *I was ready!*

Chapter Thirty-Three

Wednesday March 27, 2041 from 5.15 p.m. – Archie

As I stood behind the podium, the determination that I felt from the day before was now set in stone. The Operational Order was held firmly in my grasp while I patiently waited for the sixty-two militia members to finish their discussions and find a seat. Sergeant Lee's booming voice almost made me flinch, "Quickly find a seat and listen up."

A majority of the militia members were unaware of the big picture. This was intentional as we wanted them focused on their specific roles during the training. However, like a giant jigsaw puzzle assorted into a collection of various pieces, I now needed them to come together to make a complete picture. In order to support each, they needed to understand how their team's objectives connected to the overall operation.

I stated in a loud and clear voice, "Our mission is to free Norseman and rescue all residents. I repeat, our mission is to............"

After I had completed the briefing, the militia split into designated staging areas to receive a team briefing from their leaders.

Mitt had performed the role of logistics officer with aplomb - weapons, ammunition, vehicles, and associated equipment had been obtained, checked, and issued. After being unsuccessful in locating a next of kin for Dimoska, I decided to keep her Blaser R96 Tactical 3 Sniper rifle by my side. I found it somewhat fitting that I was about to use her weapon to vanquish her killers.

At just over 200 kilometres, the journey to Norseman would take approximately two hours. Speed limits in the State were no longer regulated and even if they were, there wasn't the available resources to police them. To mitigate drivers racing to the town on some mad adrenalin rush, it was agreed that I would lead the convoy in the Beast. We used the Old Coach Road instead of the Highway to decrease the likelihood of being spotted prior to our arrival. In the event the convoy sighted outlaws on the way to the assembly point, the enemy would be engaged and eliminated by the teams' closest to the threat.

The plan was that all vehicles would assemble fifteen minutes out of town at the Dundas Rocks Picnic Area. Alpha Team's five vehicles (Victor One through to Five) would then be provided a fifteen-minute head start. This was tactically imperative due to the distance of the mine from the assembly point. If *old Murphy* and his law keeps his nose out of it, each team will commence their mission at 8:45 p.m. on the dot. I covertly rubbed my hand over the timber podium.

Chapter Thirty-Four

Wednesday March 27, 2041 from 8.15 p.m. – Archie

Alpha Team – Gold Mine

The Beast was purring as we thundered down Old Coach Road towards a track that would lead us to the eastern side of the mine site. Mitt was next in line driving Victor Two, with Victor Three to Five following close behind. We arrived at the intersection and drove down the red gravel track, parking behind an old, rusted iron shed. One of my crew used bolt cutters to cut a hole in the fence. We'd made good time, with ten minutes to spare before executing Phase One.

As long as the NMG haven't altered their schedule, at 8:45 p.m. the guards will be escorting the residents from the processing pit, power station and workshop, to the administration carpark and awaiting buses. Mitt led eleven members from Alpha Team to the rear of the administration building where they would seek cover and wait for the NMG guards to arrive at the carpark. The plan was for Mitt to task four of his team with simultaneously assaulting the guards at the workshop, which was located behind the admin building. He wanted to avoid NMG guards approaching his six while he was engaging the enemy in the carpark.

I led five team members towards the mine's entry, where I almost lost my life after escaping the rock collapse. The decline mine was cut into the side of a rock face. A sniper and I lay down on the summit of the cut where we had the high ground. We were positioned about twenty metres above the tunnel entrance. This provided an elevated vantage point whereby we could pick off the guards, forcing them to defend from lower ground with little to no chance of escape. The remaining three team members would lay down fire, preventing the enemy from exiting the dirt ramp. It was a good plan.

I glanced at my watch - 8:42 p.m. Two guards led a group of residents from the tunnel entrance and started to link the chains to their neck-irons. When another two guards escorted a second group, the sniper and I commenced firing. With Dimoska's rifle in my grip, it should have been like shooting ducks in a barrel. My teammate shot two in the head, and I shot one in the chest. Just as I sighted the fourth guard and was about to press the trigger, he ducked behind a line of residents and scampered into the tunnel. BLOODY MURPHY!

I ordered my sniper to remain in position and left a team member to guard his six. Time was of the essence. I was concerned that the NMG guard would begin executing the residents, many of whom were chained together in groups at the tunnel entrance. I was also concerned for the safety of residents that may still be underground.

Two members joined me in sliding swiftly down the 45-degree angled rock face. Loose gravel skimmed off our boots and backsides while dust clouds rose in our wake. I was pleased with my team's firearm safety discipline as we descended; muzzles pointed in safe directions with fingers off the triggers. The last thing we needed was someone to be taken out by friendly fire.

As soon as my boots hit the ground, I placed my shoulder against the rock wall and pointed my muzzle towards the mouth of the mine. As I waited for my team to move into position, I advised the residents to place their backs against the side wall, where they at least had partial cover from fire. I noticed fear and doubt etched on some of their faces as they focused their eyes on my rifle. I suddenly became aware that they recognised me from when I was acting as a guard. I attempted to reassure them by quickly informing them that we were part of the Esperance Militia on a rescue mission. I was rewarded by a thumb-ups, smiles and nods. A pregnant lady mouthed the words 'thank you.'

I drew my revolver and torch and took a deep breath. Adrenaline was coursing throughout my body – I could feel my heart quicken – its mission to pump excess blood to my muscles – preparing me to react and fight. My body and mind were free of the opiate handcuffs that imprisoned my emotions and heightened senses. I was free to feel the adrenaline *RUSH!*

When I felt my colleague grasp my shoulder to signal for me to move forward, I entered the tunnel with my revolver and torch raised. Fortunately, most of the rock and debris from the collapse had been removed. As we travelled into the bowels of the earth we constantly scanned for the enemy. The sudden cool change in temperature and darkness accentuated the fear of the unknown. Wire mesh bolted to the rocky ceiling reminded me that men with guns were only one of the threats we faced.

We had just crept around a rocky bend when gunfire suddenly erupted. We instinctively fired towards the muzzle flashes while we sought refuge behind an underground haulage truck. The thick steel panels and colossal tyres that stood taller than a man provided the ideal cover.

I shone my torch over panic-stricken residents who were ducking and diving behind rubble and machinery. The cavernous confines of the mine accentuated the chaos that was unfolding - the sound of gunfire booming and ricocheting off the rock and metal - the muzzle flashes appearing like mini fireworks - the echoes of residents screaming, shrieking, and shouting.

An outlaw with an assault rifle swung his muzzle recklessly back and forth like he was Tony Montana from the movie Scarface. We maintained our cover behind the truck as we returned fire.

The earsplitting screams of residents and roaring gunfire transported me back to the mine collapse. The hairs on the back of my neck stood as straight as the Queen's Guard. I was momentarily frozen in place while chaos reigned around me. I snapped out of the vivid flashback when a shard of rock struck my cheek.

As I knelt behind a rear tyre I took aim and fired three rounds into Montana's torso.

I could no longer see any muzzle flashes from the enemy. I

beamed my torch over frightened faces until I illuminated an angry, desperate man. The outlaw stood behind a middle-aged woman - his arm wrapped around her neck as he pressed the muzzle of his pistol into the back of her head.

"CEASE FIRE!" I yelled.

I glanced at my sniper and slightly tilted my head. In my periphery I could see him creeping to the other side of the truck like a jaguar stalking his prey.

Unlike the movies, I didn't stand out in the open and offer to place my revolver on the ground while I negotiated with the outlaw. That would be suicide. However, I did attempt to distract him, so my sniper had time to attain a clear shot. "Look mate, we're from the Esperance Militia. If you let the lady go, you're free...."

"Let my mum GO!" shouted a teenage boy.

I started to warn him to stay put, but I was too little, too late. In a moment of madness and courage, he ran towards his mother to rescue her.

The lady squirmed in the outlaw's grasp and his gun went off. He fired point-blank into the back of her skull. A second report of gunfire jerked the outlaw's head to the right. He fell to the ground in a heap beside the woman he had just executed.

After considerable effort, we succeeded in convincing the residents that it was safe to exit the mine. Two residents helped the young man carry his mother's body from the mine. Once we'd returned to the open air I conferred with my team. They'd heard a steady rate of gunfire coming from the western side of the site, where Mitt was rescuing the residents. The gunfire had ceased shortly before we exited the tunnel. I had picked up bits and pieces of information from the radio, but at the time I'd been more concerned with my team's tenuous situation.

The first thing that caught my attention as I approached Mitt's location was a line of outlaws trembling on their knees in the dirt. Gizzarelli was standing behind a man with his Magnum forty-five calibre revolver pointed at the back of his head. He was laughing with delight as he strolled down the line, executing one man after the other.

By the time I was standing alongside Mitt, Gizzarelli had killed all fourteen captured men.

"Why did he kill them?" I asked Mitt.

He shrugged his shoulders. "Why do you think? We can't take them with us. Who's going to guard them? They'll be dead once the Judge arrives anyway."

In all honesty, I hadn't considered the possibility of a mass surrender and a subsequent mass execution. Mitt explained that he'd lost two of his team during the assault and killed four guards before the remaining outlaws surrendered. Unfortunately for their sakes, their surrender didn't save them from Gizzarelli's retribution.

I didn't have time to dwell on Gizzarelli's actions. We were in the middle of a battle, and I needed to stay focused. I had to make critical decisions that would affect the lives of the residents and militia. We asked the grateful and relieved residents to one last time ride the bus to town. I sat down on the seat just behind Mitt, who took on the role as the new bus driver. I pressed the radio's transmitter button and attempted to raise Fiona on channel four to obtain a situation report (sit-rep).

Chapter Thirty-Five

Wednesday March 27, 2041 from 8.29 p.m. – Fiona

Echo Team – High School Gym

I constantly checked my watch, anxious to move as soon as Alpha Team's fifteen-minute head start had ended. My heart thumped against my chest as my mind raced with thoughts of responsibilities and self-doubt. Once again, I glanced down at the aide-memoire resting in my lap – a notebook sized document summarising Echo Team's objectives. I stared at the words but didn't read them. I tried to calm my nerves by visualising the initial actions I would take – from exiting the vehicle, to approaching the gym door and then tactically entering the premises.

Charlie was sitting in the driver's seat of Victor Fourteen – an orange Holden 69 HT Monaro. I was riding shotgun, while a young man with bad acne was sitting in the back seat. Some smartass gave him the nickname, Spotty. His knees were knocking together as his eyes were glued to his watch. *I wondered whether I looked as nervous as Spotty.* I hoped not.

The remainder of Echo Team was sitting in a 1973 Volkswagen Kombi Van which was parked directly behind us. Spotty counted down - ten, nine, eight, seven....... Charlie revved the engine and we accelerated down the back road towards town. It was on.

My heart accelerated into a higher gear as Charlie swung the Monaro around a street corner. I'm quite sure my heart beats slower during a run. The nerves and tension I felt were vastly different to the train assault or the Lewis operation. There was no time for anticipation during those Ops. Bullets just started flying and I automatically reacted. This time I had days of waiting and worrying as my anxiety peaked. Charlie must have telepathy as he glanced in my direction and said, "You've GOT this Fiona." *Wow, he must have completed the same 'pep-talk course' as Archie.*

The journey felt like sixty seconds. Charlie turned into the high school and pulled up alongside a bus parked outside the gymnasium. As I opened the car door my nerves evaporated. I was ready - *I'm Ellen fucking Ripley.* It was bravado. But that's what I needed to tell myself, so I'd keep marching forward.

I led eight members of Echo Team to the front door of the gym. Charlie commanded the remaining four and advanced to the rear fire door carrying the door breaching tools. Spotty and I stood at either side of the gym's double door entrance. Two of our teammates grabbed the handles and pulled the outward opening doors. Without hesitation we stepped forwards and engaged two guards. I fired two nine-millimetre rounds into an outlaw's back, as Spotty fired his pump-action shotgun at his comrade. His twelve-gauge slug literally vaporised the outlaw's face. Good shooting Spotty.

My team and I fanned out into the gym. We saw forty or more mattresses spread out over two basketball courts, with residents sitting or lying down on their makeshift beds. They resembled photos I'd seen at school of malnourished prisoners of war – women, men, and children.

My attention was drawn to an obese man at the back of the gym. "GET DOWN!" I screamed. He fired his fully automatic assault rifle, indiscriminately mowing down the residents and my men. Spotty fell as I emptied my mag. I went down on one knee screaming "RELOADING."

"Cease firing. All clear. Cease firing. All clear," yelled Charlie.

Charlie and his men had breached the rear door and shot the obese outlaw as he was wreaking havoc with his M-16. This one man had killed four Echo Team members and eight residents, including two children. One of my men and five residents were also injured, some worse than others. The fucker was wearing a Kevlar bullet proof vest. I noticed that he'd failed to secure the straps around his enormous girth.

Charlie placed two Echo Team members on the front door and two on the back to secure the premises. Our medic started to triage the injured and asked for my assistance to treat them. I promised her that I'd be straight back after I gave Archie a quick update. I walked past a dead child lying beside Spotty's corpse. I'd never seen a dead child. I ran directly to the bathroom with my hands over my mouth.

I vomited on the tiled floor before I was able to reach the toilet. I continued to puke over the toilet bowl, telling myself to hurry up so I could get back out there. When I felt my hair being pulled, I franticly drew my Glock and spun to engage the threat.

A gaunt grey-haired woman raised her hands. "Don't shoot sweety, I was just holding your hair back."

I sighed with relief and bent over placing my hand on my knees. "Thank you," I spluttered.

She smiled with tears in her eyes. "You saved us angel. You'll be getting Christmas cards and invites to family dinners for the rest of your life."

Great I thought, I hate Christmas. My radio blared, "Fiona, this is Archie. Requesting a sit-rep."

Chapter Thirty-Six

Wednesday March 27, 2041 from 8.43 p.m. – Sergeant Lee

Charlie Team – Police Station

When I joined the WA Police Force as an adventurous young man in 2021, I never thought in my wildest dreams that I would be leading a team of militia some twenty years later. I'm sure there's been thousands of men throughout history that have had similar reflections – '*When I joined the WA Police Force in 1913, I never thought I'd be dodging bullets as I sprinted up these Gallipoli hills.*'

I glanced at my watch – 8:43 p.m. If the intel is correct, the NMG have been using the police station as an armoury. As I pressed my shoulder up against the door frame, I couldn't help but consider our odds of success. The scared shitless look on Senior Constable Atkins' face, certainly didn't fill me with confidence.

"Are you ready?" I asked Atkins.

He nodded nervously in reply. For fuck's sake, he's shaking in his bloody boots. One look at this bloke and any competent bookie wouldn't give us better odds than 10 to 1. After this is all over, I plan on having some stern words with my Kalgoorlie counterpart. Surely Atkins isn't his best officer. When he failed to attend the team's training sessions, I didn't make a big hoo-ha about it because I thought he was competent. I was gravely mistaken.

I ordered two of my team to advance to the rear door to prevent any outlaws from escaping. After waiting thirty seconds, I yelled, "GO, GO, GO."

Atkins went in hard and fast. He failed to wait for me to clear the main office area and just barrelled his way past the counter. Before I had an opportunity to tell him to slow down, he rushed into the break room at the rear of the station.

I heard a shotgun – BOOM!

With one hand pressed to his ass cheek, Atkins ran from the rear of the station screaming like a banshee on fire. He left a trail of blood in his wake as he ran straight out the station door.

I used the front counter as cover and yelled, "I'm Sergeant Lee from Esperance Police Station. We have five gunslingers out here that are a lot meaner than the fella you just shot in the ass. Come out with your hands up or we're coming in with guns blazing."

I didn't plan on sending my men to their death. Instead, I planned on throwing a grenade. I had seized the grenade just after the War and stored it in my armoury for just such an occasion.

"When I give you the thumbs-up, you run from the station," I whispered to my men.

I wanted to give my men time to get clear before I threw it. Who knows how many rounds or explosives are stored in the break room? There could be some impressive fireworks. I gripped the grenade in my right hand, fully prepared to pull the pin.

"I'm giving you ten seconds. Ten, nine, eight, seven."

Just as I yelled six, a skinny old barefoot bloke wearing a filthy white singlet ambled out of the kitchen with his hands raised in the air. I examined the grenade in my hand. I'm ashamed to admit that I was a little disappointed that I didn't get to use it.

Chapter Thirty-Seven

Wednesday March 27, 2041 from 8.45pm – Clarry

Bravo Team – Norseman Hotel

We parked Bravo Team's four vehicles down a side street, twenty metres from the Norseman Hotel. The streets were deserted. As planned, two of my uncles and one cousin jogged to the rear of the hotel to cover the back door. My fifteen family members and Captain Ross walked with me to the front doors of the establishment. The NMG had been using the hotel as their drinking hole. We were likely to find violent, intoxicated, and well-armed men who would not surrender without a fight.

The Captain and three of my cousins established a defensive position outside the front of the hotel, ensuring outlaws didn't attack us from our rear. I kept my promise to Elizabeth by placing the Captain out of harm's way. Just before we left for Norseman, I asked my cousins to look out for him during the Op. All three were keen hunters and sharp shooters. He was safer outside the premises than inside, that's for sure.

My eleven family members followed me through the front doors of the premises and fanned out along the entry wall. The jukebox was screaming out Black Sabbath's song, '*Paranoid*.' Ozzy Osbourne's desperate vocals along with the driving guitar and powerful bass, generated a nervous energy that sent tingles up my spine.

My cousin on the far left pulled the plug out of the wall socket. There was a moment of silence and stillness. The thirty or so outlaws either stood along the bar, around the pool table or in front of the dart board. They were holding bottles of beer and glasses of spirits. A mixture of tobacco and cannabis smoke filled the air.

The outlaws glared in our direction with a mixture of hate and fear in their eyes. I can pretty much guarantee they'd never seen so many blackfellas on their patch. My family were armed with either pump-action shotguns or assault rifles. All of which were now levelled at the outlaws' chests. I was carrying a wicked looking F92 Austeyr assault rifle that Archie gifted me upon returning from Kalgoorlie. I never had a chance to ask him how he acquired it. We also carried a backup sidearm holstered to our belts.

"We're here because some of you fellas lynched my cousins," I said with a contemptuous tone. I took a step towards the bar. "Raise your hands in the air and get down on your knees. If you comply with my instructions, I give you my word that we'll escort you to the police station."

As a Christian I had to give them an opportunity to surrender. But I knew they'd never take a blackfella's word and agree to walk towards the gallows of their own free will.

A bearded pot-bellied man near the dart board shouted, "Fuck you, you black bastard," and reached under his leather jacket. Within a heartbeat all hell broke loose. Outlaws reached for their weapons as we started firing our longarms. I focused on the men in my immediate line of sight. I mowed the pot-bellied provocateur down instantly. Blood spraying from his neck and chest. A skinny bloke with shoulder length black hair was cut down by gunfire as he raised a sawn-off shotgun.

Twelve-gauge slugs, buck shot and 5.56-millimetre rounds ripped through flesh, glass, wood, and brick, in a deafening display of pure and utter violence. Blood, bone, and flesh splattered against the wall, floor, bar, and ceiling.

In less than five seconds we had slaughtered the entire group. I doubt they'd even managed to fire a round in our direction. I could feel my heart racing. I wouldn't have been surprised to learn that it had jumped from 70 to 180 beats in a matter of a seconds. As I reloaded my rifle, I noticed for the first time that my ears were ringing. The average pain threshold from loud sounds is considered to be between 130 and 140 decibels (dBs). The rifles and shotguns we were using emit over 155 dBs. It's no wonder my ears were ringing.

I was just about to provide an update over the radio when I heard shots ring out at the rear of the premises. My uncle advised me over the radio that they'd shot two outlaws that had attempted to escape out the back door.

Nine of my family members followed me up the stairs to the second storey. Our second team objective was clearing the twenty hotel rooms. We paired up and spread out along the corridor. I partnered up with Rory, my eighteen-year-old cousin who happened to be a talented guitarist who idolised Jimi Hendrix.

Rory and I stood outside room sixteen. I was about to reach for the doorknob when a loud BOOM! erupted from inside the room. A spread of buckshot scattered the door and corridor wall. The lead pellets missed us by centimetres. I failed to hear the slide action of a pump-action shotgun, but I heard another BOOM! I made the educated guess that he was armed with a double-barrel shotgun.

I wasn't going to lose another young cousin. Before he had time to reload, I stepped in front of the room door and squeezed the trigger. It took three seconds to fire all thirty 5.56-millimetre rounds from the assault rifle's magazine. The rounds pierced through the plywood door at 930 metres per second like darts hitting balloons.

I reloaded my rifle. Rory kicked open the shredded door and we entered the room with our muzzles raised. We found an obese man wearing pink undies and a white singlet, lying spread eagle on the bed with his shotgun resting on his chest. His body was riddled with bullet wounds. Blood dripped down his chin as he spluttered his final words. I couldn't be certain, but I believe he was asking us to bury him.

One after another my family members yelled, "ALL CLEAR."

When I returned to the bar, I examined the carnage and paused to reflect on how much I missed my cousins. Now that they'd been avenged, their spirits could rest.

Chapter Thirty-Eight

Wednesday March 27, 2041 from 8.45 p.m.
– Mayor Jason

Delta Team – Railway Motel

Before the War I owned a successful commercial plumbing business. I was also a keen runner, spending my free time running day and night. Each year I competed in at least three international marathon events. I was actually quite good if I do say so myself. I managed to place third in my age division in the 2029 New York Marathon. A photo of me crossing the finish line was on the back page of the Esperance Express. When I reflect on my last competitive marathon, it's hard to believe that I was competing in China, just six months prior to the U.S. declaring war.

The previous Esperance Mayor died of a heart attack almost two years ago. Business is slow and sporting events like marathons are a thing of the past. I'm a person that needs to keep busy, so I submitted my nomination for mayor and ran for election. It turned out that I was the only person that wanted the responsibility. I enjoy most of what the job entails, even the task of leading a team of militia. On the flip side, sorting out neighbourly disputes about noise, dogs, gardens, and fences, can be an absolute pain in the rear end.

We parked at an intersection behind some large trees, fifty metres from the Railway Motel. The NMG were using the motel as their canteen, forcing the residents to cook and serve them food day and night.

I sent four of my team carrying door breaching tools to the rear of the premises. At 8:45 p.m. on the dot, they would make entry through the two rear doors. A few years back, one of my team members worked as a kitchen hand at this very motel. She was able to provide us detailed information of the property's lay-out.

The time struck 8:45 p.m. Four of my team followed me through the front door to the dining room. The guard standing inside the doorway didn't have time to react. I pointed the muzzle of my assault rifle under his jaw and took the shotgun out of his hands, while my team shouted for the two outlaws sitting at dining tables to raise their hands in the air. We then secured their wrists with cable ties.

Alex, a twenty-two-year-old baker, and Susan, a thirty-one-year-old farm hand, were clearing the rear kitchen when I heard the terrifying sound of fully automatic gunfire. It sounded like a Rambo movie. I ran to the kitchen to find four of my team standing over two dead outlaws. They had entered through the rear doors to find Alex and Susan in a shootout with the guards. The cowards must have been hiding in the kitchen.

Alex and Susan were lying side by side in a pool of blood. I knelt down beside their motionless bodies to check their pulse, before wiping away my tears.

Chapter Thirty-Nine

Wednesday March 27, 2041 from 9:30 p.m. – Archie

The mayor, sergeant and Clarry provided me a sit-rep over the radio on channel four. The sergeant's Charlie Team captured the armoury and one outlaw, reporting no friendly casualties and only one walking wounded. Senior Constable Atkins had taken a bullet in the backside. I smiled and filed a mental note to get the full story during the debrief.

The mayor's Delta Team succeeded in securing the canteen, but unfortunately lost two members when they were shot by outlaws' hiding in the kitchen. They had killed the men and captured three more.

Clarry's Bravo Team had killed thirty-nine men with no friendly casualties. I was undecided whether I would have liked to be a fly on the wall during that confrontation. I had mixed feelings to say the least. There is no doubt that revenge can be satisfying, but the violence and carnage that is imprinted into your memory can have negative consequences. *How many marbles did that conflict cost?*

Upon arrival at the school gym, I could see the relief in the residents' faces. They were hugging, laughing, and crying with tears of joy. I attained a sit-rep from Fiona as she was wrapping a bandage around a young girl's wounded arm. She was remarkably effective at multi-tasking. Fiona and I agreed to send four militia members and two medics with the wounded to the Norseman Hospital. We were unaware of the current condition of the hospital, but it had to be a better option than treating the wounded in the gym.

Phase Two of the operation had now been executed, with

Bravo, Charlie and Delta Teams rendezvousing at our location with all surviving residents. The sergeant left four militia members to barricade and guard the police station. I calculated that there were fifty-nine outlaws dead and three captured. Regrettably, eight militia and nine residents had been lost during Phase One.

I briefed the team leaders in the gym's equipment store. We decided to leave ten well-armed militia members to secure the gym and protect the residents. We formed the militia into four-person assault teams, issuing them a vehicle and advising them to report back using their Victor call sign. We provided them maps with their areas of responsibility, instructing them to clear each and every building.

Lee Mitchell performed the role of communications officer from the police station. The teams were ordered to provide her regular sit-reps over the radio, so she could record the teams' progress on a town map. She could reduce the likelihood of friendly fire incidents, by ensuring teams stayed clear of buildings that were in the process of being searched.

Fiona and I teamed up with the Captain and a young man that looked familiar. Charlie whispered in my ear, "Take care of my boy Archie." Seven weeks had passed since Sonny, Charlie's eldest boy, had aimed his rifle at my chest. Sonny's younger brother, who was a spitting image of him, had caused a misunderstanding when he fired a rock at me with his slingshot. The recollection made me smile. I squeezed Charlie's shoulder. "Don't worry mate, I'll look after him like he's my own."

I drove the Beast to the south western side of the town, where we commenced clearing Goodliffe Street. The first twelve houses we cleared were empty. Some houses had spoilt food left in the open and others had more gruesome finds, with several dead pets, and in one case, a man who had hung himself from the rafter of an outdoor pergola. Over the next two hours we continued to clear residential houses, gradually moving closer to the centre of town.

I heard over the radio that a team on the eastern side had made contact with several outlaws. When the outlaws' attempted to flee, they were cut down by militia gunfire. Teams that had witnessed the death of their friends by the hands of the NMG, showed little to no interest in capturing the enemy - *alive*. They were focused on vengeance. And who could really blame them.

We walked through the front gates of a timber church. Fiona and I made a tactical entry though the front door, with the Captain and Sonny following close behind. An elderly olive-skinned man was kneeling, his head bent forward in prayer before a large wooden cross. Fiona suddenly raised her muzzle towards a big man who entered the church through the back door. I shoved her aside just before she fired, forcing her to miss her target and instead splinter a timber pew. I yelled, "Guns down," and quick marched towards the unarmed man. The man's expression conveyed a sense of recognition as I smashed the butt of my revolver into his temple. His eyes rolled back, and he collapsed onto the church floor with a thud! I knelt down and secured his wrists with cable ties and rolled him onto his side.

"What the fuck?" Fiona asked irritably.

"Long story, but this bloke saved my life. I owe him one."

The big Samoan had intervened when I was copping a beating at the hotel. As I searched him for weapons his name suddenly popped into my head – *Iokua.*

The old man that had been kneeling in prayer now sat on a pew with his wrists clasped with cable ties. I had attempted to question him, but I couldn't make rhyme or reason out of anything he said. He spoke of his wife waiting for him at the Auckland Airport and how he needed to catch a plane. To my knowledge, there hasn't been a domestic or international flight for the past eight years. I examined a photo that was sticking out of his shirt pocket. He was standing in a park alongside a lady I presumed was his wife and Iokua as a younger man.

I pointed at Iokua. "Is he your son?"

He nodded. "My naughty boy. Needs a spank," he muttered.

"I'm not going to disagree with you sir," I said.

"Are you here to play with him? Church is finished so you can play marbles in the yard."

"Maybe later sir," I responded.

I contacted Sergeant Lee by radio and requested that he attend the church in the van. It would be near impossible to lift the giant Samoan into the rear seats of the two-door Beast, and I wasn't confident he would be amenable if he woke.

The sergeant arrived in the Kombi with two offsiders. It took four of us to carry the unconscious Iokua into the back of the van. With great difficulty we managed to lie him down in the back seat. His father stared out of a window as he muttered nonsensically.

I was concerned that if Gizzarelli set eyes on the pair, he would repeat his earlier performance and execute them both. As the sergeant was preparing to drive away, I pointed towards the back of the van and asked, "Can you do me a solid and keep these two away from Gizzarelli?"

"No problem, Archie, I'll lock them in the station cell. Do you want to tell me what this is all about?"

"Nah, you're a busy man. We'll speak later."

Just after the sergeant drove from the church, I heard the mayor's dulcet tones over the radio. He was requesting medics to attend his current location. He explained that his team had searched the Norseman Council office and found twenty South Australian residents in a terrible condition. I pressed the transmitter button and advised the mayor that we were 'on our way'.

Upon our arrival to the council building, Jarrad, the thin administrator that I'd met during my recce, was talking to Mayor Jason behind the front counter. As soon as the mayor was aware of our presence, he guided us to the council chamber. Twenty women and children of various ages were either seated in plush chairs or lying on the carpet. The mayor hadn't exaggerated, they were in a horrendous state. Most looked like they hadn't slept for days, and some had been beaten, with black eyes, split lips, broken noses, and horrific bruising. I had to take a second glance as I thought my eyes had deceived me. There were three sets of identical twins and two dwarfs amongst the group. Captain Ross, Fiona, and Sonny opened their medic packs and started triaging the injured.

I found Jarrad slumped in a chair sobbing in the front office. As I approached, he rubbed his eyes with the sleeves of his jumper, attempting to wipe away the evidence of tears.

He looked up with bloodshot eyes, "It seems you've jumped ship. I know the feeling."

I shook my head. "I'm not judging you Jarrad, but I didn't jump anything. I was gathering intel. Look, from my perspective, that's all water under the bridge. And now I need your help. I need information concerning the captives from South Australia."

"What do you want to know?"

I sat down and opened my notebook. "Can we start with why these people are here?"

Jarrad handed me a requisition form with a list of captive requirements, including identical twins, dwarves, and pregnant women.

"The gang is raiding small towns in S.A. and abducting people to work in the mine. They're also selling people to some bloke called Patterson. He's paying in gold bars and assault rifles for people with, um, certain characteristics. I've no idea why. My job is, I mean.... well, was to separate them from the group and accept payment when Patterson's man arrives to pick them up. The group in the chamber were due to leave tomorrow."

I took a second look at the list. "Explain to me what Patterson's minion looks like."

"He's not hard to spot. He looks like a character from a Marvel comic."

Chapter Forty

Thursday March 28, 2041 from 5.45 a.m. – Archie

By the completion of Phase Two we had killed an additional nine outlaws and captured another two, providing a total of sixty-seven dead and seven captured. The adrenalin had completely dissipated, and I was feeling utterly exhausted. I also had a thumping headache. My mind had started to wander, and my mood had darkened. I replayed the scenes in the gold mine over and over – the death of the mother and her son's anguish – the fear of being trapped or crushed in a rock collapse – Gizzarelli's look of pure joy as he executed the guards. The disturbing thoughts were tunnelling deep into my psyche like a vicious viral infection that refuses to release its victim.

Fiona was assisting at the hospital while I headed to the police station to receive a sit-rep from Sergeant Lee. On my way, I stopped by the town pharmacy in hope of finding paracetamol or ibuprofen. I parked the Beast out the front and kicked open the pharmacy's front door. I was not in the mood to pick the lock. I switched on the store lights and searched the shelves. Not surprisingly, the store had been ransacked, with bottles and packets strewn over the floor and counter. I found a trampled packet of Panadol on the floor and popped two pills, swallowing them down with a gulp of water from my canteen.

As I walked towards the exit, I noticed a bottle with a label that was all too familiar. The oxycodone stood on an empty shelf. In my crazed mind I considered fate's cruelty. *Did some outlaw leave the oxy to taunt me?* Drug addiction programs are no longer an option, but if they were, I'd be urgently contacting my sponsor.

In my stupor I stared at the bottle. My hands shook as beads of sweat formed on my forehead and trickled down my face. Staring my demon in the eye, I considered taking just one pill. Just one. I then thought of what Clarry and Fiona would think of me. Their disappointment!

After I recovered my faculties, I marched out the front door, leaving the bottle untouched on the empty shelf.

I needed to get out of town, settle a debt and clear my head. I drove the Beast around the corner to the police station. As I walked to the station's front door, I noticed that the jarrah gallows had been assembled on the main street. Most small towns use portable gallows that are constructed from wood or galvanized steel that can be readily assembled when required.

The station was a hive of activity, with the mayor's recovery team organising the logistical requirements for the rescued residents – housing, clothes, food, transport, and amenities. Sergeant Lee stood in the main office of the station, busily giving instructions over the radio to the militia teams. I wish I had his energy. After he concluded his transmission, he handed the radio to Lee Mitchell and asked her to coordinate the transportation of the Norseman citizens that no longer wished to reside in the town.

I nodded a greeting to the sergeant. "I'm going to grab a coffee mate. We need to have a little talk. Do you want one?"

"That sounds ominous. Give me two minutes, I'll meet you in the crib room."

I ambled into the break room to find the Esperance Judge sitting at the table having a cup of tea and reading the Esperance Express. He was an elderly gentleman with curly grey hair and thick mutton chops. He had arrived from Esperance an hour ago to try the accused outlaws.

He looked up as I entered. "Don't let me bother you sir, I'm just grabbing a coffee," I said as I grabbed a mug.

"Good morning Mr O'Connor. I'm glad to see that you fared well after last night's activities. Congratulations on a very successful mission."

I was surprised that he knew my name. "Thank you, sir. It's the Esperance and Kalgoorlie residents that should be congratulated. I just came along for the ride."

He chuckled. "How very self-deprecatory of you. You'll be happy to know that I've already conducted the trial. It only took fifteen minutes. A new personal record. Of course, it was all but a mere formality. I believe the mayor plans to lead the seven convicted men to the gallows in the next half hour or so," he said, checking his watch.

I was about to ask him why he sentenced Iokua's father to hang (*a man who on the balance of probabilities has some form of dementia and is not a member of the NMG*) when Sergeant Lee entered the room.

The Judge nodded to the sergeant and returned to reading his newspaper. As the sergeant made a coffee, I sidled up to him and asked in a low voice, "Can we talk in private?"

"Sure, bring your coffee and we'll speak in the interview room."

We took a seat in the bland interview room. "What's up Archie?"

"The big Samoan you have in the cell saved my life when I was conducting my recce. I owe him one. I know this is a lot to ask mate, but I want to take him and his father across the border."

The sergeant rubbed his tired eyes and yawned, fatigue finally starting to set in. "You want to pardon them? Well, okay, I guess we can ask the judge, but I don't like your chances."

"This is important to me mate," I said earnestly.

The sergeant let out a long sigh. "I owe you Archie. We all owe you. Without your plan and guidance, there's no way in hell we could have pulled off this operation. You take them and go. Let me handle the Judge."

"Thanks mate, I really appreciate this."

"Drive around back and I'll meet you in the staff carpark. We don't want to cause a riot," he explained.

I parked the Beast and waited for the sergeant to escort the men through the station's rear door. Both men had their wrists secured to their front with cable ties. Iokua looked how I felt – dead on his feet. Few men could sleep knowing they were about to hang.

"I'll take it from here sergeant. By the way, I owe you a beer."

"It's all good Archie. Take care."

As the sergeant re-entered the station, I opened the front passenger door and motioned to Iokua. "I'm taking you both across the border. If you try anything, I won't hesitate," I said, placing my hand on the grip of my revolver.

As we drove down the main street, the five outlaws stood in line with their wrists secured behind their backs, waiting to be led up the gallows steps. One by one, the executioner secured the rope around their necks and pushed them off the platform. A lady from the crowd stepped towards the condemned men and spat at their feet, before turning on her heels and striding away. Later that morning, the sergeant would organise for the men to be cut down, transported to the bush, and buried in unmarked graves alongside the other outlaws who had lost their lives.

We didn't say a single word during the seven hour journey. I just drove in blissful silence through the night and into the day towards the South Australian border. By the time we reached our destination, I was absolutely spent! I parked near the old bullet riddled sign that read, 'Welcome to SA.' Iokua and his father exited the Beast and stood on the side of the road. I followed them and cut their cable ties with my F-S fighting knife.

I returned to the front seat of the Beast and turned the ignition key. Iokua bent down and peered through the opened window, "Thank you bro."

"Now we're even. But I won't forget what you did to those people. If I see you again, and you're involved in slavery, I will bring you in," I replied with a steady gaze.

I accelerated down the road, leaving them in a cloud of dust.

Chapter Forty-One

Sunday March 31, 2041 – Fiona

Three days had passed since we freed Norseman from the NMG. The mayor implemented his recovery plan, assisting the surviving residents to reclaim their homes and purchase food and amenities. Almost a third of the residents decided to leave Norseman and search for a fresh start in Esperance or Kalgoorlie. Some wanted to escape painful memories, while others feared that gangs would once again cross the border to capture the town. The residents that stayed voted to demolish the mine, in the hope that their memories of misery and horror would be buried with the gold.

Archie and I returned to Clarry's home to recuperate and plan our next move. Helen had taken a keen interest in the horses and asked if I'd teach her to ride. Archie encouraged me to start as soon as possible, telling me that it would be a 'cathartic experience,' one that Helen and I needed after the chaos and violence we endured. When I asked him to clarify, he explained that it would help take my mind off the operation. I wondered if he knew the specifics of what occurred at the high school gymnasium.

Jasper's calm temperament made him the perfect mount for Helen to learn on. She was a good student and I actually had fun teaching her. Clarry suggested I speak to her about her future and the opportunity to join one of the surviving families, many of whom had lost children. I attempted to broach the subject as we trotted along the shoreline of a local beach. My good intentions backfired in a spectacular fashion, with Helen galloping back to Clarry's house and locking herself in her bedroom.

After an hour or so, I convinced Helen to unlock her bedroom door.

I sat on the edge of the bed while Helen sat in the corner of the room with her arms wrapped around her shins. "Look, I'm sorry Helen, but I'm just trying to look after your best interests." *Wow! Even to my own ears I sound like a stuck-up adult.*

"Why can't I live here with you?" she asked in a quiet voice.

"Don't you want to stay with one of the families you know?"

"No, I don't know any of them. I only got there a month ago."

I wanted to slap myself in the forehead. I'd mistakenly presumed that she was a resident of Norseman. "Where was your home?"

"In Clare Valley. We had a vineyard before the men came. They burnt our house down," she explained with tears running down her cheeks.

I had no idea where Clare Valley was located. I'd never heard of it. "Where is Clare Valley Helen?"

"In South Australia. They killed my parents and took me," she sobbed.

I sat down beside her and held her in my arms. "I want to stay here," she wailed.

I couldn't find the words to convey my thoughts. What could I say, *'I'm not ready to be a mum'* – *'I'm a bounty hunter and it's not safe'* – *'You're better off with someone else,'* she would just hear, *'I DON'T WANT YOU!'*

I woke early the following morning and had a light-bulb moment during my daily run. I spoke to Clarry, and he offered me a lift to the Ross's home on his way to work. He strolled towards the harbour as I approached the front door. After a couple of knocks, Elizabeth opened the door and rushed forward, grabbing me in her turkey wing arms. Her intense perfume almost made me gag. She offered me a piece of her delicious pavlova, which I unashamedly devoured in an unladylike manner. We spoke of anything and everything but the events in Norseman. Every time I attempted to broach the subject, she would redirect the conversation by gossiping about some sordid affair, or jump up to give her chatty galah a cracker.

I ended up blurting out in frustration, "Archie rescued a twelve-year-old girl in Norseman. She's fragile and needs a home. Can I leave her with you? You're the kindest woman I know, and I have no one else to leave her with."

Elizabeth smiled. "Of course you can. Why did you take so long to ask?"

I assisted Elizabeth in the fish 'n' chips shop until late in the afternoon and returned home with Clarry at the end of his working day.

The following morning, after promising Archie that I wouldn't drive like a maniac, he let me borrow the Beast to take Helen to the Ross's home. *Jesus, you'd think I was asking him to give me his first-born child.*

During the drive I lay my cards on the table. "I'm not going to BS you Helen. I want to be in your life and I think of you as a little sister, but you know you can't stay with me. I can't provide you a future. I'm taking you to a woman that helped me. She's kind, smart and a great cook. I'll visit you when I'm in town, I promise." Helen stared out the window pretending to ignore me. "I know you Helen, because I was you. You can have a good life here. Four words - Don't Stuff It Up!"

Elizabeth had baked a chocolate cake and made us cups of coco. She fussed over Helen as we sat at the dining room table making small talk. Helen didn't smile or engage, but she wasn't openly hostile either.

The Captain entered the kitchen and read the room like a poker pro. "Hey Helen, do you want to learn how to spearfish? Because I'm taking the boat out to catch me a massive groper!"

I was pleasantly surprised when Helen accepted the invitation, grabbing a second slice of cake as she followed the Captain to the harbour. As I was leaving the Ross's home, Elizabeth reassured me that Helen would be fine, she just needed time. *Don't we all, I thought to myself.*

Clarry and his family invited Mayor Jason, Sergeant Lee, and the Ross's to their caribberie (known in English as corroboree). The

Elders explained that a caribberie is a time to pass on stories of the Nyitting, which describes the Dreaming or Creation Time - a time before time, when spirits ascended from the land and descended from the sky to form the water, the land, and all living things.

We all sat in Clarry's backyard, full and satisfied from a magnificent meal of seafood that Captain Ross had caught and prepared. Clarry had the honour of reciting Dr Jack Davis's version of Yagan's ceremonial tribute to the Wagyl, for creating the Noongar universe.

I'm not a religious or spiritual person in any shape or form, but there's something beautiful in being connected to the land. The chant reminded me of the painting of the Wagyl on the water train, and the artist's belief that the Dreamtime creature would offer the train protection.

Helen was sitting with Elizabeth, relaxed and content in her presence. Archie was laughing as he listened to Sergeant Lee's version of events that led to Senior Constable Atkins being shot in the ass.

The rest of the night consisted of dancing, singing, and story-telling. I relaxed in the warm glow of the fire, enjoying the company of newfound friends. It had been a long time since I felt this content.

Chapter Forty-Two

Tuesday April 2, 2041 – Archie

The house was eerily quiet. Fiona was out walking the dogs and Clarry was visiting a lady friend. Clarry's family left Esperance the day before to return to their homes. My funds were disappearing fast, and I was itching to get back to work. The police had been busy dealing with border gangs and didn't have the resources to focus on local crime. New bounties were few and far between and I was considering putting the feelers out to work on the water train.

I was getting bored. The only job that we had going was the contract with Mr Singh to find his grandson. I found the blue Samsonite case in Fiona's bedroom and sorted through the material we retrieved from Patterson's thug in Kalgoorlie. I spread the posters, maps and reports over the kitchen table and perused my notes. There must be something that I've missed that will give us a lead.

I heard the front door unlock and Clarry walked into the dining room. "How is, um, what's her name?" I asked with a cheeky smile.

"What's her name is none of your business," he chided.

"Do you want a coffee?" I asked.

"Yeah sure," he replied.

"Good, can you make me one too," I said with a straight face.

"You lazy bugger, " he said, as he walked towards the kettle.

Clarry sat at the table and a passed me a cup. "What are you up to mate, completing a school project?"

"Ha ha, very funny. I found all this material at a house in Kalgoorlie. Same place I found the F92 assault rifle I gave you. It's all got to do with a contract I have regarding a kidnapping. Did I tell you about the freak with green blood?"

Clarry placed his hands on my shoulders and looked into my eyes. "Hold on. Did you just say green blood? I thought we'd beaten the drug problem brother. What are you on?" Clarry teased.

I lightly punched his shoulder and stood up. "Grab me a beer, because have I got a story to tell you."

Clarry took a couple of his home brews from the fridge, and I told him the basic gist - the meeting with Mr Singh, Sal's notes leading us to Paddy, and the monster with the green blood.

Clarry held up the poster and read the headline, "The New World Party. It sounds like a marketing campaign run by Hitler or Stalin."

I picked up one of the reports and handed it to him. "It's funny you say that, because Paddy compared Noel Patterson to Josef Mengele."

"Who?" Clarry asked.

"Josef Mengele, the crazy Nazi scientist that experimented on prisoners in the concentration camps during World War Two."

Clarry sighed. "I know who Mengele is, but did you say Noel Patterson?"

I nodded, "Yeah, Doctor Noel Patterson. He's the bloke that took Raj Singh. Mate, weren't you listening?"

Clarry stood from the table and walked to his bedroom. He returned shortly after carrying a cardboard box full of documents. He placed the box on the floor and pulled out a stack of papers, combing through them until he grasped a single document. "Aha! I knew it! I remember this bloke, he put in for a grant with the CSIRO just before the War. I specifically recall his application as it provided great comic relief in a difficult time." Clarry gathered all the reports and returned them to the box. "I need to read these."

"What, all of them?" I asked.

Clarry either didn't hear my question or couldn't be bothered answering, as he quick marched to his bedroom and shut the door. When Clarry is engrossed in a topic, especially when it's a problem that needs to be solved, he shuts himself off from all distractions, including his mates.

I sculled the remnants of my beer and walked to the backyard gym. I hit the bag with punch, kick, head, knee, and elbow combinations, working up a good sweat. After thirty minutes striking the bag, I focused on powerlifting exercises - squats, dead-lifts and bench-press.

Fiona and the dogs met me in the gym. Xena was the most eager to say hello. She ran up to me and placed her two front paws on my chest and planted her tongue under my chin. Fiona asked me if I wanted to join her for a ten-kilometre run. I was feeling pretty flat and fatigued after the workout. I was about to decline, when I suddenly recalled how exhausted I felt during the run with Helen through the Norseman bush. I groaned inwardly and placed four five-kilo plates into an old backpack and followed her down the road to a nearby bush track. Fiona set a good pace and we completed the run in just over forty-five minutes.

Upon our return, I wasn't at all surprised to find Clarry still locked in his room. When I hit the hay hours later, he was still pouring through the reports. Xena was lying at the foot of my bed, patiently waiting for me to warm up the mattress.

I was woken at a sparrow-fart by someone pushing my shoulder. I yawned and shoved Clarry's hand away. "What time is it?"

Clarry gripped a coffee with steam rising from the mug. "It's 5 a.m. already. Here, get up and drink this. I have eggs and bacon on the pan, we need to talk."

I rolled out of bed and stretched my neck, back and shoulders to the sounds of snap, crackle, and pop. As I touched my toes, I was definitely feeling the effects of yesterday's workout. My hamstrings felt as tight as a sailor's knot.

Clarry was plating up breakfast as I ambled into the kitchen. He looked like he hadn't slept a wink. "Forget bags, you've got suitcases under your eyes mate. How much sleep did you get last night?"

"I didn't. It took me all night to read Patterson's reports," he replied.

Fiona skipped in through the back door, returning from a twelve-kilometre run. I felt pain in my calves just thinking about slipping on my trainers – *oh to be young again!* Clarry picked up my notebook from the kitchen table and flicked through the pages as he sipped his coffee from his favourite mug. His treasured purple mug depicted an anchor, the logo of the Fremantle Docker's football team we barracked for in the Australian Football League (AFL). It was rumoured that former players from the Dockers and their rivals, the West Coast Eagles, met in a southwestern town after the War and played one final derby. Clarry's aware that this rumour is romanticism at its best, but he passionately wants to believe it's true.

Fiona sat down and pinched a piece of bacon from my plate. My instincts were to slam my hand down on her knuckles, but I just grunted in annoyance. "So, what's up?" Fiona asked as she chewed my bacon.

"Clarry here is going to tell us what he learned from Patterson's reports." We both looked intensely at Clarry in anticipation.

Clarry cleared his throat. "I'm not sure if you're aware Fiona, but I used to work for the CSIRO. I doubt Archie knows what unit I worked for, or even my specialisation. From the look on your face Archie, my hypothesis is confirmed."

I gave him a wounded look. "You were a scientist working on bugs and things."

Clarry smirked. "Well done Archie, I was a scientist working on bug and things. My PhD topic concerned diabetes, an autoimmune disease that my people are almost four times more likely to suffer from than non-indigenous people. I was a supervisor in the Health and Biosecurity unit. So, when Patterson's application first came across my desk, I took an interest in his proposal. But telomeres are not my area of expertise, so I asked one of my colleagues to examine his application. As I mentioned last night, his application was automatically dismissed and made light of to say the least."

"So you all took the piss out of him?" asked Fiona.

Clarry shrugged his shoulders. "I wish I'd paid more attention. After reading his research last night, I actually believe his hypothesis is plausible. In these reports, he claims to have lengthened his subjects' life spans and significantly reduced the likelihood of diseases such as cancer and diabetes, by permanently maintaining the length of the subjects' telomeres. In the past, research in this area had resulted in achieving the unfortunate result of stimulating cancer cells. To solve this problem, he's used targeted radiation within the cells of the liver and kidneys, as a countermeasure to the abnormal production of proteins. But I can't verify any of his claims without access to a lab and the process of a peer review."

I was now more confused than before Clarry started his explanation. "Sorry, what is a telomere?"

Clarry sighed theatrically. "Sorry, I'll simplify it for you. A telomere is a region of one's DNA at the end of a chromosome. It protects the end of the chromosome from deteriorating or fusing with other chromosomes. It's believed that this reduces the aging process. Over one's life, telomeres gradually shorten, until cells can no longer replicate, and we die. Patterson claims to have stopped telomeres shortening, therefore prolonging life."

I was becoming a little impatient, and to be honest a little lost in his scientific mumbo jumbo. "Okay, what about the green blood?"

Clarry picked up a book from his mystery box and opened it to a page that he had tagged. "You can see the anatomy of the Blue Tongue Lizard, which belongs to the skink family. Skinks have green blood due to an accretion of a bile pigment called biliverdin. Biliverdin and bilirubin are by-products of the liver, which humans also produce. Humans normally excrete these by-products, whereas skinks don't, so it builds up in their body and causes their blood to turn green. Patterson's irradiating of the liver and kidney cells is causing this unintentional symptom. It should also be noted that he's injecting his subjects with exceedingly high doses of modified equine growth hormone and myostatin inhibitors, to stimulate cell regeneration and turn them into man mountains."

I nodded in understanding. "This explains Chef Hulk." Clarry gave me a confused look.

Fiona chimed in, "Not only was the bloke with green blood built like a professional body builder and had an inhuman pain threshold, but he could also cook a mean chicken curry."

Clarry pointed to one of the reports and added, "Well, for no apparent reason he's also prescribing his 'subjects,' and I'm using that term loosely, high doses of methamphetamine. That could explain his ability to endure pain." Clarry opened one of the reports. "There's no mention of enhanced cooking ability in any of the reports."

"Don't give up your day job Jerry Seinfeld," I teased. I passed Clarry 'The New World Order' poster, "I think he has a warped fantasy of building an army of Super Human Mutants."

"Mutants?" Fiona asked as an afterthought.

Clarry shrugged his shoulders. "I don't have enough information to form a conclusion, but he's using a combination of radiation and animal hormones."

I showed Clarry the maps with the Blue Opal Resort, The Perth Mint and Campbell Barracks encircled with a black marker. "In all seriousness, is it possible that he's in Perth building an army?"

Clarry avoided answering my question by asking a question of his own, "Can you tell me exactly, word for word what Paddy told you about his association with Patterson?"

After Fiona and I explained everything we knew about the case, Clarry leaned back in his chair and clasped his hands to the back of his head. "I need time to think. We'll reconvene at lunch."

Fiona punched me in the arm. "Do you want to do some sparring?"

I instantly reached down and held my right hamstring. "Let's go shooting instead. We'll take the horses out and drill in the kill house."

Fiona's shooting had improved leaps and bounds. She could now count the pistol and shotgun shells as she engaged the targets and reload instantly without looking at her firearm or mag pouches. Her shot groupings were now tighter than mine, however I was still a little faster in identifying and engaging the targets. She's a natural talent with quick reflexes and smooth weapon handling.

After two hours of shooting, Fiona insisted we complete some sparring rounds. I have clear advantages when competing with her in combat activities. Not only am I twenty-five kilos or so heavier and five inches taller, but I've also been a martial arts practitioner longer than she's been alive. But I have to give credit where credit is due, she's ballsy and won't back down.

We returned to Clarry's gym and slipped on the fingerless gloves and shin pads. We touched gloves and then encircled each other testing our range. She swiftly closed the distance and threw a straight cross, left kick combination, and then immediately dove for a double leg take-down. She was determined to put me on my ass. I sprawled on top of her and rather than grappling on the ground, I immediately rose to my feet and stepped to the side. I push kicked her to the stomach and then took a half-a-step and thigh kicked her lead leg. She surprisingly checked my kick with her shin and took a big step forward, clipping me to the jaw with a left hook.

I took a step back and smiled. "You're getting better young padawan."

She jabbed and I slipped to the outside. "What the fuck is a padawan?" she asked.

"Disregard," I replied as I dove for a single leg and spun her to the ground. I then performed an arm-bar, bending her arm outward at the elbow joint, forcing her to tap my leg to signal that she was giving up. She punched the ground angrily and gingerly rose from the mats.

Clarry whistled from the back door. "After you two have finished playing, come inside and let's chat."

Clarry was standing in front of maps that he'd pinned to his lounge room wall. He was making notes on his clip board. I was still a little bewildered by his intense interest in this contract. "So, what's the story Clarry?"

Clarry looked up from his clip board. "You're going to rescue that boy and I'm going to help you."

I pointed at the Blue Opal Hotel on the map. "You actually believe they're in Perth?"

"I'm convinced of it. Look, full disclosure. I'm not going to bullshit you and say this is all about rescuing the boy. I have a selfish reason for helping you. If Patterson has actually achieved the results detailed in these reports, it has the potential to change the way we exist. We could all be protected from cancer and extend our life expectancy. We could repopulate the cities and move on from this Middle Ages existence. I can be a scientist again. Don't you see Archie, this is an opportunity we can't ignore," he explained fervently.

I was struggling to keep up with him. "Okay mate, slow down. We have a little issue of radiation exposure. We can't just drive to Perth and walk into the Blue Opal Hotel lobby. We'll be pissing and puking blood from radiation exposure before we arrive in the carpark."

Clarry leaned closer and with an earnest tone he stated, "Trust me Archie, we're going to plan this out one step at a time. I don't plan on shitting out my gastrointestinal tract either."

Over the next two days, Clarry was busier than a one-legged man in a butt-kicking contest. He worked all day and late into the night, reading copious reports, journals, and textbooks, making logistic lists, developing strategies, and considering risk management plans. He was definitely a man on a mission. I offered to help, but he refused in his candid manner, explaining that I'd just be getting in his way. He didn't hurt my feelings. I was used to his eccentricities. I learned long ago that it's wise to accept your friends' idiosyncrasies, just like I hope they accept mine. He advised me that he'd ask me for my input after he completed the draft plan.

Chapter Forty-Three

April 4 – 6, 2041 – Clarry

As I sat in the backyard gazing up at the stars, I contemplated the upcoming mission. I enjoy the mental stimulation of conducting research, analysing, and solving problems. Don't get me wrong, I love fishing for a living, but I was born to be a scientist. I have always been an inquisitive person. One of my uncle's nicknamed me Y, because as a child all I did was ask, WHY? Why do motorbikes go faster than cars? Why don't they send more people to the moon? Why does Auntie have hair on her chin? My uncle complained that not even Google could answer all of my questions.

As a young child, my cousins would be kicking a football while I was studying in the school library. As a teenager, my cousins would be taking girls out to the cinema while I gazed through a telescope. As an adult, my cousins were fighting in wars while I conducted my PhD research.

This is why Patterson's research has reinvigorated me. It's provided me an opportunity to challenge my grey matter and dream of returning to a lab. I just pray that I'm not justifying the risk on the hope of a successful outcome, like a gambler that goes all-in after a night of repetitive losses. I ask myself as I sit in the dark, am I willing to risk my life and the lives of my friends, in the hope of succeeding in this mission.

The most crucial items on my logistics list were the three Level A Hazmat suits with radiation shielding in the lining. These suits provide the highest level of protection from radiation exposure and are fully encapsulated with a full-facepiece self-contained breathing apparatus (SCBAs). Without this protection, the mission has no chance of success. We had Level A suits stored at the CSIRO Perth Office. Unfortunately, they were stored in the contaminated zone. We'd be experiencing acute radiation sickness by the time we entered the city and located the suits.

I was what you would call a nosey scientist. I wanted to know as much as I could about the various research projects the organisation was supporting. Not long before the start of the War, I toured our Geraldton Astronomy Support Hub and recalled seeing a reserve supply of Level A suits in their Secure Storage Unit. I just hope they are still there.

Archie and Fiona had just returned from a ride and were guiding the horses to the stables. I walked out to the backyard and asked them to meet me in the lounge room for a coffee and strategy meeting. I placed their mugs on the coffee table and advised them that my first goal was to travel to the town of Geraldton and pick up the hazmat suits from the CSIRO Astronomy Hub. With a guilty conscience I chose to omit my fear that the Hub had been looted and the suits plundered. My second objective was to modify scuba tanks, so we have enough air to get into Perth, complete our mission and return uncontaminated. The Captain should be able to assist us to achieve this objective.

Archie raised his eyebrows. "By our mission, you mean to rescue Raj and return him to his family?"

I needed to be very strategic in how I worded my following explanation. Archie is my best mate and he's highly intelligent, but he can tend to be fixated on achieving his priorities, without considering other perspectives. This may be due to a personality trait, or his military objective-based approach, or even a lawyer's ego. I just had to convince him that we can achieve both our outcomes.

I leaned forward in the couch. "Raj is our number one priority brother. But I also want to grab Patterson's research and capture one of his subjects alive."

Archie frowned in disbelief. "You want to do what?"

"We need to take this opportunity Archie. I can take the research and the subject back to the lab in Geraldton, build it back up and work on this breakthrough. I need this, Archie. It will change the way we live," I explained, acutely aware of the desperation creeping into my tone.

"How exactly will this change the way we live?" Archie asked, like a lawyer cross-examining his opponent's witness.

"Just imagine a vaccine for cancer and a life expectancy of 200 years," I said, hoping I didn't sound like I was trying to oversell it.

Archie looked over at Fiona and she nodded her head. "Let's do it Archie," she said. Archie didn't look convinced, but to my relief, he nodded his head in reply.

~

The journey from Esperance to the town of Geraldton should take just over eleven hours. As a majority of the 1100-kilometre journey was on major roads, it was wise to plan our refuelling stops. We packed enough food, water, and fuel for the trip, ensuring we had room for ammunition in case we came across a situation we couldn't talk our way out of.

Archie said his goodbyes to Roger and Xena, explaining that we'd be back as soon as possible. The ever-reliable Captain Ross offered to look after the dogs and horses while we were away. As Archie reversed down the driveway, Xena and Zeus stood at the security screen door and whined.

Archie drove the Beast for the first four hours, munching on anything he could get his hands on as he sang to mixed-tapes. I inserted ear plugs to drown out Archie's attempt to hold a note. Fiona slept in the back seat like a log, extending her legs over the arm rest. Archie immediately detached her feet from the arm rest, and to his annoyance he was forced to repeat the action numerous times during the trip. His obvious frustration brought a smile to my face.

I just started to close my eyes when Archie shook my shoulder and said something that I couldn't quite hear. He looked stressed. I turned my head and looked over the back seat to see a yellow HZ

Holden ute approaching the Beast at high speed. Two men were standing in the ute's tray aiming shotguns in our direction.

Two off-road motorcycles were racing on either side of the ute. Archie suddenly veered the Beast to the right in an attempt to collide with one of the riders.

Fiona woke up rubbing her eyes. "What the fuck's going on?"

"We have company," I explained.

Fiona passed me my Browning Lever Action .223 Rifle, and I leaned out the window and fired at the bike closest to me. My third round must have hit him, as the rider lost control, striking the ute and launching into the air like a cannon ball fired from a naval gun. I winced as his head struck the tarmac, cracking like a watermelon struck by a sledgehammer.

I flinched as something sharp struck my neck. The bastards on the ute blew out the rear windscreen. I pulled a thin glass shard from my skin and looked for my next target.

I was concerned that everything sounded muffled. *Have I ruptured my eardrums?* I suddenly realised that I still had the bloody ear plugs inserted. I pulled the plugs out and watched Fiona firing from the backseat with her pump-action shotgun. *Great I thought, the ringing in my ears had returned.*

"Seat belts on. HOLD ON!" Archie bellowed.

"GO TO HELL!" he yelled, before slamming on the Beast's brakes.

I placed both hands on the dash as the old seat belt sagged. I felt a massive jolt as my palms pressed against the dash mat, preventing my head from striking the windscreen. I heard a loud SMASH! and then the ear grating sound of metal scraping against metal. Two white fellas, one still holding a shotgun flew over the hood of the Beast. The second bike just kept on screaming down the highway, the rider not even taking the time to look back at the carnage in his wake.

The Beast came to a stop. Archie got out of the vehicle and walked to the ute, which was resting with a crumpled front-end against the Beast's caved-in boot. With the exception of the smashed rear windscreen, this was the only damage to the vehicle. The potent odour of burnt rubber, worn brake pads, oil and fuel hung in the air.

Archie returned to the driver's seat and started the ignition. He looked pissed. "They've killed my baby," he complained.

"She's not dead mate, she just needs some TLC. Mitt knows some great panel beaters that'll make her look as good as new."

For a split second I thought the silly bugger was about to shed a tear. "What about the driver?" I asked.

"No more dukes of hazard for him."

Archie drove past the two outlaws that flew over our bonnet and landed fifteen metres down the road. Their impersonations of stuntmen from a B-grade movie had not ended well. They had landed with their legs and arms positioned at odd angles like marionettes that have had their strings cut. Archie stepped on the accelerator as he cursed the men that had damaged his baby. I pity the second rider if Archie ever catches up with him.

About two hours after the incident, we decided to swap drivers and refuel. As Archie filled the tank, I stood on the edge of the road and took a deep breath and appreciated the fresh air. In that moment I acknowledged how easy it is to take it for granted. I thought about the contaminated city and the claustrophobia I would need to endure while wearing a fully enclosed hazmat suit. That didn't stop me praying for the suits to be waiting for us in Geraldton. *They had to be there. I need this!*

The Geraldton Astronomy Support Hub was located within the University Centre. This site was a support hub for the CSIRO's radio telescope array, located at the Murchison Radio-astronomy Observatory, 360 kilometres north east of Geraldton near a remote cattle station. The array was designed to enable astronomers to answer fundamental questions about the creation of our universe. Now it's just sitting there useless. It's a crime against humanity, which I'll do everything in my power to rectify.

As Fiona pulled into the hub's carpark, I started to feel anxious, knowing that I was minutes away from discovering the fate of the mission. Our first pivotal step. I should have expected the front door to be smashed, but it didn't prevent my anxiety from reaching new levels. I ignored Archie's comments to slow down as I marched through the damaged door.

I jogged down the side corridor and stood in front of the steel strong room door. "YES, YES, BLOODY YES!" I yelled.

Archie stood beside me and pointed at the heavy-duty lock. "What are you getting so excited about? The door is as thick as a safe door. I can't pick this lock."

"Sometimes my friend you can be a little simple," I replied tongue-in-cheek. I placed my hand on the door. "Look, it's intact. Which means the suits should still be inside. I've brought some C-4, so don't you worry, I'll get the bugger open."

"What do you mean you have C-4?"

"I've got some in the boot," I replied with a cheeky smile.

"And you're calling me simple, you could have blown us to bloody smithereens," Archie chided.

I shook my head. "You were a soldier mate, you should know that C-4 is a plastic explosive that requires a detonator to set it off. U.S. soldiers during the Vietnam War actually burned C-4 to cook their meals. You could fire your rifle directly at it and it won't trigger a reaction."

I used a jemmy bar to force open the Beast's crumpled boot to retrieve the C-4. Although I have an understanding of the chemical compounds and reactions of C-4, unfortunately I don't possess the specific formula to calculate the exact force of the blast. When planning this little operation, I read a reference from a military engineering manual that stated – 'to take out one twenty-centimetre square steel beam, it would require four kilograms of C-4'.

I was blessed to be born with an exceptional memory. If my recollection is correct, which I'm willing to bet my house on, I recall the door being approximately five-centimetres thick. I decided to only use 300 grams for the initial blast, leaving some wriggle room to reduce the risk of damaging the suits. I attached the blasting cap to the C-4 and secured it to the steel door. I then rolled the detonator cord out the front door and into the middle of the carpark. We knelt behind the Beast's engine block.

Just as I placed my finger on the trigger, Archie asked, "This is not going to damage the Beast, is it?"

I smiled and pressed the trigger. BOOOOMMMMM!!! The explosion was instantaneous. The windows of the premises that had escaped the vandals were not as fortunate on this occasion, with shards of glass blown all over the carpark.

As Archie was looking over his paint job, Fiona and I marched back into the hub and found the entire door peeled away from the frame.

I stepped over the rubble into the storage unit. I searched everywhere. "FFFUUUCCCKKKK!"

The suits were nowhere to be found.

I located a Geiger counter and five sets of breathing apparatus in steel lockers. Archie found four radiation dosimeters stored in Faraday bags in the corner of the room. The Faraday bags would have been deliberately used to protect the dosimeters from EMPs. The bags are made from a mesh material with small wires of conductive material such as copper. It was basically the same material used to make Faraday wallets to protect credit cards in the 2020s from being illegally scanned. All the good it will do us now, as the dosimeters are useless without the suits.

"Let's go home," I moaned miserably, feeling utterly deflated

My ardent objections didn't prevent Archie from stopping by the Geraldton Hotel. We were sitting at the bar drowning our sorrows with a local brew, while Fiona behaved like a social butterfly, swapping stories with the locals. I'd never seen her so amiable. I don't know what she's got to be happy about. We bloody failed!

We were five beers into our session when Fiona rested her chin on my shoulder. "Don't get your hopes up Clarry, but I think I know where your suits are."

"You little beauty," I beamed.

Fiona had spoken to a local man who stated that a kid down the road from his place wore a space suit during last year's Halloween celebration.

I bought the man a bottle of hooch and asked him to point us in the direction of the kid's home.

Archie knocked on the security screen and a pimply teenager opened the door. "What do ya want? Mum's not home."

Archie placed his palm on the kid's chest and pushed him back a couple of steps as he entered the premises. "Show us where your space suits are buddy."

The kid stuck his chest out. "Fuck you and get out of my house," he commanded with false bravado.

Archie took half an ounce of gold from his pocket and held it in front of the kid's eyes. "I'm not stealing them kid. I want to buy them from you."

The kid gawked at the gold. "I don't have space suits, but I found some hazmat suits."

The teenager explained that when he discovered that the astronomy hub had been broken into, he went inside to investigate and found the five suits neatly laid out on the carpet in the middle of the main office area. *Of course he found it burgled I thought.* More likely he was the one that smashed the front door. I can't even imagine what my former colleagues were planning. Were they also considering a trip to Perth? I guess I'll never know.

I gave the suits a quick once over and found that four of them appeared serviceable. It came to no surprise that the suit the kid wore during Halloween had a tear at the shoulder joint. I was absolutely elated! We were back in the game. Fiona couldn't escape the sloppy kiss I planted on her forehead. All three of us were up-beat during our return journey to Esperance. Even Archie's horrible singing couldn't dampen my cheerful mood.

Chapter Forty-Four

April 7 – 8, 2041 – Archie

The last time I saw Clarry this worked up was when our beloved Dockers football team won the 2029 Grand Final. They were two points up with two minutes left to play. I'm quite sure he held his breath for the entire 120 seconds. On the night of the big win, we celebrated with a momentous pub crawl in Melbourne's CBD. Our celebration lasted through the night to the wee hours of the morning. I had a severe hangover that I will never forget.

Working like a man possessed, Clarry meticulously planned our journey to Perth. After he completed the draft of the Operational Plan, he encouraged us to poke holes in the proposed strategies and tactics.

In 2031, the Australian Defence Force Radiation Disaster Team taught me how to correctly place on and remove a hazmat suit. I was instructed how to operate the breathing apparatus, voice-operated microphone, and dosimeter. I'd be lying if I said I can recall all eighteen steps in the process, and before today, Fiona had never even seen a suit. As a member of the CSIRO's Health and Biosecurity Unit, Clarry had spent numerous hours wearing the suit in an operational setting. He taught us the correct sequence to place on the suit, gloves, boots, and mask to ensure the personal protective equipment (PPE) was airtight.

Clarry stood in front of a whiteboard and scribbled on the board with a black marker. I had flashbacks of my university days. I noticed the photo of Patterson, Raj and his mother taped to the corner of the board. He penned the words Dosimeter and Survey Meter in capital letters. Clarry explained that a survey meter is a device that estimates the radiation dose deposited in an individual or object, whereas a dosimeter estimates the radiation dose an individual is receiving.

Clarry handed us the dosimeters that we found in Geraldton and demonstrated how to switch them on. He then picked up a yellow box about the size of a brick. It had a gauge at the front and a black rubber coil with a tube attached protruding from the side, which he referred to as the probe. He clarified that it was a type of survey meter called a Geiger counter. I had seen Geiger counters in use during nuclear disaster movies. They were often used in scenes to build suspense - the clicking sound of the counter would increase in speed as the cast learned of the radiation fall-out and their inevitable demise. I hope we don't experience that much drama. I automatically touched the jarrah coffee table to avoid tempting fate.

Clarry advised us that radiation is measured in units called millisieverts (mSv). A routine chest x-ray results in an effective dose of 0.02 mSv, which is equivalent to what a person could receive over five days from natural sources such as the sun, cosmic rays, rocks, soil, plants and even the food we eat. The annual limit of radiation for a member of the public is one mSv, however if you work with radiation, you can be exposed to up to twenty times that amount. He went on to tell us that people living near the 1986 Chernobyl nuclear power plant disaster received a dose of 500 mSv. This resulted in over six thousand reported cases of thyroid cancer. After scaring the crap out of us, we paid the utmost attention during the rest of the lesson. He trained us how to operate the dosimeter, Geiger counter and the suit's encapsulated breathing apparatus.

Due to the size of the hazmat suits and the associated equipment, we required a larger vehicle than the Beast. In any case, the Beast was currently out of commission. When Sergeant Lee learned of our mission and transport predicament, he sold us his 1973 Volkswagen Kombi at a bargain-basement price. We packed the suits, petrol, firearms, ammo, and packs in the van.

We were all aware of the worst-case scenarios. I accepted that our chance of survival was a flip of a coin. If something goes wrong with the equipment, we're likely to be exposed to a lethal dose of radiation. Not to mention we may have to deal with Patterson's mutant army. To ensure my mates were looked after, I arranged for the Captain to take care of Xena and Zeus, and Charlie was kind enough to agist Roger and Jasper free of charge at his Merivale farm.

The night before we were due to leave, I gave Fiona the opportunity to back out of the operation. She's only twenty-one years old and has her whole life ahead of her. We were both stretching on the mats after completing a hard workout.

"I have to say Fiona, from where I'm sitting, you've given this job your all. I don't have to tell you...."

"Hang on, you're not sacking me, are you?" she asked with wide eyes, interrupting my train of thought.

"No, no, just let me finish. Look, I don't have to tell you that this is by no means a typical contract. In fact, it's bloody crazy when you stop to think about it. There's a high likelihood that we won't make it back." I paused to let it all sink in. "There's no shame in backing out. It's actually the smart thing to do. I've taught you enough for you to go it alone. And if I make it out of Perth, then we can continue working together."

She stopped stretching and looked me directly in the eyes. "I'm a big girl Archie. I've thought about the risk. Let's face it, I can get taken out during any contract. I mean, fuck, in the last ten weeks I've been through enough life-threatening situations to last five lifetimes. I shot a bloke that was going to chop your head off, I was throttled by a mutant with green blood, I've been in gun fights on a train, and led a militia team to defeat an outlaw gang."

She actually had me lost for words. I couldn't think of a reasonable rebuttal. She could have made a hell of a lawyer in the old world.

Fiona sat on her heels. "Can I ask you something?"

"Of course."

"Why are you taking this risk? Is it because of Raj or the fifty ounces of gold?"

Damn, now she was on the attack. She asked a good question that I'd spent some time mulling over. "The priority is rescuing Raj, but

I'd be telling you a fib if I said the gold, isn't a consideration. I also have another motive that I haven't mentioned before now. Those captives that were being held inside the Norseman Council, were being sold to Patterson. He's experimenting on innocent people, including pregnant women and kids. He's an evil bastard that needs to be taken down, and I don't see anyone else lining up to do it. Maybe this is why Sal wanted me to take on the contract. I reckon, I owe it to him."

~

We woke at 3 a.m. to have breakfast and pack the van. Fiona and I had just wiped our plates clean when Clarry handed us each two tablets. He explained they were potassium iodine tablets that would help mitigate the radiation exposure. Without saying a word, I swallowed the pills with the last gulp of my coffee.

Perth, the former capital city of W.A., is located 700 kilometres north west of Esperance. The journey should take us roughly nine hours in the Kombi. We removed the Kombi's rear two seats to make room for the equipment we required for the operation. We hung the hazmat suits from a steel rack that Clarry soldered to the sides of the van, with extra care taken not to tear the fabric or damage the instruments.

I turned the key in the ignition and carefully reversed down the winding driveway, trying not to displace the equipment and ammunition. I was also a little worried that Clarry had covertly packed some C-4. Detonator or no detonator, it was better to be safe than sorry.

We had planned to rotate drivers every two and half hours, but I preferred to just keep on driving. Clarry read a ten-year-old science magazine and Fiona stripped and cleaned her firearms. After she had finished cleaning, she took a nap in the bean bag situated behind the driver's seat. Her persistent and unrelenting snoring did wonders in keeping me awake and focused on the road.

We stopped at the small town of Brookton, which is located 138 kilometres from the Perth CBD, the reported epicentre of the 2033 nuclear strike. Even though Northam is 96 kilometres from the cities CBD and had been confirmed as a low radiation zone, Clarry wanted to check the area for contamination. He exited the Kombi and switched on the Geiger counter. The device made a slow clicking sound as he pointed the probe within an inch from the surface of the road. I let out a sigh of relief when the metre displayed a low level of radiation. I wasn't keen on driving in the suit for the next three and a bit hours. Every fifteen kilometres or so, Clarry jumped out of the vehicle and repeated the procedure.

As we travelled closer to Perth, the presence of human and animal activity noticeably decreased. Upon stopping fifty-kilometres from the CBD, Clarry stated that the radiation reading was now too high to continue driving unprotected. Fiona and I placed on our hazmat suits with Clarry's assistance. We secured the dosimeters around our chests with an elastic strap and turned them on. Clarry then wrapped our wrists, ankles, waist, neck, and edges of the face mask with high-test tape before we returned the favour. After we were all suited up and air-tight, we continued on our journey.

As we entered the outskirts of Perth, Clarry reiterated the plan through the suits' internal two-way radio system. Thankfully, our dosimeter alarms were silent. I just prayed they were working. I looked out the Kombi's windows at the desolate suburban streets. Aside from the absence of birds and other animals, I was actually amazed how normal everything appeared. However, as we journeyed closer to the CBD, it didn't take long for this picture to dramatically transform into a disaster movie.

The streets were beginning to return to nature – trees, weeds, plants, and bushes were slowly but surely taking over the yards and streets. During high school I completed a project about Pripyat, the Ukrainian ghost town that was deserted in 86 after the Chernobyl nuclear Disaster. I'm confident that in another ten years or so, Perth and many cities around the world will resemble Pripyat, with the vegetation enveloping the city and destroying the buildings that lie within.

We approached from the north and noticed that many of the double brick homes were cracked, with windows smashed and roof tiles melted. The damage to homes and streets became progressively pronounced as we travelled closer to the centre of the city, with burnt and collapsed walls and roofs, bitumen roads melted, and vehicles smashed and upturned.

I rounded a corner and slowly accelerated up a steep hill where we had a clear panoramic view of the CBD through the Kombi's front windscreen. We could suddenly see the devastation of the nuclear strike - two thirds of the CBD was completely destroyed, including Parliament House, Elizabeth Quay, the Supreme Court, and a majority of Perth's Skyscrapers. Buildings had completely collapsed, leaving metal beams protruding from concrete rubble. We were all in silent shock. It's difficult to comprehend the complete and utter destruction of the CBD.

Clarry decided to park the Kombi at his former local church, Saint Bartholomew's, and walk the 1300 metres to the Blue Opal Resort. He selected the 170-year-old church, as it's set back from the road near an old cemetery and shielded from the view of the resort by a row of three-storey apartments and mature gum trees. It was comforting to find the front gates secured by lock and chain. After Clarry split the chain with bolt cutters, I drove up the driveway and parked at the rear of the church. The once beautiful stained-glass windows were shattered by the shock wave of the blast.

We walked down the street towards the Queens Gardens. I lugged my pack and rifle over my shoulders, while Clarry and Fiona were armed with shotguns and carried a rucksack over their bulky suits. We entered the western side of the garden and knelt behind a five-foot hedge that faced the underground carpark entrance of the resort. At eighty-five floors, the resort was the third tallest building in the country. I'm not sure if number one and two are still standing, so it may now be the tallest. The building has an oval structure encased in blue glass resting atop of two towers.

Even though it's only twenty degrees Celsius, the suit's triple layer fabric and airtight protection was causing me to sweat profusely. I told myself to toughen up as I scanned through a gap in the hedge. I couldn't spot any movement.

My voice relayed through the voice-activated microphones, "It's all clear. On me."

Just as we advanced towards an opening in the hedge, our dosimeter alarms started to blare. "Bloody Murphy," I swore under my breath as we quickly turned off the devices. I pondered whether the sound carried, and we were about to walk into an ambush.

As the saying goes – 'nothing ventured, nothing gained.' We jogged across the road into the entrance of the one thousand bay carpark. It appeared empty, but that was impossible to verify in the fading light. As we advanced down the carpark we hugged a side wall, while taking extra care not to rub against the concrete and tear the fabric of our suits. We had walked about 150 metres when the headlights of a truck cut through the jet-black confines of the underground carpark. We all dropped to a knee, watching, and listening. I lifted my rifle to my shoulder. My heavy breathing fogged my face mask, making it impossible to gain any type of sight picture through the scope.

The electric engine of a 2031 Ford Truck was almost silent as it glided down the middle of the carpark and drove past the vertical boom gate. I hadn't witnessed a modern vehicle running since the end of the War. I cursed at our inability to see the driver through the vehicle's tinted windows.

We walked towards the parking bay the electric vehicle had moments before occupied. There were five modern vehicles parked in a row - a Mitsubishi 4WD, a Mercedes sedan, a Porsche 911 and two Toyota vans. We continued to advance down the carpark and found a nearby fire exit door held ajar by a construction sign.

We tactically entered the stairwell. I cleared the immediate area and pointed my muzzle towards the first flight of stairs. I looked back at Fiona who gave me a look of uncertainty. It dawned on me that I hadn't taught her how to tactically navigate stairs. I signalled for her to go up ahead of me. Fiona acknowledged my instruction and moved up to the next landing and paused at the fire exit door.

I gestured for Fiona and Clarry to stay put before slipping into the expansive lobby.

It was convenient that the lights were off, as the orange hazmat suit made me stand out like a parrot at a penguin convention. I stood behind a large marble pillar and surveyed the room. It looked untouched from the devastation just two blocks to the west. I returned to the stairwell, and we continued to march up the steps, checking one floor at a time.

The tenth floor was a designated business centre where some of the most powerful companies in the world held their annual general meetings and conferences. I attended a conference here in '29. I had to represent the firm as my boss opted to play golf at some networking event. I wasn't a fan of the small talk, but the free food and booze made up for it. The floor was divided into two large convention rooms and ten smaller conference rooms.

As I entered, I instantly became conscious of the downlights. All but a few were switched on in the conference open space. I placed the butt of my rifle firmly in the pocket of my shoulder and scanned the immediate area. When I failed to sight anyone, I speculated where they were sourcing their power. They must have the generator up and running. I also noticed they'd ripped up the fancy plush carpet leading from the stairwell to the conference rooms.

I returned to the stairwell and provided Clarry and Fiona a sit-rep. "What do you reckon, should we investigate this floor?"

They both nodded and exited the stairwell gripping their shotguns. After placing my pack on the ground and retrieving my revolver from a side pocket, I instructed them to leave their packs while we cleared the floor. We entered the nearest conference room to find two desk-top computers sitting on oak office desks positioned in the middle of the room. It was evident by the thick layer of dust that the room hadn't been used since high-flyers' graced the Blue Opal with their presence and drank Moët Champagne as they discussed the latest commodity prices. Most of them would have been killed, if not from the nukes and the subsequent evacuation, then by the hands of outlaws or desperate people.

We stepped into the first of the two large convention rooms and scanned the immediate area. The expansive room had been converted into a dormitory of some sort. Plastic sheeting and false walls had been erected to construct numerous rooms, separated by a long corridor running down the centre.

We walked down the corridor and peeled back the plastic sheeting to enter a makeshift hospital room. I was amazed to see two hospital gurneys positioned side by side, occupied by a pair of identical female twins aged between ten and twelve years old. Both girls were hooked up to patient monitors and had an intravenous (IV) cannula inserted into their arms. White bandages were wrapped around their necks and their wrists were handcuffed to the gurneys' metal frame.

Fiona stepped towards the girls. Their lips were moving as if they were trying to speak but no noise left their mouths. I registered a sudden blur of movement crash into Fiona, sending her flying against one of the girl's beds. A man that bore a scary resemblance to Chef Hulk had her pinned against the mattress and was raining down punches to her face mask and chest.

The exertion of marching up ten flights of stairs with a thirty-five-kilogram pack had caused my air-tight mask to almost completely fog. I lifted my revolver but was unable to see the front or rear sights. I made a split-second decision. I sprinted towards the man and dived forwards, wrapping both my arms around his waist in a tackle that would have impressed my high school rugby coach. My revolver fell from my hand as we both crashed to the ground.

The freakishly powerful man straddled my chest before I could sit up. He then viciously elbowed me to the head. I attempted to throw him off by leveraging my hips and pushing off his thick torso, but the bulky suit and his massive frame made the move impossible to execute. Blow after blow connected to my head and neck, causing my vision to blur. Through the haze I saw doubles of Fiona standing above me holding a silver object. She swung her arm in a flash like she was hitting a forehand winner.

Like a tree that had just been chopped down, he fell headfirst onto my chest and face. With Fiona's assistance we managed to roll the giant off me. When I saw the handle of a scalpel sticking out of his right ear canal, it was clear what had interrupted his one-way slugfest.

Just as I was getting my breath back, another Hulk rushed into the room. I had a quick glance for my missing revolver before taking a deep breath and raising my fists to my chin, preparing myself for the onslaught.

BOOM! BOOM! BOOM! Clarry fired three twelve-gauge slugs into the head and chest of the man, stopping him dead in his tracks.

That was about the fourth time Clarry had saved my bacon.

I could see his grin behind the mask. "You owe me another carton brother," he chuckled.

Chapter Forty-Five

Monday April 8, 2041 2041 from 2 p.m. – Fiona

I had just taken care of the mutant pounding Archie and was in the process of gathering my wits, when another mutant launched into the room. Clarry was quick on the draw, shooting the goon three times with his shotgun. Blood splattered all over my mask. The slugs mutilated half of his face and left a gaping hole the size of a snooker ball in the centre of his chest. *Gross!*

I reached down and picked up my shotgun. Clarry knelt next to the downed giant. He appeared fascinated by the green blood, tracing his index finger around the mutant's chest wound and wiping it on his suit.

Clarry approached a long silver bench that held test tubes, beakers, two microscopes, a tiny fridge and various lab machines. On the corner of the bench stood an Apple computer that was switched on. It looked identical to one I'd seen my dad use for work. I hadn't seen an operational computer for eight years, which made me wonder how it was possible?

Clarry operated the mouse and started to search through the computer's folders. As he opened the files, he started praising the man we were looking for, "Patterson may be a freak, but he's obviously a tenacious genius. He's managed to find functioning tech and set up a lab. He's even got a working computer, centrifuge, and bloody DNA sequencer. It's hard to fathom how he managed to achieve all this."

Archie placed his hand on Clarry's shoulder. "Okay mate, settle down. When we catch up with the evil genius, you can present him with the 'Scientist of the Year' award. Until then, Fiona and I'll investigate the remaining rooms while you grab our packs and take care of the two girls. Agreed?"

Clarry nodded. "No problem. But I need time to analyse Patterson's research before we leave."

"Mate, we have to keep moving and find the boy. You can take the computer with you."

"Alright, alright, no problem," he replied as he busily opened and closed files on the computer.

Each room was constructed similar to the previous; false walls with a hospital bed and medical equipment situated alongside. In a room furthest from the entry point, we found a pregnant woman in her mid-twenties.

Like the twins, she had one wrist cuffed to the gurney and had an IV cannula inserted into her arm. I approached her and said, "My name's Fiona and we're here to help you."

With tears running down her cheeks she spoke with a strained voice, "Please let me go. I need to get out of here."

Archie walked over to the gurney. "We're not with the men that did this to you. We're here to rescue a young boy. But like Fiona said, we'll help you escape this place. But first, I have an important question to ask you. Have you seen a ten-year-old boy named Raj?"

She shook her head and wiped away her tears. "I haven't seen anybody apart from the bald assholes and this sicko doctor named Patterson. I arrived here two days ago and they've been injecting me with all sorts of shit. I'm worried about my baby!"

I noticed her chart and the patient's name written alongside. It stated, 'Subject 0182'. "What's your name?" I asked.

"Katherine. Katherine Jenkins."

"It's nice to meet you Katherine. Like I mentioned, I'm Fiona and this handsome bloke is Archie. We'll do everything we can to make sure those men never hurt you again."

We wheeled Katherine in the hospital gurney to the room occupied by the twins. Clarry was busy reading the patient charts and examining the girls. Archie grabbed his lock pick set from his pack and within seconds released their wrists from the steel cuffs.

Katherine was speaking softly to the twins. *She'll be a great mum I thought.*

Clarry gestured for us to speak with him in the far corner of the room. He switched on the Geiger counter and placed the black probe over the dead mutant. The needle barely registered. He then slowly waved the probe over our arms and chest - the needle on the metre swung to the far right and the clicking sounds significantly increased in intensity. He then turned on our dosimeters and closely examined the electronic readings.

Clarry attempted to sound calm but failed miserably. His voice quivered as he explained, "We have a big problem. We've all been exposed to a lethal dose of radiation. Even if we abandon the mission this very minute, we'll still in all probability die in the next three to twelve months from ARS."

"What's ARS?" I asked, trying my utmost to keep a stiff upper lip.

"Sorry. Acute radiation syndrome, commonly known as radiation sickness."

Clarry placed his fingers in large tears in my suit that I'd somehow failed to detect. I noticed that Archie's suit was also badly torn. I guess that's what you get when you wrestle with mutants. With his eyes filled with pity, Archie placed his hand on my shoulder. My mind was suddenly numb. Mortality was staring me in the face.

I was going through a rough trot after I lost my parents, so when I came across a self-help book on overcoming grief and loss, I paid particular attention to the five stages of grief. It was interesting, but it didn't really help me much at the time. As I stared at my dosimeter, I was well aware that I was progressing through those five stages at warp speed. I had raced straight through Denial and Anger and was now transitioning from Stage Three – 'Bargaining' to Stage Four – 'Depression.'

"So, what's the good news Clarry? Or is the headline, 'We're All Fucked'?" I asked.

Clarry waved the Geiger counter over Katherine and the twins. The needle barely moved, but Clarry's expression told me something had registered in his mind. He then did something totally unexpected. He ripped off his suit and face mask. I felt like everything was happening in slow motion. He approached the silver bench, opened the small fridge and retrieved a vial. He held the vial up to his eyes before shaking the contents. I glanced at Archie, who was just standing there like a stunned mullet. Clarry inserted a syringe into the clear liquid. "What the fuck Clarry?" I asked. Without missing a beat, he injected the substance into his upper thigh.

"I'm really sorry. I don't want to put you in this position, but you have to make a decision, and quickly! I can inject you with Patterson's experimental drug or you can take the chance and return home. I've only had access to his preliminary results, so I really have no idea of the drug's efficacy or side effects."

Clarry must have realised that we were both dumbstruck with indecision. "Look, the drug could harm or even kill you, but as you can see, I'm still standing, and Katherine and the girls seem to be healthy."

"What are our chances if we high-tail it out of here?" Archie asked.

Clarry let out a long sigh and shook his head. "Not good brother."

Archie ripped off his suit. "Well, it's not much of a choice then mate, is it?"

I followed Archie's lead and removed my suit. I took a deep breath and smelt the pungent odour of disinfectant. Clarry plunged the syringe into Archie's leg. I pulled up my shorts to expose my upper thigh. As Clarry prepared to inject me, he made an attempt at levity by teasing me about my 'chicken legs.' It fell on deaf ears. I was feeling so overwhelmed and numb, that I didn't even feel the needle go in. As I watched him inject the drug into my blood stream, I just prayed that it protects me from the radiation. And doesn't kill me.

We agreed that it was wise for Clarry to return to the van with Katherine and the twins. They had already been through an absolute nightmare, and they would only slow us down. Clarry gathered Patterson's computer, reports, charts, and vials and packed them in a

Samsonite suitcase that he found in an adjoining room.

"Don't do anything stupid mate. Just cross the street and walk through the park to the van. Then sit tight and wait for us. If we're not back by 6 p.m., then you take off. We'll take a car and make our own way back home," said Archie.

We escorted Clarry as he wheeled the suitcase to the fire door with Katherine and the twins in tow. Archie clasped Clarry's hand and wished him luck.

As Clarry started to walk back down the stairs, I whispered, "Take care Clarry, stay frosty."

He flashed his trademark grin. "Same to you little sister."

It felt good to be free of the bulky hazmat suit. I had my Glock strapped to my waist with three spare mags. I reloaded my shotgun. Archie grasped his revolver and carried his sniper rifle over his shoulder.

Archie placed his hand on my arm. "I'm really sorry about this Fiona."

I had stopped feeling sorry for myself and had moved on to the final stage – 'Acceptance.'

"Nothing to be sorry for Boss. I'm a big girl, I knew what I was getting myself into. Now let's find Raj and complete this mission."

He nodded, put his game face on and entered the stairwell. There are eighty-five floors in the Opal, and we were currently situated on the tenth floor. My gruelling runs and workouts were paying dividends as I climbed one floor after another.

"Come on old man. Keep up," I quipped as I passed him.

We cleared guest floors eleven to thirteen. Each had their hallway lights switched off and were unoccupied. As soon as I opened the door to floor fourteen, my nose was assaulted by a putrid smell of death and decay. It made me want to gag! We both switched on our torches. It took enormous discipline not to cover my face as I entered the main corridor.

We were confronted with a ghastly and stomach-churning scene. Piles of corpses - men, woman, and children of all ages were stacked along the corridor. I ran back to the stairwell and projectile vomited down the stairs. Archie handed me his water bottle. He gave me a couple of minutes to take a few sips and recover my wits.

"Sorry about that," I said, with a tone of embarrassment.

Archie shook his head. "Nothing to apologise for. I've never seen anything so disturbing in my life. And I've been around more death than most."

"Do you hear that?" I asked.

We entered floor fifteen. I could hear the rapid beats of techno music blasting down the corridor. The gold placard on the glass door read, '*Gymnasium & Heated Pool*'. Archie placed his pack on the ground and opened the door. We both entered and scanned our area of responsibility before approaching the gym door.

The pine door had a narrow panel of glass at eye level. We both had a peek and saw a mutant with his back to us performing a shoulder press exercise. As he lifted the weight from under his chin to an extended position above his head, the bar was bending from the four twenty-kilogram-plates stacked on each side.

My eyes were drawn to grotesque sores the size of bottle caps on his back and shoulders, some of which were discharging a thick white fluid. *Yuck!* I hope to God that's not a side effect of Patterson's drug. After managing to skip through the teenage acne phase, that would be a cruel fate indeed.

As the mutant continued to rep out his set, I noticed he was wearing noise cancelling headphones. Once again, I pondered where they got their modern tech? Also, why's he playing music if he's not listening to it? It suddenly dawned on me, there must be a *hardcore* techno fan in the building. Archie tapped me on the shoulder and pointed towards the pool entry. He obviously came to the same conclusion.

Through the clear glass door, I could see the outline of a mutant sitting in the spa, with his head resting on the edge, and a white folded towel placed over his eyes. I detected a silver pistol resting on the side of the spa. It was impossible to hear anything over the ear-piercing beats. I gained eye contact with Archie before making a finger gun gesture and pointing towards the spa.

Archie signalled for me to watch the gym door. He re-holstered his revolver and brought his rifle to the ready position. He nodded towards the door handle. I could feel the vibration of the music as I gripped the stainless steel handle and pulled the door towards me.

As Archie stepped through the doorway, he raised the rifle up to a firing position. Without warning, sleeping beauty suddenly came alive and reacted with incredible speed. As he raised the pistol, Archie fired the armour piercing .338 round – *craaaacckkkk* - shooting him just above his temple. His head jerked back violently. Green blood leaked down his face into the bubbling water.

We swiftly cleared the sauna and change rooms before returning to the gym door. The bodybuilding mutant was now performing bicep curls with forty-kilogram dumbbells. Archie cupped his mouth and yelled something into my ear. All I could hear was '*Alive*' and '*Interrogate*'. I groaned inwardly at the thought of going toe-to-toe with another one of these *motherfuckers*.

Archie continued to watch the mutant through the glass panel, until he madly gestured for me to draw my Glock pistol. Archie yelled the words that I mistakenly lip-read as '*Fuck Me*,' however quickly realised were '*Cover Me*.'

I had a quick glance before Archie opened the door and peeled inside. The mutant was now flat on his back bench pressing a vast weight off his chest. Archie ran to the bench and placed both hands over the bar and pushed down towards the mutant's neck. Archie's forearms and biceps were shaking as he fought against the freakishly strong mutant. They had reached a stalemate, with Archie unable to push the bar down any further, and the mutant unable to push the bar up onto the rack.

Unbelievably, the mutant grunted with exertion and suddenly lifted Archie off his feet. My index finger started to squeeze the Glock's trigger, disengaging the safety lever incorporated into the trigger. Archie explained at the gun range that it only required six pounds of pressure to fire the Glock.

Red in the face from the physical strain, Archie looked in my direction and shouted, "NO!"

I was just on the brink of firing when Archie's weight and forward momentum started to overpower the mutant. The bar slowly descended to press down against his neck. After continuing to strain against the load for almost a minute, his lips finally turned blue, and his eyes rolled back. Archie heaved one side of the bar off his neck and pushed him off the bench to the gym floor. The mutant's headphones fell from his ears as his head struck a twenty-kilogram-plate.

Archie retrieved cable ties from his pocket and secured the mutant's wrists with two sets. I guess, like me, he was intimidated by the mutant's strength, as he also hogtied him with a leather skipping rope.

I marched over to the stereo and switched it off. My ears were ringing from the deafening music. I was never a fan of techno.

Archie gazed down at the mutant and then at me. "I guess neither of us are giving him mouth to mouth."

"You've got THAT right!" I replied adamantly.

The mutant then abruptly coughed and wheezed - regaining consciousness.

"Cover the gym door while I interrogate our new friend," instructed Archie.

"Sure thing Boss."

Clarry mentioned that Archie was an expert negotiator, which I'd previously seen glimpses of when he questioned Jack, the former train station manager. Archie sat on the weight bench and peered down at the mutant.

Archie cleared his throat. "Believe it or not, I'm not a bad bloke. In fact, I'll let you live if you answer my questions."

"FUCK YOU CUNT!" the mutant roared.

Archie chuckled and looked over at me. "At least they can talk."

Archie drew his knife from the leather sheath attached to his belt and placed the point of the blade against his own fingertip. "When I fought in the War, they taught me the unpleasant business of extracting information. I hated doing it, it's just not me. But you know the saying, 'desperate times call for desperate measures.' I need to find Patterson and the boy so we can get the hell out of here. Now, are you going to help me or hinder me?"

The mutant drew phlegm from the back of his throat and spat at Archie, striking him halfway up his shirt.

"Fiona, don't turn around and don't look in the reflection of the mirrors. Understood?"

"Perfectly understood Boss," I replied as I turned to face the door.

Over the next five minutes I focused on the rich texture of the pine door as guttural screams reverberated off the mirrored walls.

Chapter Forty-Six

Monday April 8, 2041 from 2:30 p.m. – Clarry

I'm primarily a man of logic and reasoning, rather than a man of action. This doesn't make me a coward. It just means that I tend to be sensible. I didn't feel comfortable leaving Archie and Fiona, but in the circumstances, it was the most appropriate course of action. Katherine and the twins followed my lead down the stairs. I was struggling to lift the suitcase in one hand and hold the shotgun in the other. My shirt was soaked with perspiration by the time we entered the underground carpark.

As we hugged the concrete wall, I could hear men conversing nearby and saw a flashlight illuminate a vehicle. I whispered to Katherine and the girls to remain silent and kneel against the wall. I removed my boots to prevent my footsteps from echoing through the carpark. I crept towards the voices in the dark.

A car door suddenly opened. I quickly dropped to the tarmac in a push-up position as the internal light of a Porsche operated like a beacon in the pitch-black carpark. Two men and a child were standing at the rear of the German sports car. I could just make out the facial features of Raj, identifying him from the photo I'd taped to the corner of my whiteboard at home.

A Mitsubishi 4WDs internal light illuminated alongside the Porsche. A giant bald goon placed a duffle bag and a rifle onto the rear seats.

The man standing alongside Raj approached the goon. "Grab me some tins of spaghetti, chickpeas and powdered eggs, and meet me at Acacias. And don't dillydally, the boy and I are hungry," the boss man ordered in an authoritative tone.

Now that the boss man was facing my direction, it was apparent that he bore a resemblance to the photo of Patterson.

Patterson and Raj sped off in the Porsche towards the exit, leaving the goon in their dust.

I saw an opportunity and I took it. I rose to my feet and sprinted the fifty metres like a dingo closing in on its prey. I retrieved my Wüsthof seven-inch fillet knife from its leather sheath and grasped it tight. Hand-to-hand combat may not be my forte, but I know how to handle a knife. I've butchered more roos and filleted more fish than most can count.

Just as I reached the rear of the Mitsubishi, the goon shut the driver's side door. In an instant I gripped the handle and reopened the door. Catching him off guard I launched my blade under his chin. His eyes bulged as he made gurgling sounds in the back of his throat. As he gripped his throat with his big meaty hands, green blood pulsated from his mouth. I grasped his upper arm with both hands and heaved him out of the seat. His body thrashed on the concrete like a fish out of water.

I searched the interior of the vehicle for keys without success. The goon was now deathly still. I quickly searched him and found the electronic key in the inside pocket of his leather jacket. The headlights illuminated Katherine and the girls shaking in fear against the wall. Wasting no time, I sped over to their location, retrieved my boots and asked them to jump into the back.

As I exited the carpark, I pressed down on my two-way radio's transmitter button and attempted to contact Archie. I wasn't particularly concerned that I couldn't reach him, as I suspected that the resort's steel-reinforced concrete was blocking the transmission.

The only 'Acacias' that I'm aware of is a six-star boutique hotel situated at Kings Park - a 400-hectare park overlooking the Swan River and the CBD. A large section of the park is situated on Mount Eliza (known as Moora Katta to the Noongar people). My Elders tell the creation story of the Wagyl rising from the Moora Katta escarpment and forming the Swan River. Over half a million visitors would congregate at Kings Park each year for national events such as the Anzac Dawn

Service and the Australia Day fireworks.

As I drove to the church, I considered my next move. I could be audacious and rescue the boy, or I could be sensible and wait for Archie and Fiona. From the moment I reviewed Patterson's work, I've questioned my motives for advocating this mission. I've placed my friends in a perilous situation to achieve my own ends. So I could resume my career. Even win a Nobel Prize. Rescuing Raj could release me from the guilt I've carried.

I decided to drop Katherine and the girls at the church and then drive to Acacias Hotel to rescue Raj. *So much for being sensible.*

Chapter Forty-Seven

Monday April 8, 2041 from 3 p.m. – Archie

I wiped my blade on a gym towel and returned it to its sheath. "Sorry big fella but I needed the intel. And you weren't exactly forthcoming."

It was time to leave. We needed to locate Patterson and do it fast. As I opened the gym door Fiona gave me a perplexed look. "What?" I asked.

She pointed at the Hulk. "He looks fine to me. What was all that screaming about?" she asked.

"Well, he needs to see a dentist, but the toenail will grow back."

Before I walked out the door, I gave the Hulk a mock salute. His glare reminded me of the saying - 'If looks could kill!'

As we marched towards the stairwell I asked Fiona, "Did you hear what he said about Raj?"

"Yep, the last time he saw Raj was this morning in the Sky Bar," she replied.

The Sky Bar was located on the top floor of the hotel. From an outside view it was designed to resemble an oval shaped blue opal. The 300-metre-long steel structure is encased in reflective blue glass. The Blue Opal encompasses a sky bar with a large dance floor, cocktail lounge, infinity pool, and butterfly sanctuary.

With seventy floors to climb, I was tempted to try the lift, but thought better of it when I considered the possibility of a power outage. I may have the longer legs, but Fiona's a lot fitter.

I took a deep breath. "Just slow it down a bit."

"Why don't we just jog up?" she asked.

"Can't be exhausted on arrival," I explained. I took another deep breath. "Who knows what we'll be up against?"

It took us about thirty-five minutes to complete the climb. Upon arrival at the top of the stairs, my legs were burning, and I was gasping for air. Aside from redness on her cheeks, Fiona looked like she could climb another seventy floors. *Oh, to be young again!* I put my pack down and cycled through my breathing exercise to recover my breath. I had frequented this venue on three or four occasions for networking events, so I had a fairly good idea of the layout.

We stood outside the fire door. "We're entering the north side, so we should be near the lounge bar. There's a dance floor further down to our left and the pool is to the right. The butterfly sanctuary is on the south side."

I nodded to the door handle, and she responded by opening the door.

Just our luck. *Thanks Murphy!* We entered the lounge bar and sitting no further than five metres away were four Hulks. They had a bottle of whisky on the table and appeared to be in the middle of a drinking session. If I had a sense of comedic timing, I would have yelled SURPRISE! Instead, Fiona and I immediately started firing as they reached for their weapons.

As Fiona stepped towards the lounge, she shot two of the Hulks, each time moving the sliding forestock rearward to eject the used shell and then forwards to load a new shell into the chamber. She was acting on autopilot, '*slow is smooth, smooth is fast.*' *Well done, Padawan!*

Before the Hulk closest to me was able to pull the trigger, I fired two rounds into his face. I then fired four rounds into the torso of a Hulk to my immediate right. His pistol fell from his grip, but to my dismay he remained standing.

Six rounds fired. "Reloading," I yelled.

From my periphery I could see the Hulk bend down to recover his pistol. I released the rounds from the speedloader into the cylinder of my revolver. It was going to be a close-run thing - but fortunately I'd never know by how much – as we both lifted our firearms, Fiona fired a twelve-gauge slug into his chest.

All four goons were dead. Why can I still hear gunfire? I scanned my surroundings. *Whaaack.* I felt a stinging sensation to my shoulder. I'd been shot and I had no idea where the shooter was.

Fiona shouted, "OVER HERE," as she darted towards a Japanese bamboo privacy screen sitting atop of a one-metre-high concrete room divider. BANG, BANG, BANG. I sprinted and dived behind the pillar like my life depended on it. Because it did!

Wincing in pain I reached for the wound – entry and exit. I'd been shot clean through the right side of my trapezius muscle, a through and through bullet hole near the base of my neck. I'd be a dead man if the bullet had struck a couple of inches to the right - severing my carotid artery. I'm losing blood, but I reckon I'll be fine for the next half hour or so. I hope.

I crawled to the edge of the pillar to have a peek, but was quickly dissuaded from doing so when a piece of marble shattered within an inch of my face. By the rate and sound of fire, I presumed the shooter was using a bolt action rifle.

With Dimoska's rifle in her grasp, Fiona whispered, "Do you want to keep him busy so I can take him out?"

After I gave her the thumbs-up she passed me her Glock and a spare mag. I removed the old mag and inserted the new. I then slid the slide slightly back to ensure a round was chambered. Fiona crept to the other side of the pillar and gave me a nod. It wasn't the time or place for reflection, but I was pretty bloody proud of her.

With gritted teeth I threw a vase into the open. I then lifted my non-dominant arm and fired through the bamboo screen at a steady pace. I prayed that he wasn't a crack shot and sighting my hand through a scope. My nerves were frayed as his bullet holes accumulated through the bamboo screen above. When the Glock's slide locked back, I reloaded the pistol with the half-full mag.

I was about to continue firing when Fiona returned to my side with a wide grin. "All good Boss, I got the bastard."

I sighed with relief and patted her on the shoulder. "Good job mate."

"Do you want me to grab your pack and patch you up?" she asked.

"No, I'll be right. We'll clear the floor first."

We cleared the entire floor, including the desolate butterfly sanctuary. I wasn't shocked to discover that Raj was absent. I sat outside on a plastic deck chair, despondently gazing at the infinity pool while Fiona retrieved the first aid kit from my pack. She asked me to take off my shirt and said something about not having to worry about fabric in the wound. Given our current situation, it was the least of my worries. Fiona proficiently stitched and bandaged me up as I considered our next move. Conceding that we'd have to give up and return home, was a bitter pill to swallow.

A foam surfboard and two fluro water pistols floated in the crystal clean infinity pool. For the life of me, I never thought I'd once again sit by the edge of an infinity pool.

Fiona interrupted my reverie. "What's the plan? Are we going to return to the church?"

I was about to answer, when my radio started to crackle, "Ccrrsssshh Archie are ccrrsssshh there? I ccrrsssshh eyes on Raj ccrrsssshh."

The radio-frequency interference made it difficult to understand what Clarry was saying.

I pressed the transmitter button. "Give me your location."

The following twenty seconds of silence felt like a life-time. "Ccrrsssshh Acacias, Kings ccrrsssshh."

I pressed the transmitter button. "On our way mate. Stay put. Don't make a move. Do you understand?"

All I heard in response was, "Ccrrsssshh stops crrsssshh."

Chapter Forty-Eight

Monday April 8, 2041 from 4 p.m. – Clarry

Before I left Katherine and the twins, I forced the rear door of the church so they could wait in comfort and security. When I saw the hotel through the gaps in the trees, I grasped the silver cross hanging from my neck. My former colleagues at the CSIRO would often joke that I'm a complicated man - a scientist who believes in the Holy Trinity and the Noongar Dreaming. I guess you could say that I like to cover all the bases.

As I crept past a children's playground, I considered the trauma Raj must have experienced. Taken from his family - subjected to experimental drugs – a vulnerable witness to gruesome depraved acts of violence. *Poor kid!*

I located Patterson's Porsche parked near the venue's service entrance. I gripped my Browning lever-action .223 rifle. My Browning nine-millimetre pistol was holstered on my hip. I crept around the side of the building and peered through the tinted windows.

Gunfire and music suddenly erupted from inside the building. Startled by the unexpected noise, I almost fell backwards over a small hedge. I cautiously approached the hotel entry and saw Raj sitting in the lobby lounge, eating popcorn, and watching a movie on a large projector screen. The scene was from a fifty-year-old sci-fi movie - Arnold Schwarzenegger (an action star in the 90s) was shooting up a line of cop cars. I forget the name of the movie, but I'm sure I've seen it.

I retreated to the rear of the building and knelt behind a large wheelie bin. I positioned myself so I had eyes on the Porsche, but was hidden from view of the service entrance. I lifted the two-way to my mouth, "Archie are you there? I have eyes on Raj."

"Give me your location," Archie responded.

The service door abruptly opened, causing me to freeze. I quickly came to my senses and switched the radio off. Patterson didn't appear to have a care in the world as he sauntered out into the carpark. In contrast to his photo, he had aged horribly, having gained at least twenty kilos and losing his thick mane. If he had some good mates, they'd tell him that his comb-over looked ridiculous and offer to shave his head. He promptly grabbed an esky from the back seat of his Porsche and walked back inside the venue.

I switched the radio back on. "I'm at Acacias, Kings Park."

Archie's transmission erupted with static through the radio speaker, "Ccrrsssshh way mate. Ccrrsssshh. Don't ccrrsssshh move."

I transmitted my reply. "Roger that, but no scenic stops on the way."

I considered moving to another location when I saw a muzzle pointing at my chest.

"If you move a whisker, I will shoot you," Patterson informed me.

I felt like a right idiot. He must have noticed me and circled around the carpark.

"Slowly put your rifle on the ground," he commanded.

I did exactly what he asked. "Good. Now put your pistol and knife on the ground. You can keep your radio."

I wondered why he let me keep the radio as I attached it to my belt.

"Very good. Now walk towards the service entrance and be a good fellow. And switch your radio on."

He followed me inside the hotel and asked me to sit on a light green two-seater couch in the lobby. Empty food containers and drink cans were scattered over the front desk counter. The lights were dimmed, and Raj was sitting about twenty metres away watching the movie. He was so engrossed in the film that he didn't acknowledge our presence. I noted that he hadn't changed much from the time his photo was taken.

Patterson sat on a couch opposite me with his pistol pointed at my stomach. Patterson raised his voice, "Be a good boy Raj and turn the movie down."

Patterson smiled. "I received an interesting message over the radio from one of my men. He said that my residence has been shot-up and some of my men have been killed. By chance, does this have anything to do with you?"

There was nothing to be gained by lying. "Yes, it does."

Patterson leaned forward. "Who are you, and what do you want?"

"My name is Clarry Ugle, and I am, I mean, I was a scientist working for the CSIRO in the Health and Biosecurity Unit."

"How interesting. But again, what do you want?"

"I want to know what you're working on and what you hope to achieve?"

"Ahh, an answer with a question. You must like to play chess. I haven't had anyone to play with lately. My men are too stupid, and Raj has just started to learn."

Patterson stood up slowly and asked me to follow him. He gestured with his pistol for me to sit down in a mahogany chair that was facing a glass table with a chess board atop. Just moments ago, I thought I was about to be killed, and now I was being asked to play chess. As we sat at the table, I pondered how surreal this all felt.

"White or black? Guest's choice."

I smirked. "If I was a brave man, I'd say something heroic and clever, like, I always bet on black."

"Oh, Mr Ugle, I think you're both clever and courageous. I thank you for allowing me to move first. But I guess we both know this isn't your first move today." Patterson moved his pawn to E4.

I asked with burning curiosity, "How did you manage to increase the subjects' telomerase while preventing the production of abnormal cells?" I moved my pawn to C5.

"Who are you with Mr Ugle? I have men on the way. You can

save me a lot of time by putting your cards on the table." He moved his knight to F3.

With an innocent expression I countered, "I thought we were playing chess." I moved my pawn to D6.

Patterson glared at me with an intensity that made me feel decidedly uncomfortable. "You must be considered a success by your peoples' standards." He moved his pawn to D4.

The smartest thing would have been to rise above his racist gibe, but I just couldn't help myself. "Sooo, I heard you like jerking off to posters of Josef Mengele." I captured his pawn on D4 and decided to double-down, "Hey, didn't Hitler have a comb-over?"

Patterson clenched his jaw as his pistol hand shook. I heard the distinct crack of rifle fire. Patterson turned towards the sound, and I instantly reacted by grabbing his gun with both hands. He violently pulled his arm away, trying to break my grip, but I hung on for dear life. He scratched at my face, and I bit down on his wrist. It would have been comical to anyone watching. Two scientists who have no idea how to fight, battling it out for physical supremacy. I would have preferred to return to the chess board and continue the 'Sicilian Defence' chess strategy I was employing to kick his Nazi ass. As we scuffled, we lost our balance and fell to the carpeted floor in an undignified manner.

Chapter Forty-Nine

Monday April 8, 2041 from 4:30 p.m. – Fiona

After racing down the eighty-five floors as fast as we could, we exited the stairwell and saw the brake lights of a Toyota van exit the carpark. We ran to a parked Mercedes and tossed our packs onto the back seats before hastily entering the vehicle. Thank God the previous driver had left the electronic key in the console. Archie accelerated in haste towards Kings Park and the Acacias Hotel.

We parked at the very edge of the Hotel carpark behind a concrete bus shelter, about three hundred metres from the Toyota van. Two mutants carrying assault rifles exited the Toyota and plodded towards the Hotel entry as we ran towards the rear of their vehicle.

Archie passed me Dimoska's sniper rifle. "Take the shots," he advised calmly.

The mutants were about 200 metres away with their backs turned. I placed my shotgun on the ground. I then swiftly extended the sniper rifle's carbon bipod and moved to a prone position near the rear of the Toyota. I took a deep breath and let it out, held my breath and squeezed the trigger. With a projectile speed of 940 metres per second, almost three times the speed of sound, the first mutant didn't know what hit him. I actioned the bolt and took out the second mutant with a shot between the shoulder blades as he sprinted towards the hotel. The .338 calibre round was more than enough to take the big bastard down.

"I'm impressed," Archie said.

I was rapt with the compliment but didn't let it show. "Let's go get Clarry and Raj," I said.

I picked up my shotgun and we ran towards the hotel. Upon entering I instantly noticed two men wrestling on the floor in the lobby lounge. Patterson was on top of Clarry, with both men frantically fighting for control of a pistol. I rammed the butt of my shotgun behind Patterson's ear, knocking him out cold.

"You can get him off me now," Clarry exclaimed.

I covered them both as Archie pulled Patterson off Clarry and helped him up. Archie then gave him a bear hug.

Clarry squirmed. "Okay, that's enough, you're hurting me more than Patterson was."

I flinched when I heard rapid gunfire. I spun around and pointed the rifle towards the report of the shots, only to discover that the noise was blaring from enormous stereo speakers. Raj was sitting in front of a film projector playing some old twentieth century movie.

I lowered my shotgun, walked over to Raj, and introduced myself. "Hi Raj, I'm Fiona." The boy stared at me in silence for an awkward moment, and then continued to watch his movie.

Returning to the others, I secured Patterson's wrists with cable ties, rolled him to his side and made sure he was still breathing. "So, what's our next move? To be honest, I hope it's to get the fuck out of here," I said.

"Just give me fifteen minutes to quickly search the hotel for any evidence linked to Patterson's research. We can then return to the church and pick up the ladies," pleaded Clarry.

"Okay mate. But fifteen minutes, that's it," replied Archie.

Clarry started his mission by entering the stairwell.

"Go talk to Raj," Archie whispered in my ear.

"I've already tried. I just knocked out his stepdad. You go bond with him."

Archie got the message and sat on the couch alongside Raj. "Cool movie mate. It's probably best if you don't eat anymore popcorn."

After breaking the ice, Archie and Raj started to chat about time travel and the type of weapons the robot uses in the movie.

"I'm going to search for some bottled water." I walked to the kitchen area and searched in every draw and cupboard, but only found a can of peaches. I met Clarry as I was returning to the lobby. "Did you find what you were looking for?" I asked.

He looked disappointed. "Not really, just a couple of vials and some reports."

As we approached the lounge, I saw Raj kneeling alongside Patterson's prone form. Archie had his back turned watching the movie and asked with a raised voice, "Have you found that comic book Raj?"

I was about to ask Raj what he was doing, when Patterson suddenly jumped to his feet and ran out of the hotel entrance. Raj stood like a statue, grasping a small knife as he watched his stepdad escape.

Clarry and I chased after Patterson. I yelled at Archie as I grabbed the door handle, "You look after Raj."

I saw a glimpse of Patterson heading into the bush at the rear of the hotel. We both sprinted after him and entered the scrub, desperate to re-capture him. We scampered through the bush for about 200 metres before we lost sight of him. Clarry grabbed my shoulder and whispered, "Just listen." I attempted to slow my breathing. I heard the sound of movement in the bush – sticks and dried leaves breaking underfoot. We both ran towards the noise and again came to a dead stop. We couldn't hear any further movement.

"Can you track him?" I asked.

Clarry's eyes furrowed. "What, because I'm black you think I can track?"

I was a little embarrassed and tongue-tied. Clarry grinned, "I'm just fucking with you little sister."

I then suddenly heard the sound of a motorcycle's engine revving. We both dashed towards the sound to witness Patterson in the distance riding an off-road motorcycle towards the CBD. *FUCK!*

Clarry and I returned to the hotel. Raj was sitting on the couch crying while Archie stood nearby with an awkward look on his face.

Raj sobbed, "You want to hurt my dad and now he's left me. Everyone leaves me!"

I know that feeling all too well.

Chapter Fifty

Tuesday April 9, 2041 from 5:45 a.m. – Archie

I thought of Roger and Xena as I parked the Mitsubishi 4WD at the top of Clarry's driveway. I was saddened that they were not here to greet me. I had been unable to convince Clarry to join us on our return trip to Esperance. After we arrived at the church to pick up Katherine and the twins, he was adamant that he needed to collect lab equipment before returning home. He was also insistent that he go it alone. Before taking off in the Kombi, he assured me that he wouldn't be far behind.

I suspected that Clarry was searching for medical equipment to assist him in replicating Patterson's experiments. I'm undecided whether continuing Patterson's research gives me hope or terrifies me to my very core. When Clarry returns, we need to have a long chat concerning his plans.

Clarry gave us strict instructions that as soon as we arrived in Esperance, we were to immediately dispose of the vehicle and decontaminate our belongings and ourselves. I volunteered to dispose of the vehicle while Raj and the ladies placed their clothes in plastic bags and showered.

The Mitsubishi was worth an absolute fortune. However, it would be a bastard of an exercise to decontaminate the entire vehicle, and we don't possess the equipment to fix electronic faults. I drove the 4WD to a secluded beach and accelerated into the water. The tide would swallow the vehicle by 1 p.m. The only items I took from the vehicle were the firearms, which I cleaned and tested for contamination with the Geiger counter.

After I stepped out of the shower and slipped into clean clothes, I found Raj fast asleep on the couch. He was wrapped in a large towel. I didn't have the heart to wake him, so I carried him to my bedroom and tucked him under the covers. Much to my delight, Katherine kindly offered to prepare breakfast. I was craving sleep but was also starving, my stomach rumbling in complaint.

As Katherine cooked breakfast, Fiona cleaned and restitched the wound to my trapezius muscle. After shoving four fried eggs down my gullet and wishing everyone good-day, I crashed on the couch. My last thought before falling into unconsciousness was my plan to pick up Xena and Roger as soon as I woke. My restless sleep was full of vivid nightmares. I was forced to battle zombies and confront giant lizards roaming through the CBD.

Chapter Fifty-One

Monday April 8, 2041 from 10:30 p.m. – Clarry

The explanation I provided Archie and Fiona was at least half true. I did plan on picking up medical and research equipment. However, I also planned on carrying out another task. After I left the church, I doubled back to Acacias Hotel, and with great effort I managed to load one of the deceased goons into the back of the van. I then drove to the Royal Perth Hospital (RPH) which is located in the CBD. I have a thorough knowledge of the hospital's layout, as I completed my medical training at the facility.

I parked the van near the loading dock and transported the subject using a heavy-duty trolley that I found nearby. I pushed the trolley to the autopsy theatre. Thankfully, I located a patient hoist, which I put to good use by lifting the goon onto the autopsy table. It had been quite a few years since I'd last conducted an autopsy. To be precise, the last time was during medical school, but I was confident that there'd be no complaints from the subject's family or the medical board.

I stripped the subject and examined the outside of his body. He had a small tattoo on the inside of his forearm - it read 009. Patterson referred to the subjects by number within his reports. I recalled that Katherine had the number 0182 recorded on her patient chart.

I used a scalpel and made a large Y shaped incision from each of his shoulder blades, across the chest to the sternum, and then down to his pubic bone. I spread open his skin and then split the ribs using rib shears to open him up. First, I examined the lungs. And then the heart. The heart was abnormally large but looked reasonably healthy.

My heart dropped as I examined his liver, stomach, and kidneys. There were visible tumours throughout the organs. I took a tissue biopsy of the tumours and placed the samples on glass slides. I then used stains to reveal the details of the cells under a microscope. My heart immediately sank. *God damn it!* They were malignant - he was riddled with cancer.

Chapter Fifty-Two

Tuesday April 9, 2041 from 2 p.m. – Fiona

I was surprised to find Archie teaching Raj how to strip and clean a firearm in Clarry's gym. He was demonstrating how to place just the right amount of lubricant on the slide rails using a cotton bud. They had stripped my Glock and placed the parts on a white sheet. Surely, he's smart enough not to use one of Clarry's bed sheets.

I had a closer look at the sheet. "You better hide that sheet before Clarry returns."

Archie looked up at me and said cheerfully, "Good afternoon sleepy head. When you're ready, we'll go collect our babies." He was referring to the dogs and horses.

"Can I have a quick word Archie?" as I motioned him to follow me to the lawn.

Archie rustled Raj's hair. "Now Raj, make sure you don't put too much lubricant on that barrel, because Auntie Fiona will spit chips."

Archie walked over to me. "What's up?"

"When are we taking Raj home and collecting on the contract?"

Archie ran his fingers through his hair. "I planned on waiting for Clarry to return home first. I need some idea of what to say to his grandfather. I haven't checked the boy's blood. What if it's green? What if he's got radiation poisoning? Does he need medication? Clarry should be able to provide the answers."

To be honest, my main focus was on collecting the gold and radiation sickness was the last thing I wanted to think about. And if I'm going to cark-it in the next three months, I want to spend my cut of the fifty ounces first and have the time of my life.

"Raj doesn't look sick and he still has all his hair," I whispered.

Archie looked over at Raj and then took at a step towards me. "Raj told me that Patterson kept him out of the city, and he'd only just arrived in the CBD the day we showed up. He'll probably be fine, but it's better to be safe than sorry."

Archie must have suspected that I wasn't convinced. "Look, if the old man asks us questions that we can't answer, he might get upset and refuse to pay us the reward," he said.

"No problem, we'll wait for Clarry," I relented.

Archie held up a sewing needle and pricked my forearm. A red droplet of blood appeared. "I had the same result. We may be all good."

It was a tight fit, but we managed to fit everyone inside the Beetle. Upon our arrival at Charlie's farm, the whole family was excited to see us. Roger nuzzled his nose against my neck. I was delighted to see him too.

I sat outside with Katherine and the Wong family. We were making small talk and eating a delicious cake that Sonja had baked. Archie was introducing Raj to Roger. Charlie's youngest was showing off in front of the twins, knocking over cans with his slingshot.

After thanking the Wong's for their hospitality, Katherine and the twins returned to Clarry's in the Beetle. Archie and I rode Roger and Jasper to Captain Ross's to pick up the dogs. Raj hung on to Archie's waist whooping with joy as Roger galloped the final 300 metres to the Captain's home. The dogs went berserk when we entered the property. Xena couldn't stop jumping up to Archie's chest, trying to plant her tongue on his chin.

I gave Helen and Elizabeth a big hug and we caught up on recent events. Helen was working in the fish 'n' chips shop and had become a keen spearfisherwoman. Elizabeth had also been teaching her to bake. I chided myself, but I was a little jealous of Helen and Elizabeth's connection.

As we rode up the driveway, I noticed Clarry waiting for us on his front porch. We sat outside with him while Raj and the twins played with the dogs. Xena and Zeus were loving the attention.

I cut to the chase and asked, "So Clarry, are we going to die?"

"Oh, you'll die little sister, but it'll be in another sixty years or so. The good news is, the first couple of doses protects people from radiation, and actually stops the aging process. The bad news is, the protection is short lived and the subsequent doses actually stimulates cancer cells. I have carefully read through Patterson's research reports that I took from the Opal. He's a hack! He manipulated the results, only recording and focusing on his initial success. I think I knew it all along. I was blinded as I wanted it to be true. I discovered that he literally murdered 97% of his victims."

Archie nodded. "We know, we saw them piled up in the Opal. It was horrifying mate."

Clarry nodded solemnly. "Raj wasn't mentioned in the reports. I believe he was kept outside of the city. It's possible that Patterson actually cares for the boy. Anyway, I'll take blood samples from you, but I'm almost positive we're in the clear."

Chapter Fifty-Three

Friday April 12, 2041 – Archie

I enjoyed the drive to Northam. Clarry had surprised me by having a panel beater mate of the Captain's fix the Beast. She looked as good as new. I drove up to Mr Singh's front gate. One of the armed guards recognised the vehicle. As soon as he spotted Raj he jumped straight on the two-way and opened the gate.

Mr and Mrs Singh were waiting at the front of their expansive two-story home. As soon as the Beast came to a stop, Raj jumped out of the car and ran to his grandmother, almost knocking her over as he embraced her.

Mr Singh invited us to sit under the white gazebo situated in the rear garden. Two of his armed bodyguards stood close by. Mr Singh wasn't one for small talk, "Thank you for bringing Raj home. Now, how did Patterson die?"

I glanced in Fiona's direction before answering. "Unfortunately, he escaped sir."

He looked extremely upset. "Well, that's not good enough young man."

I felt like a schoolboy being admonished by the principal. "The contract was to bring Raj home sir. We have honoured that contract," I replied calmly.

Mr Singh huffed, before stating, "You are quite right."

The bodyguard passed me a leather case which I in turn opened. I had never seen fifty ounces of gold. It's a thing of beauty. Mr Singh whispered to one of the guards, who then turned on his heels and marched to the house.

Mr Singh poured us both a lemonade. I sculled the refreshment and then said, "Thank you for your hospitality, I think we'll be on our way."

"Mr O'Connor, please provide me a further twenty minutes of your time."

Mr Singh stood from his seat and walked into his premises with his head held high. He returned a short time later with a typed document in his hand.

It was a private contract to kill Patterson for a further fifty ounces of gold. This wasn't the first time I'd been asked by a private citizen to assassinate someone, and it probably won't be the last.

"Sir, with all due respect, this is not a legal contract. Civilians can't contract bounty hunters, or anyone for the matter, to kill another person."

From the expression on Mr Singh's face, my response appeared to have frustrated and angered him.

I took out my notebook and reviewed my notes from our first meeting. "Correct me if I'm wrong, but I believe Patterson owes you a substantial amount of coin?"

Mr Singh's eyes narrowed. "Indeed, he does."

"If my partner agrees, we'll attempt to locate Patterson and perform a civilian arrest. We'll then escort him to your farm so you can settle your financial dispute."

Fiona nodded. "I'd be happy to bring that scum to you sir."

Mr Singh looked pleased and typed a new contract, stipulating that we would be rewarded with fifty ounces of gold upon escorting Mr Noel Patterson to the Singh Farm.

We said farewell to Raj and promised we would send him a postcard during our travels.

I placed my foot down hard on the accelerator pedal and sped off to the sound of AC/DC's song '*Thunderstruck*.'

"So, are we going after Patterson?" Fiona bellowed over the music.

"Yep, he's on our radar," I shouted back.

I pondered the suffering Patterson had inflicted. There are countless innocents, dead and alive, that deserve RETRIBUTION!

DEFINITION OF TERMS

Area of Responsibility: When operators are tactically entering a room, the area is divided into pie like sections or sectors. The room can be cleared faster. If there are two operators in the room, they each have 50% of the room.

Bounty: Payment or reward (especially from a government) for acts such as catching criminals or enlisting in the military

Brazilian Jiu-jitsu: A martial art and combat sport based on ground fighting and submission holds.

Cark-it: Australian slang for die

Carbon Copy: Before the development of photographic copiers, a carbon copy was the under-copy of a typed or written document placed over carbon paper and the under-copy sheet itself

C-4: A plastic explosive which is one-third more powerful by weight than TNT. When C4 is detonated, the explosive is converted into gas which creates a pressure (shock) wave that demolishes the target by cutting, breaching or cratering.

Door breaching: The use of equipment (ram, jimmy bar, hinge puller, bolt cutter) to gain entry to a locked and/or barricaded door.

Dosimeter: estimates the radiation dose an individual is receiving.

Dummy rounds: Fake bullets that are used to practice malfunction drills and dry fire exercises

EMP: A short burst of electromagnetic energy. A pulse's origin may be a natural occurrence or human-made and can occur as a radiated, electric, or magnetic field or a conducted electric current, depending on the source.

A Faraday cage or Faraday shield: An enclosure used to block electromagnetic fields. A Faraday shield may be formed by a continuous covering of conductive material, or in the case of a Faraday cage, by a mesh of such materials.

Friendly Fire: An incident involving the killing or wounding of friendly forces while engaging with what is thought to be an enemy force.

Furphy: Australian slang for an erroneous or improbable story that is claimed to be factual.

Gallows: A scaffold or gibbet used for execution by hanging.

Geiger Counter: A type of survey meter that estimates the radiation dose deposited in an individual or object

HAZMAT Suit: Personal protective equipment that consists of an impermeable whole-body garment worn as protection against hazardous materials.

Kill House: Or shoot house is a live ammunition shooting range used to train Police and military personnel for close contact engagements in urban combat environments. They are designed to mimic residential, commercial and industrial spaces.

Livery: Is an insignia or symbol adorning a person, an object or a vehicle that denotes a relationship between the wearer of the livery and an individual or corporate body.

Longarms: Longarm include rifles, shotguns and machine guns

Militia: An army of non-professional soldiers, citizens of a state, who may perform military service during a time of need.

Muay Thai: A martial art and combat sport that uses stand-up striking along with various clinching techniques.

NMG: A gang from South Australia that has been wreaking havoc in Western Australia

Operational Debrief: A review of an operation in order to affirm and reinforce what worked well, and what requires improvement in order to refine and enhance future processes.

Operational Order: The order converts the Operational Plan into action and gives the team essential information and direction needed to carry out the operation. It is broken into five elements-: Situation, Mission, Execution, Administration and Command and Control

Operational Plan: An operational plan sets out the objectives, strategies, tactics and tasks that a team needs to perform in order to achieve a mission

Oxycodone: An opioid medication used for treatment of moderate to severe pain. It is highly addictive and is commonly used recreationally by people who have an opioid use disorder.

POWs: Prisoners of War

Recce: Slang for reconnaissance. Exploration of an area by military forces to obtain information about enemy forces, terrain, and other activities.

Round: Bullets

Screw: Prison warders, wardens, officers and guards are nicknamed screws

Shiv: A homemade knife-like weapon, especially one fashioned in prison.

Shottie: Shotgun

Six: It refers to the 6 position on the face of a clock. If you were standing in the centre of a clock face, facing the 12 position, the 6 position would be immediately behind you.

Wagyl: A major spirit (Dreamtime Rainbow Serpent) for the Noongar people, which is considered to be central to their beliefs and customs.

ACKNOWLEDGEMENTS

One of the main characters, Archie, is battling mental illness and an associated drug addiction. I would like to thank my wife, Ming, a qualified psychologist, in explaining symptoms of various mental illness and drug dependence. However, any errors made in this novel are mine and mine alone. I would also like to thank Ming for her patience and advice with other aspects of the book. Thank you to confidantes that were gracious in explaining their journey with mental illness. This assisted me to learn about some of the challenges Archie faces.

One of my main characters is Clarence Ugle, a Whadjuk Noongar man from Fremantle. I would like to thank my colleague and friend Sharon Ninyette - Proud Noongar Woman, for her advice and assistance. Again, I want to be clear, any mistakes made in this novel are mine and mine alone.

And a special thanks for those that provided me encouragement and feedback throughout the journey - Lynne, Graham, Jon, Ming and Knut. Thank you, Steve, for the cover work and design of the book. It is much appreciated!

FURTHER NOTES & REFERENCES

A majority of the locations mentioned in the novel are accurate, with exceptions including the Blue Opal Hotel and Acacias Hotel. Fortunately, at the time of writing this novel the Western Australian Cricket Association Ground has not been demolished to build the Blue Opal Hotel, and Kings Park has not been desecrated by building the Acacias Hotel.

At the time of writing this novel the Blaser and Austeyr (Aussie version of the Steyr) rifles are used in the Australian Army. However, the Blaser R96 Tactical Sniper rifle and F92 Austeyr assault rifle do not exist. I have adjusted the weapons' model numbers to take into account the manufacturers' future improvements and developments.

Alex Wellerstein has created an engaging and confronting website that assisted me to visualise the destruction of the Perth CBD from a nuclear strike. I placed the epicentre in West Perth and selected a ten-kiloton yield surface strike. This enabled Patterson to use the fictitious Blue Opal Hotel as his base of operations https://nuclearsecrecy.com/nukemap/

The First People of Australia's culture, customs and beliefs are rich and complex, with over 300 languages from over 500 different clan groups or 'nations' around the continent. The Whadjuk people are one of fourteen different Noongar groups. Clarry's family are also from the Wongutha people, also written as (Wongatha, Wangkatha, Wankatja, Wongi or Wangai), which encompass eight different groups. I encourage you to peruse The National Unity web page which provides an informative map of Aboriginal countries http://nationalunitygovernment.org/pdf/aboriginal-australia-map.pdf

I have chosen to use the word Wagyl for the Dreamtime Rainbow Serpent that is painted on the train to provide it protection. Wagyl is also written as Waakal, Wawgal, Waugal, Woggal and Waagal. The Wagyl is a major spirit for the Noongar people, which is considered to be central to their beliefs and customs. This creature fascinated me as a child and still does. I encourage you to learn more at the Kaartdijin (knowledge in Noongar) website https://www.noongarculture.org.au/spirituality/ Dr Jack Davis's beautiful poem of Yagan's ceremonial tribute to the Wagyl, for creating the Noongar universe can be read on this site.

The custom of 'payback' is represented in cultures throughout the world, but for many Aboriginal groups, including Noongar, it is part of their traditional culture and lore, many of which are still practiced today. The severity of payback depended on the significance of the lore broken. Payback could be invoked for a variety of offenses such as burning the territory of another group, for stealing resources or for taking another man's wife, to name but a few. In the case of a killing, a man's death had to be avenged before his spirit could rest. If you are of a legal mind, please go to the below website that explains the recognition of Aboriginal Customary Laws in the Australian Legal System. https://www.alrc.gov.au/publication/recognition-of-aboriginal-customary-laws-alrc-report-31/

A confronting video about Weewar, a Noongar man who was convicted under British Law for carrying out payback in 1842 can be viewed at https://www.noongarculture.org.au/in-1842-weewar-a-noongar-was-convicted-under-british-law-for-carrying-out-payback/

Songs Mentioned in the book (in order of appearance)

Scott, Bon. Young, Angus. Young, Malcolm. (1979). *Highway to Hell* [song]. AC/DC. Albert Productions, July 27. LP

Commerford, Tim. Rocha, Zack de la. Morello, Tom. Wilk, Brad. (1992). *Bullet in the Head* [song]. Rage Against the Machine. Epic Records, November 3. CD

Commerford, Tim. Rocha, Zack de la. Morello, Tom. Wilk, Brad. (1992). *Know your enemy* [song]. Rage Against the Machine. Epic Records, November 3. CD

Marley, Bob & Sporty, King. (1978). *Buffalo Soldier* [song]. Bob Marley & The Wailers. Island Records, May 23, 1983. LP

Bowie, D. (1982). *Let's Dance* [song]. David Bowie. EMI America, March 14, 1983. LP

Butler, Gezzer. Iommi, Tony. Osbourne, Ozzy. Ward, Bill. (1970). *Paranoid* [song]. Black Sabbath. Vertigo Records, August 7. LP

Young, Angus. Young, Malcolm. (1990). *Thunderstruck* [song]. AC/DC. ATCO Records, September 10. CD

Map of Australia

Map is courtesy of Bruce Jones Design and FreeUSandWorldMaps.com

Notebook and Journal Image

Images Purchase and licenses from Vector Stock Images

ABOUT THE AUTHOR

James Thomson grew up in the South West and Eastern Goldfields of Western Australia (WA). He served in the WA Police Force attaining the rank of Sergeant. He has completed two Master's Degrees and is the Director of a Registered Training Organisation focused on Emergency Management. James has also performed roles as a University Lecturer, Management Consultant and Training Manager. He has practiced martial arts for over thirty years, having recently been awarded a black belt in Brazilian Jiu-Jitsu under the Jean Jacques Machado BJJ Perth Academy. He resides with his wife and son in Perth, W.A.

The Retribution
Gallows Gold Series
Book 2

Written by James Scott Thomson

Excerpt from The Retribution – Book Two of the Gallows Gold Series

I retrieved the infrared binoculars from my pack and scanned the horizon. It didn't take long for me to spot a campsite consisting of an old tin shed beneath the foliage of a gum tree. My attention was drawn to a recently used fire pit. Its glowing embers were slowly dying in the cool morning. An old mine shaft with a rusted steel headframe sat twenty metres east of the ramshackle dwelling.

"So, what's the plan, Boss?" Fiona asked.

"We'll tie the horses up and approach from the west. With any luck, he'll be sleeping like a baby. And then Bob's your uncle, we'll get the drop on him."

Fiona raised an eyebrow, "We're after Gizzarelli, not some daft bank robber. Can't we just prop 250 metres out and take him down with the sniper rifle?"

"You know the code. We can't do that. When we return to Geraldton, I need to tell you about my former professor's glass jar philosophy."

Fiona chuckled, "Philosophy 101? If you're buying the drinks, I'll listen to whatever lecture you're giving Boss."

We tied Roger and Jasper's reigns to the trunk of a large eucalypt tree and hiked through the scrub from the west. I saw the tin roof through the foliage and signalled for Fiona to stop by holding my open hand up at shoulder height. We both knelt behind a weeping bottlebrush. I signalled for Fiona to enter his camp from the north and approach the rear of the shed. I planned to continue walking from the west and snake around the shrubs and mining machinery to the front door of the shed. If all goes to plan, we'll meet at the door and tactically enter hard and fast, catching him unawares.

The full moon provided enough light to avoid tripping over rusted junk and large rocks. As I approached the shed door, I was startled by the sound of bells ringing, followed by a high-pitched scream and a thud!

It was a matter of seconds before I found the cause of the commotion. Fiona was lying face down in the dirt, about four metres from the rear of the shed. Her legs were tangled in wire with small brass bells attached. Gizzarelli was standing above her, holding an empty champagne bottle by its neck.

As Gizzarelli grinned and stepped towards me, I glanced at Fiona's motionless crumpled form. "You thought you could bring me in. Shit mate, you've got dibs on yourself," he sneered.

"What did you do to Fiona?"

"She's trespassing on my property, so I gave her a bit of a whack with the old Dom Pérignon. But I think you should be more concerned about your own welfare."

I tried to keep the conversation light. There was still a chance I could reason with the man. "Dom Pérignon? I wasn't aware you had such expensive taste."

"I don't. I just found it in the shed."

"Why don't I check on Fiona, and then you and I can have a chat about where we go from here."

He spat on the ground and raised his fists. "This has been a long-time coming, Archie."

I shrugged my shoulders, "I guess it is what it is," I grunted.

I stepped backwards while Gizzarelli rolled his shoulders and followed me to the open space beyond the fire pit. I wasn't sure if Fiona was breathing, let alone conscious, but I wanted to create some distance between her and Gizzarelli, as I had no idea what was running through his mind.

I would be wasting valuable time attempting to negotiate with the man. He was stubborn, desperate, and pissed. And he was confident he would give me a flogging. At about five foot eight, he had a wrestler's frame, with thick forearms and broad shoulders. I had six inches of height on him, but he outweighed me by at least fifteen kilos.

I reached for the grip of my revolver as he sprinted towards me, dust spiralling into the air as the tread of his boots gripped the red dirt. Just after my revolver left the holster, he struck my gun hand with the bottle. I spun to the side, and the revolver flew out of my grip into scrub. I couldn't risk turning my back to search for it, and it was too dark to locate it at a glance.

Gizzarelli held the bottle like it was a sword. Forget what you have seen in old movies; ninety-nine bottles out of a hundred don't smash when you strike someone. He watched me like a hawk as I circled and tested my right hand for injuries by forming a fist. He stretched his neck to the left and right, touching his ears to his shoulders, causing his vertebrae to crack and pop in response.

As I raised my fists to my jaw, he hurled the bottle at my head, narrowly missing when I flinched like I was slipping a punch. He charged forward like a raging bull and threw a right hook toward my jaw. Reacting with muscle memory, I bobbed and weaved under his punch. With surprising speed and grace, he instantly regained his balance and rotated on the balls of his feet to face me.

I smirked, "Jeezus! You move fast for an old boy. But I notice that you're puffing pretty hard. Do you need a bit of a lie-down, granddad?"

I intended to enrage him and provoke a mistake. I just needed an opening to win the fight so I could check on Fiona. *Come on, Gizzarelli, throw a haymaker.* But unfortunately, he had other plans.

When I threw a quick cross, he slipped to the outside and launched an uppercut into my liver. I instantly doubled over, clutching my stomach in excruciating pain. He didn't hesitate to take advantage of the opening. He drove his right knee into my jaw.

My vision blurred, and I fell to my backside. Gizzarelli attacked me with the ferocity of a wolverine claiming its kill - raining down punches and elbow strikes. Reflex and instinct took over. I managed to block most of his blows with my forearms.

He pressed one of his hammy fists across my throat, forcing his weight down with grim determination. "Say goodnight to granddad, you cheeky fuck," he growled.

I struggled to breathe as I reached for my knife. Thud!